Katelyn's Choice

by

SUSAN G MATHIS

KATELYN'S CHOICE BY SUSAN G MATHIS
Published by Heritage Beacon Fiction
an imprint of Lighthouse Publishing of the Carolinas
2333 Barton Oaks Dr., Raleigh, NC 27614

ISBN: 978-1-946016-72-0
Copyright © 2019 by Susan G Mathis
Cover design by Elaina Lee
Interior design by AtriTex Technologies P Ltd

Available in print from your local bookstore, online, or from the publisher at:
ShopLPC.com

For more information on this book and the author visit: SusanGMathis.com

Brought to you by the creative team at Lighthouse Publishing of the Carolinas (LPCBooks.com):
Eddie Jones, Ann Tatlock, Denise Weimer, Shonda Savage, Elaina Lee

Library of Congress Cataloging-in-Publication Data
Mathis, Susan G
Katelyn's Choice / Susan G Mathis 1st ed.

Printed in the United States of America

PRAISE FOR *KATELYN'S CHOICE*

If you like romance, history, and the Thousand Islands all wrapped together with an inspirational message, you will love *Katelyn's Choice*. This first book in the new Thousand Island Gilded Age Series has it all. I love how Mathis tells an engaging story while weaving in river facts and history as she captures the wonder and beauty of this marvelous place. I can't wait to see what Susan has in store for Singer Castle!

> ~ **Patty Mondore**
> Award-winning author of *River-Lations,*
> *Singer Castle* and *Singer Castle Revisited*

With such splendid attention to detail, Susan G Mathis transported me to that charming historical world I so enjoy. *Katelyn's Choice* is a treasure as well as being realistic and relevant. Her characters struggle with some of the same challenges we all face, and she blends in just the right amount of biblical truth in a natural manner.

> ~ **Janine Mendenhall**
> Author of *Starving Hearts*, Selah and
> Carol Award Finalist, 2017

Reader beware: prepare to be enticed to visit the Thousand Islands yourself, to imagine The Gilded Age and to want to learn more of its history. Katelyn and Thomas make likeable but flawed characters who must deal with the inner and outer turmoil of their faults. The story unfolds around the delicate complexities of a budding romance in the 1800s with well-developed characters. I enjoyed the vivid sensory descriptions of the islands, the St. Lawrence River setting, and the almost magical lifestyle. I also appreciated the smooth weaving of history that didn't interfere with story.

> ~ **Janet Bly**
> Author of over 35 books, speaker, writing mentor, editor

Katelyn's Choice is a delightful book, filled with love, laughter, and page-turning challenges and adventures. The author is an expert at bringing characters to life and enabling them to walk off the pages and into the reader's heart. Don't miss this wonderful story!

~ **Kathi Macias**
Award-winning author of more than 50 books,
including her most recent release, *To the Moon and Back.*

Susan G Mathis created a magical story where the reader is immersed in the sights, sounds, and experiences of the Thousand Islands. Her characters are delightfully different, lending the story and plot a well-rounded, entertaining delivery.

~ **Angela Breidenbach**
Christian Authors Network president
Author of several stories including Fanned Embers in the
Second Chance Brides

Katelyn's Choice is a delightful story that pulls the reader into The Gilded Age through the eyes of a servant girl for the wealthy Pullman family. Susan did an excellent job of weaving historical details into the lives of the characters and showing the beautiful setting of the Thousand Islands. The charming characters, romantic tension, and the moral dilemmas of the characters keep you engaged and turning the pages.

~ **Marilyn Turk**
Award-winning author of *The Gilded Curse, Shadowed by a Spy*,
and the *Coastal Lights Legacy* series

Once again, Susan Mathis masterfully weaves history, faith, and romance into an endearing and moving story set in the Thousand Islands in 1872. The characters' trials and triumphs, vivid setting descriptions, and rich historical detail sweep the reader back in time to experience a time and place not to be forgotten.

~ **Jayme H. Mansfield**
Award-Winning Author of *Chasing the Butterfly* and *RUSH*

Katelyn's Choice is an enchanting read. Katelyn will strike a chord in all of us who have a bit of trouble controlling our tongue and impulsiveness. She's a loveable character. Set in the fascinating setting of Pullman Island allows us to experience a bit of the Gilded Age.

~ Diana Lesire Brandmeyer
Author of *A Bride's Dilemma in Friendship, Tennessee*

Author Susan Mathis escorts readers to the fabled Thousand Islands of the St. Lawrence River. Class distinctions cut as deeply between the wealthy and their servants as the great river's channel between the mainland and the jeweled summer playgrounds of America's Gilded Age.

~ Davalynn Spencer
Award-winning author of Inspirational Western Romances including *The Front Range Brides* books

Katelyn's Choice is a charming story interwoven with intriguing historical events on Pullman Island. Katelyn Kavanagh hopes to escape her grief and past but must first learn to face present truths about herself and those she loves. Mathis' characters are engaging. Their excitement of the president's coming visit and the author's descriptions will sweep you away into the 1870s, to enjoy a lovely visit to the Thousand Islands, and one young woman's summer journey to discovery, healing—and love.

~ Kathleen Rouser
Award-winning author of *Rumors and Promises*

Susan Mathis masterfully weaves history into her fiction in this delightful tale, reminding us all about the important spiritual lesson of conquering our own personal enemy. Her character isn't mended all at once but continues to struggle again and again, in the midst of a wild yet cultivated setting and poetic narrative. This tale is a must-read for lovers of historical romance, post-Civil War buffs, President Ulysses S. Grant fans, and readers of well-written fiction.

~ Donna Schlachter
Author of several stories including
Train Ride to Heartbreak in Mail-Order Brides Collection

Dedication

To my wonderful husband, Dale, my inspiration and my muse, who has the wisdom and goodness of Shamus and the kindness and gentleness of McCarthy. Thank you for our love story that inspires me to create novels that sparkle with love like ours. Thank you for supporting me and cheering me on in this great adventure of being an author. And most of all, thank you for sharing the amazing journey of doing life together. You truly are a gift from heaven.

ACKNOWLEDGMENTS

For years, I've dreamed of writing stories about the Thousand Islands I love so much. So many of you have helped me to make that happen, and I am so grateful for all the special people in my life who continually share their love, support, encouragement, and time.

Thanks to my readers who support my writing so faithfully and even ask when my next book is coming out. Your encouragement and excitement blesses me and spurs me on. Thanks, too, for spreading the word about my work through your reviews, social media comments, and more. I hope Katelyn, Thomas, and the others touch your heart.

Thanks to Judy Keeler, my Thousand Islands historical editor and president of the Alexandria Township Historical Society, whose invaluable knowledge and insight helped make sure everything was historically accurate.

Thanks to Laurie Raker and Amy Sasser, who so willingly and lovingly pored over the manuscript and gave me great suggestions and input to make the story even better.

Thanks to Rich Calabrese for so graciously taking Dale and me to Pullman Island and giving us a personal tour. There's nothing like experiencing the sights, sounds, and smells of the island and hearing its stories. Our time there helped me create vivid descriptions and tell a better story.

Thanks to my son, Sean, who inspired me to create Thomas, a fisherman and all-around good guy like you.

Thanks to my many writer friends who have helped me hone my craft, encouraged me to keep on writing, supported me through my writing journey, and prayed for me. There are too many to mention here, but you know who you are.

Thanks for the support of my fellow authors in the Christian Authors Network (CAN), the American Christian Fiction Writers Colorado Springs chapter (ACFW-CS), the Writers on the Rock group (WOTR), and of course, my fellow authors at Lighthouse Publishing of the Carolinas.

Thanks to the stellar team at Lighthouse Publishing of the Carolinas, especially Ann Tatlock and Denise Weimer, who have made this book everything it can be. Without your faithful, hard work, this book wouldn't shine as brightly as it does.

And to God, from whom all good gifts come. Without You there would never be a dream or the ability to fulfill that dream or even the opportunity to write *Katelyn's Choice*—or any other book. Thank You!

CHAPTER 1

June 1872
Thousand Islands, New York

Katelyn Kavanagh looked out at the sparkling waters of the mighty St. Lawrence River and the enchanting islands dotting it. She squinted, trying to shield her eyes from the glare of the early summer sun shining brightly on the placid water. Pondering the adventures to come, she brushed back a stray lock of her hair.

A gentle breeze blew off the main channel, causing her skirt to swirl around her ankles while she anxiously waited on the crowded docks of Alexandria Bay, New York. Was her dream—her mama's dream, more likely—finally coming true? Soon she would live on one of those magnificent Thousand Islands for the entire summer season of her nineteenth year.

She would be far from her father's anger and far from her brothers' meanness.

She would be free like the gulls that sailed the summer breeze.

She paced along the dock, waiting for a St. Lawrence skiff to take her and her best friend to Pullman Island. The *clip, clip, clip* of her heels betrayed her excess nervous energy, sounding her determination to get away from the mainland. As she paced, she scrutinized why she wanted to live on an island so badly.

Her parents had emigrated from Ireland just a year before she was born. She recalled how her mama had always spoken fondly of island life, and she wanted to experience it. But island life meant so much more, and her eyes filled with tears as she remembered her dying mama's last words just hours before she went to heaven. "Find your future on one of the islands, Katie, dear. Many a rich folk be looking for a fine young woman to serve them. 'Sides, you'll be far from the farm, and you'll be safe, my lamb."

On that terrible day, Katelyn had lost her dearest friend and confidant. Her loving mama. She felt abandoned, left alone with her angry father and brothers.

Three long months without Mama. Would it ever stop hurting?

She spotted the skiff approaching, so she shook off her thoughts and the sadness that clung to them. She wiped her eyes, stomped her foot, and squared her shoulders, determined to fulfill her mama's dying wish—and to make that dream her own. She smiled over at Sara O'Neill, and her plain, dear childhood friend stared at her with a raised eyebrow.

"It's a new day, sweet Sara. A whole new world is waiting for us across this river. Let us be gone." With her usual flair, Katelyn swept her arm toward the islands. Then she picked up her worn carpetbag, and Sara followed her lead. They handed the boatman their bags and boarded the skiff.

It was Katelyn's first time in a skiff, her first time on the river, her first time going to an island. It was the first of many firsts, and her excitement grew with each minute that passed.

Katelyn settled onto one of two wicker chairs and surveyed the canoe-like boat that was so famous among the islanders. The St. Lawrence skiff was long and wide, about twenty feet long, she guessed. From the keel to the gunwale, a sturdy plank floor provided a place for carpetbags and feet to stay dry, and thole pins held the long oars in place. The smell of shiny new varnish and wet wood filled her senses.

Moments later, the boatman shoved off, and they were on their way. Sara perched on the other wicker chair, pale as a ghost and looking as if she might lose her breakfast at any moment. Katelyn shook her head.

Sara never was one for adventure, not like her brother. Not like me. How can she not be excited?

Katelyn leaned in to be heard above the squeak of the oars and the grunt of the boatman. "I'm so glad your brother recommended us for hire, Sara. Thomas is quite the adventurer, don't you think?"

By now, Sara was as white as the gulls that squawked overhead. The poor girl swallowed hard before responding to Katelyn's question. "I can't believe he's been working on Pullman Island these three years now. I'm glad Thomas will be on the island, else I mightn't have the courage to stay there."

Katelyn pursed her lips and giggled at her friend's angst, but she said nothing. She closed her eyes so she could experience the boat trip to the fullest. The skiff under her glided along the waters of the mighty river to an island world far different from her own small farm. She inhaled the wild river scent, listened to the waves lap against the skiff, and repositioned a piece of her curly, dark hair that the wind had pulled out of the fashionable braid she had worked so hard to create. It was set atop her head just right and hidden under her bonnet, but the wind still had its way.

I do hope I look much older than my nineteen years. Won't Thomas be surprised to see me so grown up?

Katelyn smiled and fluffed the edges of her hairdo one more time. Out of habit, she pinched her high cheekbones to encourage some color and smacked her full lips in anticipation of meeting Sara's brother once again.

"I'm not sure I can do this." Sara's voice quivered, breaking into Katelyn's thoughts. "I'm a farm girl. Milking cows and gathering eggs are all I know. How am I to work for a man the likes of the famous Mr. Pullman?"

"I hear Mr. Pullman be a mighty tyrannical sort, and Cook is rather stern, too." Katelyn teased poor Sara, naughtily playing with her frayed emotions and pushing aside a prick of guilty regret. "I do hope we don't get a beating from either of them if we make a mistake."

At the comment, Sara's sad, grey eyes welled up with tears, and her tiny frame started to quake. The boatman looked at Katelyn and then at Sara. He shook his head and rolled his eyes, but Katelyn chose to ignore his silent rebuke.

"And can you believe Mr. Pullman had the audacity to change the absolutely perfect name of Sweet Island to Pullman Island? I, for one, will retain its proper name." She wrinkled her nose, straightened her spine, and lifted her chin. "'Tis all too arrogant to name the island after himself, that's what I think."

"I ... I don't know," Sara said, biting her thin bottom lip. "If the master renamed it, we must follow his lead."

"Not I," Katelyn said stubbornly, shaking her head and folding her hands in her lap. "Ever since I was a wee thing, I've known it to be Sweet Island, and Sweet Island it shall stay. 'Sides, I can call it by its true name, least-wise, in my head."

When Sara didn't respond, Katelyn fell silent, though she wanted to say more. She couldn't grasp how her friend held so few opinions and disliked talking about all of the intimate details of life. Whenever Katelyn shared some interesting news or a bit of gossip about a neighbor or a classmate or the teacher, Sara would withdraw into herself and not respond. Katelyn always sensed her disapproval. Why couldn't they just enjoy an exhilarating and spicy conversation?

Frustrated, she looked out across the waters toward the island that would be her home for the next several months. Lots of people commented on how Katelyn's piercing hazel-green eyes turned to a vibrant sea-green whenever she was on or near the water. She could almost feel them turning green as she looked across the rippling waves. She smiled at the thought.

"Katelyn, do you think they'll be as mean as your father?" Sara asked, her thin blonde hair blowing in the wind.

"Rest your head, Sara," she said, trying to soften her prior teasing. "Thomas would not allow such a thing, and nor will I. Anyone dare not lay a hand on you—or me."

Sara smiled, her round face widening and making her look even younger than eighteen. Since they were best friends and less than a year apart, Katelyn's mama had called them Irish twins. Katelyn sighed, thinking again of her mama.

Oh, Mama, we both know Sara is a loyal friend and a godly young woman who will execute her duties faithfully and quietly. But will I? How will I fit into a servant role to the Pullman family—and to all the famous guests who will be visiting the island this summer?

She started to fidget, excitement and nervousness filling her thoughts.

"What's wrong, Katelyn?" Sara asked.

"Nothing. I was just thinking about all the fine folks we might meet this summer. Maybe some famous New York City socialites who wear diamonds and fancy gowns? Or maybe some rich young men will come and sweep us off our feet and marry us, and take us away from the drudgery of farm life?"

"Stuff and nonsense. We'll likely be sweatin' over a hot stove, hid away in the kitchen all summer," Sara scoffed.

"Pshaw! I, for one, won't be hidden away!"

"If it be where your job is, you will, miss," interjected the boatman. "You best not be gettin' no high and mighty ideas about jumping out of your class."

Startled, Katelyn glared at him with a hint of disdain. He simply gave her a condescending and toothy grin. She didn't respond, deciding she had better keep the rest of the conversation to the confines of Sara's ears only.

Instead, she quietly continued to dream about all the interesting people she might meet throughout her summer on the island. But her thoughts kept returning to Thomas. Had he grown since she had seen him last? She remembered an older boy, a fine-looking boy, but a boy still. Yet she recalled that his dark eyes always seemed to dance and hold a secret, a secret she would love to uncover.

"Land, ho!" hollered the boatman, shaking her from her daydream. "Hands in the skiff, me ladies."

When they pulled near the dock, Katelyn saw a young man with a mass of black curls sticking out from under a captain's cap ready to pull the skiff to the landing. His face was backlit from the sun, but Katelyn guessed it had to be Thomas.

"Thomas?" she asked as the boat bumped the dock. "Are you the same incorrigible boy who teased us unmercifully when we were girls?"

"One and the same, Miss Katie Lynn Kavanagh." Thomas chuckled. He grabbed the skiff's rope and tied it up to the dock.

"It's Katelyn, if you don't mind."

Thomas shrugged and grinned, and the two laughed while the boatman helped them out of the skiff and handed their belongings to Thomas. Thomas paid the boatman the fare, and with a tip of his cap, the massive man and his skiff shoved off to return to the mainland.

Katelyn looked around and felt both excitement and a bit of trepidation. *A whole summer on this beautiful island! What magic might transpire?* She shook her head, pushed her apprehension aside, and allowed her excitement to rise within her.

She turned around and gazed at Sara and Thomas, who were hugging and talking quietly, so she discreetly observed her former schoolmate, Sara's brother. He was taller and far more muscular than she had remembered, and his mustache and well-trimmed beard were black as molasses. His chocolate-brown eyes danced while he spoke with his little sister, who looked small and fragile next to him. Thomas smiled, obviously happy to have her on the island with him.

"You must tell us everything, Thomas," Katelyn said, walking up to them and interrupting the reunion between brother and sister. "We simply must know what we will face before we face it. For your sister's sake."

Thomas laughed a deep, baritone laugh. *When did his voice change?* Katelyn smiled and awaited Thomas' comments. Sara also looked to him for a response.

Thomas clicked his heels together and stood erect as if greeting royalty. "Ladies, let me be the first to welcome you to Pullman Island, home of the famous George M. Pullman of the Pullman railroad car fame!" By the tone of his voice and the twinkle in his eyes, Thomas was obviously proud of his employer.

"Mrs. Pullman and her two girls, Florence and little Hattie, are also here, along with their nurse and others from the mainland staff," Thomas continued. "I will tell all, but just now, I am to take you to the women's staff quarters and get you settled."

"And will you show us around?" Sara asked. "I am ever so nervous about meeting everyone and finding my place here."

"Dear Sara, you are such a worrier," Thomas gently scolded. "Fear not, sister. I will give you a tour of the island before your two o'clock meeting with Cook. This summer can be the adventure of a lifetime, if you let it, for you will find a new world on Sweet—ah, excuse me—Pullman Island."

Katelyn laughed at the mistake. "I, too, aim to call her Sweet Island whilst I am here."

"Don't let the Pullmans catch you in such a transgression," Thomas warned, shaking a finger at her. "Mister Pullman has his ways, and you must not cross him."

"Then it will be our secret," Katelyn whispered and curtsied to him.

Thomas smiled but didn't respond. He loaded their bags onto a wooden cart and led them along the path toward the massive granite-and-wooden frame building that served as the staff quarters. He pointed to the beautifully rugged structure sitting high above the water's edge. Katelyn observed that it had a tall, wide stone chimney pointing toward the heavens, and a lovely large veranda sweeping halfway around the building. She looked at Thomas and smiled, while Sara walked ahead.

Thomas stopped and turned to her. "I am sorry for your loss, Katelyn. But I am frightfully glad you are not alone on the farm without your mother. Your father, he is a stern man, is he not?"

"He wasn't always so. The war changed him." Katelyn looked down at the paving stones, her face burning hot with embarrassment.

"Sorry. I didn't mean to pry. I only meant ..."

"I know you know about him. Everyone does. And I am glad to be gone."

Thomas touched her forearm with the gentleness of a feather, and he gazed compassionately into her eyes before he removed his fingers and moved toward his sister. Katelyn rubbed the spot where he had touched her. She felt warmth creep into her cheeks and turned toward the river's view to calm her racing heart.

"Coming?" Thomas called, shaking her from her wonder.

Once Katelyn caught up to Thomas and Sara, the three stopped on the pathway leading to the building. Thomas pointed at the main floor. "That is the women's quarters. The floor below is for the men, and high above you are other rooms for McCarthy and Mrs. Duncan. The turret will give you a wonderful view of the shipping channel if you want to climb it one day, and the massive chimney will keep all of us warm on chilly nights."

Thomas paused but then continued, "You will have four to your room, including Darcy from the mainland staff, and Miss Claudia Burton, who arrived a few days ago. Her parents are from Quebec but now run a French pastry shop in Watertown. I hear they have taught her well. And since the Pullmans are fond of their sweets, she will certainly be an asset to our staff." A dark shadow crossed his face, and his jaw tightened as he looked away.

"I hope, then, to learn from Miss Burton," Sara said. It was the first time Katelyn saw a hint of excitement in her friend since they had left the mainland. "I would love to become proficient in such an art."

"I trust you will learn much, dear sister, in your time here," Thomas said. "This is a very different world than you are accustomed to. It is a place of servants and masters, and we must maintain our place in the island society."

"Oh, pshaw," Katelyn declared. "It can't be so old-fashioned as all that! 'Tis 1872, and the world is changing."

"Not here. Not now," Thomas warned, shaking his head and narrowing his eyes. "Mind your place, miss, or you will regret the day you came here."

Katelyn didn't respond with words, but she felt her eyes flash with disapproval. She bit her tongue, holding back her troubled thoughts.

"Is it truly as we have heard?" Sara asked fearfully. "Is Cook as stern as they say?"

"Mrs. Stanton is a general of sorts, and she runs her kitchen with an iron fist. But she is fair and will teach both of you much. She has served the Pullmans for years, both on the mainland and on the island. The Pullmans bring her each year, for she knows their likes and loyally serves them with excellence."

"But will she beat us if we err?" Sara sucked in her breath.

"Where did you get such an idea, Sara? Cook runs a tight ship but will not abuse you."

Sara glanced at Katelyn, who had turned her eyes away, feeling Sara's silent scolding upon her.

When the three arrived at their quarters, Thomas unloaded the bags on the porch. "Here is your home for the next several months. Your room is inside and to the left. Miss Burton should be there now and will show you from here." Planting a gentle kiss on his sister's cheek, Thomas turned and tipped his cap to Katelyn. "Farewell, ladies! Until we meet again."

"*Au revoir.*" Katelyn waved. "That means 'goodbye' in French!"

Thomas nodded. "Yes, I heard that from Claudia." He turned away to return to his duties.

~~~

Thomas stopped at the crest of the hill and sucked in a deep breath. *When did that freckle-faced imp become such a beautiful woman?* He chuckled as he remembered those lovely, piercing hazel-green eyes from his boyhood days, but now they danced a little too mischievously, their message a bit too ... womanly. And now Katelyn stood nearly as tall as he, albeit rather skinny for his liking. Hadn't her father been feeding her since her poor mama died?

No! He didn't need thoughts of a woman. He was a man of the river. He shook his head, grabbed the handles of his cart, and hurried to the safe harbor of the boathouse.

~~~

Inside the staff quarters, Katelyn found the correct door and opened it. "Here we are!"

A beautiful young woman, whom Katelyn decided must be Claudia, turned and sent them a fiery glare. Her narrow, oval face accented crystal-blue eyes that appeared cold as ice. Creamy skin encircled flaming cheeks. While her sandy blonde hair was already tucked beneath her white bonnet, she was still buttoning her uniform when Katelyn and Sara entered the room.

"Don't you know how to knock?" she scolded with venom.

Katelyn moaned. *She may be regally beautiful, but she'll not send me such condescending looks and get away with it!*

"Forgive me, miss," Katelyn said with a tinge of sarcasm, placing her hands on her hips. Sara tried to hide behind her.

"Don't 'miss' me! My name is Claudia, and I hope you will be more proper in the future." Claudia turned her back as Sara quietly closed the door.

"Which bed would you like, Katelyn?" Sara whispered.

"The one near the window would be nice."

"That will be my bed," Claudia said, pointing a bony finger for emphasis. "I intended to move my things there before you two barged in like hooligans."

"Pardon me!" Katelyn shot back. "The bed was empty and unmade, so I assumed it was free."

"It is not, and don't assume anything," Claudia scolded. Katelyn stared back until, in silence, both backed down. Then, without a word, the three young women settled their living spaces, trying to avoid one another.

CHAPTER 2

The air was rife with tension and silence while Katelyn and Sara unpacked their things. Thankfully, Thomas soon returned to fetch them, knocking loudly on the outer door and shouting their names, but not venturing into the women's quarters.

Katelyn left the room and answered his call. Released from that hothouse of emotions, she laughed when Thomas bowed low, one arm bent over his stomach and the other across his back. Sara joined her and smiled when Thomas straightened and grinned proudly. "I am to take you for a tour of the island."

Before Katelyn descended the stairs, Claudia poked her head out the door, stuck her nose in the air, and dramatically waved them off. "I had a private tour. Thomas showed me all the secret places."

Thomas' jaw tightened, and his dimpled chin jutted out as he looked at her with dark, narrowed eyes, saying nothing. Claudia smirked and closed the door.

Relieved Claudia was gone, Katelyn took a moment to admire the picturesque view. From where she stood on the porch, she could see the far end of the island and the beautiful river beyond. Only then did she realize how small their new home truly was. The manicured lawn sloped gently down to the river, and to her, the island resembled the back of a turtle. Stately old oak, maple, and pine trees, and masses of thick bushes, speckled and encircled the island.

Its loveliness took her breath away.

Beyond the boundaries of the small island, out on the St. Lawrence, boats passed on either side, and in the distance, a huge cargo ship made its way along the main shipping channel between the mainland and the island. Just then, the scent of wild roses wafted in the breeze and mixed with the smell of the grand river surrounding Katelyn. She closed her eyes and breathed in the moment.

"Shall we go?" Thomas swept his arm toward the steps.

Katelyn opened her eyes and hurried to catch up. "Sorry. I see we can tour this whole island in barely a jiffy."

Sara nodded and took Thomas' arm as they descended the stairs. Her friend appeared frightened and timid, but Katelyn felt ready for an adventure, no matter how small it was.

Thomas transitioned into tour guide as they left the staff quarters and walked past the two main structures on the island. "The island may be just three-and-a-half acres, but the Pullmans have big plans for further developing it. They built the original whitewashed cottage six years ago after Mr. Pullman bought the island. It has served them well and has many modern conveniences. The steam pump provides water and light. And modern appliances are far beyond what we're used to on our humble farms."

Thomas led them to the next building and stopped. "Just this year, I had a hand in constructing the additional building here at the crown of the island. The Pullmans plan to entertain larger house parties in the grand gallery, and a few of the guests will lodge here. The bedroom berths are quite like Pullman sleeping cars, most unique indeed."

Thomas beamed with pride as he pointed to the front of the cottage to show off his work. "My boss, Shamus, says that in a few years, they want to build a proper castle that will rival those in England!"

Katelyn smiled. "It is a grand island, to be sure. And though our quarters are beautiful, they probably don't compare to this fine cottage."

Thomas agreed and continued the tour. "The Pullmans' flag, with its fancy coat of arms, designates this as their home. For now, the Pullmans will supplement their grander summer parties with tents, and mark my words, we will all be as busy as beavers when that happens. Our island staff is rather small, so each of us must be ready to take on whatever task is asked of us, even when it's above and beyond our normal duties."

"Oh, I do love a party!" Katelyn said. "And I'm sure they will entertain a very many famous persons."

"That they will. They have neighbor folk from the other islands who come to their parties, and some visit from the mainland communities as well. Each season, the Pullmans' friends from Chicago, Rochester, and even New York City often vacation here too."

Katelyn grabbed Sara's arm and gave it a gentle squeeze, barely able to contain her joy. "How exciting!"

Sara just stared at her, turning ashen, likely overwhelmed at the prospect.

They walked a little farther and stopped again. "This is the icehouse. At the winter's end, we cut blocks of ice from the thawing river and fill it full. So far, it has lasted us the entire summer, even with all the guests and parties and such. We chill the champagne and keep the larger food items cool in there, but for everyday use, the Pullmans actually have an icebox in the main house."

As they drew near to the double-seat outhouse, Sara asked, "We can use the privy, can we not, Thomas?"

"Of course. 'Tis the only one on the island presently, but I am to fix that this summer. One of my tasks will be to dig a second privy."

"Is your boss such a cruel taskmaster?" Sara asked. "Does he work you hard?"

"Oh, Sara. Settle your heart. Shamus—ah, excuse me—Mr. Hartwell is a fine boss. I enjoy the work, and I love being on this island."

With that, Sara took her leave to use the privy, while Katelyn stayed behind with Thomas. Several awkward moments passed with neither of them knowing what to say, but she hated silence. She had to speak.

"There's been much chatter in the bay about how perfectly medieval Mr. Pullman is in how he treats his workers. They say he is a hard man."

"Don't believe all the gossip you hear, Katelyn dear," Thomas warned. "He may be firm, but he is not cruel."

"And is the missus as mousy as they say?"

"You should have left all that prattle on the mainland. You'll not find contentment here if you don't hold your tongue. 'Tis too small a world on an island."

Katelyn gave him a narrow-eyed glare, stuck her chin in the air, and turned to the river view, trying not to comment on his scolding.

Just like his sister, he is. Why can't people enjoy a lively conversation now and then?

~~~

Thomas pulled off his cap and raked his hands through his hair. Katelyn had turned her back on him and squared her shoulders against his gentle counsel. He snatched a quick glance at her. *Is she so proud as that? And those stunning green eyes could bore a hole clear through a person. She's so beautiful and adventuresome on the one hand but so terribly opinionated and loose-tongued on the other. Does she always believe the town gossip? Must she repeat it? Those luscious red lips will be her downfall if she does!*

He glanced at her again and watched the sunshine paint tiny highlights of red in her auburn hair. He whispered a silent prayer for Katelyn and for his sister, entreating the good Lord to help them adjust to the new and very different world they just entered.

~~~

To Katelyn's relief, Sara soon returned to her side and took her arm. Thomas led them back to the dock to finish the tour. "The pumps and the boats are in there," he said, pointing to the large boathouse. "This is my world. In it, I am a jack-of-all-trades and a master-of-none, but I love the variety. One day I am a fishing guide, and another day I am building a cottage. One day I am fixing a boat; the next I am serving guests. 'Tis a fine life, indeed!"

"I hope we will feel the same, brother," Sara said. "I fear Cook might not be so free with our duties or our days."

Katelyn rolled her eyes and patted Sara's hand. As Thomas led them into the boathouse, she saw an older gentleman working on a large boat.

"Mr. Hartwell," Thomas said, tipping his hat and addressing the grey-haired man. "This is our new staff—my sister, Sara, and her friend, Katelyn."

"I be mighty pleased to meet you, misses," Mr. Hartwell said, tipping his cap to them. "You can call me Shamus, for that be me name."

Katelyn could see why Thomas liked his boss. His bald pate shone like it had been polished, while a rim of grey hair ran from ear to ear. His bushy eyebrows were the same grey, but they seemed to accentuate the many laugh lines around his kind brown eyes. As he smiled, his meticulously-trimmed, thick grey mustache framed his upper lip and seemed to dance when he spoke.

"Pleased to meet you, sir," Katelyn and Sara said in unison. Then they giggled, covering their mouths.

"Two peas in a pod, I see you be!" Shamus said. "I do hope you enjoy your work here, and 'may the best day of your past be the worst day of your future.'"

Thomas laughed and turned to them. "Shamus here is always putting forth a witty Irish saying for you to muddle over in your mind. 'Tis just one of his many fine traits."

Then he turned to Shamus and bowed slightly. "Best be getting these young women over to the kitchen. Wouldn't want them to be late for Cook's appointment."

"Dare not be late for the missus. She's a mighty woman who won't be taking no tardiness nor shenanigans. Off with you then, and, 'may the excellent Lord take a liking to you, but not too soon.'" Shamus laughed and picked up his tools to return to work on the boat.

Katelyn looked at Sara quizzically and shrugged her shoulders. She smiled and waved goodbye to Shamus as Thomas led them out of the boathouse.

"He talks like Grandfather," Sara whispered.

"He is Irish first and foremost, and he is a man of wisdom and goodness," Thomas said reverently as they approached the back door to the cottage kitchen. "Be sure you always enter this building through this door, never through the front."

Thomas knocked, wiped his feet on the rug, and opened the kitchen door. Inside, he paused to let them take in their surroundings.

Katelyn noticed that the large, well-stocked kitchen was obviously created to fill the needs of large parties more than that of a small family. A plump woman, who must be Cook, stirred something in a big pot on the stove, while a young girl cut potatoes and added them to an even bigger pot. Cook's ample bosom, midsection, and double chin attested that she tasted her cooking far too often. Her head snapped up at the interruption in her domain.

"Thomas, why are you standing there in my kitchen with these two forlorn faces?"

"These are your new staff, Cook. My sister, Sara, and her friend, Katelyn."

"Nothing but a wee little thing, you is," Cook said, casting her steel-grey eyes on Sara and clicking her tongue. Then turning to Katelyn, Cook lowered her chin and said, "And you willowy mite of a girl? I dare to hope you'll be ready for a hard day's work and strong enough to do the job."

Neither girl knew how to address those comments, so they remained silent.

"Well, don't just stand there, girls. Show me what you know."

Katelyn's jaw dropped open, and Sara began to shake.

Cook smacked her wooden spoon on the side of the pot. "Well. Grab them aprons over there. And you shoo, Thomas."

Thomas nodded to Cook, winked at Katelyn and Sara, and left the kitchen. They both took an apron from the hooks on the wall and put them on as they awaited further instructions. Peeking around the corner, Katelyn saw Claudia at a small adjoining alcove, working on some kind of pastry.

"Don't dawdle, you willowy thing! Come here," Cook said, pulling Katelyn from her thoughts. "My kitchen is not for daydreamers nor the faint of heart. You will learn the meaning of hard work, and you will learn much about running a proper kitchen. But be warned: you must follow my rules, or else!"

Cook began to rattle off a long list of expectations—from proper hand washing to knowing their place on the island—and much, much more. "... You are servants, the lowest of the low. You will be seen but not heard. You will hear but not tell. You will serve without being noticed. You will stay within your station. You will never betray a confidence ... or else."

Katelyn and Sara curtsied and nodded, acknowledging the volumes of rules and regulations. When Cook turned to check on the stove and the other kitchen maid, Katelyn whispered to Sara. "She's an absolute sergeant, that she is! How will we ever endure?"

Before she got another word out, Cook spun around as if she'd heard every word. "What did you say, Miss Willow? I'd better not catch you telling tales or complaining, or, mind you, I'll box your ears!"

"Yes, Mrs. Cook," Katelyn said.

"My given name is Mary Stanton, but you will call me Cook. Cook and nothing more."

"Yes, Cook. Sorry, Cook."

Cook stared at Katelyn for what seemed like an eternity before turning to the other girl. "Darcy, best be preparing the duck. You wee thing, Sara, is it? Finish peeling these potatoes. And Willow, or is it Katelyn? Get to peeling those carrots."

Claudia came into the kitchen and glared at Katelyn. She spoke quietly to Cook, who smiled and followed her into the alcove.

Katelyn grunted. *What is her problem? Why does Claudia get such kind treatment from Cook?*

For the next few hours, Katelyn and Sara peeled, cut, cleaned, cooked, and did whatever task Cook barked at them. As she worked, Katelyn made her own stew—an emotional concoction of frustration seasoned with Thomas' scoldings and anger from Cook—yet mixed with the excitement of fulfilling her mother's dream.

By dinnertime, sweat moistened Katelyn's brow as she struggled to keep pace with Cook's orders. She had barely made a peep the entire afternoon. Katelyn's many unspoken words just itched to get out. So when Cook went to consult with the housekeeper about serving dinner, Katelyn grabbed the opportunity to introduce Sara and herself to Darcy.

"Me name's Darcy Brady, and I'm pleased to meet you." Darcy's dark brown eyes reminded Katelyn of a little fawn, fearful and skittish, but her frizzy red hair sticking out from under her cap made her look like she was on fire. She appeared several years younger than Sara and Katelyn.

Smiling, Katelyn said, "I hope we will get on marvelously," and Sara nodded in agreement. "What shall we do now?"

"Rest when you can, but don't look like you're resting." Darcy's eyes darted about, landing on Claudia as she sat on a stool. "Cook will return with a flurry of jobs so we can get dinner together for the master."

"'Master'?" Katelyn repeated sarcastically. "We are not slaves. We are paid staff."

"You are my kitchen slaves, Miss Willow, as long as you work here," Cook said, stomping over to stand within inches of Katelyn's face. "And don't you be getting no high and mighty ideas otherwise!"

Sara's eyes filled with tears, and she looked like she might vomit. Darcy quickly turned to clean an already clean counter. Claudia smirked and left the room. Katelyn, however, stood her ground, aching to say something, anything, to let Cook know she would not be treated so. But something warned her to hold her tongue.

Finally, Cook gave a vigorous clap and addressed the staff. "Dinner will be served in ten minutes. You must work together to get everything ready to serve at exactly the same time. No exceptions!"

For the next hour, the kitchen buzzed with activity. Workers prepared bowls and ladles and serving spoons and trays with such beauty and grace that Katelyn couldn't help but be impressed. And pleased. And proud to be a part of the intricate dance. Only after everything was served did the girls get to sit down to their own meal, a much simpler fare, but a hearty one nonetheless. Claudia joined them, but she never said a word. Instead, she cast an air of superiority with eye rolls and glares and sighs.

By the end of the meal, Katelyn's emotional stew was thoroughly cooked, but she was so tired that she could hardly form a word. Darcy and Sara, however, happily chatted and ate their share and more. They acted as if they'd known each other forever, and Katelyn felt a wee bit jealous.

"Where's Cook?" Katelyn asked.

"She eats with the others," Darcy answered.

"What 'others'?" Sara asked.

"Housekeeper, Mrs. Duncan, and the butler, McCarthy, of course," Darcy said. "Bridget, the children's nursemaid, and Mr. Hartwell, the groundskeeper, sometimes join them. Other times, they eat whilst they work. I'm sure you'll meet them soon enough."

"It sounds like a mighty big task to serve here," Sara said, a mixture of fear and excitement revealed in her eyes.

"If it wasn't such a prison here, it might be a grand affair," Katelyn muttered.

"Don't be speaking so," Darcy warned. "If Cook hears, you'll be out on your ear."

Claudia stuck her chin in the air and said, "I quite agree. You'd better mind your manners, Miss Freckle Face."

Anger flooded Katelyn, and she searched for what she could say to Claudia. But just as she found the words, Cook returned. "Supper's over. Now get to work and clean up this mess!"

For the next hour, all four girls washed the many dishes that had returned from the dining room. They put away the leftovers, and cleaned the counters, the stove, and the floor; they made the kitchen sparkling clean. It was past nine o'clock when they were finally released for the evening.

"When the family is away, it is much quieter," Darcy said as they left the kitchen. "But when they have guests, it can be eleven o'clock or later afore we turn into our beds. Other times, we might have an hour or two off midmorning or in the afternoon if there are no other duties."

As the girls returned to the staff quarters, Sara sighed at the sight of the massive building casting dark shadows on the water. "'Tis a lovely place where we can lay our weary bodies down at night, don't you think? This grand porch looks magnificent in the moonlight, and it's so close to the water's edge. In our free time, maybe we can venture out onto it."

"If we ever get a moment free from such a woman," Katelyn complained.

"Cook's not so bad—if you know how to handle her," Claudia said, sticking her chin in the air and smirking. "Least-wise, if she finds you worth her time."

Katelyn snarled and opened her mouth to talk back, but she was so tired she had no words left to spend on such a person.

Inside their room, the four girls dressed for bed without anyone saying another word, save a cordial "goodnight." Before long, Darcy snuffed out the light, and three of the four fell fast asleep within minutes.

Not Katelyn. She continued to stew even as she struggled to embrace this new adventure. She felt the deep loss of her mother's ever wise and kind counsel, and she prayed the terrible ache might one day lessen to a manageable pain. Her mama had taught her to cook, clean, sing, and garden. Her mother had also taught her to shake off negative words or actions, to relegate them to a safe place in her mind and heart.

As her tired eyes filled with tears, Katelyn whispered into the darkness. "Oh, Mama! I miss you so. What have I gotten myself into?"

CHAPTER 3

Since the Pullmans preferred a tradition of simple breakfast fare, Katelyn's morning started out much easier than the evening before. It didn't take long to prepare the meal and serve the family. After they cleared the dishes, Katelyn and the others enjoyed their own breakfast.

Katelyn picked up the warm, flaky biscuit, split it in half, and took a whiff of its buttery goodness. Then she spread a generous spoonful of jam on each piece. Taking a bite, her thoughts returned to her mama. Every Sunday morning she had helped her mama make biscuits just like these. But instead of jam, the family had sausage gravy, thick and hot, "to give them a hearty meal and full belly as they went to church," Mama said.

Katelyn held back tears at every memory of her mama; though filled with love, the thoughts of her were also tainted with sorrow that seemed still too raw and real.

As she shook off her sad thoughts and cleaned up, Katelyn avoided Sara's gaze. She didn't want to share her thoughts for fear that her emotions might take over and cast a dark cloud on the day. Thankfully, Sara only smiled and tended to her own dishes.

Before long, Cook shook Katelyn from her reverie, barking orders for each of the girls to assume various chores around the island.

"Claudia, report to Mrs. Duncan and see what she may need. Sara, go out and weed the garden. Darcy, inventory the pantry and make a list of what we need from the mainland. Katelyn, go to the dining room and clean it thoroughly; I'll not tolerate a spot of dust or grime."

Katelyn and the others curtsied, said, "Yes, Cook," and quickly disappeared. Katelyn gathered the cleaning supplies from the closet and went into the grand dining room. She took a moment to admire her surroundings.

The soft morning sunshine streamed through the open windows, and so did the sound of the lapping waves. The muslin curtains danced gently with the breeze, and the scent of the river filled her senses.

Katelyn smiled as she scanned the room. A long, beautifully carved oak table with tapestry-covered chairs. A matching oak sideboard that held costly silver and cut glass serving dishes. A grand mantel above an open hearth. On the wall hung several trophy fish, a few larger than herself. In all her years, she had never seen a room like this.

This one room was larger than an entire floor of her farmhouse. When she added the parlor, the kitchen, and the upstairs where she guessed several bedrooms were, her head spun with the grandeur of it all. *And this is just a cottage? What must their mainland home be like?*

Katelyn shook herself from her daydreams and turned to her assigned task. She cleaned the room while pondering the past twenty-four hours. Orders. Rules. Scolding. And Claudia. How could she hold her tongue through it all? It seemed unthinkable.

As she skimmed the mantel with a feather brush, dust spun in the air, sending her into a sneezing fit. Once she recovered, Katelyn returned to dusting a wedding portrait set in a beautiful gilded frame, a baby picture of two tiny girls, and a photo of an austere man who she assumed was Mr. Pullman.

She cleaned the scuffmarks off the doorjamb. She wiped the spilled food off one chair that she assessed was one of the little girl's. She dusted the table, the chairs, the drapes, the sideboard and everything on it, the baseboards, and she finally swept the floor. And all the while, she thought about her life here on the island.

At home, her mama had always encouraged her to speak her mind. And during her schooling, her teacher was quite modern in allowing the children to openly voice their opinions, even when the thought was contrary to the lesson or different than what the teacher might think.

Apparently, Cook is very un-modern.

Katelyn understood that her teacher's way wasn't normal for all school children or even for most, especially when it came to girls. All her life she had heard the popular motto, "children are to be seen and not heard," especially from her father. That's what got her into trouble more times than not.

"Hello, miss," said a tiny, cheerful voice.

Startled, Katelyn turned to see two adorable little girls dressed in matching frills and pinafores. Big, bright yellow bows adorned their dark and neatly curled hair. Katelyn inwardly scolded herself for being so engrossed in her thoughts and her work that she didn't even hear the patter of little feet.

"Well, hello to you," she said, sitting back on her heels and smiling brightly. Before Katelyn could say more, a plump young woman rounded the corner. She guessed the woman to be the girls' nanny and her age to be five or six years her senior. She wore an impeccable grey-and-black uniform and her dark hair in a neat, tight bun. The woman's round eyes and face made her appear rather jolly, yet she lacked a smile.

"I'm Katelyn." She smiled at the woman, hoping to find a friend in her.

"I'm Bridget, the girls' nursemaid." She politely nodded, but then immediately turned to the girls and said, "You must stay with me, little ones." Both of the girls frowned as Bridget grabbed their hands.

"You have pretty eyes," said the older girl to Katelyn. "They're green like the river. And your hair is the color of the milk chocolate."

"Why, thank you! What's your name?"

"I'm Florence, and I am nearly four! This is my sister, Little Hattie. She's almost three. We call her Little Hattie because Mother's name is Hattie too, and she's big!"

Katelyn laughed as the chubby little cherub with a mouth full of teeth and a bright smile prattled on. She turned to assess Little Hattie, who sucked her thumb furiously and looked very much like her big sister, only she seemed shy and a little afraid.

"Would you mind very much if I leave the girls with you whilst I go to the privy?" Bridget asked.

"Why, not at all." Honored to be entrusted with the care of the children, even for a moment, Katelyn nodded. She stood, set her cleaning cloth on the buffet, and wiped her hands on her apron. "I'd love to get to know these two little dollies."

Bridget thanked her and left the room, while Florence whispered something to her little sister. The girls giggled, and their eyes danced with delight.

"We're not dollies," Florence said. "We are girls."

"I know. But you're both so beautiful that I could imagine you as the most perfectly wonderful dollies a doll maker could ever make."

Again, the two giggled, covering their mouths but appearing very pleased at her words.

"What's you doing?" Little Hattie asked.

Katelyn stepped closer to her, bent down, and gazed into her eyes, trying to ease her shyness. "I am cleaning your dining room so that it will be spotless for you to dine in, little one."

Little Hattie smiled and came close to her, so Katelyn knelt down to let her sit on her lap. She gently hugged Hattie and looked up to address her big sister. "What do you like to do here on the island?"

Florence beamed. "We play hide and seek, and we look at the fish from the dock, and we pick flowers, and we dip our toes in the water." Suddenly she stopped, and a shadow passed over her innocent face. "But we never, ever, ever go near the water without a grown up with us."

Katelyn squeezed Little Hattie, just a bit, and nodded to Florence. "That's a clever girl. You must be careful near the river, for the currents can be dangerous."

"Yes, but I like to ride in the boat, and Mr. Thomas, the boat driver, is so nice."

"That he is, Florence," Katelyn agreed as she imagined Thomas taking the Pullmans on a boat ride and chatting with these two little girls. The thought made her smile, hoping that one day, she would get to take a boat ride with Thomas too.

"Hello," said a prim and proper voice behind her.

Katelyn spun around and saw the woman who had to be Mrs. Harriet Sanger Pullman. Her regal beauty made her look like a larger, grown-up version of her daughters, only with dark eyebrows that accentuated a rather tight hairdo parted in the middle and pulled high on the crown of her head. Her day dress was a misty blue with wide puff sleeves.

"Good morning, missus," Katelyn said, fumbling to know whether to remove the little one from her lap and stand.

"Stay where you are. I am Mrs. Pullman, and I overheard the kind way you spoke to my daughters. Thank you. But where is Bridget?"

"She went to the privy, ma'am." She lowered her eyes, not sure what to say next.

Just then, Bridget returned, apologized for being gone, and took the girls by the hand. Katelyn stood before Mrs. Pullman. "You have a lovely island."

"I hope you will enjoy working here. What is your name?"

"Katelyn, ma'am. I came with Thomas' sister, Sara, to work in the kitchen, but Cook sent me here to clean."

Mrs. Pullman looked around the room. "And a fine job you've done, I must say. It was nice to meet you. Carry on."

Katelyn curtsied as the four started walking toward the door. Suddenly, Little Hattie broke away from Bridget, ran to her, and hugged her tight. Florence followed, and the two grabbed each of her legs, giving her a squeeze. Bridget appeared surprised and hurried over to gently pull the girls away.

Katelyn glanced at Mrs. Pullman, who had stopped and smiled at her girls' spontaneous act of affection. However, she raised a curious eyebrow at Katelyn before turning to leave the room.

"Goodbye, Miss Katelyn," Florence said, waving as Bridget led her toward the door. Little Hattie waved and smiled, too, so Katelyn waved back as they left the room.

What darling little girls!

Once she had thoroughly cleaned the dining room, she returned to the kitchen for further orders. And orders she got. Since the others had already eaten, Katelyn had a quick lunch of bread and cheese by herself. Then Cook sent her outside to pluck a freshly beheaded chicken.

Though she had done the job once before, her mama had seen her repulsion and hadn't required her to repeat the task again. The blood. The smell. The sound of the feathers tearing from the loose skin.

"Ewww! This is so disgusting. I'll simply have to fill my mind with more pleasant thoughts," she said to the chicken.

Thomas. The little ones. Shamus. Mrs. Pullman. These were the bright spots in her world now, so she would think on them. She would not dwell on thoughts of Cook or Claudia ... or chickens.

Her mind soon turned to a Scripture her mama had made her memorize just months before her death. "Whatsoever things are true, whatsoever things are honest, whatsoever things are just, whatsoever things are pure, whatsoever things are lovely, whatsoever things are of good report; if there be any virtue, and if there be any praise, think on these things." Yes, her mama had known her well.

Her mama had warned her about her propensity to think of things opposite from what this Scripture encouraged. She'd admitted to her mama that she just couldn't help but talk about things, whether good or bad. But Katelyn knew that a loose tongue would often get her into boatloads of trouble. Like when the school superintendent ranted about the schoolhouse and Katelyn spread the news about it until he paid her parents a visit. Or when the preacher's wife put on a little weight and Katelyn told everyone she was "with child" when she wasn't.

"I'm always getting into a fix," she whispered to herself as she continued to pluck the chicken. Relieved she had almost finished the nasty job, she blew out a breath. But in her distracted state, she hadn't realized the chicken blood had run down onto her shoes.

"Oh no!" She squealed as she dropped the chicken in the dirt. Looking around to ascertain that no one had seen her error, she picked it up, quickly wiped off the chicken, plucked the last few feathers, and snuck into the kitchen to wash it off, forgetting all about her shoes.

"What are you doing, you Willow? You're getting chicken blood all over my clean floor!" Cook stood there with her arms crossed, angrily staring at her. "After you clean up that mess—and my dirty floor—it seems that you're done here."

Katelyn gaped at her in shock. What had she done to be dismissed from her job? To avoid crying, Katelyn bit her bottom lip and turned to the sink, away from Cook's glare. Yet she could feel Cook's anger boring into her back as she washed the chicken and then knelt to clean the floor.

"Mrs. Pullman paid me a visit a little while ago. You didn't tell me you met The Family." The emphasis she placed on the last two words assured Katelyn they would have been written with capital letters. Cook paused, glared at her with narrowed eyes, and stepped closer. Too close. "Seems you have somehow weaseled your way into the main house. Lord knows I can't imagine how. I am the one to be choosing the dining room maid, and I would have chosen Claudia afore you. Just you mind that! But you have thwarted my plans, Miss Willow, and the missus has decided that you shall be the parlor and dining room maid."

Katelyn blinked, then stood with her feet frozen to the floor and her eyes wide.

"Close your mouth afore a fly enters, and report to Mrs. Duncan immediately. You will do as she says, but, mind you, you will report to me when she sends you to work in the kitchen."

"Yes, Cook. Thank you, Cook."

"Do not thank me. This is not my doing." Cook wiped her hands together and then on her apron. "I wash my hands of it all, and when you fail, you will return to *my* domain!"

Katelyn curtsied and left the room as quickly as she could. She looked heavenward. "Oh thank You for delivering me from the mouth of the lion!"

Katelyn scurried into the parlor to find Mrs. Duncan giving Darcy a pile of bed linens. "Change the sheets on the master's bed while they are away, and be quick about it." Though commanding, Mrs. Duncan spoke with gentleness, and Katelyn relaxed in relief.

Mrs. Duncan's soft hairstyle and kind face accented the many smile lines that framed her full lips and brown eyes.

After Darcy left, Mrs. Duncan turned to her. "Katelyn, is it? I am Mrs. Duncan. The missus has chosen you for a fine position, and I hope you will prove worthy. It seems she took a liking to you while you were tending her daughters?"

"Thank you, Mrs. Duncan. I will do my best to meet your approval—and hers." She paused and looked down at her dirty kitchen clothes, shuffling her shoes under the hem.

"I see you will need a new uniform, immediately." Mrs. Duncan winked and smiled, and took her to a large closet where several stacks of neatly folded uniforms sat on the shelf. Mrs. Duncan looked through the piles until she found what she was looking for and handed Katelyn a bundle of clothes. "The navy one is for serving, and the grey one is for everything else. I think they will fit you just fine. Mind that your apron is well pressed, and always wear the bonnet. And make sure your shoes are polished."

Katelyn nodded and went into the closet. She closed the door, quickly changed, and tried her best to shine her shoes with the hem of her soiled kitchen clothes. When Katelyn reported back to Mrs. Duncan, the woman took a long time describing her daily duties. There were many jobs to do as a parlor-dining maid, so she knew she would need to be flexible, but that was just fine with her.

This is so much better than the endless days I would have been spending with Cook!

Katelyn turned her attention back to Mrs. Duncan.

"Most of your days will be here in the main house, but there will also be times when you will work in the kitchen or run errands for me. You will also serve the table."

The hours of instruction flew by, and before Katelyn knew it, it was nearly time to serve dinner. She donned her white bonnet and frilly apron, put on a smile, and tried to keep her nerves at bay. Even though Mrs. Duncan had told her she'd be mostly observing and fetching things from the kitchen, Katelyn had never even been near such important people, much less served them, so her stomach wrenched with nervousness. She smoothed her skirt over and over again and fidgeted as she stood at attention, peeking out of the corner of her eye as the Pullmans entered the room and sat down.

Katelyn admired the elegance of Mrs. Pullman's attire, the finest pale green dress, the feather-embellished hair comb, the jeweled necklace. Her elegant hairdo accented her pretty face.

Florence and Hattie's dresses sported layers of excessive ruffles and flounces on their skirts. Their hair, immaculately curled and topped with oversized bows, shimmered under the candlelight.

Mrs. Duncan interrupted Katelyn's observations by sending her to retrieve the first course. Katelyn took a steadying breath, picked up the tray of soup bowls, and entered the dining room. She carefully set the tray on the buffet.

Mrs. Pullman spoke. "Mr. Pullman, this is Katelyn, whom I told you about."

Katelyn glanced at Mr. Pullman, and then to Mrs. Pullman, but the woman appeared frightened.

"Katelyn, I hope you will fit into our island staff." Mr. Pullman's words seemed to hold a veiled threat.

Katelyn curtsied and wondered if she should speak or stay silent. She stayed silent.

As she stole another glimpse of him, Mr. Pullman appeared quite the commanding figure. His full head of greying hair, his dark eyes and eyebrows, and his long, goatee-style beard made him appear stalwart, and from his thin lips, a deep baritone voice boomed as he turned to his wife.

"And I hope you chose well, Harriet," Mr. Pullman said, furrowing his heavy eyebrows.

Mrs. Pullman looked down, obviously stung by his words. She said nothing in reply.

"Hello, Miss Katelyn," Florence chimed in cheerily.

Mr. Pullman glared at his eldest daughter. "Florence, do not address the staff at dinner. It is not proper." His tone wasn't angry. It was simply commanding. Mr. Pullman was in charge!

Katelyn smiled at the little girl but kept silent and still while the soup was served. She stood beside Mrs. Duncan and the butler, Mr.

McCarthy, awaiting further orders. Katelyn shifted nervously from one foot to the other, pretending not to notice that the little girls kept looking at her. She didn't want them to get another scolding from their father on her account.

Mrs. Duncan continued to send her to the kitchen to bring the next course. Katelyn did as she was told, determined to keep her composure and do her very best not to cause any trouble as she moved through the dinner.

While Mrs. Duncan served dessert, she assigned Katelyn the job of pouring the tea. But as Katelyn poured Mrs. Pullman's cup, she got so nervous that she spilled the tiniest bit of tea on the tablecloth and saucer. Mr. Pullman responded by huffing and puffing as if she'd committed some grave error, and Mrs. Pullman appeared frightened by her husband's ire. Thankfully, the missus didn't reprimand her for the mistake.

Finally, the family finished their meal and retired to their bedchambers, and Katelyn sighed in relief. She helped clean up and set the table for breakfast. When Mrs. Duncan finally released her for the evening, Katelyn thanked her and returned to the kitchen to walk with the others back to their room.

As the girls made their way to the staff quarters, the thoughts that Katelyn had ached to share with Sara tumbled off her tongue. "Mrs. Pullman is so mousy and fearful of that man. He treats her positively beastly!"

"I can't understand why you are there in the first place," Claudia said, overhearing the conversation. "Cook was grooming me for the job." Claudia gave her a haughty stare and left in a fast and furious walk.

"She's just jealous, 'tis all," Darcy said. "I'm just glad Claudia has her own station and doesn't interfere with us very often."

"Is it very hard, Sara?" Katelyn asked, putting her arm around her friend's shoulders.

"Cook is not so bad. She was even nice to me today."

"Well, I'm not so sure Mr. Pullman is nice to anyone. He hollered at poor little Florence and yelled at his wife. He's simply insufferable."

"It can't be that bad," Sara countered. "We didn't hear any yelling or hollering."

"Well, he did."

For the rest of the walk to their room and as they readied for bed, the girls chatted about the small things of the day. Katelyn wanted to talk about the family and her new position, but she decided against it. It would only cause Claudia to be angry and Sara to disapprove.

Still, Katelyn thought she might burst from the force of her unused words. Mr. and Mrs. Pullman had discussed so much high society gossip. Oh how she would love to share it all with her friends, even though it was against the rules. But she must hold her tongue. At least for now.

CHAPTER 4

After a good night's sleep and a quick breakfast, Katelyn reported to the dining room for more training. But when she arrived, only the tall, regal-looking butler, whom she guessed to be in his mid-forties, awaited her. Though she had seen him, even worked with him the night before, they had not yet been properly introduced. As he busily set the table, Katelyn hesitated, biting her lip.

The man paused, tilting his head of greying, light-brown hair to acknowledge her arrival. "Mrs. Duncan is ill, so today I will instruct you in the ways of a dining maid. When she is well, she will show you your duties as a parlor maid." His well-trimmed mustache didn't move as he spoke, much less twitch with even the beginnings of a smile.

Katelyn swallowed. "Yes, Mr. ..."

"Mr. Joseph McCarthy. You can call me McCarthy. Just McCarthy, thank you. I have served as the Pullmans' butler for many years, on and off the island. They are like family to me." He looked down at her with piercing blue eyes, but she couldn't read them.

"Yes, McCarthy." Katelyn fidgeted and tried to calm herself. Just the sight of McCarthy reminded her of her father, a stern and strict man who had given her the lash whenever he thought she transgressed. Would McCarthy be like him?

She squared her shoulders and began her training with a great deal of trepidation. Throughout the morning, McCarthy taught her the proper way to set a table, the proper way to stand at attention when serving, to serve and remove the service at the proper time and in the proper way. Everything was to be proper, proper, proper.

But the most important point he made, repeatedly, was that she was to repeat nothing spoken at the table. "You are to see and not say. Hear and not share."

By noontime, Katelyn's head spun with information and exhaustion. She just had to find someone to talk to. It was her way of processing information, and if she couldn't talk, she feared her mind would explode. Thankfully, McCarthy gave her two whole hours off before she was to return for the afternoon lessons.

Katelyn went to the kitchen and found that since the Pullmans were on a neighboring island for a luncheon, Cook had given the kitchen girls the same two hours off.

"Can we enjoy an *al fresco* lunch together, please?" Sara asked Cook.

"Do what you want, but don't complain to me if ants spoil your meal," Cook said, wiping her hands on her apron.

Katelyn and Sara looked at each other and smiled with delight. Although they politely invited Darcy and Claudia to join them, both declined.

"I don't sit on the dirty ground to eat like a gypsy," Claudia said. Darcy excused herself to take a much-needed nap.

Katelyn took a clean towel and laid two hunks of bread, some cheese, and a handful of juicy strawberries in it. Sara grabbed tin cups and filled them with water from the pump. Then the friends scampered out the door and into the bright, sunshiny day.

The heady perfume of rain-washed wild roses attracted Katelyn's attention. Drawing near to inhale a full-lunged breath of the pale pink, blossoming bushes, she twirled with joy.

Giggling with delight, Katelyn and Sara hurried to choose a place to picnic. After finding a soft and dry spot of high ground, they sat overlooking the river, enjoying the meal, and relishing some time together.

"What a beautiful summer's day this is," Sara said.

"Yes, but I despise that we must spend most of our time inside. And you with Cook bossing you all day," Katelyn countered.

"I don't mind. She's just gruff on the outside. Cook isn't anything like she first appeared. She really is nice and helps me learn."

"McCarthy does, too, and he's nothing like Father, as I feared he might be. He's ever so patient, but he's also quite the perfectionist. He even uses a ruler to make sure the fork and knife are aligned properly."

"Mercy! I'm glad you have that job. I'd be so nervous waiting on such important folk as the Pullmans."

"Oh, I don't mind. It's actually quite exciting. But it's hard not to talk to the girls when I just know they want to talk. I cannot fathom how Mr. Pullman expects such tiny people to sit still, dine according to the etiquette book, and stay silent. It's barbaric!"

"I believe such high society folk aim to train their children in the proper way to behave." Sara took a bite of her bread.

"Proper. Pshaw! They are but wee children, and it's not fair to have them tied up so." Katelyn huffed out an angry breath.

Just then, Katelyn saw Thomas coming up from the boathouse, biting into a strawberry. She waved and called to him, thrilled to have an island veteran to process some of her new job duties with.

Thomas hurried over, plopped down close to his sister, and gave Sara a peck on the cheek. "Good day to you, lovely ladies! Don't you both look rosy today?"

"And good day to you, Thomas." Katelyn brushed a stray lock from her face. "Are you free, too? We have two whole hours off!"

"Do you now? I have just one, but I treasure the prospect of spending it with you fine ladies." Thomas leaned back on one elbow and casually sucked juice from another strawberry.

"I have been chosen as the parlor and dining-room maid!" Katelyn explained all that transpired until she finally stopped to take a breath.

Thomas winked at Katelyn. "Well now, that's quite a promotion. Congratulations!" Then he turned to Sara. "And you, sister? How are you getting on?"

"Very well, thank you. Cook really is nice. Not at all what I'd feared."

"See now? Your fears are often unfounded." Thomas gave her hand a squeeze and opened his mouth to continue, but Katelyn jumped in again.

She had so much to tell. So much to say. She told them all about McCarthy's kind ways, about the two wee girls, about Mr. and Mrs. Pullman.

"And did you know that Andrew Cornwall is going to pay us a visit sometime soon? I heard tell that he keeps the books on the sale of each and every island. I suspect that he's a cunning businessman who could easily take his share—and maybe more."

"Best not be making such assumptions, miss," Thomas warned. He raised an eyebrow to caution her. "He is an important leader in this community."

"But is he honest?"

"That is none of your business. 'Sides, remember the rule, 'hear and not say.'"

Katelyn wrinkled her nose, fell silent, and fretted about Thomas' comment. Now whom would she talk to? *Just like his sister. Always spoiling a fun conversation.*

~~~

Thomas prickled at Katelyn's rejection of his words of caution. He could see it in her eyes, her demeanor. Her full lips spoke so passionately, but that tongue! Well, she'd better take care to tame it, that's for certain.

His emerging feelings for her clashed within him, and his heart raced like a wild stallion. She was such an Irish beauty, with that thick, chestnut hair and creamy-smooth skin with a touchable splattering of dainty freckles. But her lack of discretion made him shudder.

Stealing glances at Katelyn as often as he could, he chewed on another strawberry as the two women chatted about the weather, about the scampering chipmunks, about their daily duties. Her laugh was like the tinkling of fine china; the sound wiped away his prior irritation like an eraser wipes clean a chalkboard.

His index finger twitched. He had to admit that he wanted to reach out and touch her arm, her face, but he flicked the impulse away as he tossed his strawberry top into the bushes.

~~~

When Katelyn and Sara returned to the kitchen, Katelyn could see that something was wrong. Cook called for Sara to stir a pot. Then Cook shot Katelyn a disapproving look.

Katelyn left Cook's glare as quickly as she could and had barely entered the dining room when McCarthy addressed her. "I have some important news for you, Katelyn. Mr. Andrew Cornwall will be our guest this very night. We must be ready. *You* must be ready, for a dinner party is no small affair in this house, even if it is with only one guest."

Katelyn's heart pounded in her chest, both from excitement and anxiety. She curtsied and looked at McCarthy with as much confidence as she could muster. "I'll do my best, sir." She rolled up her sleeves, brushed the hair from her face, and determined to do the job well.

Katelyn spent the rest of the afternoon trying to learn every detail of dinner service. With McCarthy's oversight, she set the table and readied the buffet. He talked about the order of the dinner, Mr. Cornwall's likes and dislikes, how a dinner party service was different than a family dinner. McCarthy was patient and kind, but he expected perfection, right down to the way she removed a plate or bent to serve a dish. As she memorized all the proper ways of serving a dinner party, Katelyn grew more excited by the minute. The rich smell of fish, onion, and thyme caused her stomach to growl.

"Go and change, miss," McCarthy instructed. "Our guest should be here presently. Remember the proper etiquette, Katelyn. With Mrs. Duncan ill, only you will assist me, and it must be done well."

Katelyn could hardly breathe as she slipped into her navy blue uniform in the closet. She donned her frilly white apron, fixed her hair into a bun, and pinned her starched bonnet onto her head. She peered into the tiny mirror on the closet wall, but she had little time to spare. Reporting back to McCarthy, he gently adjusted her bonnet, tucked away a stray strand of hair, and squared her shoulders.

"Well then, you look to be a true professional dining room maid. Good on you!"

Katelyn smiled, but her lips quivered.

"Fear not, lass. You have learned well and have a sharp mind. You will do fine."

As he finished speaking, Mr. Pullman and Mr. Cornwall walked into the room, barely taking notice of Katelyn and McCarthy. She stood there, still as a soldier and silent as a stone. But she listened and observed the two out of the corner of her eye.

Andrew Cornwall appeared to be well into his sixties. He was a short, stocky man with white hair, thick dark eyebrows, dark eyes, and a slight beard. He walked with a cane and a limp, and she wondered why.

"Pour us some wine, McCarthy," Pullman said.

McCarthy did as he was told.

"The missus will be down shortly. The children will dine with Nanny," Pullman added.

After several minutes, Mrs. Pullman came into the room wearing a lovely light blue dress with ivory ruffles and a full bustle. Her hair was braided and pulled back with ringlets flowing down her back. Katelyn couldn't help but gawk, for she had never seen such finery, except in pictures.

But she had no time to think on the missus' loveliness, for her work commenced. She was glad of it. Standing at silent attention only proved to make her more and more nervous.

Throughout the evening, McCarthy sent her to gather course after course from the kitchen. They had practiced well, for he barely had to say a word to her as he cued her with his eyes or a tilt of the head when to remove the dirty dishes or when to place clean utensils. Only once did he have to whisper an instruction. She loved it, the entire elegant dance.

She adored the scent of Mrs. Pullman's flowery perfume. She enjoyed the gossip and hearing the men make plans to sell the islands and seeing the animated discussion between Pullman and his colleague. And although Mrs. Pullman barely said a word, she often smiled approvingly when Katelyn completed her tasks well.

During the main course of trout, potatoes, and green beans, Mr. Pullman stopped eating, set down his fork and knife, and waited for Mr. Cornwall to do the same. "Say, I want to share some exciting news." Mr. Pullman paused again, grinned, and then continued. "I have invited President Ulysses S. Grant to be our guest and enjoy respite here from his re-election campaign. He, in turn, has invited his son and the respectable General Sheridan to join us for several days of rest and relaxation on the river. All have gratefully accepted."

"Well now. Just how did you manage that?" Cornwall asked. "I believe our president is a very busy man these days trying to win his re-election."

"We've been the president's friends for years, have we not, Harriet?" Mr. Pullman shot a glance at his wife but didn't let her answer. "We have even stayed at the White House. Andrew, I think we must make much of the president's visit. The press will surely descend upon this place like locusts, and we should be on the ready."

"Truly, it is quite an honor to have the president as our guest in these magnificent Thousand Islands. But what, exactly, are you suggesting?"

Mr. Pullman narrowed his eyes mischievously and drummed his fingers on the table. "We can use this visit as a chance to promote these islands and make them what they should be—the summer playground for the upper class." With an air of victory, he sat back in his chair, thumbs tucked in the pockets of his jacket.

Katelyn leaned in to hear more as Mr. Pullman continued. "With the press gathered about us for nearly a week, they will see what a paradise this is and tout it all over the country. Then the best of American society will flock to these shores, scoop up the treasured islands, and build fine mansions and castles all over the region."

"And my partner, Walton, and I will be rich!"

"Precisely." Mr. Pullman grinned wide. Then let out a deep, low, belly laugh that seemed to bounce off the walls.

My president here on this island? Oh, this is beyond my wildest dream! I wonder if I will meet him. Maybe ...

McCarthy nudged her, pulling her away from her daydream, whispering, "Fill the coffee cups and the missus' teacup, Katelyn. And stop daydreaming!"

"Yes, sir." As she filled the drinks, she tried to be as quiet and invisible as she could while listening carefully.

The conversation continued about preparing for the president's visit: where the honored party would stay, what they would do, who they would meet. Katelyn only heard bits and pieces of the conversation since McCarthy kept her busy running to and fro, delivering dirty dishes to the kitchen and returning with the next course. But in between, she strained to soak up all the information she could.

When dinner was done, Mrs. Pullman retired to her bedchambers, and the men retreated to the veranda to indulge in cigars and port and enjoy the cool evening breeze and twinkling stars. Katelyn happily cleared the table and set it for the morning meal. While she worked, she pondered all she had heard, but she prickled at the thought that she could not share any of this exciting information. It felt like being a child in a candy shop but unable to buy anything. How could she not share such tasty treats?

Still, they will all know soon enough, will they not? What harm would it do to share just a bit of the good news?

Returning to the kitchen, she waited until the three other girls put away all the dishes, and then the lot of them walked together through a wind-tossed evening. A storm was brewing. Sprinkles of pelting rain stung their faces and hands as they hurried to their quarters.

Once inside, Katelyn begged Sara to take a turn on the veranda with her, and Sara happily complied. Katelyn loved the rain and wanted to spend a few moments with her friend before falling into bed. Besides, she was about to explode.

"I cannot tell you what an exciting adventure has been thrust upon us, Sara," Katelyn whispered, pulling Sara close and leading her to the far end of the veranda. "It is beyond your wildest dreams. Life-changing and exceptionally wonderful!"

"Do tell. Please!" Katelyn could hear the curiosity in Sara's voice, but she could also see the caution in her eyes.

"I cannot. You know the rule. 'Hear and not say.'"

"But you have wet my wonder so." Obviously Sara's resolve had faltered.

"Well, if I tell, you must not tell a soul," Katelyn whispered, looking to and fro as if imps might be riding on the breeze, ready to snatch the information she so wanted to share.

Sara nodded, eyes wide and mouth open. Katelyn had successfully piqued her interest, and even though she knew it bent the rules, she'd tell her the news. She had to. She turned them both to look out at the river.

"President Grant is coming to our island!" Katelyn burst out, much louder than a whisper. There. She said it, and it felt so good to get it out.

"It cannot be so! How do you know?"

"I heard it from Mr. Pullman's very mouth. He's coming. And so are the president's son and the great Civil War General Sheridan. Mr. Cornwall and Mr. Pullman aim to create an island-buying frenzy whilst they are here." Katelyn swung Sara around in a circle as if starting a dance. But Sara stopped, turned white, and withered like a plucked rose.

"Oh, I am so nervous! What if I meet one of them? Especially the president himself? I think I shall faint before him."

"I shall be waiting his table, and it thrills me to my toes. Imagine, waiting on my very own president!" She rubbed her hands together like a child being handed her first dish of ice cream.

Sara's eyes darted back and forth, and she pulled Katelyn into the corner of the veranda. "Oh, Katelyn, we must cease this chatter at once! We are breaking the rules, and if they find out, who knows what might happen? We may be thrashed asunder!"

"They won't find out because you won't tell, will you?" she said confidently.

"You know I'd never betray my best friend, my Irish twin," Sara said, taking her hand and smiling. Then she looked out into the night, making sure a wind imp didn't snatch their secrets. "But we must never repeat this in front of anyone."

Suddenly, Katelyn heard a sound. She turned to see Claudia standing there, a smug grin crossing her lips. She had heard the entire conversation!

"Claudia?" Sara said in a much-too-friendly tone. "Come and visit with us, will you?"

"I would enjoy that. Thank you." Claudia drew close and cast a knowing look at Katelyn, smirking ever so softly. "So, Katelyn. What is new in the Pullman world?"

"Oh, just idle chatter, 'tis all." She tried desperately to change the topic. "Your pastries today looked simply scrumptious. The men ate them like candy. However did you learn such a skill?"

"I wonder if the president will enjoy them, too."

"You won't tell, will you?" Sara pleaded. "Please don't tell!" She grabbed Claudia's arm and burst into tears.

"Oh, I think we can avoid such a transgression since we are all becoming such dear friends. Aren't we, Katelyn?"

CHAPTER 5

Katelyn tossed and turned the entire night. Not only did the moonlight flooding her room keep her awake, but she also wondered how Claudia might betray her. Her comment was nothing more than a veiled threat, she was sure of it. She didn't trust the girl farther than she could sneeze.

She listened to the three girls breathe peacefully and occasionally stir. Katelyn tossed the covers back, heated by the thoughts of humiliation and error. She sat up, trying to catch the breeze that crept in the open window. But finding no relief, she plopped down on her pillow and silently scolded herself for what seemed like hours.

Katelyn awakened just before daybreak, long before the others. She quietly dressed and took an early morning stroll along the shore, hoping to clear her mind for the day ahead. She walked along the river's edge, not caring if the morning dew wet her shoes. She had more important things to worry about. What would she do if Claudia betrayed her?

As she neared the boathouse and docks, she saw Thomas already hard at work, adding heavy river rocks to the far end of the seawall.

A visit with Thomas will calm my jitters.

Katelyn watched him for a few minutes, enjoying the sight of the hard-working and handsome young man. She delighted in his strong muscular frame as he heaved large rocks and placed them where they would hold back the river's torrent. She smiled as he wiped the sweat from his brow and looked east.

"Thomas?" she finally called out. She tried to sound cheery and surprised to see him there.

Thomas jerked his head her way and quirked an eyebrow. Then smiled. "Well, I see we have a 'morning dove' on the island. You are just in time to give this hard-working man a much-needed break."

Thomas wiped his brow and hands and stretched like a sleeping bear. Then he walked up the bank to where she stood. At that moment, the sun peeked over the horizon, so both of them turned their attention to the sight. She sucked in a quick breath and felt a huge smile spread across her face as the yellows and oranges melted into the river's edge and cast a warm glow all around.

Birds chirped, and a few boats chortled along, creating waves that lapped against the shoreline. A rich fragrance of wild roses wafted on the breeze, mixing with the comforting scent of the river. Thomas stepped closer to her and gazed skyward. Katelyn joined him in admiring the puffy clouds that blocked the sun and scurried across the blue sky.

Thomas broke the silence. "Isn't this simply the best time of the day?"

Katelyn turned to him, smiling broadly. "'Tis magical! Truly. So different than the plainer sunrises at the farm."

"I love island life. I do. 'Magical' is a perfect word for how it feels to me too." Thomas' voice cracked.

Admiring his passionate words, deep voice, and handsome face, Katelyn felt a blush ascend on her cheeks as they enjoyed the sunrise together.

~~~

Thomas' pulse quickened and his nerve endings prickled when Katelyn stood close by his side. Her enchanting eyes, dazzling smile, and winsome words would set any morning aright. He snatched a glance her way, but she was absorbed in the summer sunrise. He couldn't help but grin wide as he admired her dark lashes and cute little nose. She was his morning dove.

That's what he'd call her. Morning Dove.

Just then, a gentle breeze carrying the scent of lemon verbena tickled his nose. Was that her mother's perfume she'd brought with her from the farm? His own mother favored it as well. He inhaled deeply and closed his eyes, wishing the moment would never end.

As the two stood side-by-side admiring the heavenly painting, Thomas listened to the rippling waves lap against a rocky shore. A deep sense of peace enfolded him like a blanket, warming his spirit, soul, and body.

~~~

Katelyn felt his eyes on her and wondered what was going through that handsome head of his. When the sun was fully up, Katelyn spoke, trying to break Thomas from his reverie. "What are you doing so early this day?"

Thomas blinked and cleared his throat. "Fixing the seawall. The undercurrents and river storms wreak havoc with it, so it must be repaired now and then. Shamus needn't do such hard work at his age, and besides, I enjoy it."

"What else do you do?"

"Oh, anything that needs doing, I suppose. Shamus is the professional boatswain here on the island. He is teaching me about maintaining the steam launch, the skiff, and the canoes, so I sometimes fill in for him. But I also act as a fishing guide, or I simply transport our islanders to wherever they need to go."

"Little Florence told me so. Seems she has taken quite a liking to you." Katelyn lowered her chin and grinned at Thomas from beneath her lashes.

"She's a sweet little thing, and so is her sister. I enjoy serving the Pullmans. All of them."

"But isn't Mr. Pullman just a brute? He barely acknowledges we exist." She felt a tinge of regret, but she crossed her arms and dug a heel into the soft grass.

"It's just his way. Let it go." Thomas raised his left eyebrow and stepped back ever so slightly.

Before she could offer a sharp retort, Katelyn heard the sound of girls' chatter and turned to see her fellow employees walking toward the kitchen. "Dear me! I must be getting to work. Nice to see you, Thomas."

"Farewell, Morning Dove." Thomas smiled a big, toothy smile and waved as she gave him a confused glance, picked up her skirt, and hurried to join the others. When she caught up with them, Sara asked where she had been.

"Oh, just taking a morning walk."

"In the direction of the boathouse? Scandalous!" Claudia snipped.

Katelyn sought safer waters by drawing Darcy into the discussion and ignoring Claudia. "How do you like the island, Darcy?"

"It is ever so different from the mainland. My parents' second story flat back home is smaller than the kitchen is here."

"And is your family large?"

"Just five. Mother and three brothers. I am the eldest. Father perished on the waters of Lake Ontario two summers ago, so I work to help feed the family." Darcy looked as though she might cry right there, so Sara put her arm around her shoulders and gave her a hug. Katelyn took Darcy's hand, while Claudia stopped and looked at the three, seemingly shaken by the news.

"I'm sorry for your loss, lass," Katelyn said, wondering why Claudia drew away.

"I lost my grandfather in the river last month," Claudia said flatly.

Before anyone could respond, Cook hollered out the kitchen door. "Stop lollygagging and be about your work! Your chatter will be the end of all of you."

Katelyn and the others snapped to attention and hurried to enter the kitchen under Cook's glare. Thankfully, she headed toward the privy. Katelyn gathered that they were all a little late, so she quickly ate her porridge without saying another word.

Cook came back into the kitchen, wiping her hands on her apron. "Claudia, you are needed this morning down at the boathouse to repair a sail. Be hasty about it, and do it well."

Claudia's eyes twinkled, and she smirked at Katelyn. As Claudia passed by, she whispered, "It will be a pleasure to see the handsome Thomas again. I believe he might be smitten with me."

Katelyn bit her tongue, but she glared at Claudia. Then, to show Sara her disapproval, she rolled her eyes and scrunched up her nose.

Cook clapped her hands. "Be about your work, girls."

Sara and Darcy began their kitchen duties, while Katelyn headed for the dining room, wondering what the day would hold. She was already tired from her restless night, but she was also excited to be a part of the dining room staff.

Since the Pullmans announced that they were going to the mainland for the morning, Mrs. Duncan and McCarthy took turns teaching Katelyn more about her dual roles, and the morning flew by. Two statements punctuated nearly every task: "when the president is in residence" and "when our special guests are present." Indeed, Katelyn noticed that both Mrs. Duncan and McCarthy seemed as nervous as she was about the prospect of the president's visit.

During their lunch break, Katelyn and Sara decided to take a walk around the island. As they strolled by a grove of trees near the boathouse, the low hum of a distant conversation, muffled by the lapping water and birdcalls, drew their attention. They followed the sound and heard Claudia's sensuous laugh.

"Oh, but you have big muscles, Thomas. Why, I haven't seen a specimen of masculine strength like this in all my life."

Katelyn and Sara covered their mouths and giggled softly, hiding behind a large wild rose bush while enjoying its fragrance. They waited until, after a long pause, Thomas responded. "I must take my leave and see what Shamus has for me this afternoon."

"Oh, must you? I enjoy your company ever so much."

"We should not fraternize so," Thomas said with a commanding, even scolding, tone.

"No one will know. They are all busy about their duties."

"As we should be. Goodbye, miss."

Katelyn peeked through the bush as Thomas turned toward the boathouse, passing them directly. She and Sara held their breath and tucked themselves tightly into the bush, receiving a prick or two from the bush's thorns in their effort to avoid discovery. Thankfully, Thomas seemed so deep in thought, even irritated, that he didn't notice them. Katelyn expelled her breath as Claudia huffed and turned toward the house. When she was a far distance away, Katelyn rubbed a thorn prick on her forearm and spoke her mind.

"Can you believe that shameless performance?"

"I think Thomas was angry with her. I know that look well," Sara said, shaking her head. "Claudia will not be able to weasel her way into his arms, of that I am sure."

"Shameful." Katelyn clucked, wagging her head for emphasis.

"We must return to our duties, or Cook will have our necks." Sara slipped her arm into the crook of Katelyn's and prodded her toward the house.

"She'll not have my neck. I report to Mrs. Duncan." Katelyn paused and changed the topic. "We dining staff are a trifle nervous about the important company coming just weeks from now, aren't you?"

Sara nodded as they joined the path that led to the kitchen. The two met Darcy along the way, and she handed each of them a small bouquet of dandelions. "To brighten your day."

"What a nice thought! Thank you," Sara said.

"I quite agree. Bless you," Katelyn said, touching Darcy's arm gently.

When Katelyn returned to the dining room, Mrs. Duncan sent her to fetch some ice from the icehouse. On the way, she stopped at the privy and found Thomas just leaving it.

"A fine afternoon, wouldn't you say, sir, even though a storm seems to be approaching?" She waved her arm toward the river and darkening sky.

"Good afternoon, Morning Dove." Thomas tipped his captain's hat ever so slightly.

"Why are you calling me that, Thomas?"

"Because, like me, you like the mornings. Besides, mourning doves are beautiful." When Katelyn felt her face grow warm, Thomas cleared his throat, changing the subject. "So how does your day fare?"

"I'm learning my way around the dining room and parlor, and I find Mrs. Duncan and McCarthy delightful to work with, even though they are both positively perfectionists."

"They must be, to meet the needs of the Pullmans. And so must we." Thomas raised an eyebrow.

Katelyn felt that his words somehow provided a gentle scolding, though she didn't know why. "And what has your day held, Thomas?" Katelyn hoped he might mention his tryst with Claudia so she could speak her mind.

"This and that. After I finished the seawall repair, of which you know, I weeded the garden and cleared the pathways this morning. It's a regular task I find always begging me to recall my humble farm upbringing." Thomas grinned like an adorable little boy. "This afternoon, Shamus and I are planning how we will expand the dock for the coming guests."

"Isn't it ever so exciting? I find my thoughts as wispy as the clouds flying overhead."

"Claudia told me before Shamus did. Now where might she have heard about the president's arrival before my superior?" Thomas bored into her with eyes that convicted without accusing. She said nothing.

"Katelyn," Thomas implored, touching her shoulder. "Mind the rules around here. Please. Your prattling ways may bring scandal to us all."

She pretended not to hear him. "I must be off. The missus needs ice." Giving Thomas a quick curtsy, she hurried to the icehouse, not even bothering to stop at the privy for fear she might again be confronted. As she gathered the block of ice, she could feel her face redden with guilt. She scolded herself all the way back to the house, remembering her school days and being told, "Your sin will find you out."

"Please, Lord. Tame my tongue," she whispered into the wind before she opened the kitchen door.

As the warm, humid afternoon drew on, Katelyn was sent to do a thorough cleaning of the parlor. Thunderclaps drawing nearer and nearer and intense light flashing through the windows announced the approach of a summer storm. She peeked out the open window and inhaled the refreshing smell of oncoming rain.

My first summer storm on the island. How I love the sound of a rainy afternoon!

The smell of leather-bound books turned her attention away from the storm. Perhaps one day she might borrow one or two of the volumes. Dickens and Dante. Longfellow. She ran her fingertips gently across the spines, wishing she could pull just one down, sit in the comfy chair, and journey to another place and time. But then she shook herself back to reality, recalling that she was a maid and needed to be about her work instead of lollygagging and dreaming the day away.

Just as she finished her thoughts, Bridget came into the room with the two girls, trying to occupy them and distract them from the stormy weather. Each time the thunder boomed, the girls would cling to Bridget.

"Are you two afraid of the storm?" Katelyn teased.

Florence and Little Hattie shook their heads violently, while Bridget nodded. *Hmmm. Nanny's just as afraid as they are!*

She walked over to the three and knelt down to be eye-to-eye with the wee ones. "Oh, there is no need to fear," she cooed, taking a hand of each of the girls. "The thunder and the lightning are friends. They are just playing a game of hopscotch up on the clouds, 'tis all. No need to fear a summer storm. The thunder is simply talking to the lightning, and then the lightning is answering back. I, for one, believe thunderstorms are lovely!"

"Truly?" asked Florence. "But they bring rain, and sometimes fire."

"The rain is a gift from God, but fire is indeed a tragedy. Yet it will not happen here. I promise." She looked up at Bridget's white and fearful face.

"You should not promise the wee ones such," scolded Bridget. "That is in the hands of Providence."

Katelyn gave the girls' hands a gentle squeeze before she stood and whispered in Bridget's ear. "Hush or they will fear all the more."

Just then, Bridget jumped as a loud thunderclap boomed, quickly followed by lightning that lit up the room. Florence and Little Hattie, however, stood still, watching Katelyn.

Florence clapped her hands and turned to her sister. "Let's play 'storm.' You be the lightning, and I'll be the thunder since I'm louder than you 'cept when you cry." Florence's face beamed with excitement as she went on to tell Little Hattie the rules.

Forgetting about her duties, Katelyn giggled, entranced as she watched the two create this new game.

"You play too, miss!" Florence said, grabbing Katelyn's hand. "And you, too, Nanny."

The two young women obliged the childish gaiety until Mrs. Duncan came into the room. "What's the meaning of this foolishness?" she asked, addressing Katelyn. "Do you not see that rain is coming in the open windows? Look at the floor. And the curtains. And the table is all wet! Be about your business, miss, and fast!"

Katelyn apologized and glanced at the girls in apology as well.

"Please don't be vexed with her, missus," Florence said, tugging on Mrs. Duncan's skirt. "It is my doing."

"Go about your play, little one," Mrs. Duncan said in a soft, gentle voice, patting Florence on the head.

Katelyn hurried to close the window and dab up the rainwater. "I must fetch a dry cloth to finish the table," she told Mrs. Duncan.

"The missus is vexed with me," she whispered to Darcy as she passed by her in the hallway.

When she returned to the parlor, everyone was gone, even Mrs. Duncan. As Katelyn dried the curtains, the table, and the knickknacks on it, she listened to the rain on the roof and scolded herself for the second time that day. How could she be so distracted, so irresponsible, so improper?

Yet those tiny cherubs can steal my heart in a butterfly's flutter. Oh why does everything here have to be so ... so proper?

Once she finished the task, she adjusted her uniform and returned to the dining room, where McCarthy and Mrs. Duncan had already prepared for the evening meal. Katelyn looked at the table set with extra places and turned to Mrs. Duncan for answers.

"Mr. and Mrs. Cornwall will be joining the Pullmans for dinner tonight, so we have much to do," Mrs. Duncan said. Then she whispered in Katelyn's ear. "We will not repeat today's tomfoolery, will we? And we will not speak of it again."

Katelyn nodded but saw a sparkle in the missus' eyes. A tiny smile crossed Mrs. Duncan's lips as she nodded ever so slightly.

Katelyn turned to her tasks and smiled. *Mrs. Duncan understands the wiles of the wee ones.*

That evening's dinner was much like the night before, only Mrs. Cornwall occupied Mrs. Pullman with island gossip and womanly interests. The two seemed to be grand friends, even though Mrs. Cornwall could likely be the younger woman's mother. Her pure white hair and wrinkled skin made her look much older than her husband, but her inner beauty hinted of a peaceful existence. Katelyn liked her.

All through dinner, the men talked about how many journalists might descend upon them for the president's visit and how to persuade them to promote the Thousand Islands in their writing.

"We shall treat the journalists as our guests, only we will keep most of them off the island. They may stay in the bay or camp on the empty islands, for all I care," Mr. Pullman said.

"But if we keep them away, how will they gather their stories?" asked Mr. Cornwall.

"We will manage them with carefully guided opportunities—tours of the islands, fishing trips, and such. We'll show them our best!" Mr. Pullman's face turned foreboding. "Andrew, we have much planning to do concerning these journalists. They must be for us, else they will be against us."

While she retrieved empty plates and returned from the kitchen with new courses, Katelyn watched the men out of the corner of her eye. She poured coffee and tea, cleared the table, and kept silent. But before the meal concluded, she was sent to help in the kitchen.

"Mind that you change and not dirty your serving clothes," Mrs. Duncan reminded her quietly.

"Yes, ma'am," she said with a quick curtsy.

Drat! I wanted to hear more. I wonder how many journalists will descend on our tiny island, and where the president and other guests will stay.

In the kitchen, Katelyn noticed that the drainboard needed cleaning. She set to it, trying not to disturb the graceful dance the others had settled into. She felt a little like an outsider here now but remained grateful to work in the dining room.

"Katelyn, thank you for cleaning up that mess. Now, if you'd please go and fetch some more ice. Seems the missus can never get enough on these warm, summer days." Was that Cook speaking to her? Katelyn swiveled to see. She spoke kindly, smiling even. "Did you hear me?"

Katelyn shook herself from her surprise and murmured, "Yes, Cook. Right away, Cook." As she stepped out into the cool, night air, she wondered about Cook's attitude and what other changes the morrow might bring.

CHAPTER 6

"Today we must polish the silver for the president's visit," McCarthy told Katelyn on the third day of her training. "All of it must sparkle."

"Yes, sir," Katelyn said with a smile.

McCarthy gave her a startled, eyebrows-raised stare.

Until coming to the island, Katelyn had never seen silver, never seen fine china, never seen fine porcelain or the kinds of treasures this house held. She admired their beauty and took great pride in caring for them.

To her surprise, McCarthy picked up a cloth and began polishing a large platter.

Katelyn broke the uncomfortable silence. "Do you like the island, sir?"

"Very much. The change from the mainland is always welcome. When Mr. Pullman bought the island in '64, it was an empty plot of ground, so he quickly built the cottage. Then he built the staff quarters, and just this past year, the larger building. He has great plans to build a castle here one day soon."

"But he should not have changed the name from Sweet Island, I think." As soon as Katelyn said it, she dropped the silver bowl that she held, knowing she had said too much.

"That is not your concern, and be careful with that bowl," McCarthy scolded.

Katelyn apologized, and then she sealed her lips, not wanting to anger the butler. Thankfully, McCarthy said nothing more and went on polishing the platter.

What is the matter with me? As Mama always pointed out from the Good Book, out of the abundance of the heart my mouth speaks.

McCarthy continued his casual history lesson. "Mr. Pullman's mother visits, and his brothers summer on nearby islands. Reverend James Pullman used to own Nobby Island until last year but now resides on Summerland Island. Reverend Royal Pullman summers on Wells Island and his brother, Albert, on Cherry Island."

Katelyn nodded. "All those wonderful islands? I have heard of such places but didn't know who abided there. It is too much to take in, sir. But oh, it would be splendid indeed to see a castle on this island!"

"Indeed," McCarthy agreed. Then he paused and turned the conversation to Katelyn. "And how are you faring here?"

"Oh, it is wonderful! I especially relish the thought of serving our president. 'Tis such an honor."

"That it will be. I have served him before, and he is a good man. But I have yet to meet the general."

"Please, sir, do tell me more about our president. I know he is a war hero, but my schooling didn't lend me much more information than that." Katelyn set aside the shiny silver bowl and picked up a bread tray to polish.

"You are correct. President Ulysses S. Grant is indeed an accomplished war hero. He led the Union Army to victory over the Confederacy in our great Civil War. But as our president, he has worked tirelessly to remove the vestiges of slavery and Confederate nationalism and has tried hard to defeat the wickedness of the Ku Klux Klan and protect our freed slaves." McCarthy paused and smiled at her. "Did you know that the Underground Railroad came all the way up here? Residents of Wolfe Island actually helped many slaves cross into Canada."

"I had no idea!"

"Moreover, our fine president has implemented the gold standard and increased America's trade and influence around the globe. He is a wise leader, and I will certainly vote for his re-election."

"I would, too, if women could vote." She smiled and fell silent. She liked McCarthy. A lot. He treated her like an adult, and he was patient and kind. Not like her father or Mr. Pullman.

Just then, McCarthy was called away to help Mr. Pullman, so she continued polishing the silver on her own. Her thoughts steered toward the day when the president would be in residence.

"I simply must change my ways. I will not speak my mind or gossip," Katelyn whispered.

Mrs. Duncan interrupted her private vow when she came into the room all in a flutter. "We must remove all this at once! Mr. Pullman has called for a luncheon with Mr. Cornwall to be served at one o'clock. I don't know how we will do it, but we must. It's nearly ten. Put the silver back on the shelves for now, clean up the mess, and then report to Cook to help her prepare the meal. I will attend to the table setting. Go!"

Katelyn curtsied and did as she was told. When she entered the kitchen, chaos reigned, and Cook was in a tizzy.

"Katelyn, go down to the boathouse and gather the fish Thomas caught this morning. If he's not yet cleaned them, assist him and bring them to me at once. And be quick about it!"

"Yes, ma'am."

Katelyn nearly ran to the boathouse and found only Shamus there.

"Please, sir, where are Thomas and the fish?"

"Steady, Katelyn. He is down by the seawall cleaning the catch. And 'may you always have a cool head and a warm heart,' dear girl."

"Thank you, Shamus."

Katelyn found Thomas where Shamus had indicated, standing over several fish on a makeshift table. She watched him raise a knife and chop the head off a large one. She recoiled at the sight, and her nose revolted at the odor of dead fish and worms and mud, but she knew she couldn't delay.

"Good day, Thomas. Cook has sent me on an urgent errand. Mr. Pullman is to dine with Mr. Cornwall at one o'clock sharp, and we are to have the fish ready for the luncheon."

"Mercy! I was preparing them for the dinner hour. We must make haste."

Katelyn surveyed the fish, amazed. "However did you catch so many?"

"They are hungriest at dawn, Morning Dove." Thomas smiled at her, and she felt her cheeks grow hot again.

"What kind are they?"

Thomas continued cleaning the largest one. "These are largemouth bass. See how big their mouths are?"

"If he were a bit bigger, he could swallow Jonah!" Katelyn laughed.

Thomas laughed with her. "These walleye are the tastiest. But enough chatter. We must hurry, or Cook will skin us alive!"

"Proceed then." Katelyn wasn't sure how to help, but she found the process both disgusting and interesting. "My brothers have caught bass, but I've not had walleye." She paused but felt uncomfortable with silence between them. "What are you to do before the president's arrival?"

Thomas continued to clean the fish as he responded. "Shamus and I have much to do. The steam launch is in disrepair, so all of his attention must be cast on that. All else is in my care at the moment—the dock needs repair and expansion, the pathways must be widened, and many, many supplies must be gathered for such a grand affair. We will erect tents for an open-air party the Pullmans will host. Thankfully, Shamus says the Pullmans will hire extra help."

"How will we ever complete it all in time?" Her head began to spin at the list.

"We must!" Thomas said so adamantly that she couldn't help but agree.

~~~

Thomas felt Katelyn's eyes on him and tried not to be self-conscious as she watched him work. He finished one fish and took up another, beheading it and removing the bones as fast as he could. He snatched a quick glimpse of her as she enjoyed a momentary sunshine bath, tilting her face to its warmth and embracing its glow. Her hair sparkled with tiny touches of burgundy, warming her crown—reminding him of her moments of temper that reddened her cheeks. Thomas smiled at the thought. *Oh if she would tame her temper and her tongue, she would be nearly perfect!*

Thomas stole another gaze at his Morning Dove. He caught her crinkling her delicate nose as the strong smell of fish wafted up to her, and that little action all but bid him to touch it. He imagined tracing his fingers along her cheek and tapping her nose playfully. He snapped out of his reverie and turned his attention back to the much less appealing work of preparing the fish.

~~~

Just when Katelyn grew so absorbed in admiring Thomas' swift skill with the blade that she forgot about the luncheon, he handed her the platter of fish. "There are plenty for the two men and likely some for us. Take these, and save Cook from having a seizure."

She giggled at his comment as he touched her hand and looked into her eyes.

"You have a lovely laugh," he said. "Now go. Until we meet again."

Katelyn scurried off to the kitchen, her heart beating wildly in her chest. His touch, his words, his smile all sent her adrift on a river of dreaming, and she had to shake it off before returning to the cottage. She took a deep breath to compose herself, entered the kitchen, and found it as she had left it, the air thick with stress and worry.

"Thank you," Cook said, taking the platter. "Now, grab an apron and help Sara and Darcy with the potatoes, carrots, and beans. Claudia is working on lemon cookies and hot rolls. And I will tend to the fish. We simply must accomplish this in time." Cook wiped her brow and grunted. Katelyn wondered if she'd have a stroke with all her worry. She thought of Thomas' comment and giggled.

"What's so funny?" Sara asked in barely a whisper, handing her a knife and pile of carrots.

"Nothing. Thomas is funny, 'tis all."

"Yes, he is. From my earliest recollection, he always made me laugh. What did he say?"

Katelyn drew near Sara's ear and whispered, "He said I needed to hurry, else Cook would have a seizure."

Both girls laughed quietly but were startled when Claudia came up from behind. "What's so funny that you stop your work?" she said, loudly enough for the entire kitchen to hear.

Sara's eyes filled with fear and Katelyn's with anger. Both looked around to see if Cook had heard. Thankfully, she had gone outside.

"Nothing, and we *are* working!" Katelyn said, turning her back on Claudia to peel the carrots.

"Humph! I am nearly done with the cookies, and they are splendid indeed." Claudia went to the oven to check on them; a blast of heat made the kitchen even more uncomfortable on such a humid summer's day.

Claudia took the cookies from the oven, gave a sniff, and tossed her head. "Perfect! As always."

"That girl always gives herself airs," Katelyn muttered.

Once they'd completed the vegetable preparation, Cook sent Katelyn back to Mrs. Duncan. It was nearly noon. She wiped off the kitchen sweat and soil and changed into her navy serving uniform.

Mrs. Duncan now appeared calm as she hovered over a complete, perfect table setting. "Mrs. Pullman is going to join the men, but Bridget has fallen ill. Mrs. Pullman requested that you take charge of Florence and Little Hattie since Mr. Cornwall is quite contrary to having children around."

"I would be delighted, Mrs. Duncan. Thank you." Katelyn curtsied, went to change into a clean, grey uniform, and hurried to the nursery. There she found Mrs. Pullman reading to the girls.

"You are a pleasing sight," Mrs. Pullman said. "Bridget is ill, and I must prepare for the luncheon at once. I would like you to take the girls on a picnic and then put them down for a nap."

"Yes, ma'am. It would be my pleasure."

Mrs. Pullman gave each of the girls a peck on the forehead and instructed them to be good and mind Katelyn. The girls smiled widely.

"Summer staff is much too sparse for such times as these. I must speak with Mr. Pullman about rectifying the situation," Mrs. Pullman said to herself as she walked out the door.

Katelyn turned her attention to the girls. They were focused on the book their mother had been reading to them, the story of Little Red Riding Hood, and it was in color. Katelyn had never seen a colored storybook, and she couldn't wait to peruse it.

"May I finish reading this before we have our lunch?"

"Start from the beginning, please," Florence said, sounding very grown up.

"Gladly." Katelyn chuckled and sat on the window bench as both girls snuggled up on her lap. Little Hattie popped her thumb into her mouth and rested her head on Katelyn's chest.

"I'll turn the pages for you," Florence said, sitting quite erect and proper.

Little Hattie stared at Katelyn's nose and finally gave it a gentle touch.

"Is something wrong, wee one?"

"Your nose. It's so wittle. I wike the dots that dance on it."

Katelyn laughed and hugged the little girl. "They are called freckles, and I'm glad you like them."

She continued to read the book to the girls, amazed at the beautifully colored pictures. She pointed and asked questions, and the girls answered all of them. They obviously had read the book many times.

"The end!" Katelyn said as she closed the cover. "Let's go and see what Cook has for our picnic."

The girls hopped off her lap and took her hands. Little Hattie yawned, and Katelyn picked her up. "Are you tired, wee one?"

"Not very much," Little Hattie responded. "Picnic!"

Katelyn smiled at the tot. Then the three went to the kitchen and found the heat stifling.

"Too hot," Hattie said.

Katelyn took them to the back door and set Hattie down next to Florence. She bent down to bid them to be quiet. She wasn't sure if the men were already in the dining room and feared Mr.

Cornwall would be vexed. "I'll be just a minute. I need to fetch our lunch. Florence, would you hold your sister's hand? Let's see who can be quiet as a mouse."

Katelyn quickly gathered the picnic basket and headed out the door with her charges. The fresh air felt invigorating, but the hot summer sun beat down on them. "Let's find a shady spot in the forest over there. Then, after we eat, perhaps we can play Little Red Riding Hood."

"Pway now!" Little Hattie said, excitedly.

"We will eat first. Then play."

"Pway now!" Little Hattie demanded, stomping her little foot.

"Let's find some shade first," she said, hoping Hattie would forget about playing once they set up their picnic.

The three found a shady spot among a grove of tall oak trees. It was several degrees cooler there, and a gentle breeze off the river made it quite comfortable.

"I be Widing Hood," Hattie said.

"I'll be the wolf," Florence said.

"Girls, look at all this good food for us to partake. Riding Hood and the wolf need food to play and be strong," Katelyn teased.

"Growl!" Florence said as she sat down on the blanket, pretending to be a wolf.

Little Hattie popped her thumb in her mouth and sat on Katelyn's lap. She wasn't quite sure how to get Hattie to eat when she had her thumb in her mouth or how to get Florence to sit like a lady and eat properly when she was pretending to be a wolf. So she decided to pray first.

She took the girls' hands, and they looked surprised. She began to pray—first for Bridget to feel better and then for the grownups' luncheon. Finally, she prayed for the food and for their time together.

Florence sat up on her knees. "I like to pray, but we only pray one prayer and only at night. 'Now I lay me down to sleep. I pray the Lord my soul to keep. If I should die before I wake, I pray the Lord my soul to take. Amen.'"

"Well done, Florence! You are a clever girl." Katelyn patted her hand.

"But I don't want to die," Florence whined, tears welling up in her eyes.

"Oh, wee one, not to worry. The good Lord has plans for you. The Bible says they are good plans, to give you hope and a future."

"What's a Bible?" Florence asked.

"Sweet child! It is God's very words written down for us so that we will know who He is and how to behave." Katelyn smiled and handed Florence a ripe strawberry. Little Hattie happily ate a piece of cheese and seemed to forget all about the game.

How lovely it would be to have such sweet cherubs one day! I will certainly teach them about the Bible and how to pray.

"Pway now!" Hattie said, jumping off her lap and putting a napkin on her head. "My hood!"

Katelyn and Florence laughed together as they watched the tiny girl pretend to be Little Red Riding Hood, sweeping her dress around and carrying the now-empty picnic basket on her arm.

"You be Grandmother," Florence said, grabbing Katelyn's hand. "You are sick, but you won't die, because the Lord has plans for you."

She joined the two as they acted out what they remembered of the story. Florence growled and scratched the air with her pretend claws and looked terribly wolf-like, even in her pretty summer dress. Little Hattie tried desperately to keep the napkin-hood on her head, but when a tree branch picked it off, Hattie cried so loudly that Katelyn feared the grownups would hear her clear inside the house.

Katelyn calmed her down, retrieved the napkin, and placed it back on her head. Then she pulled a hairpin from her hair and fastened the napkin securely on the little one's head. "There now, your hood will stay secure." She gave her a little pat on her head, and Hattie happily returned to the game.

When they were finally finished pretending, Katelyn said, "The end. Well done! You are quite the wee actresses. I'm proud of you."

The three sat down and let the cool river breeze dry their sweaty brows. When Little Hattie yawned and lay down on the blanket, Katelyn and Florence gathered up the remnants of crusty bread, the discarded strawberry tops, and the tin cups. She loaded them in the basket, and with Florence's childish help, folded the blanket and laid it atop the basket.

Katelyn picked up and awkwardly carried Hattie, the handle of the wicker basket in one hand, while Florence held onto Katelyn's skirt. They stopped by the privy before heading back to the house for the girls' much-needed naps.

After Katelyn dabbed a cool cloth on the girls' faces and removed their shoes and socks, Florence yawned and snuggled beneath the coverlet that Katelyn tucked about her. "Today was fun! I like you, Miss Katelyn."

"Me, too!" Little Hattie said, popping her thumb out of her mouth just long enough to say so.

"Well, I like the two of you very much. Now sleep, and I will be here whilst you dream."

Katelyn gave each of them a kiss on the forehead and moved to the far end of the room. She picked up the storybook again and sighed, admiring its colorful pictures.

I think Bridget's job may be even better than mine!

CHAPTER 7

After the staff served a simple, light supper to the Pullmans, their day ended early. At barely seven o'clock, Katelyn was released for the evening, Bridget faring better and taking over. Once the girls returned to the staff quarters, Sara, Darcy, and Katelyn settled on the veranda to enjoy the summer breeze and watch the stars reveal themselves, one by one, in between the big, puffy clouds.

"Today was rather difficult, do you not think?" asked Darcy. "I was frightfully worried that we would not have the luncheon ready on time."

"But we did it, and that's that," Sara said. She sounded quite confident and cheery, and Katelyn liked seeing her friend like that. "Katelyn, do tell about your day with the girls."

"Charming little cherubs they are, but they are next to heathens. I prayed with them, and they seemed not to know anything about the practice. Florence even asked what the Bible was."

"Surely you err," Darcy said. "Society folk aren't heathens. The Pullmans are not heathens. You mustn't say such things about our employers. Someone might hear."

"Like me?" Claudia said, rounding the corner and scoffing at Katelyn. "You have a mighty big opinion of yourself, miss. I wouldn't allow it if I were your boss."

Katelyn felt her face turn bright red, and she scowled at Claudia. "Well, you aren't, and I would appreciate it if you didn't stick your nose where it doesn't belong!"

"Humph! I've never endured such beastly treatment!" Claudia turned on her heal and stomped away, her shoes making a loud *clomp, clomp, clomp* on the wooden deck.

"And good riddance," Katelyn said. "Now, where were we? Oh yes, about the cherubs." She told them more of her afternoon and how much she enjoyed being a surrogate nanny.

After Darcy and Sara shared about their days, they decided to dip their feet in the river. The three splashed and laughed as they frolicked in the cool water. Then they washed up and returned to their room.

They found Claudia already asleep, so they silently went to bed. But before she closed her eyes to sleep, Katelyn remembered the veranda incident and asked God to help Claudia forget all about the "heathen" comment.

Why, oh why, can I not keep my opinions to myself, just for once? Will I forever be cursed with such a mouth?

She suddenly missed her mama, her wisdom, and her counsel. Her mama was the one who had taught her to love and trust God, and to hide Scripture in her heart. But ever since that terrible day of Mama's death, Katelyn's faith had begun to waver, her prayers to falter. Somehow, wee Hattie and Florence reminded her of her mama and all she had taught. She whispered her gratitude, sending it to the heavens as a silent plea to God. Yet Katelyn struggled to let go of her cares, and it took a long, long time to fall asleep.

The following morning they woke to rain, so Katelyn and the others pulled their aprons over their heads and ran to the kitchen as quickly as they could.

"What a downpour!" Katelyn said, scurrying inside. "We are wet all the way through."

"Well, you'll be getting no mercy from me," said Cook. "Eat your porridge and get to work."

The girls consumed their breakfast in silence. Cook ate with them at the far end of the table, but she huffed and puffed her way through the meal.

"What's wrong with her?" Darcy whispered.

"She's in a terribly sour mood this morning. Better steer clear of her wrath, ladies," Katelyn said.

"What did you say?" Cook asked, rising from the table like a bear from her den.

"Nothing, ma'am. I best be getting to the dining room and attend to my chores for Mrs. Duncan." Katelyn curtsied and hurried out the door before Cook could ask more.

"Whew! I nearly caught it again," she said to herself.

Mrs. Duncan and McCarthy were already setting the table.

"Goodness. You can't wait the breakfast table looking like that!" Mrs. Duncan said. "Change your uniform and fix your hair."

"Yes, ma'am," Katelyn said as she scurried to the closet to change out of her wet uniform.

"Everyone seems in a stormy mood today," Katelyn mumbled as she hurried to put on a clean, dry uniform and fix her hair.

Upon returning to the dining room, Katelyn found the Pullmans already seated at the table. She slipped in next to McCarthy and stood at attention, waiting for orders.

"You are late, miss!" Mr. Pullman said, not taking his eyes off the paper he was reading. "I will not tolerate tardiness."

"Yes, sir. Sorry, sir," Katelyn said timidly, wanting to justify herself ever so much but knowing she must hold her tongue.

"Do not let it happen again. Florence, sit up straight. Hattie, take that thumb out of your mouth at once."

Katelyn peeked at the girls, watching their eyes well up with tears.

"Really, dear, must you fuss at the children so?" asked Mrs. Pullman.

Mr. Pullman glared at his wife over the top of the paper. "I am their father, and you, my dear, will not counter me in front of others." He slammed his hand down upon the table, shaking the silver and china. "Where is my coffee?"

McCarthy hurried to tend to his coffee cup, pouring the dark liquid flawlessly. Mr. Pullman looked at it and shook his head. "There are grounds in this. Be off with it!"

"Yes, Mr. Pullman, sir." McCarthy removed the cup and saucer, setting it on the buffet. Mrs. Duncan handed the pot to Katelyn and sent her to the kitchen. The enjoyable smell of coffee wafted up to her nose as she set the pot on the counter.

"Mr. Pullman is mighty vexed to find grounds in his coffee. We need more—quick!"

"There are no grounds in the coffee. I tasted it meself," Cook said. "Claudia, strain the coffee. Again. Now!"

Claudia did as she was told and handed Katelyn a freshly strained coffee, smiling. Katelyn couldn't tell if her smile was genuine or not, but she had little time to ponder it.

She returned to the dining room and gave McCarthy the pot. Both Florence and Little Hattie were now crying, and Mrs. Pullman stared at her husband in disbelief.

"Maybe now they'll learn to behave at the table," Mr. Pullman said flatly. "And they may not leave this table until we are through."

Mrs. Duncan sent Katelyn back to the kitchen to gather the main breakfast. Katelyn's anger rose, and she grunted her disapproval as she entered the kitchen.

"He's terrorizing those wee babes, that he is! The man is a barbarian," Katelyn whispered to Sara as she took the tray of food. "He should be jailed—or worse."

Before giving Sara a chance to respond, Katelyn rushed out of the kitchen and back to her station. Mrs. Duncan, McCarthy, and Katelyn served the food as a dark cloud of sadness and—what was it?—fear?—hung heavily over the room. The girls picked at their food through sniffles and sobs, and Mrs. Pullman moved the food around her plate. But Mr. Pullman ate heartily, smacking his lips, even burping once. Katelyn's ire grew like an ugly storm cloud, and she felt her face and neck grow crimson.

The beast! How dare he torture his family!

Katelyn worked herself into a frenzy with theories of what Mr. Pullman might have done to create such an atmosphere. When Mrs. Duncan told her to pour the coffee, her hand shook with so much anger that she spilled some onto Mrs. Pullman's saucer.

"Clumsy girl!" Mr. Pullman hollered at her and turned to his wife. "Mrs. Pullman, you should have allowed Cook to choose the proper girl for this station, not poke your nose into such business." Mr. Pullman paused to give Katelyn and then his wife a tyrannical glare. "I am off to my study. And see that I am not disturbed." He lay down his paper, wiped his mouth, and left without anyone responding to him.

Katelyn pinched her lips together, feeling her throat tighten and her heart thump. After their employer stalked out of the room, both Mrs. Duncan and McCarthy simultaneously released a deep sigh.

Both girls burst into tears. "Why does he hate us so, Mother?" Florence asked through her sobs.

"This is not the place for such talk, darling. Let's go to the nursery." Mrs. Pullman glanced at Katelyn and the others, gathered her girls by the hand, and whisked them out of the room.

"The poor woman. Imagine being married to such a man," Katelyn said under her breath.

Mrs. Duncan snapped her neck in Katelyn's direction. "What did you say?"

Katelyn didn't realize she had spoken out loud. She was so angry, so frustrated, so offended by the pain of the two wee ones. "Ah, nothing, ma'am! What shall I do now?"

"What did you say, miss?" Mrs. Duncan demanded.

"Nothing, ma'am." Katelyn lowered her eyes and felt that infernal blush on her face, hoping beyond hope that she would not have to confess what she didn't mean to say.

"You had better not say anything like I just imagined you said, Katelyn. This position is one of trust and honor, and if you will not be trustworthy and honor your employers, then we will find someone who will. You are to hear and not speak, is that not true?"

"Yes, ma'am." Katelyn's voice shook with a mixture of fear, regret, and anger. Did she sound as if she were a whining child? She balled her hands, willing the tension to move down her arms and away from her face.

"I expect you will never presume to speak your mind again?" Mrs. Duncan's eyes held a dire warning.

Swallowing the lump in her throat, Katelyn answered in a small voice. "No, ma'am. Sorry, ma'am."

"All right then. Once you have cleared the breakfast service, I need you to tidy the parlor and then return to the task of polishing the silver. You must accomplish all the polishing that you can today, for we have very much to do in the days to come. Mrs. Pullman has decided to host an outdoor tea party in just two days. Her guests will be her mother-in-law, Mrs. Simmons, and Mrs. Cornwall. And when she has a tea party, she expects it to be perfectly proper. Do you understand?"

"Yes, ma'am," Katelyn mumbled, but then she stood stick straight, raised her chin, and squared her shoulders.

"Be about your work, then. You are excused."

Katelyn curtsied and hurried into the kitchen with all she could carry. She took a deep breath, and then sighed, holding back tears of embarrassment. A heavy cloak of guilt enveloped her, and regret weaseled its way into her thoughts.

How could she? How could I?

Katelyn had to get away, if only for a moment. After a quick trip to the privy, she returned to the house to finish cleaning up the dining room. She was thankful to find neither McCarthy nor Mrs. Duncan present. She needed to be alone with her thoughts. She couldn't understand Mr. Pullman or Mrs. Pullman or even Mrs. Duncan. How could they tolerate such abuse of sweet babes like Florence and Little Hattie?

As she completed her cleaning, McCarthy came into the room. "Sit, please, Miss Katelyn." He seemed so serious, so somber, that Katelyn feared another tongue lashing—or worse. He pulled up a chair facing her and looked directly at her.

"I know you are young, but you must honor the ways of the Pullmans. Marriage is a difficult thing, and some marriages are more difficult than others. Parenting is hard as well; you and I are not skilled in such tasks, so we must not judge."

McCarthy paused and looked deep into her eyes as if he examined her very soul. "You were not here when Mr. Pullman disciplined his children. Always remember that assumptions and judgments are rarely accurate. Even if they are, it is not your place to judge, and it is certainly not your place to speak such judgments."

Katelyn's eyes brimmed over with tears, and McCarthy took her small hands in his large ones. "There, there. All of us are human and err. When I was young, I also held many opinions that were not for me to speak. But I will tell you a secret; I found a leash for my tongue in one place, and in one place only."

Katelyn grasped at the small glimmer of hope. "Where, dear sir? Do say."

"In the Word of God. In the book of Proverbs, mainly, but in other texts as well. They hold the keys to control, if you will but apply them."

"Thank you, sir. I will look for the keys." Katelyn wiped at her tears.

McCarthy handed her a napkin, and she blotted her eyes. "Now go to the parlor and do your work, and tell no one of our words. But know that I am here, Katelyn, and know that as you struggle against the fires within, I will pray for you."

Katelyn burst into tears again and whispered "thank you" as her superior shooed her into the parlor. As she worked to tidy and dust and sweep and mop, she tried to recall the memory verses of her childhood. Her mama had taught her many Scriptures, especially about the tongue. But her mind was too full of regret, of embarrassment, of failure.

"Katelyn," Mrs. Duncan said, interrupting her muddled thoughts. She again dried her eyes before turning to address her. "For heaven's sake! Are you still moping over this morning? Be done with it; we have work to do!"

"Yes, Mrs. Duncan." She curtsied, not quite sure what more to do or say.

Mrs. Duncan's tone softened, but she was still not herself. "Mrs. Pullman has decided that you and Thomas will solely serve the tea. I'm certain I don't know why, but we must do as she requests. The rain has stopped, so I need you to go and fetch Thomas. Then I will instruct you both in the proper ways of a garden tea service. Thomas has done it before, but it has been a year, and I am certain he needs a reminder."

"Yes, ma'am. Thank you, Mrs. Duncan."

As Katelyn passed by her, Mrs. Duncan placed a gentle hand on her shoulder, stopping her and addressing her quietly. "None of us is perfect, dear girl. Mind your manners, and learn from your transgressions."

"Thank you, Mrs. Duncan. I will."

Mrs. Duncan's kindness nearly undid her again. She held her tears in check, but they threatened to brim over and burst like a dam.

I will not cry, especially in front of Thomas.

Katelyn stopped and gulped the summer breeze, thankful to be out of the hothouse of emotions. She looked up to see the clouds gathering and wondered if there would be yet another summer rain coming, so she hurried down to the boathouse. She found Thomas working on the dock, gave him Mrs. Duncan's message, and urged him to come with her back to the house.

"I have so much to do afore the president's coming, and now I have to relearn and serve a garden tea?" Thomas complained as he walked with her.

Was the entire island grumpy?

~~~

Thomas tried to shake off the irritation he felt. It wasn't Katelyn's fault that he was being summoned to serve tea. Well, at least he would be near her as they worked, and that would be a pleasant distraction. As he walked beside her, he sensed that Katelyn was upset. She seemed tense, stoic, and all too quiet. Oh how he longed to calm her jitters, to comfort her, to hear of her cares!

He glanced at Katelyn's face. Her eyes were red, and her porcelain skin held fading blotches. She had been crying. Why? If only he could hold her in his arms and soothe her stormy day.

No! He must tend to his duties and not get so involved with Katelyn—or her cares or her secrets. Lately, she was nearly all he thought about as he worked, but how could he help it? He shook his head and rolled his shoulders, hoping to unhinge his neck muscles from their stubborn tension and his heart from its wayward path.

~~~

Katelyn feared Thomas sensed the dark secrets she held and had questions that she didn't want to address. How could she tell him her days were too often filled with regret and remorse? How could she bear to let him see her true self, a heart that yielded to her terrible, awful, wicked mouth far too often? No, she would keep her composure and smile.

She walked with Thomas in silence, occupied with her private and stormy thoughts. When they got to the dining room, Mrs. Duncan spent over an hour laying out the tasks of tea service. She demonstrated the correct way to pour, to serve the delicacies, to remove the used items. She talked about the proper etiquette of a garden tea and discussed what to do if something went wrong.

Proper, proper, proper! Katelyn was so thoroughly tired of proper and in no mood for it on this sour day. She just had to turn her mind to more pleasant things, so she looked at Thomas. She imagined him in fine service attire and smiled. She pondered how closely they were to work together in serving the tea.

Like a dance!

"Katelyn? Are you daydreaming again?" Mrs. Duncan's words snatched her away from her thoughts and pulled her back to reality. "You must listen and learn, young woman, or I will find another to take your place! Thomas, you are dismissed."

"Yes, ma'am," Thomas said, bowing, clicking his heels, and stealing a quick, reassuring glance at Katelyn.

"Sit, please," Mrs. Duncan said gently.

Katelyn sat, fearing she would receive yet another scolding. She sucked in her breath and steeled herself for the worst.

"This has been a difficult day for you, Katelyn, and I fear you'll not recover as you must. Settle your heart and learn. Life is a series of lessons in becoming a better person, and we must take these lessons to heart and change accordingly. If not, we will become most miserable.

"Yes, you erred repeatedly this dark day, yet it is but a day. The sun will shine again, and we will begin anew tomorrow. But I beseech you to not speak of it but to the Father, for He alone can help you in your present misery. We have all been there in one form or another, so I shall not be the one to judge. Furthermore, I also want to warn you to steer clear of the feelings you have rising within you concerning Thomas."

Katelyn blinked, shocked to hear such words. *Can this woman read my mind? How shall I endure?*

"I see, Katelyn. The daydreams are of one handsome young man who will work with you closely two days hence. Beware of the danger of allowing such thoughts to run wild, or you will endanger your position as well as Thomas' fine reputation here on this island. Tame them, Katelyn. I entreat you."

Katelyn lowered her eyes and fought back the tears that threatened to come until she could finally speak. "Yes, Mrs. Duncan. Thank you for being so patient with me." Her voice cracked and her words were but a whisper, but she meant them. Mrs. Duncan gave her a potion of maternal concern and encouragement, a mixture she sorely needed just then.

Mrs. Duncan patted her hand and told her to take the basket of mending. She should get a bite of lunch and spend the afternoon in her room sewing. She wanted to hug her like she did her mama when she had scolded her. But that would not be proper. Instead, she curtsied and looked into Mrs. Duncan's understanding eyes in silent gratitude.

Bless you, Mrs. Duncan! You know I need to be alone.

CHAPTER 8

Katelyn settled into a wicker chair on the veranda and began to mend Hattie's tiny, white pantaloons. Visible through the overhanging branches of a tall maple, dark clouds billowed across a tattered sky. The scene reminded her of her heart.

Her mama-ache had returned, as it always did when things were difficult. That dull pain too often reared its ugly head and made it hard to live, to love, to speak without erring. She longed for the hurt to stop. She wanted her joy back, but she had no idea how to make that happen.

She picked up Florence's dainty nightgown and mended it. Then she turned to work on the tear on the sateen hem of Mrs. Pullman's lemon-colored skirt.

She had to admit that Mrs. Duncan was right. She did have feelings for Thomas. Yet when she thought about his repeated scolding, she clenched her teeth and shook her head.

"How can men be so exasperating?" she said aloud as she sewed a button on the scratchy woolen fabric of Mr. Pullman's trousers. "Ouch!"

Distracted, she had pricked her finger. Startled that she could hear her own voice, she quickly looked around, just to be sure no one had heard. Then she sucked her finger, pressing her lips tight to stop the bleeding.

She swatted a mosquito, annoyed by its ever-present threats to bite her. They irritated her almost as much as the incessant scolding of Sara and her brother. Katelyn stood and stretched, then she sat and bent down to dab her bloodied finger on the inside hem of her dress.

Men. She thought of her father and brothers and brushed away an unbidden tear with the sleeve of her uniform. Her brothers were just plain mean, and Father had never paid her much attention, save a scolding and a swat. But her mother's love and gentle care had made up for the lack of it.

She finished the button of the trousers, folded them, and put them in the basket as she pondered her present situation. She had been on the island barely a week, yet she had already learned so much about island living, the ways of a servant, and the life of the wealthy folk like the Pullmans. But she had also learned a few things about her heart, things she didn't like.

"Oh help, Lord! This tongue is my curse."

Her eyes brimmed over with tears; she had to let her emotions out. In the midst of the beauty of this island paradise, she felt so overwhelmed. She cried many tears as she watched a flock of gulls fly overhead, just off the shore. They were free. Free of making all the foolish mistakes a prattling girl can make. Free to fly where they dared to go. Free of having to choose the proper words or hold their tongues. As if to punctuate her thoughts, the gulls honked in unison and made her smile.

God does have a sense of humor.

Finally, she dried her eyes and returned to her mending. She darned Mrs. Pullman's under-shift. Then she carefully folded each finished garment and set them in the basket. She swallowed the growing lump in her throat and pondered the troubles she had put on herself.

Soon massive clouds gathered, and the wind picked up. A distinct chill in the air carried the smell of coming rain, so she took her work to the warmth and quiet of her room.

As she opened the door, Katelyn was surprised to see Claudia getting into bed. "Are you all right, Claudia?"

"Not very. I have a horrid headache and feel quite ill."

"I'm so sorry. I wonder if it's the illness Mrs. Duncan and Nanny had, do you suppose?"

"You never know about these things. What are you doing here in the middle of the day?"

"Mrs. Duncan set me to mending this basket of clothes and said I could do it here."

Claudia climbed into bed and put an ice pack on her head, while Katelyn settled into the hard chair in the far corner of the room. She sewed the rip in a petticoat and began to darn a pair of Mr. Pullman's socks.

"Isn't it ever so exciting to think about dozens and dozens of fine, young journalists coming to the island?" Claudia asked, even with her eyes closed. "I weary of being so isolated."

"The journalists may be old and ugly for all we know," Katelyn said darkly.

"Oh, I suppose there may be a codger or two, but I imagine there will be many handsome writers who will come to gather story after story of our illustrious president and honored general. I plan to meet them all ... somehow."

"I suspect we will be quite busy and have little free time for socializing. 'Sides, I doubt such men would give us a second look."

"They are no better than we, and I plan to find a way. Perhaps there is a match for me, and maybe even one for you."

"Pshaw! I daren't dream such dreams."

"No, you only dream of Thomas."

"He is but the brother of my best friend!"

"And more."

Katelyn shook her head and fell silent. How could she contest Claudia's words without lying? Ever since she set foot on Pullman Island, her feelings for Thomas had been muddled and mixed.

"He is a rather handsome lad, to be sure," Claudia continued. "But he loves this dreadful island so. I fear he might be one of those strange men who like the pioneer life far from society. Men such as they grow old in the wilderness or plains or on an island barely saying a word, and when they do, it's only about fish or fowl or furry things. I want a man who aims to rise in the ranks of society, a man who loves frills and fashion and balls, and most of all, a man who has money."

"Oh, money is fine, but it won't buy love, least that's what my mama always said." At the thought of her mother, Katelyn bit her lip to avoid crying again, but it was no use. Sobs came as unwelcome intruders, and even though she tried to cry quietly, her roommate heard her.

Claudia pulled the ice pack off her head and rose up on an elbow. "What's wrong? Can I help?" The compassion in her voice was welcome albeit alarming at the same time.

"My mother died three months ago. She was my best friend, my confidant, my ally."

"And my grandfather passed last month. It's a heartbreak, to be sure."

Consoled by another soul understanding her pain, Katelyn's sobs slowly subsided. "I am sorry for your loss as well. How can we bear such sadness and do our duty here?"

"We must. I must. I have no desire to stay in Watertown and grow old in the station to which I was born. My parents are poor shopkeepers, and many shun us because we are French Canadian. I aim to find a wealthy husband and live above such misery."

"My family are Irish immigrant farmers, and we feel similar prejudice, so we keep to our own kind. 'Tis a shame, I must say."

"I will not let the stairway to the upper class elude me. Perhaps my golden staircase will find its way to the island in the form of a successful journalist."

"But I hear tell that journalists are scoundrels and cads who lie and cheat and draw scandal out of every nook and cranny they find."

"I don't care a wit about any of that if it will bring me status and fortune," Claudia said matter-of-factly.

"Have you ever entertained a beau, Claudia?"

Claudia lifted the ice pack and surveyed Katelyn as if she were deciding to answer or not. "I've had several beaus, but my little sister, Clara, stole from me the one who really mattered. We were to be married, but Pa found the two of them in the back room of the bakery together and made them get married the very next day. I'll never forgive them. Ever."

"Oh, Claudia, I am so very sorry." She didn't know what else to say, but her heart pricked with compassion—and a little better understanding of the girl who had become something of her nemesis.

Claudia lay back down on her bed, returned the ice pack to her head, and closed her eyes. "I think I should nap now."

Claudia's astonishing admission gave Katelyn much to contemplate. *What kind of person would marry for money? And what kind of sister would do such a thing?* Katelyn felt sorry for Claudia, and the reasoning behind the girl's high aspirations stirred Katelyn's admiration.

What do I believe about such things?

As she mulled that over, Katelyn returned to her darning. Mama once had a dream, had aspirations for her, but it was to find her future—a future birthed in integrity. Of course, Katelyn appreciated having enough money to live comfortably, but to push and shove her way into another class? That was a new thought!

Soon the sun began to shine through the window, so Katelyn decided to take her work outside again. She left the pile of mended items on the chair and gathered the things she still needed to work on, then left the room, careful not to awaken Claudia. She returned to the veranda. It was quickly becoming her favorite spot on the island.

With the weather's clearing came humidity so dense that it felt hard to breathe. The mosquitoes also came, tormenting her as she worked. And though she sat in the shade, perspiration dripped from her forehead and wet the nape of her neck.

Nothing seemed to be going right today.

Katelyn worked on a few more items and finally got to the bottom of the mending basket. Mrs. Pullman's corset. She fingered the beautiful, ornate lace and found where the stitches had come free, so she began to repair it. What would it be like to wear such finery? The satin, the lace, the frills. Mama's corset had been plain and sensible, but this? She'd never seen such a beautiful thing; even Little Hattie and Florence's clothes were finer than she had ever dreamed of. Was Claudia right to want such a life?

"No, I mustn't covet," she said aloud. A squeak of the floor alerted her that someone was near.

"What did you say, Morning Dove?" Thomas asked, ascending the stairs, chomping on a stalk of rhubarb and carrying a tray of food.

She hid the corset from his view, cleared her throat, and swept the sweat from her brow. "Nothing, I was just thinking."

"Thinking aloud can get you into trouble, Miss Katelyn." Thomas smiled a crooked, teasing smile, which she didn't appreciate just then.

"Yes. 'Tis all too true."

Thomas set the tray on the table beside her. "Cook sent this supper to you and Claudia."

"Cook isn't at all what I thought she was. She can even be nice."

"Most people aren't all good or all bad. Nearly everyone has redeeming qualities, even if we don't see them very much. May I sit a spell?"

"Of course." She welcomed the intrusion that took her far from her dark mood and thoughts, especially of him.

Perhaps the day will brighten yet.

~~~

Thomas shivered at the mood Katelyn seemed to be in. Had her tongue gotten the better of her again? Her words could be venomous, and her opinions lacked wisdom, but this beautiful woman likely held a mystery he longed to unlock.

Yet she seemed sad and hurting, not guilty and errant. What could be troubling her heart so? Thomas ached at the thought that she might be in pain.

Thomas studied Katelyn's downcast demeanor. She was so beautiful on the outside, and he had seen her tender heart with the wee ones, even way back when they were school chums. She had willingly and happily helped the younger students and showed herself to be a faithful daughter and neighbor. Maybe she would be the woman he hoped she was?

He leaned forward and shook his head, resigned to try and keep his distance. He didn't need to fall for a woman who could ruin his chances for a quiet, peaceful life here on the island he loved. He should keep her at arm's length. She was his sister's friend, not his, though he longed to be her friend, her very good friend.

Just then, her confounded lemon verbena wafted on the breeze, tickled his nose, and threatened to weaken his resolve.

~~~

Katelyn caught Thomas watching her before he averted his gaze. He sat on the railing, swinging his legs.

He turned her way. "It's been a hide-and-seek day, has it not? I had set my mind to work on the landscaping, but the rain and wind have thwarted my efforts repeatedly." He looked out at the lawn and the landscape beyond. "Did you know that Mr. Pullman has carefully kept the wild and natural landscaping on purpose? As we built the cottage, he instructed us to keep the island nature intact. He loves the island, most certainly."

Katelyn nodded and noticed, for the first time, how the pathway from the docks wove its way around the wild rose bushes, oak trees, and shrubs. She turned to the tray of food, picked up a piece of buttered bread, and nibbled on it as Thomas continued.

"Moreover, Mr. Pullman plans to work the island's natural beauty around the new castle he'll have built in the coming years. 'Tis a mighty fine plan, I think."

"For such a gruff man, I am surprised he cares for nature so," she said condescendingly, scrunching up her nose.

"He is a good man, Katelyn. You should be honored to work for him."

Ire rose up within her. Why must he always counter her? "He's a mean man, that's what I think. He makes his children cry and pains his wife. He treats the staff like we are chattel, and he is a merciless businessman. I do not care for him."

Thomas shook his head and turned to look deep into her eyes. His silent stare reminded her of Sara's, but just then it seemed to be sad. Disappointed. She knew it well. "What you see and hear is only one part of the story, Katelyn. Judge not lest you be judged. Remember Luke 16 that we learned in school? 'He that is faithful in that which is least is faithful also in much.' This is not just about money. Trust is also about words and attitudes and judgments."

"Then don't judge me!" She shouted, stood, stomped her foot, and glared at Thomas even as she felt the heat rise in her face. She grabbed her mending basket and stormed off, clicking her heels hard against the wooden floor.

As she stomped away, Katelyn didn't know where she could go to get some peace and quiet. Suddenly, the island seemed claustrophobic. She glanced here and there, seeking a place to go. To be away from him. She thought of the dock. No! Though she loved sitting there and dipping her feet in the cold river, she couldn't take the risk of running into Thomas again. Not now.

She couldn't go back to the house in such a state. And she couldn't go to her room. The terrible day closed in on her, and she felt trapped. Like an animal.

So she walked. Walked around the shore of the island, as far from people as she could go until she found an outcropping of rock that she had heard would someday become an overlook with stairs going down to the water's edge. It would one day be the grand entrance to the island. Today it would be her hiding place.

She realized she had thoughtlessly carried the mending basket with her, and it was heavy, so she set it down and looked out at the river. Spotting a large cargo ship passing by, she wished she could hop aboard and sail away from this place.

Anywhere but here. Any place where there was not a Thomas or a Mrs. Duncan or others to scold and shame and embarrass her.

She plopped down in the crook of a tall oak tree, and a cool breeze blew, delivering a heady scent of wild roses from the nearby bushes. Katelyn smelled the intoxicating fragrance and remembered her mama anticipating the break of spring as she inhaled the scent of the bush's bloom just outside her kitchen window. Her mama had loved wild roses.

That lovely smell stirred her grief yet again, reminding her that the open wound within her needed a healing balm. Tears filled her eyes as she recalled her mama's tender touch, warm hugs, and gentle love. How she needed her now, yet it could never be.

Unbidden, she recalled the final moments of her mother's life. Her face, so vibrant and exuberant just weeks before, had become pale and blank. Her mouth had drawn down into a frown, which Katelyn had only seen when Mama was disappointed. Her eyes stared at nothing, glassy and emotionless. Her mama's strength left as her life ebbed away.

At the funeral, Katelyn shed so many tears that her father slapped her hand and whispered, "Stop that whimpering, girl, or I'll give you something to really cry about." That's when hope had been ripped from her heart, and grief took its place.

A great blue heron swooped just feet from her and jarred her from her thoughts. She caught a glimpse of his wingspan—nearly as wide as she was tall. She blinked and whispered into the breeze, "I cannot bear to think of Mama just now. I must address today's troubles afore I go mad."

She steeled herself to recall the day's details as she followed the heron with her eyes. Oh that she could hop on its back and ride away!

Katelyn cringed at the memory of all the terse words spoken of her, but she had to admit they were true. She pondered Claudia's comments and felt her face grow hot. Finally, she remembered what McCarthy said about the book of Proverbs holding the keys to control. Could she truly find the Scripture's keys to unlock the secret to control her tongue?

Katelyn held her breath, feeling her heart pound fast in her chest. Every nerve in her body seemed frayed, like the tattered shawl she gave for the missionary barrel last year. Would her heart ever mend? Would she ever be able to change?

For a long time, she prayed and implored the heavens to show her the keys to help her open the door to her soul. At long last, a measure of peace flooded her as she humbled her heart and trusted for better days ahead. But what would tomorrow hold? How could she face those who had seen her flaws and even spoken of them?

As she trudged back to her room, the full moon and bright stars began to pop out, lighting her way in the darkening night.

Chipmunks scattered at her footsteps, and an owl hooted in the distance. Fireflies twinkled all over the island, delighting her eyes and raising her spirits. Oh that a new day would dawn soon!

"Katelyn? Is that you?" Sara asked, panic tight in her voice.

"Yes, 'tis I, Sara."

Sara ran down the path and threw her arms around Katelyn. "I thought you were drowned. I couldn't find you. Oh, Katelyn. I'm glad you're safe. I was just going down to the boathouse to have Thomas help me look for you!"

"I am fine, dear friend. I was just walking and getting a breath of fresh air."

Sara looked out into the darkness and then down at Katelyn's basket. "At night? With a basket of mending?"

"It's a long story and an even longer day. Let's take our rest, Irish twin." With that, Katelyn slipped her arm in Sara's, and the two returned quietly to their room.

CHAPTER 9

Early the next morning, Katelyn awakened with puffy eyes. Her roommates were already dressed and making their beds. "I cannot be late today! Why didn't you wake me?"

Sara touched her forearm gently. "I was about to. I just wanted to give you a few extra minutes of rest."

With a smile at her friend, Katelyn hopped out of bed, splashed cold water on her face, and grabbed a towel. She dressed quickly, then found that Sara had already made her bed. "Thank you, Sara."

Sara nodded, and they hurried out the door. Claudia and Darcy had already left for the kitchen.

Sara took Katelyn's arm. "A new day dawns sunny and warm. Don't you love island life, Katelyn?"

Before she could answer, Thomas popped out from behind a tree, scaring the two.

"Thomas! Up to your usual tomfoolery, are you?" Sara scolded with a nervous laugh.

"As Mother always said, sister." Thomas smiled and gave his sister a quick hug. "May I have a moment to speak with Katelyn?"

Sara cocked her head and winked. When Katelyn shrugged her shoulders, Sara left the two to talk.

"Forgive me, Katelyn," Thomas said, touching her arm lightly. "Too often my opinions get the best of me."

She shook her head as she felt the heat of embarrassment color her cheeks and run all the way down her neck. "As do mine. Yet you speak the truth, Thomas. Let us start this day anew."

Thomas agreed. He stuck his hands in his pockets, and kicking the grass, said, "See you later, Morning Dove." Just then, he looked like the little schoolboy she knew so well. This change from boyhood to manhood was unsettling, yet also appealing.

Katelyn bid Thomas farewell and hurried into the kitchen to find everyone eating in silence. Cook threw her a disagreeable look but said nothing. She grabbed a bowl, ladled a full portion of oatmeal into it, and sat down, trying to catch up with the others. But before she finished her oatmeal, Mrs. Duncan came to fetch her.

"Where is the mending basket? Did you finish it?" Mrs. Duncan asked, furrowing her brow.

Katelyn blinked. "Oh, I'm sorry. I must have left it in my room. I'll go get it and bring it to you right now." She rose to scurry off, but Mrs. Duncan stopped her, planting a gentle hand on Katelyn's shoulder. A watch dangled from Mrs. Duncan's shirtwaist. She opened it, checked the time, and snapped it shut.

"Finish your meal, get the mending, and report to the dining room. We have much to do to prepare for the tea party."

Today! Katelyn had forgotten all about Mrs. Pullman's garden tea party.

She took one last bite and washed her bowl, then hurried to her room. She grabbed the basket and hurried to the dining room as fast as she could. "All finished," she said, handing the basket to Mrs. Duncan.

"Well done. Are you better today?" Mrs. Duncan smiled, tilting her head. Her eyes showed kindness.

"Yes, ma'am, and thank you for the reprieve." Katelyn looked down at her shoes.

Mrs. Duncan took her hand and patted it, just like her mama used to do. "It's a new day, filled with promise. Let's gather the tea settings and be about our business. Thomas will help us set up for the tea shortly, but mind your manners with him, Katelyn."

"Yes, ma'am." Katelyn curtsied and began gathering the party things. When her arms were full, she went outside to find that Thomas had already taken the wicker furniture from the porch and placed it under the shade of the great oak.

Katelyn returned to the dining room, and with Mrs. Duncan's guidance, she gathered the rosebud china tea set, the finest crystal, the best silver, and the whitest napkins. This must be quite an important affair!

Since Katelyn had never been to a formal garden tea party, she was a bit surprised that an *al fresco* tea would be so fancy. Her excitement grew as she made several trips back and forth to take everything out to the garden table. After Mrs. Duncan inspected her work and gave her a "well done," Katelyn covered the table with a sheet to keep the bugs away.

Katelyn stopped and wiped the sweat from her brow with her shirtsleeve. She watched as Thomas spread two quilts on the ground for Florence, Little Hattie, and their nanny.

"Won't it be grand to see those two little cherubs all dressed up in their Sunday best?" Katelyn said, helping Thomas smooth out the quilt. Perhaps she would get a moment with them? They would surely bring sunshine into her busy day.

"They are beauties, 'tis true." Thomas took off his cap and ran his fingers through his wild hair.

Katelyn and Thomas worked side-by-side, yet she kept her distance while they finished preparing for the party. She could feel him gazing at her more than once, but she would not be chided on such a day, nor would she be distracted by his handsome grin, strong muscles, and charming ways.

Soon Thomas left to change into his serving attire. Katelyn headed to the kitchen to see how she could help with any last details before she changed into her best serving uniform, the light blue one with the lace collar. Katelyn's excitement grew with each step she took.

Entering the hot and busy kitchen, Katelyn gasped. Cook and her staff had prepared a wonderful feast for the luncheon—scones and teacakes, finger sandwiches, and fruit.

She stepped over to the pastry station and observed the delicacies. "Claudia, these teacakes are a work of art. Truly. And the butter cookies? Perfect."

Claudia smiled and handed her a cookie. "Try one."

Katelyn accepted the treat with an open hand. She had only tasted such delights a few times in her entire life including once at a funeral. She nibbled the cookie, savoring every morsel. "Heavenly!"

Mrs. Duncan popped into the kitchen and drew her away from her enjoyment. "Best fix your hair, Katelyn. They will be here soon."

Katelyn curtsied and hurried to change. She fixed her hair, pinned her cap, and straightened her uniform. Then she returned to the yard to wait for the guests. When she got there, Florence and Little Hattie already sat on the quilt with Bridget. Dressed in pink frills, buttons, and bows, the girls looked like fine porcelain dolls. Their hair was curled and fashioned just right, and they both had long strands of pearls about their necks.

"Hello, Bridget, and hello to you sweet wee ones." Katelyn walked toward them as the two girls got up from the blanket and ran to her, hugging her legs tightly.

Florence looked up. "Hello, Miss Katelyn. We're playing with our paper dolls. Do you want to play too?" Both of the girls took Katelyn's hands and tried to pull her onto the quilt.

Katelyn tugged gently away. "I'm sad to say that I cannot. I am to serve the ladies their tea on this lovely morning. But I will watch you as I work." Katelyn bent down and picked two clover flowers from the grass, handing one to each of them.

"Thank you, Miss Katelyn. I shall put it in my hair," Florence said, trying to push it into her thick tresses.

"Best not do that. A bee might think you are the mother flower and settle on you."

Florence's eyes grew wide. She crinkled her little face and held her flower away from her. Little Hattie threw it on the ground and said, "Bees sting!" Then she popped her thumb in her mouth.

Katelyn squatted and stroked her hair. "Yes, but only if you scare them."

Just then, Mrs. Pullman walked down the path wearing the prettiest blue lawn dress that Katelyn had ever seen. Katelyn stood, curtsied, and nudged the girls back to Bridget and the blanket.

A moment later, Thomas came up the path from the boat dock, and the sight of him took her breath away. She had never seen him dressed in a serving uniform—a fine black suit with a starched white shirt and vest, shiny shoes, and bow tie. How handsome he looked!

Katelyn couldn't help but stare. His tanned and smiling face, his calloused hands, and his darkened fingernails had so recently attested to the hard, outside work he embraced. But now, here he was, dressed as a butler, with clean nails, combed hair, and regal appearance. How did he manage it so swiftly?

Katelyn blinked away her stray thoughts and turned her gaze beyond him. There she saw the three invited ladies, resplendent in their finest lawn dresses. One by one, Thomas announced the party. Katelyn listened and watched to learn their names.

As mother-in-law to Mrs. Pullman and grandmother to the girls, Mrs. Emily Pullman came first. Her face lit up when Florence and Hattie caught her eye, and she swept up the pathway to give them a hug. Her lovely lavender dress with a full bustle and her veiled silk hat with a peacock feather made her look like she was going to a ball, not just a tea.

Mrs. Cornwall appeared as pleasant as ever. She wore a soft yellow shirtwaist-skirt combination with a full bustle and straw bonnet, and Mrs. Walton, Cornwall's partner's wife, wore a soft pink lawn dress with a white shawl and hat covered with tiny roses.

Katelyn thought they looked like a summer flower garden.

Mrs. Pullman glided to her guests, beaming like the sun, greeting each of them with grace and elegance. She was in her element as she kissed her mother-in-law's cheek and bid everyone to take a seat.

Katelyn stood quietly and waited to serve, while Thomas slipped into the shadows, presumably to allow the women their greetings without his male presence. Yet Katelyn knew he was observing her while he waited to help. She could feel his eyes on her, which made her quite self-conscious, but it also made her feel special. Still, she would not—could not—let anyone know.

~~~

Thomas stepped back, waiting for his cue to serve and wishing he weren't there. A garden tea was no place for a man. He caught himself scowling and pasted on a smile.

A gentle breeze tiptoed across the lawn as he trained his eyes on Katelyn, and his frustrations flew away on the wings of the wind. The sight of her, the very thought of her, made his heart race and his emotions soar. He sucked in his breath, knowing he had to keep his thoughts at bay, even though they threatened to take command of his very being.

The sweet fragrance of wild roses danced in the air, yet he'd rather draw close to Katelyn and catch a whiff of her endearing citrus scent. He admired how Katelyn flitted around the party from guest to guest, like a beautiful butterfly alighting on the spring flowers.

She caught his gaze, and he gave her a discreet wave, fanning his hand and gifting her with a subtle wink. She responded with a confident and genuine smile, chin high in the air. Despite her weakness of speaking her mind too freely, she was a sweet-spirited woman, one he longed to know better.

~~~

Katelyn quietly attended the ladies as they talked. She brought them a cold drink of their choice, and after they greeted one another and chatted a bit, the ladies settled down for their lovely summer tea party.

Thomas fetched the tea and handed the tray to Katelyn with a slight bow and kind smile. She curtsied and smiled back as formally as she could, but her heart skipped a beat each time she looked at him all dressed up and formal like that. This was surely not the farm boy of her childhood.

Katelyn poured the tea while the women gossiped, waiting to fill any need one of the ladies might have. Thomas brought out the delicacies one by one, presenting them in fine fashion to Katelyn. She, in turn, presented them to each of the women. What a wonderful team they made!

"He is quite a handsome young man," Mrs. Walton said, fanning herself furiously against the growing heat.

"Yes, he is, and a fine worker, too," the elder Mrs. Pullman said. "He's got the makings of a footman or butler, I do believe."

Katelyn blinked. A butler? Thomas? How little they knew of whom they were speaking. She turned to gather the plate of teacakes from Thomas as she continued to listen to the women.

"And that one is a lovely little thing, though she's awfully skinny," said Mrs. Walton, pointing to Katelyn. "Perhaps if she were fattened up a little, she'd be a fine match for the young butler."

Her cheeks grew hot as she glanced at Thomas. She could feel the evidence of her nervousness glistening on her face, so she discreetly wiped the sweat from her brow. Smelling the tang of the river that the breeze blew in, Katelyn turned her face to it, refreshing herself a bit.

"Ignore them," Thomas whispered as she took a plate from him. His face was also red.

"Well now, let us turn our attention to other matters, shall we?" Mrs. Pullman, the elder, said. Katelyn sighed, relieved at the turn of the conversation.

"As you know, my son has invited our wonderful president and the great General Sheridan to our island oasis—and they have accepted. We will hold a grand masked ball to honor the president, and we shall invite the cottagers from all the surrounding islands. It will be a gala like none other!"

Mrs. Walton clapped her gloved hands. "Oh, bravo! And let us invite all the upper-class mainlanders and move heaven and earth to make it an historic affair. I will lend my expertise and my staff."

"We must all lend our staff, for we are woefully shorthanded here on the island," said the younger Mrs. Pullman.

Just then, Little Hattie, who had been sitting quietly on her grandmother's lap, let out a piercing wail.

Grandma Pullman abandoned all pretenses of propriety, turning into an alarmed, doting grandmother in an instant. "What it is, baby?"

"Bee!" Little Hattie said through her screaming.

"Bridget, take her inside at once and tend to her," Mrs. Pullman said. "Florence, you go with them."

Despite her disappointment at the lack of motherly compassion displayed by her employer, Katelyn managed not to frown.

Florence looked at Katelyn, and Katelyn waved the tiniest goodbye. Florence saw it, and said, "Goodbye, Miss Katelyn!"

"Well, I never! Speaking to the help instead of to me, their grandmother?" Mrs. Pullman sent Katelyn a glare.

Katelyn continued pouring tea, serving the food and retrieving the dishes, while Thomas took them to the kitchen.

She was more than grateful to hear the party return to the previous discussion. Mrs. Pullman glanced at her mother-in-law. "This island must be spick-and-span. Everything must be perfect! Thankfully, we have several weeks before the Grand Affair, as we shall call it. We will plan every detail together, shall we, ladies?"

Katelyn had never seen Mrs. Pullman so authoritative, so composed, so confident. Around her husband, she was so different, and Katelyn wondered why. Although her father was much like Mr. Pullman, her mama had never appeared to be two different people. Her mama had been a strong, lovely, competent person whom Katelyn nearly worshiped. Tears formed in her eyes as she thought of her.

"Katelyn! More tea for Mrs. Cornwall."

At Mrs. Pullman's quiet scolding, she blinked back to the present. Katelyn curtsied her contrition, quickly pouring tea with a sweet smile. She hoped, she prayed, that her daydreaming hadn't gotten her into trouble. Again.

The ladies didn't seem to even notice as they continued to plan the Grand Affair and gossip about other families who summered on the islands. Mrs. Pullman sent Thomas to fetch paper and pen and take notes on the guest list and plans. Thomas did as he was told, executing his duties like a seasoned butler.

Perhaps he would make a fine butler or valet? No, Katelyn decided. *He's too much a man of the islands and water to hold such a formal, stuffy role.* She smiled to herself, pleased to know more than those whom they waited on.

As the sun rose higher and the air thickened with heat and humidity, the ladies said farewell and beckoned Thomas to have Shamus take them home. Mrs. Pullman escorted them to the docks and, returning from her farewells, walked up to Katelyn, who was busy clearing the last of the food and dishes. Mrs. Pullman wore a smile on her face.

"You did well, Katelyn, though the episode with my daughters was perplexing to my mother-in-law. I scarce know why you attract them so, but I notice their eager faces each time they see you." Mrs. Pullman gave her a kind look and turned to go into the cottage.

Before she finished placing the teacups on the silver platter, Thomas joined her. He had changed into his work attire so he could return the furniture to its rightful place.

"This be quite a morning," Thomas said, placing the last chair on the porch. "You nearly caught it from a jealous grandmother, did you not?" Thomas laughed, and she joined him. It was nice to laugh together instead of being scolded.

"You there! Miss Willow," Cook shouted from the kitchen door. "Come here at once!"

CHAPTER 10

Cook glared at Katelyn as she walked through the door, though Katelyn felt unsure of what she had done to elicit her anger. The kitchen was empty, and Katelyn wondered where the girls had gone.

"I need you and Sara to go with Thomas to the bay to get baking supplies and such for the coming events," Cook said. "Mrs. Duncan has given permission. I don't have time, and I need Claudia and Darcy here to clean up these dishes and prepare dinner."

"Yes, Cook."

"Go and meet Sara and her brother at the docks. You three need to be back afore dark."

Katelyn hurried along as instructed, excited to go to the bay and have an adventure. The siblings were already in the launch when she got there, and Thomas helped her into the boat.

Katelyn smiled as she took his hand. "Why are we taking the launch instead of the skiff?"

Thomas answered as he untied the boat. "We are bringing supplies back, so we need the bigger boat."

Katelyn gave Sara a hug, then felt the cushioned seats and admired the highly polished wood. She sighed in gratitude for the canopy that shielded them from the hot summer sun and for the spaciousness of the large boat. "She's a beauty!"

"Yes, she's a steamer launch. Mr. Pullman is quite proud of her. Shamus says Mr. Pullman sees her as a quite modest launch and plans on a bigger one, but I sure like the way this one handles." Thomas donned his captain's hat and grinned.

Katelyn thought it a grand boat. As she surveyed the vessel, she guessed it was over twenty-five feet long and about eight feet wide. The steam engine chugged along at a fairly good speed, and Thomas told them that the rotating, bladed propeller provided the smooth ride.

Sara scooted closer to Thomas. "You handle it well. Until we came to the island, I had no idea what a talented brother I had." Sara winked at Katelyn and beamed with pride.

Thomas smiled. "Thank you. We have a lot of merchandise to gather, ladies, while we are in the bay. If we get it all done, perhaps we can get a root beer at the cafe. We have to be back before dark, but it's barely one now. What do you think?"

"Oh, Thomas, I'd be delighted," Sara said, rubbing her hands in excitement.

Katelyn wasn't so sure she wanted to stay in town very long. Her father had been all too happy to banish her to the island, and she knew her brothers would tease and mock her as a "servant" if they saw her. They always found some way to belittle their younger sister. Besides, just being there would make her miss her mama even more than she already did, and that would ruin a perfectly fine day.

Katelyn retreated from her thoughts and took in the river view. Her senses filled with the wonder at the river's freshness, sounds, smells—the life-giving magic of the mighty St. Lawrence. She bent over the side of the boat and wet her hand, drew it up to her lips, and tasted the clean, cool water.

Several islands dotted the waters, and Katelyn wondered how God made them all. Did He sweep His finger through this part of the earth, separating one chunk of land from another to create the great St. Lawrence? Did the crumbs He left behind become the Thousand Islands, even the very island she worked on? The thought of it made her toes and fingers tingle with awe. She shook herself from her reverie. She had to address the reality before her.

"I, for one, would be happy to return to the island as soon as we're done."

Sara and Thomas looked at each other knowingly. Thomas raised an eyebrow but said nothing.

Relieved at the silence, Katelyn studied the horizon and her hometown, Alexandria Bay, in the distance. Lumbermen, farmers, and fishermen found the sleepy little town on the shore of Northern New York to be an important stop for supplies. The islanders found it a good place for procuring temporary summer staff for the islands. Katelyn crinkled her nose and furrowed her brow. Her hometown now felt more foreign to her than the tiny island she worked on.

I'll never be content here again, of that I'm sure.

Sara broke into Katelyn's musings. "What do we need to get, Thomas? Cook's not one for sharing the details with me."

Katelyn smiled at Sara's cheerfulness. Her timid friend was beginning to blossom, and she had adjusted well to both island life and her work. Katelyn patted Sara's arm as Thomas answered.

"Since everything must be brought to the island, Cook is planning well ahead. We need wood to build a platform for the Sunday church service whilst the president is here and for the second privy and extended dock, which I am to build. Cook has a long list of cooking and baking supplies she wants to stock up on, and Mrs. Duncan has a list of linens and other things that must be ordered and made by a seamstress. And Katelyn, would you please post these letters as well?"

He handed Cook's list to Sara and Mrs. Duncan's list to Katelyn, along with a dozen or more letters addressed in beautiful handwriting. She supposed they were invitations. They looked over their lists, and Katelyn said, "Mercy, this will cost a small fortune!"

Sara waved her list in the air. "Mine too!"

Thomas grinned. "The Pullmans are sparing no expense whilst the president and guests are in residence."

Katelyn slipped her arm through the crook of Sara's. "Mrs. Pullman said it would be called the Grand Affair. It's a fine name for it, don't you think?"

Both Thomas and Sara agreed as Thomas drew into the bay and alongside the dock. Once they were off the launch, the three hurried off in different directions to conduct their business.

Katelyn visited the postmaster first. After posting the letters, she went to the seamstress.

Upon opening the screen door, her rosy-cheeked former schoolmate met her with a welcoming grin. "Grace? I didn't know you worked here." Katelyn gave her full-figured friend a hug, and they chatted for a few minutes.

"Mrs. Thomson will be back shortly," Grace said. "I started working here a few months ago, and I love it. I think I shall grow into an old maid sewing my fingers to the bone."

"Oh, you'll marry and have lots of babies one day," Katelyn countered.

"Not likely in this town. Who is there to marry?"

Katelyn whispered. "Have you heard about the Grand Affair? Perhaps you'll stumble across a handsome journalist who will scoop you up."

Grace shook her head, and Katelyn caught her up to date. Feeling sorry that her plump, plain friend lacked her own position to be privy to such exciting information, Katelyn might just have added a few of the private details as well. But before she had a chance to clarify and ask Grace to keep their conversation a secret, and before she even felt guilty about overstepping her bounds, Mrs. Thomson came through the door.

"Katelyn? What a pleasure to see you! What brings you to our shop?" Round and rosy like Grace, Mrs. Thomson possessed black hair with a wide streak of grey running from her forehead straight back to her bun. Katelyn smiled at the thought of her resembling a pregnant skunk.

She gave her the list of the Pullmans' needs and with a small smile, handed her some money. After looking it over, Mrs. Thomson plopped down on her chair and held her heart.

Was she having an attack?

"Just think, I will get to sew for my president. What an honor!" She began fanning herself furiously until even Grace became alarmed.

"Are you alright, missus?"

"Fine, dear. Just overcome with joy! To think that he will be wiping his mouth on the napkins I make."

Katelyn rolled her eyes as Mrs. Thomson's words trailed off. She always was dramatic, even when she sang a solo at church.

"They simply must be done by July twentieth. No matter what," Katelyn said, pointing to the Pullman instructions written on the bottom of the list.

"If I have to hire a hundred others to do the rest of the work, I will do this all myself—and on time!"

"Thank you, missus. It was good to see you. And you, too, Grace."

After giving both of the women a hug, Katelyn left the store with a sudden pang of loneliness. All around her were so many reminders of her mama, who had loved the village of Alexandria Bay and the people in it. Katelyn had visited most of these establishments hand-in-hand with her mama. She squeezed a fist at the bittersweet memories.

Katelyn crossed the dirt street and stepped onto the boardwalk, eager to meet up with Sara at the Cornwall & Walton Store. When she opened the door, she nearly ran into her brother. "Albert? What in heaven's name are you doing here?"

"If it isn't my little sister," Albert said flatly, stepping back from her open arms. She knew Albert hated hugs, but she wanted to connect with him. "I live here, 'least on the mainland. You're now of the island lot. The better question is: what are you doing here?"

"We're fetching supplies for the Grand Affair." Prompted by Albert's blank stare, Katelyn prattled off all she knew about the event, the island, and her job. When she finally stopped, Albert said, "I swear, your tongue must be forked in the middle. You talk more than ever. 'Fraid I don't have time for it today, runt. I'm about farm business."

Albert left without another word, leaving her standing there alone and feeling very forsaken. Did he even care for her? She doubted it. Deep sadness filled her, and she turned toward a shelf of dry goods to keep from crying.

"Katelyn? I'm glad you're here." Sara stood there with arms full of packages. "I could never carry all this to the launch without you. What's the matter, my Irish twin?"

"Did you see Albert?"

"No, I must have missed him when I was in the back."

Katelyn dropped her gaze. "Just as well. He acted like we weren't even related."

"Please don't let him spoil the day. He's always been a rather prickly fellow."

"Like a trio of porcupines the three of them are!" Katelyn said, picturing her father and brothers.

Sara laughed in response, balancing the packages on her knee so she could wipe the sweat from her brow. "It's so much hotter and more humid on the mainland, don't you think?"

Katelyn nodded and took several packages from Sara, grateful for the change of topic. "I expect it is. After we take these purchases to the launch, what must we do next?"

"The butcher, the baker, and the candlestick maker," Sara teased.

Katelyn smirked. "Very funny. Let's split up and see who can finish first!"

After setting the packages in the boat, off they went, running from errand to errand and bumping into each other more than once. Katelyn saw several of the locals she knew from church and other community gatherings, but she only gave the briefest of details about the Grand Affair to several of them. She loved doling out hints of information like treasure. If she were a man, she would probably be a journalist, scooping the story and sharing all the latest news with the world. She chuckled at the thought as she walked back through the town.

Katelyn found Thomas near the general store. "All done?" The mischievous sparkle in his eyes seemed to draw her to him in reckless abandon. He reached for an errant curl that had stuck to her moist cheek, tucking it behind her ear. With the other hand, he shielded his eyes from the sun as he cocked his head and lifted an eyebrow, waiting for a response.

At his tender touch, Katelyn's heart leapt in her chest, and her breath left her with a deep sigh. She wished she didn't have perspiration drenching the back of her cotton dress and making her hair all sticky. She finally found her tongue. "All done."

Thomas sucked in his breath and took a step back, clearing his throat. "I saw Sara at the butcher. She's waiting for the lamb chops and will meet us at the launch. It's been a full day, has it not?"

"It surely has." By now, Katelyn was all out of words, especially for Thomas. The sight of him in his serving attire kept flashing through her mind, causing heart palpitations and stealing the words from her mouth. And then there was his touch.

"Aren't you the quiet one this fine afternoon, Morning Dove."

"I'm just taking in the day's experiences, 'tis all."

"What was your favorite thing about today?"

Katelyn looked into his chocolate-brown eyes. *Being with you, silly boy*, she thought. But instead, she said, "The few short moments with Florence and Little Hattie, I reckon."

"Well, that beats all. I thought it would be the fine tea or the launch ride or the trip to the bay. Those babies are adorable, but the best?"

Katelyn shrugged her shoulders. "What's yours?"

"You." He smiled and tucked another stray tendril behind her ear.

Katelyn stopped dead in her tracks, her mouth dropped open, and her mind went blank. She felt her cheeks flush and nervous sweat shimmer across her forehead. She discreetly wiped the evidence of her embarrassment. But she couldn't will the rosy blush away.

Before she found the words to reply, Sara joined them. "All done! Do we have time to visit the cafe?"

Thomas' handsome face went blank. With a twitch of his strong jawline, he diverted his attention to the sky, looking for nature's clock. "We don't have much time, but I 'spect there's enough for a cold glass of sassafras."

Katelyn, Sara, and Thomas entered the cafe and ordered their drinks. Sara sat facing the street and seemed to be enjoying the comings and goings. Katelyn sipped her drink while Thomas cast perplexing glances at her until she inhaled a shuddering breath, hoping to hide her growing emotions.

Just then, Mrs. Thomson came through the door and lumbered up to them. "I hear you three are going to be quite busy for the next several weeks, with the Grand Affair and all."

"Where did you hear about that?" Thomas said, turning narrowed, accusing eyes on Katelyn.

An apprehensive shiver ran through her body. She looked down at her hands, digging her fingernails into the palms. Her head began to spin as the air seemed filled with her guilt. Her mind grasped for an answer, but she found none. Her words, her mouth, had overstepped her boundaries yet again.

"Oh, it's all over town. To think that President Grant is coming *here!*"

Thomas and Sara glared at Katelyn, shaking their heads. Thomas' eyes narrowed, and he pursed his lips. She studied her dust-covered boots as her face turned as hot as a fire poker.

Katelyn reasoned, *Well, they are coming, and everyone would know about it sooner or later!*

"If you need to rent a cow and some chickens, I know a few farmers who have an abundance this year. I'm sure they'll give the Pullmans a deal—for the president and all."

Thomas said, "I'll tell them. Thanks, Mrs. Thomson."

~~~

Thomas' first impulse was to grab Katelyn by the arm and march her straight to Mrs. Duncan for a proper scolding. He was so livid he could barely breathe, and the lump that lodged in his throat attested to his disappointment. Again.

How could he voice his anguish? How could he make her understand the error of her ways? The tongue had the power of life and death, but the careless speech of his beautiful Morning Dove could destroy herself and others. And turn this lovely creature into a vile one.

There was so much at stake here. Not only Katelyn's job, her friendships, her future, but his reputation as well. She had no right to share the Pullmans' news, news that was not hers. Didn't she understand how idle gossip could take on a life of its own? People's reputations hung in the balance—the Pullmans, the staff, the president himself. Oh that she would tame the monster within her.

He must dissuade her of her tongue's folly. But how?

~~~

Katelyn turned to look out the window. The news of the president's visit already spread, unleashed by words she never should have uttered. She clenched her jaw, bracing herself for another scolding. Her temples pounded, and her heart raced, but she remained silent. Time passed slowly, like it did after a convicting sermon.

But no scolding came. Instead, Thomas and Sara completely shut her out, talking only together. They chatted about their family, their farm, and their work on the island. Not once did they draw Katelyn into their conversation, even though it sounded strained, stilted, stifled.

Katelyn was both sad and glad. She was glad she wasn't confronted with her runaway mouth, but she was sad because she felt a terrible distance from both of them.

At the silence, panic began to fill her mind. What had she told the others? Was there a secret or two she had divulged that might get her fired, or worse? She tried to recall all that she had said, but the conversations became muddled in her mind. Then she thought of her mama, who would have been so disappointed in her.

As they headed back to the island, the guilt of her errant words filled the air like an unwelcome ghost of a guest. Katelyn bit her bottom lip, trying not to cry as they traversed the river. She had spoiled a beautiful day. She looked at the sky and prayed that the Pullmans or the other staff wouldn't hear about her transgression.

As they pulled up to the Pullman Island dock and unloaded the purchases, Katelyn worked in silence, while Thomas and Sara bantered back and forth. She might as well be invisible. Darkness fell as Thomas pushed the cart of goods toward the cottage. Katelyn and Sara said goodnight and took the path to their quarters.

"I'm sorry, Sara," Katelyn said, barely above a whisper. Sara didn't respond, and they continued to walk in awkward silence.

Katelyn glanced at Sara's face. Was she mad, sad, or disappointed?

Sara turned the door handle to enter the staff quarters and stopped midway. "Remember our memory verse from childhood, Katelyn? 'In the multitude of words there wanteth not sin; but he that refraineth his lips is wise.' Teacher had us memorize that for a reason, don't you think? Will you never learn?"

CHAPTER 11

When they entered their room, Darcy and Claudia were already asleep, so Katelyn and Sara got ready for bed in silence. Sara's anger was palpable, and that turned Katelyn's contrition into indignation.

How dare she judge me; she's just like her brother!

Katelyn sucked in a breath as she lay in the moonless darkness, the implications of her folly flooding her mind. The nameless nightmare she so feared again found its way into the reality of her world, both on the island and in her hometown. As she tried to recall the gossip she'd shared, and with whom, the wild beating of her heart increased until she could not control it. She hugged herself, trying to calm her fears, but it was no use. She began to shake, so she rolled over and tugged the covers to her chin, but she felt her world closing in on her. She couldn't breathe. She couldn't think. She couldn't sleep.

Katelyn tossed and turned her way through a sleepless night, waking ready for a fight. Sara and Darcy had slipped out of the room early, so that left her and Claudia to walk to work together. Katelyn was grumpy, but Claudia was sweet as sugar.

"How was your trip into town? I wish I could have gone too," Claudia said.

"Fine, but I'm glad to be back on the island. It feels more and more like home every day."

"Not for me. It's claustrophobic. After the season is up, I hope to find work in the big city."

"What city is that?"

"Oh, I don't know or care. Maybe Montreal or New York. Or, if I meet my journalist prince, any place he lives will be just fine. As long it's not an island, or Watertown, for that matter."

As they ate breakfast, Sara chatted happily with Darcy, casting a dart-ridden glance at Katelyn every so often. Claudia continued to talk to Katelyn, but Katelyn found it terribly hard to concentrate; she was cross, tired, and distracted. She felt her life tumbling down deeper and deeper into a pit of her own making.

By the time breakfast was finished, Katelyn was fuming and muttering under her breath on the way to the dining room. "I'll show her who needs an Irish twin. Not me!"

She nearly ran into McCarthy. "What did you say, miss?"

"Nothing. Um, what shall we do today, sir?"

"We'll be having several guests for dinner tonight. The senior Pullmans, the Waltons, and the Cornwalls—the newly established Grand Affair planning committee, I assume." McCarthy smiled and winked at her. "It will be a formal setting, so we have a busy day ahead of us."

She nodded, knowing that meant ironing the table linens, polishing the silver, and setting a spectacular table. She loved the beauty and grandeur of the wealthy's way of dining. She enjoyed the finery and the frills. She even felt a little jealous about the ease of their lives.

Katelyn could also imagine the emptiness of it all and wondered how they could live without any of the salt-of-the-earth ways that she'd grown up with as a farmer's daughter. Her mama had cared for her three children tirelessly. Always engaged with them, she continually showed her love and affection. Everyone pitched in to do chores and care for the land and the animals. They worked together through the long winters, and even though Katelyn's father and brothers were not the kindest human beings in the world and often made her feel cast off, shared labor had connected their family. *So how, exactly, does this disengaged upper class work?*

Mrs. Duncan walked into the room. "Katelyn, before we work on the dining room, I'd like you to help Claudia prepare the vegetables for tonight's dinner."

She turned from her pondering, said, "Yes, ma'am," and headed for the kitchen.

"It's going to be a scorcher today," Claudia observed in a pleasant tone.

"Yes, and this dinner party will occupy most of our day's work. How will we ever have time to prepare for the Grand Affair?"

"We have a month, and that should be enough."

Katelyn continued to grumble. "Not if we have to build things and make things and acquire things."

"It will be fine, friend."

Katelyn looked at Claudia. *Friend?* When had they become friends? Her heart lightened at the thought as she began peeling carrots.

"We'll have to buy lots of fresh produce from the bay," Claudia said.

Katelyn nodded, and as they worked, she told Claudia about the plans she had heard the society women making at the tea, including bringing staff from the other islands. "They even plan to have Mr. Crossmon cater much of the Affair."

Claudia looked a bit concerned. "The hotel owner? I hope he won't bring a senior pastry chef to thwart my efforts."

Katelyn placed the carrots in a pot, but as she reached for the beans, Cook stopped her.

"We'll finish this. You go out and sweep the porch and the walkway—all the way down to the docks. We can't have our guests soil their gowns on fallen berries or such things."

Katelyn curtsied and left the kitchen with the broom. She swept the porch and started down the path, listening to the music of the songbirds calling from the trees. Watching a huge tanker passing the island on the main channel, she stopped to wipe her brow.

She resumed the sweeping, considering how she could make amends with Thomas, if not with his sister. What could she say or do to soothe his ire and bring peace? More importantly, how could she change her loose-tongued ways?

Katelyn swept furiously as her worry mounted. She rounded a bend of the path hidden by bushes and nearly ran into Thomas, who was working on the same pathway, widening a narrow section by placing new stones along the edges.

"Oh, so sorry. I didn't see you there."

Thomas stopped his work, dried his brow on his shirtsleeve, and stood up. He seemed to eye her with suspicion, or was it anger? Katelyn gripped the broom so tightly that her knuckles turned white.

Rather than address her, he turned his attention to someone beyond her and said, "Good day, Claudia. What's new in the cottage?"

Claudia joined Katelyn, nodding a silent greeting before turning to Thomas. "We're having a dinner party tonight. Have you heard?"

Thomas' eyes darted between the two women and landed on Claudia. He smiled at her. "I hadn't. I'd better ask Cook if she needs some fish."

Claudia stepped closer to Thomas, nearly blocking Katelyn's view. "No need. Looks like it's duck tonight, but Cook says you're to take me to the bay so I can get the spices we need, and some sugar. She says a man has no mind for such things."

Claudia giggled, turned toward Katelyn, and shrugged her shoulders. Thomas and Claudia excused themselves and headed to the boat just as Darcy came down the path on her way to the privy.

Katelyn stopped Darcy with a hand on her arm, the gesture bidding the girl to pause and be her friend. She needed that just now. "My, it's a whirlwind day. What do you think of the Grand Affair, Darcy?"

"'Tis mighty exciting but will be so much work. The Pullmans haven't held such an event, least-wise since I've worked for them."

"It's been a busy few weeks, but I like it here, don't you?"

"I like the mainland better." Darcy crinkled her nose. Katelyn wondered how Sara got this girl of few words to talk so much. Darcy excused herself, and that was that.

"So much for friendship," Katelyn whispered to the wind.

She finished the pathway and swept the dock as she watched Thomas and Claudia in the distance. "Glad it's not me going there this time," she murmured.

She turned to go back to the cottage as a bald eagle flew over the river, searching for its breakfast. It reminded her of the last time she attended church with her mama, and she closed her eyes to remember the day. The preacher had talked about renewing hope. Her mama had held her hand, stroking the back of it with her thumb. Ripples of sadness rose up in Katelyn. Oh to have her mama back. She would know how to help. She always did.

Katelyn opened her eyes and studied the regal bird, wings spread, catching the wind. "Will I ever soar like that eagle, Lord?"

Her heart pinched with a combination of grief over her mama and regret for her gossip. She watched as the eagle swooped down and caught a fish.

"No, I'm more like that fish. Trapped and helpless."

At hearing herself voice those words, Katelyn's emotions ran amuck like the river's current, threatening to overpower her again and drown her in grief. Her uniform clung to her, while sweat rolled down her back, her face, and her arms. She wiped her face, but moisture returned as soon as she'd bid it goodbye.

She walked down to the river, scooped up the cool water, and splashed it on her face and neck. *Oh where is the river breeze? It's still and stuffy as a cave.*

She shook herself from her daydreaming and returned to the cottage, wanting to avoid a scolding. Upon Katelyn's entrance to the kitchen, Sara glanced at her and stiffened. Katelyn gave Sara's back a glare as she passed through the suffocating room.

She gnashed her teeth and sucked in a deep breath. *I'm so glad I don't work in the kitchen.*

She found Mrs. Duncan in the dining room, setting the noonday table. The missus mapped out the day's work and the dinner menu and sent Katelyn to clean the parlor and do the ironing.

As she dusted and mopped, she looked around the room, enjoying the pretty decorations and furnishings. *If this is a cottage*, she mused, *how much grander must their main home be!* She daydreamed about living in such luxury, owning so many fine things, and running in the social circles that the Pullmans did. Katelyn dusted the bookcase, running her fingers over the bindings of so many stories she would love to read.

"Would you like to borrow one?"

Katelyn spun around to see Mrs. Pullman standing mere feet from her, smiling.

"Why yes, if it is proper to do so. I love to read. What would you suggest?" Katelyn lowered her eyes in submission, but Mrs. Pullman gently lifted her chin with two fingers.

"You may choose, my dear. Just be sure to put it back when you're finished." Katelyn curtsied and thanked Mrs. Pullman as she turned to leave the room.

Katelyn scanned the titles and quickly chose *Little Women* by Louisa May Alcott. She had heard about the novel that was only a few years old, and she'd always wanted to read it. But when would she find the time? She shrugged, smiled, and whispered, "I'll simply have to *make* the time!" Setting the book on the side table, Katelyn patted it gently and left to finish her cleaning.

When she was done, she gathered the pressing basket and turned to the ironing. She thought about how elegant and kind Mrs. Pullman was as she ironed her dinner dress, admiring the low neck, short mutton sleeves, and soft fabric. Maybe she had misjudged her about her children? Maybe she misjudged many.

Katelyn pressed the little girls' pantaloons and pretty dresses. She even ironed the under-drawers. Lost in her thoughts, she took longer about the ironing than expected. She forgot to have lunch until McCarthy reminded her and sent her into the kitchen.

Seeing that Sara and Darcy chatted at one end of the table, Katelyn paused in the door, uncertain what to do. Unaware of any simmering drama, Darcy invited her to join them, and Katelyn did, but Sara shot her a disagreeable look. To avoid bringing any more ire into the situation, Katelyn ate her bread, cheese, and fruit without saying a word.

As she put away her dishes, Sara bumped against her, setting off Katelyn's pent-up frustration in almost a shout. "Watch what you're doing, you clumsy girl! What's your problem, Sara?"

Sara slowly shook her head, shoulders slumped. "You are." Her voice quivered just above a whisper as she shuffled out the door.

Darcy turned a shocked face to Katelyn. Mrs. Duncan stood frozen in the doorway looking just as puzzled, and Cook came out of the pantry with fire in her eyes.

"What's the meaning of this outburst?" Mrs. Duncan demanded.

"Nothing, missus," Katelyn said. She turned her eyes to the floor and walked past Mrs. Duncan, hoping not to hear any more of it.

Mrs. Duncan followed. "That was not nothing, Katelyn. We cannot have such outbursts in this house. I like you, but understand this—either find your way out of whatever your problem might be, or you will be dismissed!"

Katelyn curtsied and nodded her apologies, returning to the duties at hand. There was silver to polish. As she worked, she wondered how she could ever change. She missed her mother's wise counsel and gentle correction. She needed a friend to help her and not scold her. She needed to be free of herself. But that was impossible.

As she polished, she sank farther and farther into the pit of despair. How could she ever go on without her mother? Ever since Mama went to heaven, Katelyn seemed to be getting into trouble, especially with her words and her temper! And why were Sara and Thomas so angry with her? Sure, she'd shared a few things that she probably shouldn't have, but really, what was the big deal?

Katelyn continued to fume, to think, to worry, polishing the silver coffee pot over and over.

"I think that pot is done, Katelyn," McCarthy said with a chuckle in his voice. "Got a lot on your mind today?"

She looked at him, not even sure when he had come into the room. She wondered if she could talk to him. Oh how she needed someone to help her just then. "I miss my mama."

"I'm sure she misses you, too." The kindness in his voice melted her resolve.

Katelyn felt her eyes brim with tears. "She died three months ago, and I don't know how to get on without her wisdom and love." She could no longer hold the tears at bay, so she let them flow.

"There, there," McCarthy said, patting her hand. "I didn't know, and I am sorry for your loss. But I do know this: God is wisdom and love, and He can fill those places left vacant by your mother. He can give you the love you need and provide the wisdom to move forward from these difficult times."

"I feel so empty—and alone."

"You are never alone, dear girl, as long as He is in you. And He can fill you with all that you need, if you'll just trust Him."

Then McCarthy actually embraced her, held her in a fatherly hug, crossing the vast ocean between servant and superior. Katelyn stiffened in surprise; her father hadn't hugged her since she was a tiny girl. Her mama had done all the hugging. But she needed it so badly. She longed for a warm embrace, so she fell into his arms. It was but for a minute or two, but that hug filled her with hope.

After several precious moments, Katelyn sat up straight and dried her tears on a hankie McCarthy held out to her. "Thank you."

"It won't always hurt this badly. When my mother died, I was just a boy, and I wanted to die with her. I was angry and defiant. Then my father died just a year later, and I was sent to live in an orphanage. I lived a very lonely life. After much pain and sorrow, I began to work for the Pullmans and have been here ever since. They are my family."

She took a deep breath and cocked her head. "Your family? I can't imagine."

"Family is sometimes a collection of those you love and those who love you."

Katelyn had never considered that idea before. Her family consisted of a mishmash of personalities—a loving mother, a gruff and often unloving father, and two brothers who tortured her because she was a girl. Now that her mama was gone, who did she have left? Even her Irish twin seemed to have abandoned her. Could someone like McCarthy ever be considered family?

McCarthy bent his head near hers and spoke gently. "We must get back to work if we're to be ready for the dinner party, Katelyn.

Trust God, and find those who will love you and help you grow into the person God wants you to be."

"Thank you, sir. Truly."

McCarthy smiled, patted her hand again, and handed her the silver platter to polish. She smiled back at him, grateful for his kindness and care. She wasn't at all sure what to think about all he had said, but his sincerity and love comforted her.

Katelyn, McCarthy, and Mrs. Duncan were still setting the table when Cook announced that the dinner guests were on their way. Mrs. Duncan sent Katelyn to quickly change into her serving uniform. She did hurry, but when she returned, the Pullmans were already in the dining room, awaiting their guests.

"Are you always tardy, miss?" Mr. Pullman scolded. He shook his head condescendingly and turned to the others. "Mrs. Duncan, I do not want her waiting on the guests tonight!"

How dare he judge me like that! I'm innocent.

Nevertheless, Katelyn quietly took her place as the gopher girl. All night long, she ran dishes to and from the kitchen, trying not to drop or spill or cause any trouble. McCarthy and Mrs. Duncan did all the serving, and although they were kind, they barely said a word to her all evening, and she felt ostracized.

Several times during dinner, as she breezed through the kitchen, Claudia smiled or commented on something or made a point to hand her a dish. Sara, on the other hand, completely ignored her, even avoided her.

"It looks like Sara won't be my family," Katelyn mumbled as she returned from the kitchen with the main entrée and nearly bumped into McCarthy. He gave her a "be careful!" look as she handed him the platter. Again and again, she took deep breaths, trying to calm her nerves.

The conversation that evening entailed how many staff the Pullmans would need for the Grand Affair, how they would house them, who they would report to, and how they would manage such a big endeavor. She was overwhelmed by the complexity of it all. Where would she fit in the mix?

"Katelyn, stop daydreaming and bring some fresh tea," Mrs. Duncan whispered.

She nodded, turned, and saw Mrs. Pullman staring at her. *What must she be thinking? Am I a disappointment to her too? To everyone?*

Katelyn took the teapot and returned to the kitchen with a sigh. *Will this day never end?*

CHAPTER 12

Thankfully, the day did end. And thankfully, Sunday was a new day.

The Pullmans had a tradition of visiting Mr. Pullman's mother at her cottage on the eastern end of Cherry Island. Every other Sunday, Shamus took the family on the trip, for his son also worked on the island.

At breakfast, Mrs. Duncan announced that they'd all have Sunday off. Katelyn cheered along with the rest of the staff. When Thomas came into the kitchen, Sara begged her brother to take them to Alexandria Bay for the day, and he agreed.

"Anything to get off this stuffy island," Claudia exclaimed, crinkling her pretty nose.

"I agree," Darcy chimed in timidly.

Katelyn decided to join them, but her apprehension about being with Sara and Thomas threatened to overshadow the day. As Katelyn got in the skiff, she took Thomas' hand but wouldn't look at him. Just behind her, Claudia pretended to lose her balance and fall into his arms.

She fairly swooned. "What a strong man you are, Thomas! Thank you for being my knight in shining armor."

Thomas said nothing as he helped her into the boat, while several of its occupants rolled their eyes. Katelyn shook her head. *Next she'll be flirting with the pastor!*

Claudia took a seat next to Katelyn, while Sara and Darcy shared the bow seats. Claudia whispered to Katelyn, "He is a handsome fellow, don't you think? I think he likes me."

Katelyn ignored her.

Once they arrived at the bay, it was but a short walk to the church where Pastor Olsen was beginning the Sunday service. Katelyn looked around for her father and brothers but didn't see them. When Mama was alive, they wouldn't miss a service. *What is to become of all of us without her strong faith and love to guide my family?*

Katelyn spent most of the service remembering how her mama had taught Sunday school and even cleaned the church once a month. She had been such a vital part of the church community that Katelyn wondered about all the others who missed her too. During a particularly quiet part of the service, she was so engrossed in her memories that she let out a loud sigh. That sent a dozen or more heads turning to scold her impertinence.

"What was that sigh about, Katelyn?" Claudia asked once the service finished.

"Thinking about my mama, 'tis all."

Several friends and neighbors came up to greet Katelyn. "I haven't seen head nor tail of you since the funeral," one elderly woman quipped.

Katelyn tried to shake off the memory of that sad day, but she failed miserably. She held back her tears.

As she turned to leave the church, she saw her father in the far corner. She hurried over to him.

"Hello, Father. Where are Benjamin and Albert?"

"Home. Bessie birthed a calf yesterday. What are you doing here?"

"We have the day off. This is Claudia," Katelyn said, introducing her friend.

Her father nodded but said nothing. Both physically and emotionally, he kept his distance, as if an invisible wall protected him. Katelyn could feel it, and she despised it.

Thomas, Sara, and Darcy joined them, gave their greetings, and said their goodbyes. Darcy had decided to join Sara and Thomas for the jaunt to their family farm. That left Katelyn to spend the day with Claudia.

"Do you want to go out to the farm?" her father asked unexpectedly. "I suppose one of the boys could bring you back."

"Oh, let's do, Katelyn." Claudia grabbed Katelyn's hands and begged before Katelyn could think.

Katelyn shrugged her shoulders. "All right. But we must be back before four."

With that, they joined Katelyn's father for a buggy ride back to Katelyn's childhood home. The sun beat down on them fiercely, but the breeze from the moving wagon helped to relieve the humidity and discomfort.

Claudia seemed happy to be on an adventure, but Katelyn couldn't share her enthusiasm. Too many memories. Too many unknowns. She wasn't prepared to fight any more emotional battles that she knew would rage within her at being home without her mama.

On the way to the farm, Katelyn pointed out several things to Claudia—her one-room schoolhouse that desperately needed new paint. Her neighbor's large dairy farm. Their own fields, planted and growing in the summer sun.

All the way, her father didn't speak, didn't ask how she was. Nothing. He just drove the horse and wagon on until they came to the two-story, whitewashed farmhouse that had seen better days. Katelyn felt a little embarrassed and very apprehensive about what Claudia might see. Though she had only been gone two weeks, it felt like a lifetime. Besides, who could tell what three rough bachelors might be doing?

"So this is home, is it?" Claudia asked with a raised eyebrow.

"Yes. That's my room, up there." Katelyn said tentatively, pointing to a window over the porch.

Katelyn and Claudia followed her father into the house. Dirty dishes were piled on the drain board. Rope and tools lay on the davenport. Papers and more dishes covered the table. Clothes, grass, and trash littered the floor. Katelyn shook her head and glared at her father, biting her tongue.

Mama would be so sad to see her once-immaculate home turned into a pigsty!

"I 'spect we bachelors don't take to housekeeping much," her father said flatly. Just then, her two brothers came through the back door and stopped in their tracks.

"What are you doing here?" Albert asked as if he'd seen a ghost. His dirty, bibbed overalls covered his body, but he didn't have a shirt on, and one strap was unhooked. At the sight of Claudia, he turned a bright shade of red and disappeared up the stairwell.

"And who's this?" Benjamin scanned Claudia up and down as he ran his fingers through his sandy brown hair and grinned at her. Katelyn noticed the mischievous twinkle in his eyes. This ruggedly handsome brother of hers loved to flirt with anyone he could.

"This is my friend, Claudia." Katelyn dreaded what might come next.

"Claudia. Beautiful." Benjamin sauntered up to her, took her hand, and kissed it.

"Go and clean up, Benjamin," their father said, brushing him off. "I'm going to check on Bess and the calf." With that, her father went out the back door, leaving Katelyn to handle the shenanigans of her flirty brother.

"Pleased to meet you, Benjamin. My, what muscles you have!" Claudia smiled and batted her eyelashes, just like Katelyn had seen her do with Thomas.

"How are Bess and the calf?" Katelyn asked, hoping to draw the two away from each other.

"Fine. Bess had a rough time of it, though." Benjamin tore his eyes off Claudia to glance around the room. "Sorry about this. My brother is such a pig."

"Not just me!" Albert countered, rounding the stairwell. "This is your doing too. And Father's."

"Let me show you my room." Katelyn grabbed Claudia's hand and headed for the stairs. She had to get away from her two brothers. Had to protect Claudia.

"It's my room now," Albert commented. "We put your things in the barn."

Katelyn stopped in her tracks and glared at Albert. *How dare he? That was my room and my things!*

Albert smiled boastfully. "Father said I could."

Claudia gave Katelyn a blank look before turning to Benjamin. "May I see the calf, please?"

The flirtation in her voice and her mannerisms made Katelyn nauseous. Too stunned to say or do anything, she stood in the center of the room, appalled that she had been pushed out of her childhood home and that Claudia was flirting with the likes of her brother. Moreover, everything she owned was packed up and put in the barn?

How could they?

Benjamin flashed Katelyn a look of victory and led Claudia out the door toward the barn, leaving Katelyn alone with her thoughts—and the sight of a filthy house.

Mama would be shocked and disappointed to see this mess!

Katelyn found one of Mama's aprons and, with a lump in her throat, tied it around her waist. First, she cleared the table and picked up the things scattered on the floor. Socks, shoes, papers, tools, rotting food. As she cleaned up, Katelyn tried to wrap her mind around it all. In just two weeks, she was cast aside and no longer had a home to come to, at least not one where she belonged.

She stopped what she was doing—scraping days-old food from plates—and stomped her foot.

I won't be their slave! No! If I'm not a part of this family, I most certainly will not clean up their mess!

With that, Katelyn removed the apron and climbed the stairs to what used to be her bedroom. Sure enough, Albert had overtaken her retreat and made a complete mess of it.

She looked around, remembering how meticulously she had kept her room. Instead of a neatly made bed with her mother's handmade quilt stood a dirty, unmade bed, bedcovers hanging to the floor, the feather tick mussed and misshapen, and the pillow teetering on the edge. A coat hung on the wrought-iron bedstead, clothes scattered the floor, and her prized mirror was covered with fingerprints and tilted precariously on its nail. Just like that, every vestige of her nineteen years in her tiny, precious domain was gone.

She turned on her heel, ready to run away, wanting never to return.

Mama is dead. I am not!

Too angry to think straight, Katelyn stomped to the barn, ready to gather Claudia and leave, even if they had to walk the nearly three miles into town. When she got to the barn, Katelyn stood in the doorway watching her father gently care for the calf as Claudia and Benjamin looked on. The two smiled at each other, and Benjamin scooted closer to Claudia, almost touching her.

"We must get back to the bay, Claudia. Now!"

"But we just got here. I'd like to stay for a while."

"Why don't you fix us some vittles, Katelyn?" Father said, not even looking her way.

"I must go! Are you coming or not?" she asked Claudia, not even addressing her father's question.

"Yes, fix us dinner, Katelyn. It's what you do best." Benjamin smiled at Claudia and winked.

"I'm leaving! Goodbye." She turned and began walking toward the road.

"Wait!" Claudia said, running her way.

Katelyn stopped and waited for Claudia to catch up. "I will not be their slave. Not now. Not ever!"

Claudia looked at her and then to Benjamin, who stood in the doorway of the barn. "Let's stay a little while and have Benjamin drive us back to town."

"I won't stay!" she shouted. "Not like this!"

"Wait here," Claudia said. "I'll talk Benjamin into driving us back."

Katelyn watched as Claudia ran back to Benjamin. The two talked for a few minutes. Then Benjamin shook his head and turned to go into the barn. Claudia walked back to where she stood.

"He won't. Not without us cooking lunch for them. Your father said."

Fisting her hands, Katelyn turned toward the road and began walking. She brushed away the unbidden tears running down her cheeks.

"It's too hot and too far," Claudia begged.

"I won't be their slave. Mama would not approve." She glared at Claudia, knowing she had fire in her eyes. She didn't care. No amount of begging would make her relent. Apparently, Claudia understood, for she stuck her hand in the crook of Katelyn's arm and matched her pace. Still irritated by Claudia's behavior around the men, Katelyn stiffened but refrained from pulling away. She needed the support right now. After several minutes of silence, Claudia spoke.

"Your brother is a handsome lad, and I thought him nice at first. But a gentleman would never let us ladies walk back to town on such a day."

"They're badgers, all three!" Katelyn's voice came out harsher than she had ever heard, and it shocked her. *She was no longer sad; she was mad!*

Mad at God.

Mad at her mama for dying and leaving her alone.

Mad at her father for not being a father to her.

Mad at her brothers for being ... badgers.

They trudged on in the heat of the summer day for over an hour, finally making it to the bay, hot and sweaty. The wispy white curtains of Ann's Café were pulled back, welcoming customers to take a seat at one of the tables covered with checkered cloths. They stepped into the cheery yellow interior, glad to be out of the sun and heat. Katelyn felt grateful that Ann's Sunday crowd consisted mainly of widows and bachelors, which meant the dining room was virtually empty just now.

Ann came out of the kitchen wiping her hands on her apron and looking like she'd seen a ghost. "Why Katelyn, what in heaven's name are you doing here, and why do you look like you've just run a foot race?" She waddled up to Katelyn and embraced her. Then she nodded a hello to Claudia.

Katelyn sighed and wiped her brow. "We walked from the farm, and it's hot. May we have some cold water, please?"

Claudia cleared her throat. "I'm Claudia, and I work with Katelyn."

"Nice to meet you, Claudia." Ann smiled kindly, handing each of them a glass of water and bidding them to sit at a nearby table before she turned back to Katelyn. "Why are you in the bay?"

"Mr. Pullman, our employer, gave us the day off. We were at the farm and walked back."

Ann's eyes narrowed as she scowled. "Why on earth didn't one of those men give you a ride? I daresay they have become imbeciles since your mother passed on."

Katelyn smiled despite her seething anger. Ann was a widow, and she always had strong opinions. And she never feared sharing them. Since she had been a good friend to her mama, Katelyn appreciated her just then, more than she ever could have imagined.

"I'm so sorry for your loss, lass," Ann said, pulling up a chair and sitting beside her. She patted Katelyn's hand, and then she swept Katelyn's matted hair off her forehead, just like her mama had always done. "It must be hard for you."

Katelyn dropped her gaze to the table and bit her lip.

"Excuse me, please." Claudia scooted her chair back, seeming to show a rare sensitivity. "I'm going to take a walk along the boardwalk, but I'll be back soon."

"All right," Katelyn said. *Good. We both need some space and still have hours left before Thomas and the girls return from their family farm.*

After Claudia left, Ann took Katelyn's hand. "Are you all right, dear? You seem rather down in the dumps."

"My father. My brothers." Katelyn's eyes brimmed with tears, of anger or embarrassment she could not tell.

Ann shook her head. "I know. I see them in town from time to time. They are angry and bitter men, all three. I'm sorry, dear. That happens when people can't deal with death well. And you?"

"I miss her."

Ann brushed her hair back from her face again and pulled Katelyn into her massive chest. Ann held her tight, stroking her hair and saying in a sing-song voice, "There, there. There, there."

Katelyn soaked up the maternal love, even though Ann felt hotter than she was. After a few minutes, Ann went to the kitchen and brought back a cold cloth, encouraging Katelyn to refresh herself. Then she said, "Ah, I have something I'd like to give you, dear girl. I'll return in a jiffy."

Katelyn ran the cold cloth over her hands, arms, face, and neck, grateful for a few moments to cool off and calm down, and also that Claudia had disappeared. Though Claudia was kind when they were alone, she was also part of the problem. Flirting with Thomas and her brother? She couldn't reconcile the double-edged person who said they were friends. How could she trust such a girl? And why did Claudia seem so determined to be her friend, anyway?

Right now, Katelyn lacked the emotional energy to dissect her confusing and frustrating relationships. She had to find a way to stop hurting and protect her heart. But how?

Ann returned and handed her a tintype of Katelyn's mama. "I knew I had seen this just weeks ago. It was made at my daughter's wedding a few years back. I want you to have it."

Katelyn stared at the portrait set inside a paper mat. Her mama wasn't smiling, but she could still see the twinkle in her eyes and the love in her heart. She wore her best Sunday dress, the striped one with the big, white bow. Her hair was pulled back in a bun, as usual, and her hand lay on a pedestal. Someone had colored her cheeks pink.

Katelyn held the photograph to her chest and said, "Thank you. This is the greatest gift I've ever received!" Her eyes welled up with tears again, but she smiled just the same.

Ann hugged her. "You are so welcome, my girl. She is beautiful, is she not?"

"Very. Inside and out." Katelyn closed her eyes and thought of her mama while Ann continued to hold her. When Ann finally let her go, Katelyn was startled and a little embarrassed to see that Claudia had slipped back into her seat.

She wiped her face on her shirtsleeve. "I didn't realize you came back."

Claudia smoothed her skirt with her hands. "It's too hot out there, and I am tired. When will Thomas be back?"

"Not until four. What shall we do until then?"

Ann chuckled. "Do? You shall keep me company and eat some of my chicken and dumplings. That's what you shall do." With a smile, Ann rose and went to the kitchen.

"But we didn't bring any money," Katelyn said, starting to rise. Claudia did the same.

Ann bid them both to sit. "It's on me. In memory of your mother."

CHAPTER 13

Even though she enjoyed Ann's company, Katelyn couldn't wait to leave the mainland. It seemed a long time before Thomas, Sara, and Darcy finally returned to town. On the way back to the island, the three laughed and talked about their day. It had obviously been a much better one than Claudia and hers had been. Embarrassed and ashamed that her family had ruined Claudia's day off, Katelyn watched the gulls swoop down to catch their dinner. But Darcy aborted her attempt to shut out the chatter of the group.

"How was your day?" she asked.

Katelyn looked at Claudia, begging her to be silent. Apparently, Claudia didn't get the hint.

"Horrid! We went to Katelyn's farm, and it was awful. Her father ignored us, her brothers—well, one of them—was beastly. And they wouldn't even give us a ride back to town unless we cooked for them in their disgusting kitchen. Can you imagine?"

"Claudia, hush!" Katelyn glared at her as her face burned like fire. Her eyes darted from Sara to Thomas to Darcy. She hid her face in her hands. To Katelyn's surprise, Sara scooted closer to her and rubbed her back.

When they arrived at Pullman Island, Katelyn ran ahead of the others, went straight to the veranda, and had a good cry. How could she face them, face Thomas, who now knew her family secrets?

An intrepid wind rose from the river to whine through the trees, and an owl's hoot interrupted her grief. Footsteps sounded on the stairs behind her. She steeled herself, hoping whoever it was would not see her and go straight to their room. But the steps approached.

Sara handed her a plate with a hunk of bread, a slice of cheese, a handful of berries, and a cup of water. "You need to eat something, Katelyn."

"Thanks." Katelyn set the cup and plate on a nearby table and started to move away.

"Don't leave, Katelyn," Sara implored.

Katelyn returned, embarrassed but stoic. "They're badgers, all. I'm going to take a walk."

"Aren't you tired after such a terrible day?" Sara asked, trying to smooth over the moment.

"Yes. After having to walk all the way back to town, I *am* tired." Katelyn couldn't keep the sarcasm from her reply. "But I'm still so upset I need to walk."

"May I join you, please?" Sara asked, running after her.

Katelyn nodded, and the two left the veranda. Sara let her take the lead on the path that went around the perimeter of the island. Neither spoke for a long time until finally, Sara broke the silence.

"I'm sorry I've been so mean, Katelyn. Pastor's sermon set me straight. No matter what I think, I should be charitable."

Katelyn's throat tightened, and her voice shook. "Forgive me, too, Sara. It's been a hard two weeks. And now, with Claudia seeing my family, who knows what she'll tell?"

"Stuff and nonsense. Her opinions matter little."

"But tales do."

Sara's grey eyes pressed the truth. "Yes, tales do."

Even as she'd said the words, Katelyn felt the sting of truth. The tales she told stung others too.

As they walked along the shore, Sara seemed as lost in her private thoughts as Katelyn. Yet smoothing things over with her Irish twin brought a bit of healing balm to the day. They stopped to admire the sunset, the passing birds, fish feeding on bugs. When they rounded the pathway toward the docks, they saw Thomas fishing.

"May we join you?" Sara asked.

Thomas looked at Katelyn, who turned her gaze out upon the water, willing herself not to make eye contact with him. "Please. Sit."

Katelyn and Sara sat on the dock, watching the waves beat against the seawall that Thomas had recently finished repairing. Fireflies blinked on and off as the day turned into night, and fish jumped as they tried to scoop up their supper.

The purple twilight enchanted Katelyn, settling her heart, her mind, her emotions. The sound of birdcalls and boats mixed together in a lovely song.

"Magic time," Katelyn murmured.

"I like that. Yes, it truly is magical at this time of night. Barely a sound. Barely a breeze. Peaceful." Thomas turned to her and smiled. "Magic time."

~~~

Thomas couldn't be vexed with her forever. It wasn't God's way. It wasn't his way. Besides, Katelyn's zest for life, her innocent charm, her sweet spirit, and even her family heartaches—not to mention her beauty—drew him to her over and over. He fiddled with his fly rod, avoiding her gaze.

As the island fell under the spell of a fiery sunset, a glimpse of Katelyn lured Thomas into his private thoughts as he waited for a bite. *Her narrow face, high cheekbones, and fair smooth skin. Lovely.* Thomas' pointer finger twitched, wanting to touch, but he grabbed the rod with both hands, willing the twitch away.

Katelyn. Her petite frame made her appear younger than she actually was. Yet the truth was, she was an alluring though vexing woman. And she was hurting. He wished he could hold her, help her through her family trials. How? And how could he settle the butterflies she brought him?

~~~

Katelyn held her breath when Thomas got a tug on his line and began the battle to bring in his catch. It took a few minutes, but he pulled in a largemouth bass, ugly as could be. Both girls applauded, and Katelyn crinkled her nose at the sight of the fish.

"Well done, brother!" Sara gave Thomas a pat on the back as he turned to put the fish in his bucket. He grinned and nodded, returning to fishing without a word.

Katelyn pondered if Claudia was right. *Are all island men ones of few words and even fewer relational skills?*

But then Thomas spoke. "I expect these next few weeks will be a hubbub of activity. Dozens of day laborers will soon ascend on our island to prepare for the president's visit. Some will help me strengthen and lengthen the dock and clear the beach. Others will erect a stage for Sunday services and help me build the new privy, and it'll be a three-seater!"

Katelyn laughed at the thought, and Sara joined her. *A three-seater? Who but men would venture together into such a private world?*

Sara turned and spoke to Thomas. "And Cook said the rest of the mainland staff will come for the entire week as well as the elder Mrs. Pullman's staff and other temporary workers."

Katelyn nodded. "And they'll bring trunks of silver and china and bedding. Can you imagine?"

"Shamus said they're even going to bring a piano over from the bay!"

Katelyn's excitement grew. "It will be an event like no other! Yet the cottage won't contain them all. Whatever shall we do?"

"Not to worry, Morning Dove. They will bring tents from the mainland for the gatherings." He smiled at her, then gave a blissful sigh. "I'm looking forward to taking my president on fishing trips. Imagine sharing such a journey with the president of the United States of America!"

Thomas looked like a contented child rather than a big, brawny man. Katelyn liked that look and wished she might one day be content like he seemed to be.

They sat there for a long time until it was fully dark. Finally, Thomas pulled in his line and stood. "Best be getting a good night's sleep. Tomorrow is another busy day."

Sara rose on her toes and gave her brother a peck on the cheek. "I fear every day between now and August will be busy. Goodnight, brother."

"Goodnight, Sara. And Katelyn." He looked right into her eyes, and she saw a softness she hadn't seen before. It challenged her. Scared her. Excited her.

Thomas destroyed the notion that all men were like her father and her brothers. His tenderness, his mercy, his compassion were remarkable, and Katelyn hoped to one day trust a man like him.

~~~

The following day began with anything but contentment. Katelyn awoke to a cloudy dawn warning of imminent storms. Storm clouds gathered around her and Claudia as well.

Katelyn couldn't look at Claudia without feeling angry. She could tell that Claudia was none too happy with her, either. The two girls sat, stewing over their bowls of oatmeal, ready for a fight.

"Why did you tell the others about my family? It's my family, and you had no right," Katelyn hissed.

"Why did you make us walk in the heat of the day?" Claudia shot back.

"Another tiff?" Cook stood over them, glaring, before Katelyn even realized she was there. "Will you girls start acting like women instead of petty schoolchildren? And why, Willow, do you always seem to be at the center of drama?"

The oatmeal Katelyn had just eaten churned in her stomach.

Neither said anything. They just sat there like scolded schoolgirls. Cook continued. "Shamus is nearly finished with the launch, but he needs a woman's touch. There are ripped boat cushions and covers that need repair. Mrs. Duncan has released you to go and do that, Willow. I suspect it will take near the entire day, and I expect you to do a good job. Then be back here to serve the evening meal."

"Yes, Cook."

Katelyn cleared her place, gathered the sewing basket, and headed for the boathouse. As she walked down the path, she recalled the look of contentment on Thomas' face. What would it feel like to be content? She hadn't felt that since she was a young girl, sitting under the apple tree, alone with her dreams.

When she reached the boathouse, she found Shamus sanding the front of the launch. "Ah, Katelyn. Do come in, lass!"

She smiled and awaited his instructions.

"I hope you can help. Look at those cushions. Bachelors like Thomas and me have five thumbs when it comes to mending things." Shamus laughed a long, low laugh, deep from his belly. "Do you mind working alongside an old coot?"

"I'm glad to. Where shall I begin?"

"At the beginning, I 'spect." Again he laughed, and then he coughed. "Ain't no spring chicken."

Katelyn climbed into the launch and began to sew. To her untrained eye, the launch looked perfect, save the cushions and the one small spot Shamus worked on.

The air in the boathouse hung musty and thick with humidity. "I think it may rain," she said, hoping to converse with Shamus.

"I 'spect so, and welcome it'll be. On days like this, neither fisherman nor pleasure-seeker wants to be on the mighty river, that be sure. Have you ever been on a river excursion?"

"Not I. In fact, the first time I was ever on the river was a few weeks ago, when I came here."

Shamus laughed again. "Well, lass, 'tis a shame, to be sure. The mighty St. Lawrence is a beauty with all its islands and bays and narrow channels. It wasn't but a decade ago when folks started buying up these fine islands for recreatin' and buildin' summer cottages. Then folks like Xavier Colon of Clayton built his tour boat called Rambles. It be a mighty fine St. Lawrence skiff—I seen it meself—and he used it to give tours around these here islands. Since the boom struck, lots of folks got themselves excursion boats. You'll see plenty of 'em poking around here, especially when the president and his party comes."

"How will you keep tourists off the island?"

"Oh, don't be fretting your pretty head 'bout that, lass. We'll hire some big, brawny fellas from the mainland, or maybe even Canada, to watch out for intruders, so they'll not be stepping a foot on our Pullman Island 'less they be invited."

As they talked, Katelyn busied herself sewing a cushion, admiring the fine fabric and soft batting. She watched Shamus carefully sand a spot that was worn and weathered.

Apparently, Shamus enjoyed conversation as much as she did, for there was little silence. "Fishermen come from all over the United States and Canada every summer, and they bring their families. The wives and children need to be entertained, and so do the friends and guests who come to visit. I 'spect touring them around the river be a rewarding way to keep them busy while the menfolk fish. Mr. Colon and the likes of him have found themselves a fine way to earn a living, 'leastwise when the winter winds aren't a'blowin'." Shamus burst into such joyful laughter that Katelyn laughed with him.

No wonder Thomas loves his work!

"Where is Thomas?"

A loud thunderclap followed Katelyn's question.

"He went to the bay to fetch some supplies. Hope he returns afore the skies open up. I 'spect it'll be a torrent today."

Katelyn nodded and continued her work, worrying about Thomas as she listened to the wind howl outside.

Finally, he banged through the door. "It's getting fierce out there. Here's the last of the supplies, Shamus. Took the rest up to the cottage."

Shamus stood and stretched. "I best be visiting the privy afore the storm stops me. Be back soon."

As Shamus left the boathouse, Thomas walked to the launch and ran his hand around the edge of it, feeling the boat with his hands like a physician examining a patient. At last, he smiled and nodded. "Ahhh, she's a beauty!"

"Yes, and it's a privilege to work on her. Will she take the president on excursions?"

"I expect she will." Thomas began sanding an area in the bow, whistling while he worked. Another thunderclap and a strong wind blew from the north, giving the boathouse an eerie feel. "It almost sounds like a winter wind today." Thomas clicked his tongue.

Katelyn paused her work. "Don't you feel forlorn and lonely here during the winter's cold, Thomas?"

"On the contrary. I rather enjoy the solitude. It helps me connect with my maker. Actually, I enjoy every season here on the island, though they are rather dramatic at times. The summer with all the people and busyness. Autumn with its winds of change and vibrant colors. The winter's slow but steady way. And the spring's muddy awakening."

Katelyn pressed a palm to her cheek and smothered a smile. To think she had doubted his eloquence!

Thomas concluded his reflections. "But the best part of life here on Pullman Island is learning from the wisdom of Shamus. I never tire of it."

"He is like a father to you, is he not?"

"Indeed he is. For all his funny ways, he has taught me a lifetime of how to live and work well."

"But do you not miss your family and the mainland?"

"Oh, I see them enough, though my mother would disagree." Thomas grinned sheepishly.

Katelyn surveyed Thomas' calloused hands as he worked, and she shifted even closer, hungry to be near him. As she continued to sew, Thomas continued to sand, and the silent connection between the two of them felt both exciting and a little unnerving.

The creaking door, the musty smell, the scattered light through the boathouse cracks set an eerie mood. Katelyn stopped her work and looked around. The boat pulley, the straps around the skiff, the wood planks that held the launch out of the water, the boat slip. They gave her a window into Thomas that she hadn't noticed before.

Earthy. Simple. Content.

A thunderclap split the silence, and she instinctively turned its way. Light burst through the doorway, causing her eyes to ache with its annoying brilliance and startling her to stand. The boat rocked, but with a quick hand, Thomas caught her, their faces just inches from one another.

Katelyn blinked. "I'm saddened by your anger with me."

"And I with you."

"Forgive me, Thomas. I fear my tongue often runs away with the thoughts that I hold in my head."

"Oh, my Morning Dove, it isn't for me to forgive. Still, I urge you to respect the power of the tongue. It can be deadlier than you realize." Thomas moved closer to her and paused, the silence pregnant with emotion. "All of us must know our adversary, the thing that would destroy us. For you, sweet Katelyn, that enemy is your tongue."

~~~

Thomas held his breath as he strained in the dim light to see Katelyn's reaction to his loving chastisement. A blush rose on her fair skin and made her more beautiful than a summer sunset. She looked at her hands, and a single tear ran down her cheek.

He swept the tear away with the tip of his pinky finger and touched an unruly curl that cascaded down her temple. Then he ran his finger along her ear. The feel of her skin made his very being tingle, enlivening his senses, drawing him to her even more.

Katelyn gazed into his eyes with sadness, a heaviness he couldn't comprehend. Like a helpless doe frightened by the words he spoke. Or was it his touch? He withdrew his hand as if a wasp stung him, and she jumped when another thunderclap sounded.

Thomas smiled at her, his wordless affirmation beckoning her to smile in return, to feel safe again. He wanted nothing more than to protect her.

~~~

As the squeaking door announced Shamus' return, Katelyn quickly scooted away from Thomas, pretending to be hard at work. Apparently unaware of the intimate moment he interrupted, Shamus walked up to her and patted her cheek. "You best be getting back to the cottage, lass. Looks as though this storm might be a doozy. Much obliged for your help today, and 'may you count your joys instead of your woes; count your friends instead of your foes.'"

"Thank you, Shamus. I will." Katelyn cast a shy glance at Thomas. Then she packed up her sewing box and bid the men good day.

Outside, she picked up her skirt and ran, trying to dodge the first sprinkles. By the time she got to the kitchen door, the sky seemed to open up with a vengeance, pelting down sheets of rain.

"Whew! Just made it," she said to no one in particular. The smell of burned food and smoke filled the kitchen. "Gracious me. What happened?"

"Claudia burned the cake," Darcy said timidly.

Katelyn flashed Claudia a lofty eyebrow and slight grin and scurried out of the kitchen.

After changing her uniform, Katelyn found Mrs. Duncan setting the dining room table with the Wedgewood china. "All done at the boathouse?" she asked.

"Almost. There is one more cushion to finish, but Shamus shooed me away before the storm came. He's a nice man."

"That he is, but his health is not the best these days, poor man." Mrs. Duncan handed her the silverware. "Finish setting the table, please. I have other business to attend to. Then grab some lunch, and do try harder to put some meat on those bones." Mrs. Duncan smiled and gently touched her shoulder.

"Yes, Mrs. Duncan."

McCarthy passed Mrs. Duncan in the doorway, stepping aside to let her pass. *Always the gentleman. Like Shamus. Why could my father not be like them?*

Katelyn sighed as she continued to set the table.

McCarthy made a similar inquiry to Mrs. Duncan's about her day. "How was your work at the boathouse?"

"Just fine, sir. Shamus says the most interesting things."

"He's been a good friend to me ever since Mr. Pullman bought this island and hired him on. We've spent many an hour talking over good times and bad, always with an Irish saying thrown in for good measure. It's sad his health is failing; don't know what we'll do without him."

Katelyn's heart skipped a beat. "Is he really in danger?"

"I fear so, lass. I fear so."

CHAPTER 14

After a day and night of stormy weather, Katelyn's inner storm finally passed as well. She and the girls awakened to a sunny, already-warm dawn. Katelyn dressed and then let in the fresh morning air and daylight by tying the muslin curtains back.

Someone knocked on the outside door of the women's quarters. Sara answered, peeking from behind the door with Katelyn close behind. "What are you doing here, Thomas, at this hour?"

"I have a very special surprise—for all of you. Shamus talked to Cook and Mrs. Duncan, and after you have your breakfast, I am to take you all on an excursion—to try out the repaired launch."

Sara slammed the door in Thomas' face and told the other girls the news. They ran out to thank him, squealing and cheering, and Sara hugged her brother.

Thomas laughed and shook his head. "Silly girls. Have breakfast, bring your shawls, and come to the dock."

After a quick meal, Katelyn, Sara, Darcy, and Claudia climbed into the newly renovated launch for a tour of the mighty river and surrounding islands. The boat was shiny and clean, and very luxurious with the padded cushions Katelyn had repaired. She smiled at her work, pleased to be a part of making it special.

Katelyn couldn't believe she was on this adventure. "I've never been farther than this island—in a boat or otherwise. This truly is a dream come true!" Katelyn wiggled like a schoolgirl thrilled to her toes, while the rest of the company expressed very different reactions.

"I hope the boat won't sink. I can't swim." Darcy clung to the seat, her face turning white, while Sara nodded vehemently. Thomas gave her a "stop worrying, sister" look.

"I've seen many of these islands," Claudia said, shaking her curls in the wind as she sat straight and tall, her face relaxed, almost bored. "My uncle has taken us around them lots of times. But it's good to be away from Pullman just the same."

Thomas rolled his eyes at the comment. Then he grinned as he powered up the steam engine, gently steering them away from the dock. He obviously felt pleased to give the girls such a treat.

"Relax, sister. And you, too, Darcy. This is a sturdy ship and will not topple, even in a storm. On this fine, calm day, you will find her to be a gentle and pleasant ride. Sara, come and pull this." Thomas motioned for Sara to take a rope and whispered something in her ear. Sara smiled and gave it three quick tugs, causing the launch whistle to blast.

"'Tis a St. Lawrence River boater's tradition. Three short blasts signal our departure and tells others that I am operating the astern propulsion," Thomas said proudly.

Katelyn giggled with glee as the steamer slowly backed up and then moved along the water much faster than the skiff. She surmised that captaining such a fine vessel must be a delicate feat of skill and expertise.

"I just learned how to navigate this launch last summer," Thomas admitted. "This summer it will be used to ferry many important guests around the island, and I expect I will captain most of the excursions." Thomas took a deep breath and grinned with anticipation.

Hearing this, Katelyn realized what a great privilege this ride was, and she felt special. Imagine. Trying out the very craft that her president would soon ride in!

"This trip is thanks to you, Katelyn." Thomas turned to her and winked. "After you told Shamus you'd never been beyond this island, he weaseled his Irish way into the good graces of Cook and Mrs. Duncan so that you all could have the time off to experience this fine piece of the world. They all agreed that if you live and work on one of these islands, you should know your way around them. So let's give Katelyn a big 'hurrah.'"

Katelyn couldn't help but laugh as they all shouted, "Hurrah. Hurrah. Hurrah!"

Thomas gracefully turned the craft to the north, making his way along the shores of Wellesley Island, careful to avoid what he told them was the dangerous, sometimes deadly, Pullman Shoal. Then he began his tour guiding.

"To your left is the very large Wellesley Island. Folks call it 'Wells' for short, and many people live there year round. Mr. Pullman's brother, the Reverend Royal Pullman, is one of the summer residents."

Katelyn thought the mass of land looked more like the mainland than an island.

"And on your right are Welcome Island and Nobby Island. And Friendly Island is beyond that." He pointed to an island in the distance as he made his way through the narrow channel.

Along the way, they saw several other boats, but none as nice as the launch they were in. They waved to the occupants of each boat as they passed by, which Thomas told them was also an important Thousand Islands' tradition.

What must it be like to own such luxury and to be free to go fishing and boating and touring—on a Wednesday? Katelyn couldn't imagine such a life. Then she realized that here she was, enjoying that very thing—at least for a little while.

"We are now passing St. Elmo Island, and up ahead is Florence Island. Many of these islands have been bought recently, just in the past decade or so. Mr. Pullman was one of the first to buy an island and settle here for his summers. If you look off the starboard bow, you'll see Alexandria Bay in the distance."

Katelyn and the others looked at each other quizzically, so Thomas pulled back on the throttle and brought the launch to a near-standstill. "You girls don't know your nautical terms, do you?" His eyes twinkled, and he grinned as if he held a jolly secret. Then he assumed the role of a seaman's instructor.

"If you look straight ahead, that's the bow. The very back of the boat is the stern. To your left is the port side, since a ship will dock on that side of the boat. The right-hand side is starboard." He put his hands on his hips and cocked his head, waiting for them to show him they understood. "All right, ladies. If I say 'look off the starboard bow,' where should you look?"

Darcy and Sara pointed front and left. Katelyn pointed front and right. Claudia just sat there like she was bored.

"Katelyn is correct. See? That land over there is the bay."

"It's so close," Darcy said.

"It is." Thomas continued to steer the launch past two more islands before turning toward the bay. "On your port side is Hemlock Island, now called Hart after it was bought last year by the Honorable E.K. Hart of Albion, New York."

"We're not going to the bay today, are we?" Katelyn asked. That was the last place she wanted to visit.

"I'd like to go there; least-wise there'd be civilization to see," Claudia grumbled.

Thomas glared at Claudia and pursed his lips. Katelyn couldn't discern what he was thinking. He shook his head. "No, we're continuing our boat tour. As we turn, Alexandria Bay will be on your port side, and the islands we just passed will be on your starboard side."

Claudia stared longingly at Alex Bay as Sara and Darcy chatted, the two girls becoming more relaxed on the water.

A few minutes later, Thomas shared a bit of history with them. "Did you know that in 1842, Charles Dickens took a steamer down the St. Lawrence from Kingston, Ontario—which would be several miles downriver on your starboard side—to Montreal? He was quite impressed by the beauty of the islands and of this river, from what I've heard. But it wasn't until after the Civil War that these Thousand Islands really started to develop. There have always been fishermen and hunters and Indians here, but travelers and vacationers? Not until now."

As Katelyn took in the magnificence of the mighty St. Lawrence River and the Thousand Islands, she could hardly breathe. She imagined herself a great lady of a castle on one of the islands, with a handsome husband and several little ones playing on the green lawn. She again felt Thomas' eyes on her, and when she looked at him, her heart nearly stopped. He smiled the warmest, most gentle smile she had ever seen, as if he could read her thoughts.

~~~

Thomas couldn't help but smile. He could tell that Katelyn was falling in love with the river as much as he had. Sunlight flickered on her hair as her eyes danced with curiosity. Just seeing her excitement, her desire to learn the nautical terms, and her enchanting joy as she experienced the river for the first time gave him a thrill.

Then, when their eyes locked, she sucked in a trembling breath. Her gaze softened with warm ... what was it? Admiration? Awe? Desire exploded in his chest. It took his breath away and caused his palms to sweat.

Thomas thought of her father and brothers and what Claudia said about how they treated Katelyn. He gnashed his teeth and squeezed his eyes shut, balling his fist. He wanted to protect his Morning Dove. Always. From them. From everyone. Even from herself.

How could he resist such a rare jewel? He felt heat creep into his cheeks and turned away to stare at the river and calm his racing heartbeat.

~~~

Katelyn studied Thomas, watching for an expression or clue that would tell her what he thought. One minute he seemed happy. Another he appeared angry. Still another embarrassed. What was going on in his head? Before she could analyze it, Thomas cleared his throat and turned his eyes from her. He slowed the boat and then picked up a book and turned to a dog-eared page.

"I recently read this book, *Perham's Pictorial Voyage*. I'd like to share a passage with all of you. The author says, 'More and more travel was being experienced on the St. Lawrence as the tranquility of the islands and the excitement of the rapids further down the river served to bring much recognition to the area.'" He set the book down and added, "You can feel the excitement of that growth here on the river today, and increasingly with every year that passes."

Katelyn glanced at Thomas, and their eyes met again. He seemed to be seeking her out, and his gaze was strong. Solid. Filled with love ... for this river? She looked away, embarrassed by the growing feelings for him that welled up inside her.

Revving the engine and returning to his tour guide persona, Thomas cleared his throat and swept his arm in a wide arc. "See all these islands? For years, Mr. Cornwall and Mr. Walton have had the timber cleared on portions of several of them. Then they put the land up for sale with the stipulation that every second island remains vacant. Moreover, those who purchase an island are to have a cottage erected on it within three years. Savvy businessmen, don't you think?"

Noticing that she was the only person who seemed to be listening, Katelyn nodded. Claudia yawned openly, while Sara and Darcy laughed about something. Thomas frowned.

"What island is that?" Katelyn asked, pointing in hopes of keeping him engaged. "There off the port bow."

"That is Cherry Island. Albert Pullman, Mr. Pullman's brother, lives on the far eastern side."

Katelyn nodded. "That's where the Pullmans went on Sunday."

"Precisely." Thomas winked in agreement. Then he turned the launch northwest, back toward Pullman Island.

Disappointed, Katelyn noticed the other girls seemed sad as well, all but Claudia.

"Must we go back so soon?" Sara asked.

Thomas shrugged his shoulders. "I'm afraid so. They gave us two hours, and that's almost up. I 'spect there's a busy day ahead for all of us."

Upon docking, Katelyn thanked Thomas for the fine tour, and the others followed suit. Katelyn and Sara agreed to stop at the boathouse to thank Shamus, but the others went on to the privy and then to the cottage.

When Katelyn and Sara entered the boathouse, Shamus seemed nowhere to be found. But on the other side of a pile of canoes, Katelyn found him.

On the floor. Unconscious.

"Shamus!" Katelyn screamed. "Thomas! Help!"

Thomas burst through the door a moment later and bent down where Shamus lay. The old man's face was ashen, but he was still breathing. "Sara, run for Mrs. Duncan. She knows a little doctoring."

Sara ran to the cottage, and within minutes returned with Mrs. Duncan. "It appears to be heart trouble. We must get him to the bay at once."

With great care, Thomas and the women carried Shamus to the launch and laid him on the padded bench. By then, he had awakened and groaned, a sheen of sweat on his pain-contorted face, his breaths short and ragged. Mrs. Duncan stayed by his side, tending to him as best she could. "You come too, Katelyn. We may need you. Sara, tell Cook and McCarthy what's happened."

Sara nodded and hurried for the cottage as the launch left the dock. A calm Mrs. Duncan stroked Shamus' forehead with the wet cloth she had brought with her, took his pulse, and spoke soothing words to him.

Thomas sped through the waters, careful to avoid waves that might jolt the patient, while Katelyn silently prayed. *Dear Lord, please take care of this kind man. Don't let him die!*

Crystal clear memories of her mama's death flooded her mind—like it was happening all over again—and tears welled up in her eyes. Her mama's beautiful face, thin and ashen. Dry lips and tired eyes. So much like Shamus looked now. Her mother's will to live—gone.

"Don't die! Please don't die!" Katelyn said aloud, just as she had to her mama those three months ago.

"Katelyn. Hush," Mrs. Duncan scolded gently. "Please pray quietly."

"Sorry. I ..." Katelyn remembered the way her mama stared into her eyes, imploring her to find a better life, a life far different than the hard farm life Mama had known. Her mama knew. Mama knew she would wither up and die on the farm with her father and brothers.

"Hurry, Thomas! His breathing is getting shallower."

Mrs. Duncan's words took Katelyn away from her memories. She could see the concern on the older woman's face, the stillness of Shamus' body, the panic in Thomas' eyes. She prayed harder.

As they neared the Alexandria Bay dock, Thomas shouted at the man waiting to help. "Get a buggy, and hurry. We have a man here who is deathly ill!"

A flurry of activity began onshore. The man ran to the road, beckoning a farmer to lend his wagon. Another man grabbed a board lying near a shed. Four others ran to the launch, carefully laid Shamus on the board, and carried him to the wagon. Shamus groaned, his face twisted with pain.

"He's alive!" Thomas said, blowing out a huge breath as if he'd held it in for way too long. Then he bent close to the ear of his boss, his friend, his mentor. "Shamus, you're in the bay, and we're taking you to the doctor. Be still. We're getting you help."

Katelyn could see his tears spilling onto Shamus' shirt, but Thomas didn't seem to care as they bumped along the road, nearer and nearer to the help Shamus needed. Thomas patted his shoulder gently and bent close to his ashen face. "Shamus, I love you."

It seemed like hours, but it was really only a few minutes before they got to the doctor's tiny office on the side of his house. The doctor hurried Thomas and Shamus inside but asked that Katelyn and Mrs. Duncan wait on the porch.

"What if he dies?" Katelyn mumbled.

"He's in the hands of Providence, Katelyn. Trust and pray." Mrs. Duncan patted her shoulder, but she had a sad, faraway look—and tears—in her eyes. "It was like this when my husband died."

CHAPTER 15

Mrs. Duncan patted Thomas on the arm. "Mr. Pullman is a good man, Thomas. He will understand."

Katelyn realized she wasn't the only one who'd noticed how deeply the young man cared for his elder.

Thomas nodded and rolled his slumping shoulders. "I'll say goodbye to Shamus and take you back to the island. Then we must speak with the Pullmans."

Thomas went back into the doctor's office and returned a few minutes later. Katelyn and Mrs. Duncan were also allowed to go in to give Shamus their love and prayers. At the sight of Shamus' ashen face, Katelyn tried her best not to cry. Yet unbidden tears trickled from her eyes anyway. She kissed his wrinkled cheek and promised to pray for him. Then Katelyn, Thomas, and Mrs. Duncan walked to the boat and returned to the island without him.

Mrs. Duncan went directly to the Pullmans while Thomas and Katelyn gave the news to the staff. While they all expressed concern, none of their emotion felt more palpable than Thomas'.

"What will the Pullmans do, now that he can't work? Will they toss him out on his ear?" Claudia asked.

McCarthy fixed her with a sharp eye. "They shan't! You mind that."

When Mrs. Duncan came back, Mr. Pullman accompanied her. He addressed his staff in the same manner that Katelyn imagined he used when speaking to a corporate board. "It seems we are one man down for the time being. Shamus is an important part of our staff, and he will stay here while he recuperates—if you are willing to care for him *and* do your work, Thomas."

"I will. Absolutely!" Thomas exhaled a deep breath.

"Good. We will all have to work harder while Shamus is under the weather if we are to be ready for the Grand Affair."

Sensing the compassion in Mr. Pullman's voice and on his face, Katelyn began to soften her attitude toward him, just a wee bit. *Mr. Pullman really does care.*

Their employer cleared his throat. "That's about the size of it. Back to work!"

The rest of the staff murmured their thanks and returned to their duties, while Katelyn hesitated, noticing Thomas standing there like a forlorn boy.

"Thomas, you will report to me for the time being. Let's talk." McCarthy laid his hand on Thomas' shoulder and led him out the kitchen door. The two of them took the path toward the boathouse, Thomas' head hanging low and McCarthy talking to him as they went.

McCarthy will help him through this, I'm sure of it. At least Thomas won't be alone.

Katelyn went over to Sara and gave her a hug. "He'll be all right," she whispered. Katelyn gave Sara a reassuring smile before heading into the dining room to clean up the lunch dishes and prepare for the evening meal. *What an up and down day this has been!*

"Thank goodness Cook and McCarthy were able to get lunch on the table in time," Mrs. Duncan said, entering the room. "But look at this mess!" She pointed to the tablecloth stained with tea still dripping down on the floor.

"One of the wee ones must have done this, don't you think?"

Mrs. Duncan gave her an unreadable look before departing for the kitchen. When she returned, she chuckled quietly. "It seems poor Claudia got so nervous serving that she spilled hot tea all over Mrs. Pullman's afternoon dress."

Imagining the horrible scene, Katelyn fluttered a hand over her mouth before recovering and defending her co-worker. "It can be daunting to serve such people."

"So true, and you've become a fine old hand at it. Now let's get these things cleared and set for dinner. Of all the days for a crisis! Mr. Walton is coming again for dinner." Mrs. Duncan bit her bottom lip and rubbed her hands on her apron like she always did when she was stressed.

For the next few hours, Katelyn scurried here and there, grabbing a hunk of bread to nibble on, cleaning and prepping for their dinner guests, and ironing dinner linens.

Two very different worlds co-exist here. The Pullmans ... and us. What would I prefer if I had the choice?

As she ironed, she pondered the magnitude of making decisions that affected the likes of Mr. Pullman—or the president of the United States. What it was like to be the missus with all the expectations and obligations weighing on her? Even the little girls faced daunting challenges ahead—expectations of marrying just the right men and carrying on the Pullman name.

My decisions are few, and not ones of any magnitude or import. But the choices I make are of the heart, and out of my heart come the words I speak. Please help them be good ones, Lord.

"Almost done?" As Mrs. Duncan interrupted her thoughts, Katelyn nearly burned Mr. Pullman's nightshirt. "Finish that shirt and then take a message to Thomas, please. Tell him to pick up Mr. Walton promptly at five p.m."

"Yes, ma'am."

Katelyn quickly finished the shirt and stopped by the dressing closet to wet her hair, combing the rebellious stuff straight back into a bun. Looking in the tiny mirror, Katelyn frowned at her curly hair and freckled face. Some days, she felt awfully plain. Like today. Yet the way Thomas' eyes had twinkled and subtly danced over her that morning on the boat caused her to rethink her appearance. Deciding that no one had time to ponder such folly, she smiled and shrugged her shoulders.

Hurrying to the boathouse, Katelyn shivered with excitement even in the summer's warmth. Just the thought of seeing him again tickled her innards. She placed a hand on the doorknob and sucked in a breath. The half-opened door squeaked loudly as she opened it.

Thomas worked on a canoe and seemed not to hear her enter. She touched his arm, relaying the message in a gentle tone. He didn't smile, nor did he respond to her. His downcast face and slumped shoulders alarmed her. His deep sadness permeated the room, making Katelyn shudder.

"Shamus will be fit as a fiddle in no time, Thomas. Just you mind that." Katelyn smiled and infused as much encouragement into her voice as she could.

"I am grateful for Mr. Pullman's kindness, but I am also worried about doing all this work myself, and about taking care of Shamus besides. I love him like a father, but it may be more than I can handle. Then what will happen to the Grand Affair? Or to Shamus and myself if I can't keep up?" He waved his hand around the boathouse and glanced outside. "There is so much to do here." His eyebrows pinched in worry.

Katelyn drew close and touched his arm again. "I will help. We all will. And the Pullmans already said they'd be hiring others."

~~~

Thomas stiffened when a whiff of lemon verbena assaulted his senses. Katelyn's hand innocently touched his arm, making his heart jump. Being so near her unnerved him, and mixed with his present concerns, he wasn't sure what to do, what to think, how to respond. He felt paralyzed, and he didn't like that feeling one bit.

Then she reassured him, and that tentative, caring smile crossed her lips, softening her lovely face. *She is a rare jewel. When she touched me, did she—could she—feel the same as I?*

He pulled off his cap, raked his hands through his curls, and rubbed his sweaty palm on his pants. *What shall I do?*

~~~

Katelyn recognized the moment Thomas' gaze shifted from some distant place, back to the present. Then he laid his hand on hers. "You're beautiful, Katelyn."

Katelyn felt an emotional lightning bolt travel through her hand to her head. Her mama had told her she was beautiful many times, but she never really believed it. Besides, she hadn't heard that from a man since she was a little girl when her father had told her so a time or two. Her face grew hot, and she managed to whisper, "Thank you."

Thomas said nothing more, so Katelyn excused herself and returned to the cottage. *He thinks I'm beautiful?* The words shook her, confused her, but pleased her even more than the idea of meeting the president.

He said I'm beautiful!

Katelyn entered the kitchen all grins, but Sara scurried up to her, her face pinched with concern. "I'm so worried about my brother. How is he? He loves Shamus dearly."

"He is good. Shaken but good." Katelyn laid a tender hand on Sara's quivering arm.

Sara sighed. "I was so worried Shamus would die. But ..." Sara paused when she looked at Katelyn's face. "Why are you smiling so?"

Darcy joined them, shaking her head and wiping her hands on her apron. "Can't be having no dead people on the island. It'd be bad luck afore the president's visit."

Claudia came over and hissed into Katelyn's ear. "I sure didn't appreciate you being gone. I had to do your job and serve the lunch, and I nearly cooked my own goose. But I know now what you've been saying, about the Pullmans, I mean. How can you do such difficult work, and put up with two wiggly children, and an overly nervous mother, and such a stern man?"

"You get used to it." Katelyn cocked her head and turned to go to the dining room, but Cook stepped in front of her.

"Did you eat any lunch, girl?"

Katelyn stared into space as she tried to recall. "I nibbled on some bread. I guess in the confusion of the day, eating wasn't a priority."

"Well now. We can't be having someone starve to death, especially one as willowy as you! Sit and eat something." Cook pulled out the bench and motioned for her to sit. She put a plate of meat, cheese, and fruit in front of Katelyn. Then she bent down and whispered in her ear. "Thank you for helping Shamus."

When Katelyn turned to glance at Cook, tears filled the woman's eyes. Katelyn nodded in acknowledgment, whispered a "thank you" for the food, and then popped a few blueberries into her mouth. The others watched the interchange, probably wondering what Cook had said.

Katelyn felt strange and rather uncomfortable, sitting there while the others worked. But when she realized they had already had a lunch break, she relaxed and ate her fill. The girls chatted about the evening's menu, the next day's plans, and hopes for Shamus' health.

When she had finished her food, Katelyn cleared her plate and returned to work, stopping by the uniform closet to change into her serving attire.

Before long, Mr. Walton arrived, and dinner got underway.

"Thomas told me about Shamus. Are you going to retire him?" Mr. Walton asked as Katelyn poured the tea.

The rather large man possessed a long grey beard that extended halfway down his chest, and Katelyn couldn't help but compare him to St. Nicholas. His tiny, round spectacles hung precariously on the bridge of his nose, only serving to underline that impression. But he didn't appear to share the charity of St. Nick.

To Katelyn's relief, Mr. Pullman replied with firmness, "No. Shamus is a valued member of our staff. He can direct Thomas, even from his bed."

"But with the Grand Affair? How will you do it all? You haven't the staff you do on the mainland." Mr. Walton took a large bite of salad and crunched noisily.

"Hire from the bay if we have to." Mr. Pullman changed the topic, avoiding more interrogation. "Tell Mrs. Pullman about how your father became partners with Cornwall. I don't think she's ever heard the whole story."

"Back in '45, he paid three thousand dollars to purchase these Thousand Islands, most of them anyway, when he found out that the owner, Colonel Elisha Camp, was finally ready to sell them. Andrew Cornwall joined him in partnership in '53. Before that, the islands were undeveloped and mainly used by lumberers for timber."

"And then you hired men to have some of the land cleared on many of the virgin islands, correct?"

"Yes, it makes the property easier to sell." Mr. Walton laid down his fork and stroked his long beard as he talked. Katelyn smiled at the funny sight. "Folks can imagine a summer home on it much better if they have a spot to build that home, I expect."

Mr. Pullman chuckled, and Katelyn enjoyed the sound of it. It was the first time she had heard him laugh. It was one of those deep belly laughs that put everyone at ease. He seemed so much more relaxed with Mr. Walton than she'd ever seen him with Cornwall or even his family.

"Have you sold many of the islands so far?" Mrs. Pullman asked, dabbing her lips with her napkin.

Mr. Walton nodded. "Some. But after this Grand Affair of yours, the islands will surely be national news, and I believe lots of people will flock to them and buy them for top dollar. Leastwise, that's what Cornwall and I hope. Speaking of the Grand Affair, how shall my wife and I help?"

Katelyn was sent into the kitchen to return salad plates and bring out the entrees, so she didn't hear the answer. She hoped the Waltons would be a big part of the event. Despite the man's old-fashioned views where servants were concerned, Katelyn could tell he exerted an uplifting influence on Mr. Pullman.

On her way back into the dining room, Katelyn somehow bumped one of the plates up against the wall, sending it crashing loudly to the floor. Thankfully, she kept the other plate intact and handed it to McCarthy.

"Mercy! What's happened?" Mrs. Pullman, whose back faced the door, asked.

Katelyn bent down to scoop up the mess, her face hot and her hands shaking.

"Clumsy girl," Mr. Pullman muttered.

"So, so sorry," Katelyn said quietly. Mrs. Duncan took the spilled plate from her hands and sent her back into the kitchen to get a new plate of food while she cleaned up the mess. Katelyn returned to find Mr. Pullman engaged in a conversation with Mr. Walton, and thankfully, he just gave her a disagreeable look. Mrs. Pullman, however, pursed her lips in a compassionate gesture.

The rest of the meal went without incident, but Katelyn continued to inwardly scold herself for the error. She tried to stay in the shadows, avoid eye contact, and not make any more mistakes. After dinner concluded, the three at the table rose to leave.

While the men made their way to the study, Mrs. Pullman approached Katelyn. "Don't fret, Katelyn. We all have our moments."

Katelyn tilted her head. "Thank you. How are the girls doing?"

"They are good, and Florence asks about you often."

"Oh, I so do cherish your little cherubs."

Mrs. Pullman laughed. "I know, and they know." Mrs. Pullman gave Katelyn's forearm a gentle squeeze and bid her goodnight.

Katelyn curtsied in gratitude.

McCarthy helped her clean up since Mrs. Duncan had not returned from the kitchen. While Katelyn cleared the table and reset it for breakfast, she wondered what the wee girls' Grand Affair party frocks would look like. What would it be like to be a small child and meet your president? *Do they even know what a privileged life they lead?*

"I'm so glad you'll be helping Thomas sort out his duties," Katelyn said, taking the clean breakfast plates from McCarthy's hands.

"Thomas is a fine young man, but it's such a shame to hear of Shamus' troubles."

"I was so frightened that he would die. Like my mama." Katelyn set the plates around the table.

"Shamus has a deep and abiding faith. He will be fine." McCarthy nodded and left the room to take the bin of dirty dishes to the kitchen.

Katelyn wondered how deep her mama's faith had been. Yes, she had helped the women in the church with childcare and other domestic needs, and she'd even sung in the choir at special events. She'd taught Katelyn Scripture verses. But other than that, Mama never had talked much about her faith. *Did she really know God like McCarthy does? Do I?*

When the room was clean and the table set for breakfast, Katelyn bid McCarthy goodnight and went to the kitchen to walk with the other girls back to their room. Cook, however, shooed her on her way, saying that Katelyn had had enough for one day.

Katelyn returned to the staff quarters alone. She intended to light a candle and ready herself for bed, but the wicker chairs on the veranda—now her favorite place for sorting out her thoughts—beckoned. The pale light and deep fog hovering over the island signaled her to be silent. Contemplative. Prayerful.

What a day! From the magic of the excursion to the horror of finding Shamus on the floor to her emerging feelings for Thomas. Did he feel the same as she? Even if he did, how could they cross the boundaries of work and private life here on the island to begin a romance?

Instead of stewing about all these unknowns, she prayed for McCarthy and Shamus—and even Thomas and Sara.

CHAPTER 16

Before Katelyn and the others even sat down to breakfast, Cook informed them that today Mrs. Emily Pullman would arrive to celebrate Little Hattie's third birthday with the family tradition of ice cream-making. Katelyn had never tasted ice cream; would she get to taste it now?

After the staff breakfast, Katelyn was sent to the icehouse to get two buckets full of ice. On the way, she enjoyed the bright morning sunshine and fresh river breeze. As she passed by the wild roses, a swarm of bees flitted among the flowers, and the sound of fishermen out for their early catch caught her attention. *Might Thomas be one of them?*

When she opened the icehouse door, the chill that swept out caused her to catch her breath. *Ah, how refreshing!*

Katelyn had only fetched the ice a few times since she started working on the island, and it took a moment for her eyes to adjust to the dark. She still found the size of the ice chunks amazing. Some blocks were bigger than she was! How did they get here? Who could carry such massive, frozen blocks?

The ice sat in the sawdust-laden dark, intact and unmelted. She found a few smaller pieces, but for nearly a half an hour, she jabbed and poked with an ice pick until she chopped all she needed to fill her buckets.

Katelyn was nearly done when a gust of wind slammed the door shut. The darkness and the cold took her breath away. Rushing to the entrance, Katelyn tried the handle, but the door didn't budge!

She pushed and pulled and kicked to no effect. Growing colder and more scared by the moment, she began to yell, "Help! Help!"

It was several minutes before a deep voice spoke from the other side. "Hold on. I'll get this open presently."

Thomas. Thank God for Thomas!

Katelyn stood back as the door shuddered under his attempts to pull it open. Finally, it jerked free, and he stood in a bright shaft of light before her, shaking his head. "I need to fix this. Today. Sorry, Morning Dove. Are you all right?"

Katelyn threw her arms around his neck. "Thank you. You saved me!"

She held onto him for a few moments before she realized what she was doing. Katelyn jerked her arms back to her side and felt her face grow red. "Pardon me. I must have been overcome with relief." She hugged herself and turned her eyes to the river, trying to calm her racing heart.

"Fear not, Morning Dove. I shan't tell a soul." Thomas rubbed her arms, smiled, and gave her a wink. "You must be chilled to the bone. I'm just glad you're all right." Thomas continued to touch her for longer than he needed to, and Katelyn's heart soared like an eagle. When she caught his eyes, he bowed and sheepishly excused himself, a silly grin planted on his handsome face. "I must be on my way to the bay to get some cream. Then I am to pick up the girls' grandma for the birthday celebration."

"Be gone then, but know you are my hero." Katelyn curtsied and smiled, grateful to be safe.

Cook met Katelyn at the door of the kitchen, where a flurry of activity had commenced. "Where have you been?" she scolded. "You've been gone nearly an hour, and we have so much to do."

"Sorry, Cook. The icehouse door jammed and held me captive. Thomas rescued me just now."

Cook's eyes popped open wide before she shook her head in regret. "That door has always been a bother."

"Thomas said he would fix it this very day."

"Very well then. Be about your work, lass, and be quick about it."

Katelyn nodded and hurried into the dining room, where McCarthy and Mrs. Duncan had already served breakfast and set the table for the evening dinner. Mrs. Duncan instructed her to gather the churn and the rock salt and take them to the veranda, where the ice cream making would take place. There, Katelyn found Sara arranging the table and chairs for the event.

Sara grabbed Katelyn's hand. "Cook wants both of us to go pick the wild strawberries from the patch on the far side of the island to be served with the ice cream."

Katelyn grinned. "That would be lovely, Sara. Besides, the sun will warm my skin."

Sara felt Katelyn's cheek. "You're still cold. I heard about your mishap, and I'm glad you're all right."

Katelyn nodded and chuckled. "News travels quickly on this island."

Carrying the bowls they had chosen to put the berries in, they walked in silence to the strawberry patch. Katelyn basked in thoughts of her fortunate meeting with Thomas, but she still sensed tension between Sara and her.

When they began picking, Katelyn cleared her throat. "Sara, my Irish twin, I'm so sorry for my foolish words. I'm trying to mend my ways. I really am. It's just that my propensity to jabber too often gets the best of me. I don't want to lose your friendship over this transgression. Please have patience with me."

Sara took her hand and looked into her now-teary eyes. "Gracious, Katelyn, I may get angry with you now and then, but I will never forsake you. Just you mind that."

Relieved, Katelyn hugged her friend, and they returned to their berry picking. *Now, to not disappoint her—or her brother—again.* Soon they had a large bowl full of berries, so they returned to the kitchen and set to cleaning them.

By noon, the Pullmans gathered on the veranda for high tea. Katelyn observed Little Hattie with delight. She wore all pink—from a huge bow in her curly locks to the stockings on her tiny feet. Frills and lace made her look like a fine porcelain doll, and the smile on her face let everyone know she was happy to be celebrated. Still—though Katelyn found the habit adorable—her thumb-sucking continued to betray her shyness.

Florence looked like the sunshine that bathed the veranda in her yellow frills and lace. She sweetly doted over her little sister, like a servant to a princess. Florence handed Hattie a cucumber sandwich, helped her drink from a china cup, and dabbed her sister's mouth. Katelyn tended to the table, but she also kept an eye on the girls, pleased to see the two little ones care for each other so.

My brothers always treated me as a slave. What would it be like to have such loving siblings?

When the Pullmans had finished their luncheon, it was time to begin the ice cream-making process. Katelyn packed the churn with rock salt while Sara added Cook's creamy mixture. Then the two took turns turning the crank. Every now and then, Florence or Hattie tried to crank the churn, laughing with glee. Grandma Pullman even allowed the little ones to dip their finger into the sweet mixture to check the consistency.

Katelyn enjoyed every moment of her first ice cream-making experience, even as she struggled to turn the crank. The longer they churned the mixture, the harder it got, and soon, perspiration rose from her skin and dampened her dress. When the cool breeze blew up from the river, Katelyn turned toward it, hoping to catch some relief.

Finally, the ice cream was almost solid. They added the berries, then Katelyn scooped out spoonful after spoonful of the pink, creamy mixture and served a bowl to each of the Pullmans. As she imagined what it might taste like and wished she could dip her finger into it too, Katelyn's mouth watered.

The family gave Little Hattie a pretty dolly as a gift. She had a porcelain face and hands, thick, curly, yellow hair, and a pretty painted face with blue eyes. Her dress was a pale yellow, with frilly lace, buttons, pleats, and bows, very much like Hattie would wear. Tiny black boots completed the doll's ensemble.

"I wuf her, Papa and Ma," Hattie said as she hugged her parents. Then she thanked her grandmother and turned to Florence. "She will be our wittle sister."

Florence and Hattie admired the doll as they finished their ice cream.

"Let's all go for a boat ride on the river and deliver Grandma back to her island, shall we?" Mr. Pullman suggested.

When the family set out for the boat, Mrs. Duncan addressed the staff. "The Pullmans have granted permission for us to enjoy the rest of the tea—and the ice cream. Have a sandwich and then partake of a little ice cream as a treat on this lovely day."

Katelyn's excitement caused her to squeal with the other girls, something she had vowed not to do, especially after her father had given her a slap the last time she displayed such ecstatic delight. But she shook off any guilt over her impulsive reaction and grabbed a sandwich, eating it quickly so that she could taste the creamy ice cream she worked hard to make.

Claudia and Darcy were already enjoying their ice cream, so Katelyn scooped bowls for Sara and herself. Her mouth watered as she handed Sara the bowl and sat down.

"It isn't as good as the ice cream at the Woodruff Hotel in Watertown, that's for sure." Claudia wrinkled her nose as she took a big bite.

Katelyn countered her. "I've never had ice cream before, but I think it's the best treat I have ever had. And if you don't like it, I'll gladly finish yours. It's simply divine!"

McCarthy chuckled as Claudia covered her bowl with her hand. "The strawberries make ice cream all the more luscious. It's my favorite flavor. Well done, Sara and Katelyn."

The staff enjoyed their own impromptu party for nearly an hour, chatting on the veranda like they were part of the upper class. *Is this what it's like?* Katelyn wondered. *Sitting and talking in the middle of the day? Not a care in the world?*

Unthinkable!

It was nearly three when Mrs. Duncan told them to clean up, but she pulled Katelyn aside and said, "Mrs. Pullman wants you to accompany Nanny and the girls to the bay tomorrow to have the children fitted for their Grand Affair party frocks. Since you will be gone much of tomorrow, I need you to get ahead on the ironing today, before the Pullmans host his brothers for dinner."

"I'd be happy to, ma'am. After this tasty respite, I feel quite refreshed." Katelyn giggled. "And to see the wee ones and their party frocks? That would be a treat as well."

Mrs. Duncan nodded and patted her hand. "Very well, then. Spit spot."

Katelyn gathered the ironing. While she hated ironing back at the farm, here it was different. There was always so much to think about while she worked, and that made all the difference. Ice cream. Birthday parties. And Thomas.

What must he think of her, so boldly throwing herself at him? But she was so overcome with relief; surely he knew that. Katelyn began to fret and nearly burned the under-drawers. Pushing back several strands of hair, she wiped her forehead. She shook herself from her worrying and pondered more pleasant things—the wee ones, to be specific.

Katelyn finished the ironing and even had time to change her uniform and help with the final dining room preparations. *Funny how time flies one day and crawls another.*

Soon Mr. Pullman's brothers, James and Royal, entered the cottage laughing and slapping each other on the back. Katelyn had overheard McCarthy remind Mrs. Duncan that Royal was the older brother. He lived in a canvas tent in Camp Royal on Wells Island. James, on the other hand, was three years younger and lived on Summerland Island, where cottagers shared a communal kitchen and dining hall.

My, what strange ways to live, especially coming from the upper-class Pullman heritage.

As Katelyn served them, she enjoyed hearing the brothers bantering about their recent fishing trip near Wells Island. Then Mr. Pullman sat forward and cleared his throat. "The Presidential Gala will be the highlight of the Grand Affair, and I would like my two brothers to help me plan it."

Royal responded first. "I'm not so sure James and I are the ones to plan such a high class, pomp-and-circumstance to-do as the president would expect."

"I agree." James nodded. "Look how we live, brother. I in a communal setting and the old man here in a tent." James pointed to Royal and both let out a belly laugh that shook the crystal. "We are not like you. Nor can we be."

"But I require your services, for there are many things to do." Mr. Pullman slapped the table, rattling the silver. "Cornwall and Walton have their hands full, and so does Mother. Can you not give me a hand?"

Royal stared at his brother for a long time and shook his head. "Do you not know me better than that? I will be glad to help, but as you know, my expertise is more of the salt-of-the-earth kind. I can build stone walls, plant gardens, prune trees, fix boats, or skin fish. Set me about such tasks if you will. You know I cannot plan a party."

James laughed. "You are as rough around the edges as the hero in James Fenimore Cooper's *Pathfinder*—one who would rather fight Indians, survive storms on the lake, and protect fair young maidens."

"Yes, and like in *The Last of the Mohicans*, I've definitely learned that the treachery and danger of guiding a woman through the wilderness can be deadly," Royal quipped.

Mr. Pullman slammed his hand on the table again, startling Katelyn along with everyone else in the room, and spilling his coffee. "Enough of this nonsense! I need your help, not your foolishness. You, miss, come and clean up this mess."

Mr. Pullman's glare fixed on Katelyn. She curtsied, grabbed a cloth, and proceeded to clean up the spilled coffee. Being so close to him in the midst of his anger scared her to death, but she willed herself not to shake. Instead, she silently did her duty.

Nevertheless, Katelyn's ire rose again. *The nerve of such a man, talking to his brothers like that. Talking to me like that!*

Katelyn returned to her post. But as she watched, Mr. Pullman got up and paced the room, hands behind his back, face red as a beet, mumbling to himself. Mrs. Pullman stared at her plate of food. Shifting ever so slightly in her seat, she dabbed her eyes and nose with her napkin, obviously embarrassed and saddened by her husband's outburst.

Meanwhile, the two brothers rolled their eyes and continued to eat their meal in silence. Katelyn, McCarthy, and Mrs. Duncan stood in silence too, eyes straight ahead, pretending to see and hear nothing. But Katelyn's mind was all a-whir with feelings of anger and resentment toward her employer.

How dare he make his wife cry and ruin a fine evening with his brothers?

Mrs. Duncan whispered to her, shaking her from her thoughts. "Katelyn, fill the missus' teacup. It's empty."

Katelyn did as she was asked.

Finally, Mr. Pullman returned to his seat and let out a huge sigh. "All right. I'll tell you what. Since Shamus is ill, Thomas has the weight of the boathouse and the property on his shoulders. Talk to him, the two of you, and see how you can help him ready the grounds and the boats for the Grand Affair. Will that suit you?"

Royal smirked. "Well now, compromise isn't so painful after all, is it, brother?"

Mr. Pullman groaned. "Blast you! You may be older, but you are surely none-the-wiser."

Katelyn nearly smirked at that comment.

The four Pullmans spent the rest of the evening in neutral small talk, and soon James and Royal were ready to find Thomas and return to their islands. Katelyn and Mrs. Duncan cleaned up and set the table for breakfast since McCarthy had gone to attend to Mr. Pullman's needs. Little was said between them as for once, Katelyn held her tongue and didn't comment on the dinner conversation.

It was nearly eleven p.m. by the time the staff finally headed to their quarters. Sara, Claudia, and Darcy seemed too tired to talk, but Katelyn's anger boiled over. "You wouldn't believe how Mr. Pullman acted during dinner. Like a spoiled child he was—pacing and huffing and puffing, and ruining the mighty fine dinner you made. No one could please him. He drove Mrs. Pullman to tears, and his brothers were appalled. I was too."

"Katelyn, hold your tongue. Please," Sara pleaded. "We do not need to hear the dining room gossip." She grabbed Darcy's hand, shook her head, and hurried away.

"She's right, you know," Claudia said, rather kindly.

"I cannot seem to get a handle on my words," Katelyn confessed. "When I am angry or frustrated or see injustice, my tongue takes over. However will I stop?"

Claudia shrugged her shoulders.

As the girls readied for bed, Katelyn felt the tension thick in the room. She wanted to apologize. She wanted to set things right. But now she had no words. When Darcy turned out the lights, Katelyn turned heavenward with silent prayers begging God for grace and mercy and help to change.

CHAPTER 17

When Katelyn entered the dining room the next day, Mrs. Duncan gave her some startling news. "Bridget's father passed away yesterday, so she must travel to Rochester and will be gone for a week, maybe more. Mrs. Pullman has requested that you fill her role as the children's nursemaid, and the trip to the seamstress is canceled. I don't know how I'll get along without you for a whole week—with preparations for the Grand Affair—but I have no choice."

Katelyn tried not to show her excitement—or her trepidation. "Yes, ma'am. I am sorry to hear about poor Bridget."

Katelyn started for the nursery, but first, she made a stop by the kitchen to tell Sara the news. "I'm not sure how to nanny. Watching them for a few hours is one thing; all day and all night is another."

Claudia overheard their conversation and commented as she continued kneading the bread, "I'm just glad it's you and not me. Children are a bother!"

Sara encouraged Katelyn to simply be herself and do the best she could. After gathering a few things from her room, Katelyn climbed the stairs to her new job.

When Katelyn got to the nursery, Mrs. Pullman greeted her cheerfully. "Thank you for filling in for Bridget; I know you weren't hired for this position, but the girls do like you so."

"I'm happy to serve you and your daughters, Mrs. Pullman." Katelyn could feel a grin break over her face as the girls ran over and hugged her legs, squealing with excitement.

Mrs. Pullman smiled and took their hands. "Hush, girls." She gently pulled them back and sent Katelyn to Bridget's room that adjoined the girls' room. There she found a teary woman not yet packed. Katelyn rushed over to encourage her. "I'm sorry this has happened to you, Bridget, but you must hurry if you are to catch the morning train."

Bridget nodded, and Katelyn helped her pack. She had so many questions, more than Bridget could answer. "Please tell me how to manage your position while you are gone. What is the schedule?"

Bridget dried her tears and began to rattle off the children's routine, the bedtime rituals, and other things pertaining to the girls.

"When do the parents spend time with them?"

"Hardly ever, especially with making plans for the Grand Affair and all." Bridget shrugged her shoulders and picked up her suitcase. Katelyn followed her back into the nursery.

"Might I please accompany Bridget to the bay to finish hearing how to manage the position?" Katelyn asked Mrs. Pullman.

"All right, but do hurry back," Mrs. Pullman agreed. "I have much to do and cannot do it with little ones running around."

Katelyn curtsied, Bridget said her goodbyes, and off they went to the dock to have Thomas take them to the mainland. On the way to the bay, Bridget prattled on about all the little quirks and habits each of the girls had, their favorite books and games, their tendency to hide and be sneaky. Bridget told her how Hattie tended to be clumsy and hurt herself and how Florence could be stubborn and refuse to obey.

By the time they docked and let Bridget off, Katelyn's head swam with more details than she thought she could manage. Yet she was pleased to have such information to rely on.

Katelyn thanked Bridget and wished her well, while Thomas found Bridget a ride to the Clayton train station and sent her on her way. When he returned, Katelyn felt ready to burst. "That woman is a textbook on those children!" Katelyn took a deep breath.

Thomas pushed off from the dock. "She should be. She spends more time with them than their parents do."

"But that's so wrong. Parents should care for their children; that's what I think. I wouldn't care if I was the richest person around and could afford the best nanny in the world. I, for one, want to care for my own children—when I have them."

Thomas shook his head and glared at her as he veered the skiff toward the island. She knew what was coming. "Katelyn, I care about you, but your tongue is poisonous. You have no right to judge the Pullmans nor spread any of their news without their consent. It is their news, not yours. The girls are their children, not yours. How they manage their children and their affairs is not for you to judge or to have an opinion about. You've got to find a leash for your thoughts and your words, Morning Dove." Thomas rubbed the bridge of his nose with his thumb and forefinger, then raked his hand through his hair.

Something in his tone begged her to meet his gaze. Katelyn looked at his face, expecting his eyes to mock her, to shame her, to judge her, but she saw only compassion and sadness. His kind, understanding expression melted her guilt and shame, and the tears she had determined to hold back spilled over her lashes. She held her lips tightly together and refused to release the avalanche of emotion raging within her. Katelyn wanted him to hold her, to make the pain go away, but he could not. When she started to wipe her face with her shirtsleeve, Thomas handed her a handkerchief from his pocket. She refused it, but he held it to her nose and bid her to blow.

"I can do it myself. Thank you." Katelyn took the hankie. She wasn't offended. Rather, she was touched by his gentle way.

He waited for her to compose herself, then he put his hand on her shoulder. Sliding it down her arm, he took her hand and gave it a tender squeeze.

Swallowing the tightness in her throat, Katelyn freed her hand, afraid it might somehow betray the confusion in her heart. She sucked in a deep breath and shook her head. "I am trying, truly, so I thank you for your mercy."

"I know, and I am far too outspoken and lack the patience to allow people to grow and change." Thomas' voice sounded taut and timid. "Forgive me, Morning Dove."

Finding his tenderness more confusing than his scolding, Katelyn felt her face flush.

When they arrived at the dock, Thomas helped her out of the skiff. She thanked him, but he said nothing. He seemed reluctant to let her go. But there was no time to ponder the relational challenges she faced with Thomas. She had a job to do and children to care for.

When she returned to the nursery, Katelyn fired off the first item of concern she'd assumed from Bridget, before Mrs. Pullman could escape. "Begging your pardon, missus, but how will we manage the editors' and publishers' gathering without Bridget? It's just twelve days hence?"

Mrs. Pullman cocked her head and smiled. "Charles Crossmon and Son will cater it, so the onus will be on them. Bridget should be back, so you will serve the table as usual." She rose, standing over the rug where the girls played with their dolls.

Katelyn smiled at them. "Thank you, ma'am. I'm ready to care for your wee cherubs."

Mrs. Pullman nodded, kissed the tops of the girls' heads, and scurried off while the children pulled at Katelyn's skirt. "Let's have a picnic and feed the ducks, please, Miss Katelyn." Florence's eyes implored her, and Little Hattie nodded in agreement.

"Why, that be a fine idea!"

Katelyn and the children stopped in the kitchen to request a picnic lunch, and then she took the girls to the privy. Thankfully, the two-seater outhouse possessed a small seat for little ones such as Hattie, and she was able to help both girls at the same time without incident.

My! I thought my dining room responsibilities were challenging, but caring for these wee cherubs is ten times harder.

Upon returning to the cottage, Sara silently handed her the picnic basket, and Katelyn couldn't read her face. She touched Sara's arm and said, "Sara, I'm sorry about last night. I'm trying. Really, I am."

Sarah hung her head and whispered, "I know."

Katelyn squeezed her hand and was about to say more when Florence interrupted her.

"I'm trying to learn my ABCs, Miss Katelyn." The child pulled Katelyn out the back door, with Hattie in tow. "I know the song!"

Florence proceeded to sing dramatically—at the top of her lungs—as they walked down the path toward the island's crown. Little Hattie tried her best to join her sister, mumbling her way through the tune.

"Well done, wee ones." Katelyn stopped under a grove of trees. "Let's spread our blanket here and enjoy the boats passing by."

Florence bent down and whispered in Hattie's ear, and the two little girls grinned mischievously. They ran to the nearby patch of wild violets, picked tiny bouquets, and handed them to Katelyn.

"Thank you, girls! You make me feel like a princess." Katelyn hugged both children at the same time.

"I want to pway 'pwincess.'" Hattie clapped her hands. "I am Pwincess Hattie."

Florence picked up a stick and handed it to her sister. "This can be your scepter, princess."

Little Hattie smiled and waved the stick in the air, nearly poking Katelyn in the eye.

"Let's be careful not to poke anyone, shall we? And come. Sit down and enjoy your princess picnic."

Holding hands, the girls alighted on the blanket, very prim and proper. Katelyn handed each of them buttered bread and a piece of cheese and put a bowl of blueberries near them to share. While they were eating, Hattie and Florence giggled and pointed at two chipmunks that scurried around the blanket and then up the tree nearest them. Katelyn observed them, trying to remember all that Bridget had told her.

After they had eaten their fill, Katelyn wiped the blueberry juice from Hattie's chin and packed up the basket. "Now, let's have some adventures, shall we?" Katelyn gave them her most expectant smile.

Florence and Hattie clapped their hands and jumped up and down. Katelyn bid them to walk along the island's path as they played "I spy"—pointing out the geese and jumping fish, the daffodils and tulips, and, of course, her favorite wild rose bushes.

When they bored of that game, Katelyn presented another plan. "Let's take a walk near the far shore. But remember, you must stay close by me, for I want neither of you to fall in the river."

The two nodded their heads vigorously and said, almost in unison, "Yes, Miss Katelyn." They took Katelyn's hands, but Florence glanced at the picnic basket, furrowing her brow.

Katelyn smiled. "Don't worry, Florence. We will come back for the basket after our walk."

As they set out, the girls talked about the large cargo ship that passed very near the island. Geese honked overhead, and seagulls soared and dipped down toward the river. Butterflies danced around them, evading the girls' attempts to catch them. The river's breeze swept the scent of the great St. Lawrence over the island, and Katelyn breathed it in. Every now and then, a fish jumped out the water, and the two girls pointed and squealed. As the childish wonder of Hattie and Florence brightened the day, Katelyn felt renewed, refreshed, reenergized.

Suddenly, Florence let go of Katelyn's hand and ran in the direction of the *chirp-chirp* of baby birds. There, barely ten feet from them, a nest of goslings lay nestled under a bush—and a large, angry mother goose stood guard nearby! Florence froze as the goose looked her way, then gave chase. The child ran to Katelyn, grabbed her skirt, and held on tightly. But the goose kept on coming, so Katelyn took the girls by the hand and darted back the way they had come.

Around the bend, Katelyn could no longer see the mother goose. But Hattie tripped on a tree root, fell down, and began crying. Katelyn picked her up and saw that her hands were slightly scraped. Florence came close, white as the winter snow, and kissed her sister's hand.

"She's forever falling and scraping her hands, Miss Katelyn. My magic kisses make them all better."

"It hurts," Hattie whined, showing Katelyn her hands. "Kiss them." Katelyn looked back to make sure the goose had gone before she knelt down.

She kissed all four of the girls' hands, then helped the children forget their upset with a tickle fest. They giggled and squirmed in a patch of soft grass.

After Florence rolled over on her tummy, she jumped up and clapped her hands. "Look, Miss Katelyn. Shamrocks! Let's find a four-leaf clover so we'll have good luck!"

"Do you really think we can find one?" Katelyn asked, and immediately, the girls began to explore. When they lost interest, Katelyn picked a three-leaf clover and showed it to the girls. "Did you know that back in Ireland, Saint Patrick taught people about God with the shamrock? Tell me, how many leaves does it have?"

"One. Two. Three." Florence smiled broadly.

"Well done. Yes, and there are three beings in God—the Father, the Son, and the Holy Ghost."

"I don't like ghosts, Miss Katelyn." Florence crinkled her nose.

"But the Holy Ghost is good. He is kind of like the wind. See how the wind blows your hair and keeps you cool? And see how it helps the birds fly? You can't see the wind or the Holy Ghost, but He helps us like the wind helps the birds."

Florence took the shamrock and stared at it. "Oh, I see. You are very clever."

Katelyn laughed as she noticed Little Hattie yawn. "Let's go back to the cottage and clean up. Then we will read a book before nap time."

On the way back, Katelyn and the girls stopped by the privy and then gathered the picnic basket. The cool silence of the nursery closed around the weary explorers like a welcome embrace. Katelyn smiled, awed by all the beautiful full-color picture books sitting tall and majestic on a shelf, just waiting to be chosen. It took a few minutes before the girls could agree on one, but once they did, they cuddled up next to Katelyn.

It took barely a minute for the two to fall asleep, and after tidying the nursery, Katelyn sat down for a moment's peace and quiet. Unaccustomed to such a luxury, Katelyn got up and went to the adjoining nanny's room to settle in, keeping the door ajar so she could hear the little ones.

The room wasn't much more than a closet, but there was a window, a bed that looked rather comfy, and a small chest of drawers. Bridget had left most of her things in the drawers, but Katelyn had little more than a handful of personal belongings, so she placed her things on top of the chest as quietly as she could before returning to the nursery. She wanted to examine all the beautiful books and then read *Little Women* while she had the chance.

Tiptoeing her way to the bookcase, Katelyn slid book after book from its place on the shelf and marveled at each of them. In all her life she had never seen a colored book until she came to this island.

What must it be like to grow up with such luxuries? To have such fine things? To experience life on an island in the summer and on the mainland throughout the rest of the year? And what must it be like to be the child of a famous and wealthy man who can host the president of the United States?

Katelyn could hardly imagine, but here she was, caring for those who did. She looked at the wee ones now chasing dreams as they slept, and she smiled. Thinking of them also made her sad. Sad that these two had so little time with their parents, and when they were with them, their father often scolded them. Like her father. Katelyn shook her head at the thought.

She turned her attention to the book in her hand. *Little Women*. How grateful she was for Mrs. Pullman. For the time to read. For time with the girls.

Soon the wee ones began to stir, and after another trip to the privy and a stop in the kitchen for a snack, it was nearly time to get them ready for dinner. Mrs. Pullman came to the nursery to choose their dinner dresses, and Little Hattie ran to show her mother her scraped hands. Her mother kissed them and laughed. "All better, right?"

"Yes, Mama," Little Hattie said, cuddling up in her skirts.

Florence prattled off all they had done. She started telling her mother about the goose when Mrs. Pullman stopped her. Thank goodness!

"Before I forget to tell you, Katelyn. Mr. Pullman received a letter from the president today that said he would not arrive until August the second. That gives us so much more time to prepare, and everyone seems quite relieved about it. I, most of all." Mrs. Pullman let out a big sigh and smiled.

Katelyn nodded. "I'm so glad. With Bridget gone, Providence has smiled upon us, don't you think?"

"What's province?" Florence asked.

Her mother answered. "Pro-vi-dence, Florence. That means God's divine guidance upon our lives." Then she turned to Katelyn. "You will find that my eldest daughter loves to use big words, so be prepared." Pride glowed on Mrs. Pullman's face.

Katelyn laughed, reassured by the evidence of affection between mother and daughter. "My mama always said the same of me." She patted Florence on the head. "We must be two peas in a pod, wee one."

CHAPTER 18

Two weeks later, a promising golden sun began to rise over the rippling river as Katelyn stood on the veranda and surveyed the island she had come to love. Large tents speckled the open area, awaiting the two hundred or so members of the Editors' and Publishers' Association of the state of New York who would soon descend upon them. She took a deep breath, anticipating an exciting and busy day, yet wondering how they would successfully manage such an important reception.

Sara interrupted Katelyn's thoughts, joining her along with the other three girls. "It's a perfect June day for an *al fresco* party, and I'm so glad Mr. Crossmon is catering the event."

Katelyn slipped her hand into the crook of Sara's arm. "It's made all the difference that the family has been on the mainland for the few last weeks, though I've missed the wee ones."

Darcy nodded. "And can you believe all they brought back with them? Dozens of trunks just full of party dresses, woolen bathing suits, linens, silver, and china, as well as fishing equipment and even more bedding. The cottage is bursting at the seams!"

Claudia rolled her eyes and huffed. "The journalists' reception is what's important today. I do hope there will be some handsome and eligible bachelors for us to meet."

"I believe we'll have little time for magical trysts with journalists." Katelyn winked and grinned. "Not to disparage your desire for such a man."

"Since I am to serve the dessert table, I will likely meet lots of these fine men!" Claudia glanced toward the boathouse and then at Katelyn. "And although you only have eyes for one man, you will be around them too."

Sara rolled her eyes and started down the stairs. "We'd best hurry to breakfast, ladies, else Cook might have a seizure."

Katelyn followed the others toward the cottage. Yes, she had to admit Claudia was correct. Each day of the past two weeks, she and Thomas had grown closer and closer. Thomas felt the same as she, of that she was sure. Although they were forbidden to fraternize, he discreetly made his feelings known. A wink. A tender smile. A knowing nod of his head. And much patience with her occasional wandering words.

She, in turn, was quickly learning to hold her tongue—well, most of the time—although she had to admit that it was, indeed, daunting. But she had taken McCarthy's advice, searched the Good Book, and asked for divine help.

Katelyn turned her thoughts back to Thomas. Once he had brought her wildflowers and rained down words of affirmation and affection—all in secret, of course. Then, one evening under a moonlit sky, he kissed her. Yes, it was only on the cheek like he'd kiss his sister, but so close to her mouth that a tiny, minute movement would have caused their lips to meet.

Katelyn touched her cheek at the memory and nearly tripped over a paving stone, squealing in surprise.

"Are you all right?" Sara grabbed her arm to steady her as they entered the kitchen.

"I'm fine. Just excited about the day, I suppose."

Inside, Katelyn tossed a few berries into her porridge and sat down to eat, shaking her mind free of Sara's brother. Before she had finished her breakfast, Cook cleared her throat and tapped a wooden spoon on the table.

"Listen up, all of you. Mr. Crossmon will take the lead on the reception food and even bring some of it—already prepared—from his hotel in the bay. But I will oversee all that goes on in my kitchen, so no monkey business from a one of you!"

Cook paused and wrinkled her face so that her eyes were barely slits, revealing her disdain for the guests who were coming. "The lot of them journalists will be traveling from Watertown to Cape Vincent by train. Then they will take a steamer down the river, have an excursion through the islands, and finally come here for the midday reception. I expect they will all be mighty hungry."

Entering the room, Mrs. Duncan added, "A musical band from Watertown will join us, and the mood must be festive all the way around. We want every member of the press to rave about the beauty of the area with articles in their papers and magazines. Their impression of Pullman Island and the entire Thousand Islands region begins with each one of us, and we must do our utmost to make them fawn over the experience they have this day!"

Katelyn spoke up. "We will all do our best, Mrs. Duncan."

The rest of the staff murmured their affirmation as they squirmed in their seats.

At that moment, Katelyn realized what a responsibility she had, mingling with such influential folk. *This truly is an important day for the Thousand Islands!*

After the staff was reminded of their assignments, Katelyn headed toward the newly enlarged dock, still yellow and smelling of fresh cut oak. Thomas had already set up a table for her, and someone else had left pitchers of drinks and glasses.

"I hear you're the drink girl for the day," Thomas quipped as she neared the boathouse. "Lucky you."

"I'm not sure that I'm so lucky. Two hundred thirsty journalists on this warm, summer day may be more than I can handle."

Thomas chuckled. "I doubt that, Morning Dove." He bid her farewell with a wink and headed down to the docks as the first boat of the morning arrived.

Katelyn smoothed her skirt and fussed with her hair, making herself as presentable as she could. After all, besides Thomas, she would be the first of the Pullman staff these important people would meet.

As each guest set foot on the island, Katelyn's job was to offer him a drink of his choice: iced tea, water, or lemonade. She greeted everyone with her most confident and friendly smile and handed out drinks as beads of condensation from the glasses wet her fingers. Later they would serve stronger drink, and Thomas would put on his handsome suit to serve with her.

Throughout the morning, several boats dropped off passengers for the reception. Between the arrivals, Katelyn noted that ships, barges, and boats continually sailed along the channel in front of the island, providing entertainment while she waited. Launches, skiffs, and steamers sailed close to Pullman Island, and friend or stranger waved greetings and surely wondered what the party was about. A ship tooted two short blasts at the vessel passing by it. Fish jumped high above the waves and dove back under with such grace that it caused her to smile. Quite often, she glanced over her shoulder to see Thomas working with the boats on the docks.

Such is life on these wonderful Thousand Islands.

As the last boat pulled up to the dock, the churning water splashed against the wood, threatening to wet Thomas through. Several older men disembarked, and then two younger journalists followed behind. The last man waited patiently until the others had been served and were heading toward the tent on the upper lawn.

"May I serve you, sir?" Katelyn asked. The utterly handsome man, whom she thought to be in his early thirties, sported a wide smile, chiseled jaw, and a scar near his ear. He carried himself with an air of importance, yet he seemed approachable, even welcoming.

"Richard Stockton's the name. I'm a war correspondent now covering the president's re-election campaign, so I expect to be back here next month. I'm also a local. From Watertown. And what is your name, my lovely one?"

Rather than answer his bold question, Katelyn gulped in a deep breath, cast a quick glance toward the boathouse, and surveyed this Mr. Stockton further. He sported a well-worn suit that looked a tad small and stiff, and he held a felt bowler-style hat that likely ill-fitted his large head. His short, jet-black hair was combed back from a simple side part. Chin whiskers and a scant mustache barely framed his mouth. His lips lifted in a charmingly sly grin, while his eyes appeared to glitter with secrets.

Mr. Stockton gazed at her with a raised eyebrow, appraising her from her cap to her boots. Then he winked, shaking her from her observations. His roguish smile caused her to wonder what was in his mind, and the rakish gleam in his eye warned her to be wary. But his charming smile overcame such caution. "Cat got your tongue?"

Katelyn offered him a tentative smile and a glass of water. Then she curtsied, turned on her heel, and scurried toward the safety of the boathouse, where she fairly flew into the arms of Thomas.

"What's the matter, Morning Dove? You look like you saw a ghost!"

"'Tis all the excitement of the day, I fear. I'd best hurry to the tent for my next assignment."

Thomas placed both hands gently on her shoulders and chuckled. "Steady, my sweet, or you'll spill whiskey all over the men with those trembling hands."

Hearing Mrs. Duncan calling for her as she approached the boathouse, Katelyn stepped back a safe distance from Thomas. "Where have you been, Katelyn? Stop lollygagging and come. Your daydreaming will be the end of you."

Katelyn mouthed a "thank you" to Thomas and followed Mrs. Duncan up the hill to the open-sided tent. Before entering, she paused to adjust her cap and apron, paste on a smile, and square her shoulders. The small ensemble of musicians was warming up. They would fill the air with gentle music, not to dance to, but to set a spirit of gaiety and generosity. So would the buffet Mr. Crossmon and his staff had prepared. The Pullman staff members shooed away persistent flies determined to land on the *al fresco* luncheon. Nothing would spoil this day, not even flies.

Katelyn took a silver tray of drinks and scooted under the tent awning as sounds of conversation like a beehive filled the air. Men chortled and chattered with one another, bragging about their latest article or award or accolade. Katelyn hurried about, serving from tray after tray as the men took the drinks nearly as fast as she could present them.

Finally, Mr. Pullman took the stage, and a hush fell over the crowd.

"Welcome to Pullman Island, my fine friends. As members of the Editors' and Publishers' Association of the state of New York, I thank you for the fine work you do day in and day out to educate and entertain your readers around the country. Furthermore, Mr. Cornwall and I are pleased to introduce you to the glories of this divine Thousand Islands region, which is ripe for you to present to your readers. As mentioned on the earlier excursion, many of the islands are for sale as we speak. We hope you will feel compelled to rave about this beautiful section of the country and create a swelling desire for thousands to view this scenery for themselves, or even acquire their own little piece of this heavenly neighborhood.

"We have spared no expense so that you will be handsomely entertained this day. Eat, drink, and be merry, my friends! Enjoy a stroll around the island. Hear the music and partake of the food and drink. It is your day to celebrate God's grand creation here on the mighty St. Lawrence River and in the majestic Thousand Islands."

In unison, the men hollered, "Hear, hear!" and clapped until the sound rolled like thunder. Katelyn wove in and out of the crowd, smiling and passing out drinks and even taking some special drink orders. Thomas swept among the guests as well, gracefully reaching into the circles of conversations with his silver tray full of the caterer's special hors d'oeuvres. Several times, she and Thomas nearly bumped into one another or met at the same group of men. Thomas would cast her a wink or a grin, and she would return his greetings with a special smile that was just for him.

In the far corner of the tent, quite near the band, Katelyn could see Mr. Stockton standing alone, leaning against a tent pole, watching her every move. She had felt his eyes on her for some time but resisted the urge to return his gaze. She tossed her head in an attempt to shake away her self-consciousness.

But Mr. Stockton beckoned her with a jerk of his head and an outstretched hand, apparently desiring a drink. A wave of his licorice-colored hair fell over his forehead and obstructed one eye until he shook it out of the way with a quick raising of his chin. His lips curved into a sensuous smile. He frightened her, yet he also intrigued her. Besides, she had a job to do.

Katelyn sucked in a deep breath and walked his way, her heart fluttering and her tray strategically placed between him and herself. "Would you care for a refreshment, sir?"

"You have yet to tell me your name, lovely one." He pouted as if terribly offended.

"Katelyn." She curtsied and turned to leave, but he grabbed her arm.

"Sir. What is your order? Please." She felt frozen to the ground, and she swallowed a nervous giggle that threatened to bubble up. Something about Mr. Stockton was far different from the boyish charm of Thomas. His handsome maturity took her breath away, even paralyzed her, and his forwardness both attracted and alarmed her.

Stockton took in a slow intentional draw of his cigar and then blew a series of smoke rings while Katelyn awaited his order with quivering hands. Then he smiled, drew close to her ear, and whispered, "I'd rather like to get to know you better, Katie dear. When are you finished with work?"

"Much later than you'll be on this island, sir. Please let me pass. I have work to do." Katelyn tried to sidestep his advances, but he met her in turn. Then Katelyn's foot caught the edge of the tent platform, tossing her back in what felt like slow motion. She thought that she would land on her head and bust it open, but suddenly Stockton caught her, sweeping her into his protective embrace just as Thomas came around the corner, his icy glare, knit brows, and pursed lips telling her he believed the worst.

As she disengaged from Stockton's arms, Katelyn stepped away and straightened her uniform. She noticed a tic in Thomas' cheek. He stiffened, anger flaming in his eyes.

Embarrassment mixed with anger burned Katelyn's cheeks. Her breath came in short puffs as she held it, let it out, held it again. Her heart pounded, beating loud in her ears and threatening to overpower her. She shook, deep on the inside, but willed herself to feign confidence as she picked up the silver tray and sole glass that had been tossed into the grass during her fall.

Thomas drew close and hissed in her hear. "Your foolish boldness amazes me, Katelyn." It was the first time Thomas had called her that since the day she stepped onto the island.

~~~

Thomas exhaled as his muscles tensed. What was going on there? Who was this scoundrel?

And Katelyn? She stood stick straight. She seemed undaunted by the incident. Defiant.

He looked around, relieved to confirm that no one else was paying any attention to them. *Could she be ...? With him? No!*

Katelyn was a good woman, and even though she too often became enmeshed in the threads of gossip, she exuded a depth of character well beyond her years. Surely she hadn't fallen prey to the cad's wiles.

Thomas tipped his chin up and glared at the taller man. "What is the meaning of this, sir?" When he spoke, his voice came out taut and sterner than he had planned.

Flashing a roguish grin, Stockton casually clapped him on the shoulder and gave a laugh that was altogether insincere, even mocking.

"A simple mishap, I do believe. She tripped, and I saved her from harm." Stockton winked at Katelyn.

Taking a deep breath, Thomas returned to his role as a servant. He stepped back, acknowledging the journalist with a tip of his cap, and casting a concerned glance at Katelyn before walking away.

~~~

As Thomas headed toward the Crossmon serving table, Stockton did the unthinkable—he took Katelyn's hand and touched her fingertips with his lips—an unwelcome and very public gesture.

Katelyn froze in disbelief, feeling heat rise from her belly to her bonnet. Perspiration popped out on her face, neck, and chest, dampening her uniform. She let out a deep puff of air and stepped back. "Sir! I must be about my work."

Stockton's rogue smile and slight bow bid her to be on her way, but for the rest of the day, the hair at the back of Katelyn's neck prickled as the man's gaze followed her.

CHAPTER 19

Katelyn tugged a letter from her pocket and waved it in the air as she and Claudia pulled up the metal croquet hoops so the gardener could cut the lawn. "That confounded journalist, Richard Stockton, has been writing me for nearly a month, and I don't know what to do. I received the fourth letter when we went to the bay last week and was barely able to hide it from Thomas."

"Do you write back?"

"No! Never. But ..."

"But what?" Claudia teased.

"Oh, Claudia. I can't help reading them. He's so entertaining and interesting. Such a man of the world. He seems to know everything about everything and goes on for pages and pages with his vivid descriptions and entertaining stories. Not that I'm attracted to him. I'm simply intrigued by his writing."

"I wish I would have met him before you," Claudia confessed. "Now you have two beaus, and I have none. Not fair!"

As a gust of wind crept over the river, an errant curl tickled her temple. Katelyn swept it back, feeling beads of perspiration forming on her skin. "I do not have two beaus. Mr. Stockton is just a flirt, 'tis all. As you've said before, I only have eyes for Thomas."

"But are you intrigued by Thomas? Will he hold your interest through the years with talk of fish and boats?" Claudia wrinkled her nose.

After dropping the hoops into a basket, Katelyn clenched her hands. *Would* Thomas intrigue her?

"Do I detect an air of stress on this fine summer day, ladies?" Thomas appeared, seemingly from nowhere.

Katelyn's heart fairly jumped from her chest at the sound of his voice. She smoothed her hair and spun around. A heavy cloak of guilt fell upon her as Thomas' lips spread wide in a sincere smile. Had he overheard their conversation?

She wiped her hands on her white cotton apron and shook her head to see the dirt stain they left behind.

Claudia spoke before she could respond. "Not so, Thomas. We were just having a lively conversation." Claudia flashed him a fake smile. "I'd better go and see if my rolls have risen. Can you finish this, Katelyn?"

"Of course. Thank you for your help." Katelyn lifted her chin to bid Claudia an appreciative goodbye. Then she blew out a deep breath as if she'd been holding it for a long time.

"What's the matter, Morning Dove? You seem to bear the weight of the world on your shoulders." As light as a feather, Thomas touched her forearm.

Katelyn allowed her gaze to shift from his hand to his face. The contact caused a swarm of butterflies to rise within her, making her lightheaded and red-faced at the same time.

"Are you well, Katelyn? You appear to be flushed."

She swallowed and blinked back her cares. "I am well. I fear the imminent arrival of our president gets me all in a flutter."

Thomas chuckled. "Steady on, girl. President Grant is a fine man. But he is just a man, and we will fare well enough. After all, we are more than ready and yet have two weeks to spare. We've accomplished so much, thanks to all the extra day workers." Thomas took off his hat and ran his fingers through his hair. "Just think. Shamus has nearly recovered. The Grand Affair platform and new outhouse and larger dock are finished. The guest quarters are prepared. Menus and schedules and plans are nearly complete. And the Crossmon caterers are coming to our aid as they did with the journalists' reception. And you know how smoothly that went."

Though a dark shadow passed over his face as he mentioned the journalists' reception, Thomas' tender eyes exuded the concern for Katelyn that she longed for. How she wished her mama was here just now, helping her navigate these complicated waters of men and emotions.

"Thank you for that wise perspective, Thomas." Katelyn smiled at him.

Turning to hide her inner struggle, she watched a huge, rusty freighter make its way downriver, creating a large wake. The resulting waves beat against the island shore as her bewildered thoughts about these two men plagued her, held her prisoner, captive to her mixed up feelings. Oh that she could find the key to unlock her cage of emotions and be set free.

As Katelyn pondered her feelings, she decided that under no stretch of the imagination could she imagine her life with a journalist, no matter how charming. This man next to her was the one who birthed butterflies in her with every word he spoke. He was her match.

And yet ...

Cook's gruff voice broke into her thoughts. "Katelyn! Mrs. Duncan needs you in the dining room immediately. Give Thomas those croquet hoops and get in here."

Katelyn handed Thomas the basket of hoops with a "thank you" as she rushed toward Cook's domain.

For the rest of the day, Katelyn scurried here and there, preparing for their dinner guests, Mr. Henry Heath of Nobby Island and Mr. Walton. She hadn't yet met their nearest island neighbor, Mr. Heath, so Katelyn wondered about him as she dusted the parlor and dining room, set everything aright, and worked on the pile of ironing.

She pressed the dinner napkins with near-perfect creases. Then she ironed the missus' dinner dress, admiring the finery. She accessed all the skills she had honed in the past month and grinned with satisfaction at the result.

Before long, the grey, dull light of the late-day sun spread like wet plaster on the walls, and the heady scent of yeasty bread and seasoned mutton made Katelyn's stomach growl, reminding her that it was nearly time for the guests to arrive. She hurried to put away the ironing basket, change into her serving uniform, and grab a bite to eat.

Katelyn enjoyed Sara's company as they shared a plate of fruit, bread, and cheese. As she handed Sara a wedge of cheddar, her friend said, "I can't believe how the days are flying by—like the gulls fly above us."

Katelyn nodded and had just taken a bite of bread when Mrs. Duncan swept into the kitchen in a flurry. "Quick, Katelyn. He's here already! And I hope you're quick on your feet tonight, because Mr. Walton is an infamous coffee drinker."

Katelyn swallowed and hurried after her, hoping to take her place in the dining room before Mr. Pullman accused her of being late again. She assumed her post moments before McCarthy led Mr. Henry Heath into the dining room. The handsome young man's dark hair, mustache, and goatee, along with his dark eyes, caused him to appear rather regal, but something about his gait hinted of feebleness.

Mr. Pullman came into the room, slapped him on the shoulder, and gave him a rare smile. McCarthy handed both of them a drink as Mr. Walton and Mrs. Pullman entered the dining room together. The missus wore a lovely dusty rose gown bedecked with shimmering accents. Katelyn must have shown her admiration, for Mrs. Pullman caught her eye, dipped her chin, and smiled demurely. Katelyn curtsied and turned to gather the bowls of clam chowder.

As she served the first course, Mr. Pullman grinned at his guests. "I predict that this summer's Grand Affair will launch the Golden Age of our great Thousand Islands."

At the comment, Walton lifted the coffee he already seemed to prefer over wine or water. "Hear. Hear. And I've been told that several of the local businessmen are already planning to build hotels on account of us, Pullman."

They all toasted to their success, and Katelyn felt a nervous flutter in her innards, hoping they were correct. This would undoubtedly help Alexandria Bay to grow into much more than a struggling little village.

She refilled Mr. Walton's coffee cup, thinking it odd that he would drink coffee so early in the meal. The portly man's belly shook as he laughed. Before reaching for his soup spoon, Mr. Walton scratched an itch in his unruly salt-and-pepper hair and then rubbed his bushy eyebrows, causing them to scatter hither and yon until he looked a little disheveled. Katelyn backed away, trying to hide her amusement.

"How are your war wounds treating you, Henry?" Pullman inquired.

"Fair to middling, I 'spect, though my lungs took a beating from that cannon accident. Still, I believe that this river life does me good. So glad you had me up here two summers ago, Pullman, old friend, and even more pleased your brother was willing to sell me Nobby Island."

Mr. Pullman sipped his soup before answering. "You and Goodwin built a fine, modern cottage. I'm proud to be neighbors with you. You set a high standard for the rest of us to follow, although I may surpass you with the castle I'm planning to build."

Katelyn enjoyed the bantering and lightheartedness that both guests seemed to bring to the Pullman cottage. Noticing Mrs. Pullman's teacup was empty, she hurried to refill it and then helped clear the table for the main dish of mutton and vegetables.

As Katelyn set a plate before him, Pullman raised a finger in the air. "By the way, Walton, I keep forgetting to remind you that my original deed to the island was lost in the Great Chicago Fire last year. As you know, this island cost me forty dollars back in '64. Guess you'd better draw me up a new deed."

Walton nodded. "Will do, but it likely won't be until after the president's visit."

Katelyn went to the kitchen for another pot of coffee and scooted close to Sara. "I've never seen anyone drink so much coffee, especially before we even get to dessert. I doubt Mr. Walton will sleep a wink tonight." She giggled as she filled the silver pot and returned to her place in the dining room.

Mr. Walton was still speaking of the Grand Affair. "With Cape Vincent being the closest train stop to Alex Bay, we simply must get the railroad here soon. By wagon, coach, or steamer, it takes nearly two hours to get to the train station from here. Thank heaven for Captain Sweet and his side-wheel steamer that can pick up the train passengers and deliver them to us in the bay."

Heath massaged his chest as if it hurt. "Have you not heard that the Black River-Utica Railroad is extending the tracks to Clayton and that the town of Clayton is building their first depot and turntable so the locomotives can make return trips back to the bigger cities? After this presidential shindig, Alex Bay, Clayton, and the Seaway islands will most certainly become the most desirable summer spot in all of America for the wealthy upper class."

Mrs. Pullman spoke for the first time that evening. "That is good news, Henry. It would be a blessing to have the train closer to us."

Mr. Pullman nodded. Mr. Walton smiled. And Mr. Heath winked. "It surely would, missus. And how are your little angels faring this summer? I've seen them from afar as I've passed by the island, and they look like they've grown a foot or more."

Mrs. Pullman laughed her dainty, wind-chime laugh. "Not that much, but they are thriving, especially here." She darted a glance at Katelyn and nodded, and Katelyn knew her eyes sparkled at the thought of the girls.

Mr. Heath steered the conversation back to the presidential visit while they enjoyed strawberry shortcake. "What about this Babcock fellow who controls so much of Grant's life? Is he truly the source of all this corruption within the president's administration?"

"I daresay he might be, Henry." Mr. Pullman sat back and crossed his arms. "Hadn't thought of that. I know personally that Grant is an honest man, but he is loyal and overprotective and likely blind to the corruption of others. Guess it's part of his military training, expecting his men to follow his orders precisely."

Walton shook his head. "That railroad bribery scandal could derail his second term if he doesn't get a handle on it. Grant shouldn't shield his friends and take the fall if Babcock is to blame."

Mr. Pullman slapped the table. "I've known Grant for years and am sure the charges of his misconduct in the treasury and interior are false. He probably can't admit that this Babcock fellow is the problem. Maybe I can address our concern whilst he is here."

As dinner wound down, Mrs. Pullman excused herself, and the men rose to take a turn in the warm summer eve and smoke their cigars outdoors. Katelyn helped McCarthy and Mrs. Duncan clear the dining room and then set the breakfast table.

"You did a fine job today, Katelyn," Mrs. Duncan said, patting her forearm. "Not once did I have to remind you of your duties, and you kept that coffee cup of Mr. Walton's filled."

As she chuckled, Katelyn laughed with her and expressed her appreciation for the praise.

Katelyn was dismissed even before the kitchen staff, so she enjoyed a quiet sabbatical on the veranda. Fireflies flitted about, and the full moon cast shimmering light on the tranquil waters of the St. Lawrence. She enjoyed watching it dance on the tiny waves like birds dancing on the wings of the wind.

"All alone tonight, Morning Dove?" Thomas asked from behind her.

Katelyn giggled, grabbing her chest. "You scared me!"

He touched her arm and scooted a chair close to her. As they sat in silence, the soft rhythm of the waves slapping against the rocky shoreline nearly hypnotized her. She breathed in the muddy scent and relished the kiss of the gentle breeze on her cheeks and hair. Yet worry tickled her mind like the evening's gnats. Anxiety filled her bosom with a heavy weight. A frown must have betrayed her.

Thomas leaned toward her, rested his elbows on his knees, and reached for her hands. "You hold secrets, my sweet." He stared deeply into her eyes as if he was trying to rip away a veil. "What is it?"

"The president's scandals. I didn't know." She folded her hands in her lap as sweat dotted her palms.

Thomas' forehead scrunched into train tracks of uncertainty. He parted his lips as if he were going to answer her but paused to consider his reply. Finally, he said, "There are always scandals around elections. Many are fabricated." Still, a question seemed to pull at his dark brows. He tented his fingers and set his chin upon the tips of them.

Katelyn blurted out her worries. "Mr. Pullman said President Grant was blind, deaf, and dumb when it came to his friends. That he was negligent in his duties to appoint fair and honest folk, and that corruption and bribery are all around him. My disappointment overwhelms me, Thomas." As soon as the words left Katelyn's lips, a twinge of guilt fluttered in her heart.

Thomas scratched his jaw and gently wagged his finger at her. "He said all that? Might there be a bit of blarney in your words?"

~~~

Katelyn's lowered lashes spoke of contrition. She seemed to be pondering his question as she chewed her bottom lip, and Thomas had to smile at the depth of her concentration. She rose and walked to the railing, standing with her back to him, her shoulders rising and falling.

When he realized her pain, compassion filled his chest like a tidal wave. He hurried to her side, turned her toward him, and wiped away a stray tear with his pinky finger. She fell into his chest, burying her face in his shirt. As he held her, he could feel her rapid breaths and gentle sobs through her cotton frock. He drew her nearer and stole a whiff of her hair. The warmth of their closeness both frightened and invigorated him.

Thomas turned Katelyn's face up to his and gazed into her glistening eyes. Moonlight danced between them, casting a heady glow on her lips. Fireflies twinkled, swooping around in an intricate reel. He touched his hand to her cheek as hot emotions threatened to overwhelm him.

She spoke, breaking the spell. "Forgive my errant tongue. I never meant to vex you."

~~~

Thomas' eyes spoke of empathy for her plight. "You misunderstand me. I wasn't vexed, just wondering how much of what you say is fact and how much is embellishment. You've come so far, Morning Dove. You rarely speak amiss anymore."

Tears overflowed onto Katelyn's lashes. She blinked them back, but it was no use.

"*What* is going on here?" Sara stood at the corner of the veranda with her hands on her hips, glaring at her brother, then at Katelyn, then back to her brother. "This isn't proper, Thomas."

Claudia stood beside Sara. She snickered in a manner that managed to be both chastising and threatening. "If this were to be reported ..." Her words trailing off, she turned on her heels and left with a huff.

"It isn't what you think, Sara." Thomas stepped toward his sister, but she, too, hurried to the women's quarters before he could explain. Thomas turned back to Katelyn, eyes wide with fear. "What are we to do now?"

CHAPTER 20

Katelyn tossed and turned the whole night through, barely on the edge of sleep, wondering, worrying, wishing her life was far less complicated. Sara had judged her unfairly. Again. Claudia had threatened to report her. Again. It had been an innocent moment, but if it was reported, she and Thomas could both lose their jobs in such a scandal.

Barely after sunrise, Katelyn quietly left the room and climbed the turret which had become a place of respite. Today, like so many other times, it provided a private place to think, pray, and draw strength from the solitude. From here she could gaze on the main channel of the mighty St. Lawrence, and in the far distance, Alexandria Bay. Through the morning mist, she could also glimpse other islands, including Mr. Heath's Nobby. She watched the storm clouds gathering in the distance, and she could almost smell the rain that was bound to come.

Katelyn wrung her hands and sighed deeply. How could she address the misconceptions? How could she make them understand? Her quandary reminded her of Jo and Laurie in *Little Women*, and how did that work out? She drew in a deep breath and asked God for His hand of grace and mercy.

A door slammed below, and she could hear Claudia's accusing voice. "I don't know where she went at this hour. Maybe off to another tryst with your brother?"

"She wouldn't dare. Thomas knows better, even if she throws herself at him." *Sara? How could she?*

The words pierced Katelyn's heart like a dagger. She pushed away her hurt and anger, knowing she needed to find her composure, so she paced, trying to calm her nerves. Finally, she unfisted her hands, climbed down, and hurried to the cottage, still feeling betrayed and confused.

"You're late, Katelyn." Standing at the sink, Cook shook a wooden spoon in her direction. "Eat quickly. Mrs. Duncan and I have an assignment for you."

Katelyn nodded and sat down to a plate of biscuits and sausage gravy, refusing to look at Sara and Claudia. Instead, she jabbed a piece of biscuit and took a bite, swallowing her sadness, anger, and fear with it. Usually her favorite, today the dish tasted like paste and rocks. She picked at it and finally scooped it in the trash when no one was looking.

She found Mrs. Duncan in the dining room, ready to serve breakfast to the Pullmans.

"I need Thomas to take you to the village to run some errands and gather supplies for the larder and tomorrow's luncheon. You're the only one I can spare today. And no tomfoolery, Katelyn." Mrs. Duncan flashed a warning with her eyes and pursed mouth as she handed her a lengthy list.

"Yes, ma'am." Katelyn curtsied, glanced through the list, and scurried away.

At the dock, Thomas prepared the launch. "Ready?" He didn't smile or look at her. His demeanor seemed thick and closed, like the morning mist on a cool day.

Confusion swept through Katelyn's mind as Thomas navigated the skiff through the choppy waters of the mighty river. Only the creak of the wooden bench broke the silence.

"Did you know that Charles Dickens made a steam voyage down the St. Lawrence from Kingston to Montreal in 1842? He was quite taken with the area."

Rather than serving as the bridge Katelyn hoped for, the formal words Thomas spoke only increased the chasm yawning between them. The churning waters under the boat made the river water murky. Like her feelings. Like their relationship.

Katelyn straightened her spine and looked into his eyes. Did they hold sympathy, anger, or was it rejection? She swallowed hard, knowing not what to ask or say. Her emotions churned deep in her belly, threatening to make her sick. The sensation reminded her of churning butter, thick and greasy. She bit her bottom lip, watching the massive black clouds gather overhead.

Thomas' muscles surged as he manned the skiff's oars. Katelyn knew that navigating the river was no small task. The hidden sandy shoals could damage the underbelly of the launch, but Thomas had been trained well, even in stormy weather.

Once they docked, Thomas looked skyward and helped Katelyn out of the skiff. "We'd best be quick. It appears that a storm is approaching."

Katelyn nodded. She fairly flew through her errands. At her final stop, the newspaper office, she almost bumped into her father. "Father. 'Tis so good to see you. How are you?"

Father looked down his nose at her. "Busy. What are you doing in town?"

Katelyn stood tall and beamed, hoping he would be proud of her. "I'm ever so busy getting ready for the Grand Affair." She put out her arms to hug him but then quickly tucked them against her sides when her father took a tiny step back from her.

He scoffed and said flatly, "You've gotten awfully high-minded for a lowly servant girl."

Katelyn pressed her lips tightly together and bit the inside of her cheek, trying not to cry. Swallowing hard, she gave him a bitter smile.

Father rubbed the back of his neck. "Well, I best be on my way." With that, he patted her shoulder, mumbled goodbye, and left her standing there. Alone.

Katelyn winced. She tried to shake off her dismay as she trudged back to the boat, but she couldn't help replaying the conversation in her mind, causing her to stumble in mid-step. She stopped and gulped in a deep breath to regroup.

She found Thomas heaving a large sack of potatoes into the skiff. The summer gale swept in angry storm clouds. Glancing at the sky, Katelyn handed him the parcels and wicker basket. "I've completed my list. The tin-ware store, the butcher, and the dressmaker—who still didn't have the missus' dress ready. I even got the last copy of *On the St. Lawrence*." She handed Thomas the paper.

"I got everything else from the general store and the apothecary. I also talked to the fishermen about holding their catch for the gala. Then I went to the post office. 'Tis a surprise I didn't see you there." Thomas stopped loading the skiff and stared at her. His jaw twitched. Slowly he pulled out a letter and handed it to her. "It seems this scoundrel writes you regularly, least-wise, that's what the postman says. Why have you said nothing to me, Katelyn?"

She steeled herself against his judgment. She would not flinch at his scrutiny of her. With a shake of her head and an open palm of warning, she gathered her skirts and stepped into the boat.

Shaking his head, Thomas unfolded a tarp and covered the crates of dry goods and food that filled the floor and threatened to sink them with their weight. So did the anger between them.

An embarrassed flush refused to subside, even as the harsh gale slapped Katelyn in the face. "I did not ask to receive letters from the man."

Thomas said something, but the wind stole his words away as the skiff left the dock.

"What did you say? I can tell by your face that it was probably another harsh comment."

An angry frown and creased forehead told her all she needed to know as Thomas stayed silent and fought the waves and wind pelting the skiff. The rigging creaked in the screeching fury of the wind, and the wood groaned against the waves. Whitecaps threatened to capsize the skiff. The skies turned as black as Thomas' hair.

A large steamer chugged past, seemingly unaffected by the waves as its stack belched black smoke. The fierce wind pulled at the oars and whipped a lock of Katelyn's hair across her face. She brushed it away. "'Tis no time to be crossing the channel. Shall we turn back?"

Thomas shook his head and struggled at the oars.

Barely halfway to the island, the storm unleashed its full fury. The distant thunder moved closer and closer until it felt like it would enter Katelyn's very being. The sky grew black and the air thick. Lightning lit up the skiff, as bright as midday, and caused her to squeal. Thomas' eyes shone more fearful with every lightning strike. Rain pelted hard against them, waves beat against the skiff, and the skies opened up like a massive bucket, drenching them and the contents of the boat. The wind whipped their hair and ripped the cover off the supplies.

Katelyn decided she had to cover the goods, so she let go of the side of the skiff and tried to catch the cover before it flew away, and the rain ruined all they had bought. Just then, a gust of wind and a large wave slammed against the skiff and tossed her into the churning river!

She fought against the current, her skirts pulling her down, her boots feeling like lead weights, her hair covering her face and choking her. The river water filled her mouth, but she spat and sputtered between gasps of air and screams for help.

Katelyn flapped her arms and flailed against the current and her skirts, until finally, Thomas grabbed ahold of her and held her tight, kicking and working his way back to the skiff. Then everything went dark and quiet.

~~~

The boat pitched from side to side as Thomas stared at Katelyn's motionless form. Her layers of skirts had weighed her down like an anchor, and her lungs were likely full of river water instead of air. She gazed at him through vacant eyes.

She wasn't breathing!

A fog swept through his brain as Thomas thought of Katelyn leaving this world forever. The numbness, the emptiness, crept into every chamber of his mind. *No!* Fear and panic coursed energy through his veins. He wouldn't let her go.

Thomas remembered what his aunt, a midwife, would do. He pinched Katelyn's nose tightly and sucked in a breath. He blew into her mouth and watched her chest rise. He blew again and prayed. She coughed, coughed again, spat out a torrent of river water, and breathed on her own.

Her eyelids fluttered, and finally she looked into his eyes, desire mixed with relief. He cradled her head, tenderly speaking security, willing her to be safe in his arms as the storm quieted to a sprinkle. He held her slight frame longer than necessary.

"I thought we could beat the storm. I could have lost you, Morning Dove! I am so sorry."

With the tip of her tongue, Katelyn moistened her lips and turned her dazed face upward. His gaze rested on her trembling smile, while colliding feelings caused him to gulp in air. Words of love trampled on his tongue but would not leave his mouth, yet Thomas could resist no longer. He bent and touched his lips to hers. Just once, just for a second, but just enough.

Then he knew. He loved her. He wanted her. With all her flaws and foibles. With all her delights and detriments. And without that scoundrel's influence. Despite her strong, even stubborn demeanor, she was vulnerable and needed protection. His protection.

He would fight for her.

~~~

Katelyn felt the skiff sway and bob as the storm began to subside, but Thomas just kept looking at her, staring at her. He said something, but the words melted in her ears. Then he bent down and ...

She blinked. Shook herself awake. Alive.

Did he really kiss her? Was it a dream?

The rain slowed to a sprinkle, a bank of clouds parted, and the sun broke through, momentarily blinding her. Katelyn struggled to sit up, and Thomas helped her. He returned to the oars with a gentle smile and started rowing.

Katelyn looked down at the rain-soaked goods. She summoned her courage to once again apologize to him. She sucked in her bottom lip and held it in her teeth as tears welled in her burning eyes. "I'm so sorry, Thomas. About this mess. About the letters. About last night. About me." Her quivering hands betrayed her nervous energy.

He shushed her by holding his finger to his lips, whispering a gentle "shh." His eyes overflowed with tears, and he returned to his rowing. "I didn't lose you, Katelyn. That's all that matters."

Katelyn shivered. Quaked. Then cried. Happy. Embarrassed. Ashamed. Afraid. Amazed. *Too much fear. Too many failures.* Her emotions scrambled in a mixture of desire and wonder. Then she realized he stared at her, his eyes like dark pools of compassion and love.

"Thank you, Thomas, for your mercy and grace." Heat swept through her body—from the humidity or shame, she couldn't tell. She suddenly became aware that both of them were sopping wet, and she giggled nervously. "We must look a sight! Whatever will we tell Cook and Mrs. Duncan?"

Thomas picked his oars out of the water and rested his elbows on them. "I have no idea, but this I know. We will figure it out ... together."

They remained silent until they docked the skiff. Shamus waited for them, shaking his head. "For mercy, young 'uns. What happened?"

Thomas helped Katelyn out of the skiff. "We tried to make it back to the island before the storm but got caught in the very center of it. Katelyn was swept into the river and nearly perished."

Placing a hand on his heart, Shamus sucked in a breath and plopped down on the nearby wooden piling. "Thank the good Lord you be all right, missy."

"We best get the goods inside and dry them off," Thomas suggested as he gave Shamus a hand up. "I'm not sure how much we can save. Cook will tan our hide, she will."

Shamus chuckled and picked up the dripping newspaper. "This here rag is useless. Good thing it's last week's edition. Ah, fear not. Accidents happen, and I will accompany you to meet Cook and put a leash on her temper."

At the thought of another confrontation, Katelyn shrank back and held her breath. So much had transpired in the last twenty-four hours, so much that could threaten their jobs and reputations. She took a damp hankie from her uniform pocket and dabbed the tears that filled her eyes.

Shamus patted her hand. "There, there. We will sort it all out presently." He slipped Katelyn's hand in the crook of his arm and led her to the boathouse, where he wrapped her in a blanket. "You sit here while Thomas and I make a quick inspection of the goods."

Katelyn's teeth chattered as Thomas helped Shamus dry the supplies with towels. As they worked, Thomas shared the details of their near-fatal river crossing. At last, Shamus stood up and let out a sigh of relief. "'Tisn't as bad as I feared. Only the flour was ruined. The tins and brown butcher paper kept the rest of it dry enough, and I believe it be a miracle by the hand of the Almighty." He turned to Katelyn. "Let us go, dear girl, and face the den of lions together."

As Thomas helped Katelyn to her feet, they shared a parting smile.

When she and Shamus reached the kitchen door, Shamus said, "Follow my lead."

After summoning both Cook and Mrs. Duncan, he began an eloquent explanation of the incident. But as soon as they understood the danger Katelyn had faced, Cook took Katelyn's hands and said, "Glory be we didn't lose you, girl!"

Then Mrs. Duncan gathered Katelyn in a tight bear hug. "I should never have sent you on such a stormy day. You must have a long, warm bath and rest. Come. Let's get you warm and dry, and Cook, please send a tray up to her room. 'Tis a quiet evening tonight, and we will need you healthy and well for the days to come."

CHAPTER 21

Fresh from her warm bath and layered in dry clothing, Katelyn cradled the tiny portrait of her mother in her hands. Oh how she longed for her wisdom! After finishing the bread and soup Cook sent to her, she took her blanket, climbed up the turret, and formed a little nest where she could gaze at the river and ponder all that happened—the confusion with Sara, Thomas' strange mood, meeting her father, the journalist's letter, the storm and near-drowning that very afternoon. And the kiss? She squirmed and shifted, unable to get comfortable. Was that kiss real or was it a dream?

Her stomach churned, and her heart fluttered. What if Thomas withdrew from her again? She couldn't bear it. What if Sara continued to judge and misunderstand? Her heart ached at the thought. What if Claudia …? She no longer cared.

As thoughts swirled in her brain, she began to hyperventilate. "Help me, Lord! I need you." She sucked in a quivering breath as she tried to sort it all out, but she could not. "I don't have the answers, but I know You do." She continued to pray, fervently, honestly, until her cares flew away on the wings of the wind. Peace, that gentle, secure blanket of peace, finally enveloped her. She sat in that peace for a long while until finally, she climbed down the steps to her room and fell into a deep sleep.

Katelyn awoke with the golden glow of the sunrise and determined to start afresh. After all, if she could survive a near-drowning, she could surely survive the many petty dramas of staff life on Pullman Island. Besides, today, her pastor and the New York City preacher would visit the Pullmans to plan the presidential Sunday service that would occur on the island just a week hence.

As she and the other girls walked to the kitchen, Sara slipped her hand into the crook of Katelyn's arm, hugging her as they walked. "I thank God you're safe, Katelyn. I'm sorry I was angry before."

"I'm glad you're okay too. It must have been quite a scare," Claudia added.

"Thank you, Sara. Claudia." Katelyn swallowed her amazement. The storm—or more likely, her fervent prayers—must have blown away their anger from the days past. She waved her arm to avoid further discussion and pointed to the lawn and beyond. "Look what the storm did to our lovely island!"

Fallen branches and twigs, and stray leaves and flowers made a mess of it, while driftwood and other debris had washed up along the shore overnight. The privy door lay on the ground, pried off its hinges.

After breakfast, everyone worked together to clean up the island. When Katelyn and Sara saw Thomas heading toward the shore, Sara waved. "May we help you work the shoreline?"

He nodded. When Katelyn drew near enough to gaze into his eyes, Thomas gulped in a breath and held it, a soft blush coloring his cheeks and neck.

"Good morning, my valiant rescuer." Katelyn smiled and giggled shyly.

Sara grabbed her brother and hugged him. "Thank you for saving my best friend. Really. You don't know how frightened I was to hear the tale that Shamus gave Cook. Tell me from your own lips."

Clearing his throat, Thomas proceeded to tell his side of the story. Katelyn avoided adding much by picking up the debris that littered the sand and stone, but she listened to his accounting, pleased with his rendering of it.

Claudia came around the stand of trees and stood there a minute, hands on her hips. "Are you quite finished? We have a luncheon to prepare!"

For the remainder of the morning, Katelyn worked with Mrs. Duncan and McCarthy preparing for the luncheon. She could now set a proper table, ready the buffet, and tidy the dining room without direction.

Mrs. Duncan took the soup spoons from Katelyn's hand. "I must say, you have become quite the professional dining room maid. I applaud you for your quick wit and able-bodied skill. Moreover, you seem to have learned to tame that tongue of yours." Her eyes twinkled with mischief and approval.

"I didn't doubt for a moment that Katelyn would excel," McCarthy commented. "She is a fast learner and is motivated by something deep within her."

"Oh, you're an old softie, you are. But I concur." Mrs. Duncan patted his arm and winked.

Katelyn curtsied, eyes glistening. "Thank you both for your confidence in me. But it is you two who are to be commended. You are excellent teachers, and I owe you my eternal gratitude."

Comfortable silence followed, but not for long. Katelyn couldn't have it. "Where is the reverend staying?"

McCarthy handed her napkins. "At the parsonage in the bay. He's been friends with Pastor Olsen since seminary."

Katelyn sighed. "What an adventure life is! One never knows whom we will meet in our lifetimes."

McCarthy threw back his head and laughed. Mrs. Duncan giggled like a schoolgirl. "And youth has a wonderful way of keeping us young, right, McCarthy?"

He nodded and gave Katelyn a loving pat on the shoulder, while she controlled her urge to hug them both.

Before long, the guests arrived, and the Pullmans joined them in the dining room. While normally Mr. Pullman wouldn't invite a small-town pastor to his island, the visit of the New York City preacher necessitated the presence of the local one as well.

Mrs. Pullman greeted both men with an air of royalty. "Welcome, Reverend Street and Pastor Olsen. Please, take these chairs facing the river."

Before sitting, Reverend Street gazed out the window. "These islands give every onlooker a picture of God's amazing creation. The rocky shores and crevices and woods. The birds and animals and men who inhabit them. The flowers and fauna and the river itself speak of none other than the Creator God who made them."

He turned and took his seat. "My, but this is a slice of paradise. Let us rejoice in the beauty that surrounds us. I cannot fathom that I live in the same state and didn't know this grandeur existed until the president's staff bid me to come."

The Pullmans and pastor applauded his speech. Then Pastor Olsen slapped Reverend Street on the back. "If you speak like that on Sunday, we'll have the lot of them weeping at the altar."

After another outburst of delight at the table, McCarthy poured wine, while Mrs. Duncan and Katelyn served the salads. Reverend Street asked Mr. Pullman, "How do you know our president?"

"The Grants were our neighbors at Long Branch, that fashionable New Jersey seaside resort. Do you know of it?"

Reverend Street shook his head.

"We've enjoyed several holidays with them, including a visit to the White House."

When Katelyn returned from the kitchen with the dinner plates, she caught what seemed to be the tail end of a conversation about the railroads.

"Journalists raise a stink about anything that can sell papers!" Mr. Pullman's voice was harsh and his face red. "Though the Credit Mobilier Scandal involved the transcontinental railroad, our president had nothing to do with it, of that I am sure."

"You should read the latest stories in the newspaper." Katelyn's pastor made a bold protest. "The buck stops with him, even though they say it was the mischief of his vice president and secretary of the treasury. I put a measure of trust in journalists like that Richard Stockton and the talented Brenner Matthew."

Mrs. Pullman changed the topic quickly, obviously aware of her husband's disdain of journalists. "Speaking of railroads, when is our Black River-Utica Railroad scheduled to be finished? It will be fortunate for those who purchase islands to have it so close."

Pastor Olsen smiled. "It should be completed by the Christmas holidays, though few travel to these parts during the harsh winters here in the North Country."

For the rest of the meal, the talk revolved around the Sunday service—who was invited, what should be said, sung, done. Reverend

Street cleared his throat. "I personally know that the president's favorite hymns are 'Amazing Grace' and the new one, 'Onward, Christian Soldiers,' so they must be prominently included. Will we have a piano?"

Mrs. Pullman nodded as she dabbed her lips with a napkin. "It will be delivered tomorrow, and we will have an ensemble and a soprano at our disposal for the entire week. The community is keen to be a part of the Grand Affair."

After the luncheon, Mr. Pullman invited the pastors on a tour of the islands. Katelyn cleaned up, but as she reset the table for dinner, Mrs. Pullman entered the room and whispered to Mrs. Duncan. Both looked at her and nodded. Then Mrs. Pullman approached Katelyn.

"Of all times, Bridget is ill, and I must accompany the gentlemen on the tour. I need someone to care for the girls. Mrs. Duncan has kindly agreed to let you help. Do you mind very much?"

Katelyn clapped her hands. "Oh, Mrs. Pullman, I'd be delighted! Thank you, Mrs. Duncan. It's been ever so long since I've enjoyed their company."

The women grinned at her response. "Wonderful."

Mrs. Pullman led her upstairs to the nursery, relaying a list of things the girls could and could not do. When they arrived at the room, Florence and Hattie were already fast asleep. So was Bridget, Katelyn assumed, since her door was shut tight. She tidied the nursery, read a few of the colorful picture books, and watched the cherubs dream.

When the two girls awoke, Florence wanted to read a book. Little Hattie remained groggy, so Katelyn cuddled her, admiring her angelic, heart-shaped face.

Soon the girls enjoyed a snack of berries and hot cross buns. Florence built a tall tower with her blocks, while her little sister made a long, disconnected snake. Laughing at their childish play, Katelyn joined them on the ornate Oriental rug. While they created, they sang, "Mary Had a Little Lamb" and "Baa Baa Black Sheep."

When the children's voices grew louder as they repeated the verses, Katelyn glanced at Bridget's door. "Let's go outside and get some fresh air, shall we? But first, let's tidy up." Katelyn began putting the blocks in the bucket, but the girls just watched. When she stopped and waited for them to help, Hattie popped her thumb out of her mouth. "Nanny cweans up."

"It's always good manners to help clean up after yourself."

"All right," Florence said, and the three of them made a quick job of it.

As Katelyn and the wee ones entered the kitchen, Sara joined them. "I've been waiting ever so long for you. I made a picnic supper, and Cook says I can go with you to help. May I?"

"Absolutely!" Katelyn grabbed her arm and faced the girls. "Have you met my friend, Sara, girls? She's made us a special picnic supper. Aren't we excited to have her join us?"

The girls stared at Sara, likely because the fact that she still wore her kitchen clothes made them uncertain of how to address her. But Hattie finally took Sara's hand, and off they went.

"Can we dip our toes in the water and see Mr. Thomas, please?" Florence begged.

"Thomas is gone just now. He's driving the boat for your father's river tour. We can dip our toes in the river, but you mustn't get your clothes wet."

The girls agreed to be careful, and before long they were sitting on the dock, splashing their feet in the cool water. Florence turned to Sara. "Is Thomas a very good brother? I think he should be a fine husband. Maybe I shall marry him."

Sara giggled and glanced at Katelyn. "He is a fine brother and will be a good husband, but don't you think he may be a wee bit old for you?"

"I shall grow up by and by. He could wait."

Katelyn swallowed a laugh, while Sara's eyes danced with amusement. She pointed out several fish and told them funny stories about growing up on a farm. Sara added a few stories of her own farm life. Before long, Shamus hobbled up and joined them.

"I dare say that on this here dock sit four of the prettiest young ladies I have ever seen! How you be, young 'uns?"

Florence hopped up and gave Shamus a hug. "We are fine, sir, and you?"

"Well now, I reckon I'm nearly back to my old self, thank you. Are you excited about the presidential parties that will soon be upon us?"

Florence put her hands on her hips and frowned. "Oh yes, but Hattie and I must be with Nanny or Grandmother every minute so we don't get into mischief or trip anyone."

Katelyn tweaked an eyebrow. Sara smirked, and Shamus belly laughed. Hattie ignored them all and kicked the water, splashing herself.

Katelyn scooped her up and set her feet on the dock. "Dearest, you're all wet! What shall we do?"

Shamus rolled his eyes. "No need to worry. Set her in the sunshine for a spell, and she'll dry just fine. I best be off to polish the skiff, but before I go—'May you always walk in sunshine. May you never want for more. May angels rest their open wings, right beside your door.'"

As Katelyn and Sara expressed their thanks for the Irish blessing, the wee ones grabbed Shamus' legs and hugged him. Once he left, Sara turned to Katelyn. "I'll fetch a towel and a change of clothes for Hattie while you three set up the picnic. How does that sound?"

Katelyn agreed, pleased to see the confidence Sara had gained over the summer. She really had blossomed while on the island. "We'll be by the big rock, near the shore."

Sara headed toward the cottage, and Katelyn took the girls to the high end of the island, stopping first by the privy.

"I don't want to change. I wike this dwess," Hattie complained.

"But you might catch a chill and miss the party."

Hattie's little mouth made an "o," and her wide eyes showed her concern. "I cannot! I have a fancy new dwess to wear."

"Mine is blue with white lace," Florence told Katelyn. "Hers is pink. Mama said we can stay up and see the fireworks if we take a good nap."

Katelyn grasped their hands, led them to the picnic spot, and took out the picnic things, waiting for Sara to return. "I have never seen fireworks, and I'm keen to do so."

"It is the beautifulest thing ever! Truly." Florence motioned with her hands as if she were creating fireworks. "They explode and make loud noises, and Hattie cries."

Hattie shook her head as she munched on a carrot. "I'm big now. I won't cwy."

When Sara returned, Katelyn patted the blanket for her to sit and turned back to the girls. "I might cry at the wonder of it."

Hattie nodded. "Me too."

After Katelyn helped Hattie change her frock, the girls enjoyed their picnic of ham, cheese, and bread, and a bowl of fruit. They talked about the days to come and the excitement of the parties. While they ate their plums, Florence asked Katelyn, "Why does the president have sandals?"

Katelyn and Sara scrunched up their faces, wondering what she meant, but understanding dawned on Katelyn first. "Oh, do you mean the president's scandals?"

Florence nodded. "What do his scandals look like? Are they like slippers?"

Katelyn laughed and pondered how to explain a complex situation to such a tiny person. "Oh no. A scandal is a disgraceful thing that can ruin a person and sometimes send him to jail. It's usually when someone does something bad. But sometimes it's caused by gossip."

"What's gossip?" Hattie quirked a confused eyebrow. Sara shrugged her shoulders and turned to Katelyn.

Katelyn's eyes grew wide, and she glanced at the clouds for an answer. "Let me see if I can explain. Gossip is when a person is given to tattling or telling tales. It's when a person talks about others or spreads rumors or shares idle talk. And sometimes it hurts people." At that moment, Katelyn flinched as the nausea of guilt rose, filling her mouth with a bitter taste.

"Miss Katelyn. Are you unwell? You look sick," Florence said as Hattie hopped on her lap and stroked her arm, giving Katelyn time to swallow the bile.

"I'm fine, wee one." Katelyn's weak smile couldn't fool anyone.

Florence quirked her head. "But I still don't understand about scandals."

"Well, if our president did something bad, like steal money from the railroad, that would be a *scandal*." Katelyn emphasized the word to help her learn it.

Florence smiled and nodded. "I see."

After their picnic, Sara returned to the kitchen while Katelyn and the girls played tag and walked around the island, picking flowers. When Florence found a tickly caterpillar on a stem, Katelyn explained how they became butterflies. Then, naturally, the girls wanted to chase butterflies.

An hour later, very ready for some quiet time, Katelyn took Hattie and Florence to the shoreline to try to skip rocks and watch the sun begin its descent below the water's edge. The setting sun cast ripples of pink, orange, and even red, before bursting below the horizon, leaving only a memory of its resplendent beauty.

Hattie scooted close to Katelyn. "It makes me want to cwy."

Katelyn picked her up and hugged her. "Beauty does that sometimes. Let's go back to the nursery before it gets dark."

Katelyn held Florence's hand and carried Hattie to the cottage, where they met Mrs. Pullman returning from the dock.

When the girls saw their mother, they ran and hugged her legs. Florence stepped back, gazing up at Mrs. Pullman with a glowing face. "We had ever so much fun, Mama. We had a picnic and saw the sunset and talked about the president's sandals."

Mrs. Pullman tilted her pretty head, questioning Katelyn with her eyes. Katelyn sucked in a breath and stumbled for an explanation. "She meant 'scandal.' She asked me what the president's scandal was, and I tried to explain it to her."

The woman's face turned a deep shade of scarlet. She furrowed her brow, and her eyes bored through Katelyn. "You told my little girls *what*?" She shook her head, grabbed the girls' hands, and turned to leave. Then she scowled over her shoulder at Katelyn. "We will discuss this matter later!"

Good heavens! It seemed that Katelyn couldn't go a day without committing some unknown transgression to land herself in trouble.

CHAPTER 22

Katelyn stood next to McCarthy and Mrs. Duncan, waiting for the Pullmans to come to breakfast. When they did, Mr. Pullman wore a suit and the missus a wispy muslin day dress. Her leather slippers padded across the room, feather light and barely noticeable. She didn't smile, didn't address the staff, didn't even greet them as she usually did.

The floorboards squeaked when Katelyn swept in to pour the missus' morning tea, and still no acknowledgment. Mrs. Pullman hadn't spoken to her about the "scandal" talk with the girls, so Katelyn continued to fear she'd be scolded ... or dismissed. What was wrong with explaining a word to the child?

"Stop daydreaming and fetch the eggs," Mrs. Duncan whispered, pulling Katelyn away from her thoughts.

She nodded and scurried to the kitchen, where Sara handed her a tray with two plates. "Careful. They're hot."

The aroma of cheesy omelets made Katelyn's stomach growl, and the smell of warm croissants caused her mouth to water. She entered the dining room and held the tray as McCarthy placed the plates in front of Mr. and Mrs. Pullman.

Mr. Pullman set his paper down and looked up at McCarthy. "When does the extra staff arrive?"

"They should be here by eleven, sir." McCarthy made the slightest bow and stepped back.

Mrs. Duncan cleared her throat. "The piano, milk cow, and chickens will be here before that, and Thomas has a pen ready for the animals. The farmer's daughter will see to them."

"Very well. I will speak to the entire island staff at two o'clock sharp. I will give a hearty speech and fair warnings to the lot of them. See that everyone meets on the front lawn."

"Very good, sir." McCarthy bowed his head.

The rest of the meal was all too quiet. Katelyn wondered if the Pullmans were nervous about the Grand Affair.

Following the after-breakfast routine, Katelyn was sent to give the parlor a final cleaning. The sunshine peeked playfully through the window, teasing her to escape her assigned work, but instead, she opened the window to let in the fresh, morning air.

Katelyn surveyed the fine, dark-paneled room, made cheery by family portraits, handsome doilies, and carefully placed trinkets and treasures. How did they get all these lovely things across the water? She rolled the thought over in her head as she made sure to remove every speck of lint and dust from the wing chair and matching sofa. Everything had to be perfect for the president's arrival on Thursday.

"I must speak with you, Katelyn."

Katelyn nearly dropped the tiny porcelain figurine she had been dusting when she heard the missus' voice. She turned to see Mrs. Pullman's stern, almost sad face.

Katelyn gently set the figurine down. "Yes, ma'am." She couldn't bear to look at her, so she stared at the missus' shoes rather than her face.

"I was most dismayed by your chatter about presidential matters with my little girls. It is never your place to discuss such things. I fretted all night long." Mrs. Pullman sighed and pushed a stray hair from her face. Then she stepped closer to Katelyn. "Yet after considering it with fresh eyes, I realize Florence listens to everything within earshot of her and can be far too inquisitive." She gave a pretty, feminine chuckle that made Katelyn look up at her in surprise. Mrs. Pullman's eyes danced with amusement.

"I am warning you, not scolding you. Be careful to avoid any talk of such private matters. You are young, but your position here is one of trust and honor, and I expect you shall abide by this. I have said nothing to my husband nor to your superiors, and I shan't. But learn to avoid such discussion, whether with a child or an adult. Is that clear?"

"Oh yes, ma'am. Thank you. I shall." Katelyn curtsied, nodded, and blew out a giant breath she had been holding for far too long.

"That is all. Continue your work." With that, Mrs. Pullman turned and glided out of the room like a gentle breeze.

Before Katelyn had time to consider her employer's words, McCarthy entered the parlor with a rag and a bowl. Her nose tickled at the strong smell of vinegar water.

"We need to clean the windows as well. What did the missus want?"

"Oh, just a mention about the girls from yesterday."

"Yes, well, they are sweet things." McCarthy cleaned the glass until it squeaked before turning to the next window. "Summer is nearly over already. What do you have in your future after Pullman Island?"

Katelyn blinked. "I hadn't much considered the future, but I have fallen in love with island life and hope I never have to return to the farm again."

McCarthy grinned and nodded but said nothing. He went to work on the final window while Katelyn dusted the credenza. "Would you consider working in the city?"

"Not I! Claudia has such aspirations, but my heart is here."

McCarthy frowned. "I see."

Mrs. Duncan poked her head into the room. "The extra staff is here!" She didn't wait for a response before whisking away.

McCarthy handed Katelyn the glass-cleaning supplies. "Finish the windows in here and in the dining room. I must see to the temporary staff."

Katelyn nodded as he hurried away. She heard many voices clamoring outside and peeked out the window to see more than a dozen workers. "My! Where will they all stay?"

"In the bay. We haven't room here." Mrs. Duncan had returned without Katelyn hearing her. "A ferry will transport them morning and night." She shook her head and furrowed her brow. "I hope they won't be more bother than they're worth with all we have before us. Training doesn't happen in a day, as you well know."

Katelyn finished her work, and soon it was time for the Pullmans' luncheon. After helping Mrs. Duncan serve the meal, Katelyn joined the other staff on the lawn for Mr. Pullman's speech. They stood in little groups, chatting quietly in the summer sun. All in all, there were more than two dozen workers present—some she knew, some she didn't know, and a few who looked so lost or afraid that she wondered if they'd make it. *Did I look like that when I first came here?*

Katelyn welcomed the intermittent clouds and gentle breeze that provided relief from the incessant heat. She swatted a few determined mosquitos and said to Sara, "Curse the heat, the humidity, the bugs! I tire of them all."

Sara nodded and shifted from foot to foot. Claudia gazed at the crowd, likely looking for some eligible bachelor. Darcy bit her nails, her eyes darting to and fro. Katelyn giggled and pushed Darcy's hand away from her mouth. "Don't fret. He's not as cross as he seems. He will likely give us a pep talk and send us on our way."

Sara's eyebrows crinkled. "Or he'll threaten us. I've heard his wrath more than once this summer."

Katelyn put her arm around Sara as Mr. Pullman came out the door and stood on the porch. He scanned the crowd, then stuck his chin in the air and his thumbs in his pockets. "Greetings to all of you. In three days, we will have an historic visit from our great president, Ulysses S. Grant. But to make these days a success, each one of you must give his or her utmost. Some of you have worked with us before, but many of you have not. The hours will be long, but the pay will be fair. And know this: I will tolerate no tomfoolery, laziness, or the like. You will work hard. You will be pleasant and respectful. You will have no opinions and share no gossip. Is that understood?"

In unison, the group murmured, "Yes, sir!"

"Before you receive your assignments, I want to give you a good understanding of our president, the elegant and wise first lady, Julia, and their son, Frederick, who is a military man of distinction. General Philip Sheridan, a major general who helped save our Union, and General Porter will also accompany the president.

"Ulysses S. Grant, the commanding general of Civil War fame, has, as president, dutifully administered reconstruction after the war. He has stabilized our nation and worked tirelessly to protect our black citizens by defeating the Ku Klux Klan and passing the Fifteenth Amendment, ensuring the freedmen's right to vote. He has implemented a national gold standard and increased international trade and influence. He has rightly been called 'the savior of the Union.' His re-election campaign slogan is 'Let us have peace,' and to that I say, 'May it be so.' There is none like him, and I believe there will never be one like him."

The entire staff shouted "Rah! Rah! Rah!" and, although Katelyn had never been to a political meeting, she felt proud of her country, proud of her president, and proud to be an American like never before. As her eyes misted over, she gazed over at Thomas, who was wiping his own eyes with his shirtsleeve.

Mr. Pullman waited for the crowd to calm down before continuing. "So to honor such a brave hero and great man, we must make his visit to our island community a most memorable one. Indeed, we want to grow our little-known piece of heaven into a bright and shining light that will welcome thousands to these shores."

The crowd hushed in awe until Katelyn could hear the birds chirp and boats chug along the river. Butterflies rose in her stomach, and she sucked in the excitement of it all.

"Each of you will be assigned your duties by McCarthy, Mrs. Duncan, Cook, and Shamus, and you will follow their instructions completely. McCarthy, the platform is yours. Good day."

Everyone clapped as Mr. Pullman retreated into the cottage and McCarthy took the porch. After introducing Mrs. Duncan, Cook, and Shamus, he rattled off a long list of duties. Katelyn thought him to be very gentleman-like, a great leader in his own right. She even dared to compare him to Mr. Pullman himself. She listened to all the jobs from caring for the animals, setting up the platform and tents, and tending the grounds, to cooking, cleaning, serving, transporting guests, washing, ironing, and much more. But what surprised her most was that no one else was assigned to wait upon the family table. Apparently she, McCarthy, and Mrs. Duncan alone would serve their honored guests!

As the group dispersed, Katelyn grabbed Sara's arm. "I thought we'd have help. I'm not so sure I can serve them, especially after all my transgressions. Whatever shall I do?"

"You've honed your skills and will do splendidly."

As Thomas joined them, Katelyn pressed her palm to her heart, half afraid it might sprout wings and burst from her chest. "I'm ever so nervous. Serve our president and his family? How can I?"

Thomas leaned in and whispered in her ear, tickling her senses and increasing her lightheadedness. "Stuff and nonsense. I shall be taking them fishing and boating and touring, and I shall love every moment. You shall too. This is a once-in-a-lifetime opportunity that we can tell our children about."

Sara snorted an unexpected laugh, while Katelyn felt her face go red. Surely Thomas didn't mean …?

"No tomfoolery, Katelyn," Mrs. Duncan called from the porch. "We have much to do."

Nodding her somewhat grateful farewell to Sara and Thomas, Katelyn scurried to catch up with the housekeeper as she strode into the house, toward the dining room. "Excuse me, Mrs. Duncan, but will we have no one else to help us serve the table?"

"McCarthy and I decided you are quite proficient enough for the task, and the missus agreed. Now, we will have someone from the kitchen meet you in the hallway with the trays and such, but yes, the three of us alone will maintain the sanctuary of the dining room. That way, the party can talk freely. Mind you, Katelyn, I've heard some shocking tongue-wagging from you. But I now feel you have tamed your weakness sufficiently to claim such an important role."

Mrs. Duncan patted her shoulder, took out her list, and began to go through Katelyn's duties for the days ahead. In one short moment, Katelyn actually felt special, privileged, important, for the first time in her life.

As Katelyn walked to her quarters that evening after being released, she found Sara, Claudia, and Darcy already relaxing on the veranda. "How did you three get done so quickly?"

"We have so many extra kitchen hands, we even prepared much of the food for tomorrow, cleaned up, and have been here for a while." Claudia shook her curls and leaned back in the wicker chair nearest the river's edge. "I see they gave you no help. Poor girl."

"I count it a privilege, although I admit it will be taxing." Katelyn took a chair near Sara.

Sara smiled. "With the Crossmons catering so much of the Grand Affair, I doubt we kitchen staff will be likewise taxed."

Katelyn shook her head. "Oh, I'm not so sure. Mrs. Duncan said that we'd all be pitching in wherever and whenever we are needed, so we must be flexible."

The girls fell silent as they watched the boats churn along the shoreline, stirring up the silt bottom and making the water murky. Waves frolicked and splashed on the rocks that jutted out along the shore.

"Did you hear about the Whiskey Ring scandal?" Darcy asked. "When Cook sent me for eggs today, the dairymaid, Prissy, told me how the president's cronies stole money from the liquor taxes. Why can't such a powerful man stop his friends from doing those things?"

Claudia shook her head in dismay. "I agree. Papa doesn't like the president because his secretary of war took money from the Indian posts. I think it was called the Belknap Bribery Scandal or some such strange title. Can you imagine those poor natives abused like that?"

Katelyn shushed them. "Ladies, our president has many scandals thwarting his campaign efforts, but—"

"Katelyn. Enough!" Thomas appeared from around the corner, his eyes flaming. "Do you want to endanger all our jobs?"

"I—"

Thomas raised a palm to stop her from saying more. "'Those who guard their mouths and their tongues keep themselves from calamity.' Please, Katelyn. All of you. Did you not hear what Mr. Pullman said?" Thomas shook his head, then met Katelyn's widened eyes, giving a nod toward the far end of the veranda. "May I speak with you over there?"

"You two will bring scandal upon us!" Claudia pursed her lips and set her hands on her hips.

Sara took Darcy's hand and grabbed Claudia, pulling them both toward their room. "For heaven's sake. They are not improper here in the sight of God and all the river folk. Let them talk this out."

Thomas nodded to his sister as he led Katelyn toward the veranda's edge. Then he turned to her with narrowed eyes. "You cannot speak so, Katelyn. You will lose your position, the trust of this family, and the respect I have for you."

"But I ..." Katelyn croaked, gulping back a sob.

"Stop the excuses. I am tired of it. Your twittering gossip is detestable to me, Katelyn." He crossed his arms as if awaiting a reply, but his expression made it clear he'd already condemned her.

Katelyn turned away and held on to the veranda railing, steadying herself against his unfair accusation. She puffed out unsteady breaths, holding back the tears, holding back the hurt, holding back the dashed dreams of a possible future with this man. A man who falsely accused her. A man who didn't trust her. A man who thought the worst of her. She had worked so hard to tame her tongue. Come so far. But now he judged her even as she was actually trying to stop the gossip of others?

Heavy footsteps, brisk with anger, drummed Thomas' departure. And Katelyn's floodgate of tears unleashed as the setting sun streaked the river with purples and pinks and dazzling orange. Why should she even bother to do right?

CHAPTER 23

Before daybreak, Katelyn shook Sara gently. "Can we talk before the others wake? Please?"

Sara rubbed her eyes and nodded. "I'll meet you outside."

Trying to dispel the nervous energy that had kept her awake for most of the night, Katelyn paced the length of the veranda. When Sara joined her, she grabbed Sara's hand and pulled her to the far end. "Thanks for supporting me last night, but things went poorly with Thomas. He wouldn't listen."

Sara rolled her eyes. "Thomas is too much like Papa. He has a long fuse, but when it's lit, he goes deaf and blind."

Katelyn almost cracked a smile, but the night before left her too distraught to be amused. "He thinks I am a twittering gossip. He said he detests me!"

"Oh, he'll cool down in a day or two and come to his senses. Men are like that."

"Do you not care that he falsely accused me? That he hates me?"

Sara pursed her lips and shook her head. "You don't understand, do you?" Her eyes narrowed but—strangely enough—twinkled.

"Apparently not. What?"

"Katelyn, my brother is in love with you."

Katelyn sucked in a breath, crossed her arms, and furrowed her brow. "He says he detests me, hates me, and you say he loves me? I cannot understand it, Sara."

Sara took her hands and pumped them up and down. "I've known him my whole life, and believe me, he doesn't hate you. But still, he can be as dense as a rock, so I will speak with him. Today if I can. I will shake some sense into him if it is at all possible. Fear not, my friend."

Katelyn sniffled, and one silent tear trickled down her cheek. She swiped it away with the back of her hand. "Thank you, Sara."

~~~

The noonday sun rode high when Katelyn flew into the kitchen, slamming the door behind her. "Misters Cornwall and Walton have arrived already. I saw them at the dock when I left the icehouse. Aren't they early?"

Cook huffed, her eyes wide with alarm. "Nearly an hour. Why wasn't I told? Go and ask Mrs. Duncan to stall them. The mutton is not yet done!"

"Yes, ma'am."

Katelyn alerted her superiors, and after consulting Mrs. Pullman, the women decided they could stall the men with drinks on the porch. A gentle breeze blew, and the porch roof would keep them from the heat of the summer sun.

When the men finally entered the dining room, Mr. Cornwall was laughing. "I hadn't heard that one, Walton. I'll have to tell it to the missus." His massive frame shook like jelly, making Katelyn recall the black bear that wandered into her farmyard last fall, tipping over the trash barrel and trying to break into the barn. His cane pounded on the wooden floor as he limped in.

Mr. Walton followed. His thick, unkempt hair and large nose tipped with red reminded her of her father on a cold winter's day. Katelyn frowned at the thought of him.

The two men bantered for a few moments until Mr. and Mrs. Pullman entered the room. Both men stood, and Walton tipped his head. "My, but you look beautiful, my lady."

The missus beamed. "Thank you, kind sir!" Mrs. Pullman wore the lovely lavender gown Katelyn had pressed just days before, and a delicate necklace trimmed her throat. "Please be seated."

Katelyn poured the pink lemonade, and their luncheon began. Though she'd never cared for stewed liver, the vegetable medley and boiled mutton smelled scrumptious. So did Claudia's yeasty, hot, cloverleaf rolls. Katelyn had to admit Claudia really was a gifted baker.

Mr. Walton tore his roll into three pieces. Then he ran an arthritic hand through his hair, thrust it into his waistcoat pocket, and removed a hankie. His eyes crinkled as he wiped his nose.

Mr. Pullman shook his head and playfully scolded his old friend. "You're not getting ill, are you? You'd best not abandon us now."

"Just a touch of the hay fever, I'm afraid. Always get to sneezing and such at this time of year."

Mr. Pullman set down his fork. "I haven't dealt with such nuisances, but I hear out West hay fever and the like can be even worse. Still, I sure would brave the elements to see Grant's newly formed Yellowstone National Park."

Mr. Walton slapped his thigh. "I'll join you! After all, it's the world's first national park of that sort, and I'd relish seeing it for myself. Our President Grant seems to make history no matter what he does these days." He paused and turned to Mr. Cornwall. "Would you like to join us?"

Mr. Cornwall shook his head. "I'm too old for a trip like that, so count me out." Then he motioned to the window. "I see it's a beehive of activity out there. I'm glad the plans are moving along so well. The platform and tents are nearly up, and the staff appears to have it all well in hand."

"We've entrusted W. A. Angel with the decoration of the island. Indeed, the orchestration of the entire affair lies in his skillful hands. He has superb taste, as I am sure everyone who visits will agree. Yes, Mr. Angel deserves most of the credit—along with my man McCarthy and his assistants, of course." Mr. Pullman jerked his chin at the silent servant standing near the sideboard. McCarthy gave the barest of smiles in acknowledgment.

As Katelyn and Mrs. Duncan placed crystal dishes of custard before the diners, Mr. Walton turned to the Pullmans. "And what are the plans for the guest and press lodging? I dare say there aren't enough rooms for all of them in the bay or even at the Anglers Hotel or Poole's Guest House on Grenadier Island combined."

Mrs. Pullman dabbed her lips. "No, but Mr. Angel made provision for rooms in Clayton and even Watertown. The Globe Hotel should be sufficient for those who aren't locals. Mr. Angel has arranged all that and their transportation besides. It is, indeed, a Grand Affair like we've never before attempted, and though the logistics be overwhelming, I am sure it will be well worth all the work that's going into it." Mrs. Pullman stood and placed her napkin on the chair. "Now, if you'll excuse me."

Once Mrs. Pullman left, the men continued to talk. Mrs. Duncan guided Katelyn into the hallway and whispered to her. "As these men have shown us today, we will need a lot of ice chunks in the days to come. Please go and work on breaking as much of the ice into smaller-sized cubes until you are too cool, and then come back here."

~~~

Thomas could hardly breathe as he saw Katelyn heading toward the icehouse. He'd been watching for her all morning. He slipped behind a stand of trees to wait, glancing at the letter in his hand. He'd almost succeeded in shaking off the disappointment he'd felt last night when another missive from that lecherous reporter arrived with the morning post.

When Katelyn drew near, Thomas stepped into her path. "Delivery for you," he fairly snarled as he thrust the letter at her. "His interest goes beyond a news story, Katelyn. Surely you see that."

Katelyn quirked her eyebrows, took the envelope, and read the address. "You are mistaken, Thomas. What you are intimating is ridiculous, to say the least. He has no claims on me. And I? I'm curious, nothing more."

Thomas' ire settled into startled astonishment. "Curious? Of what?"

"Of the glamor of the newspaper world. Of publishing. Of words that light the imagination. Of the world outside our own." She swept her hand in a circle, then held it out, imploring him. "Can't you understand that?"

Thomas dug his fingernails into his palms. "I can't understand you allowing him to continue to court you with his letters, while you behave the way you do around me."

"I'm not letting him court me! You falsely accused me, Thomas! Last night, and now you're doing it again." Katelyn covered her face with her hands and began to weep as if her heart was breaking.

This time her tears wouldn't work. "Really?" he said in disgust, steeling himself against the sight of her distress. "Falsely accused you, did I? The truth is, I caught you in the act both times, gossiping about our employers again last night, and this morning, I brought you the evidence that you're leading two men on at the same time. Well, I'll have no more of it, Katelyn. I'm done."

When she jerked her face up with an expression of astonishment and hurt, Thomas shook his head, rubbing his throbbing temples. He couldn't allow her tears and her silver tongue to stir his compassion again. He strode away, leaving her with her precious letter from the outside world.

~~~

Katelyn heaved a shuddering sigh as she followed the path toward the icehouse. He hadn't even let her speak, let her explain. His cold, narrow-mindedness shook her to her toes. Good riddance.

But it didn't feel like good riddance as Katelyn trudged into the icehouse, took up the pick, and stabbed at the large chunks of ice like a woman possessed. At first, all she could feel was pain. But with each thrust of the pick, she grew more angry and indignant, until the cool of the ice felt soothing on her hot skin.

How dare Thomas? She hadn't invited Richard to write to her. Still, she had to admit that she enjoyed his eloquent letters beyond anything she had yet read, save *Little Women*. And the things he wrote about seemed innocent enough, ordinary things—like a story he was doing on Burr's Mills, a sawmill and a gristmill built in 1801 that was soon to be converted into a cider mill. He wrote about how he would like to become a renowned journalist, maybe even work in New York City one day. In his last letter, he mentioned that he was looking forward to being back on the island and seeing her, but he never spoke of any interest in a relationship or wrote one inappropriate thing. There was nothing between them, of that she was sure.

It seemed that Thomas misjudged her about that, too.

Finally, Katelyn began to shiver, and she realized how tired she was, so she piled the small ice chunks into the wooden bucket and closed the door.

Maybe she had misjudged both Thomas and Richard. Maybe it was best to have neither of them in her life.

Twilight embraced the island as Katelyn left the cottage that evening. She had polished so much silver that her hands ached, and she felt physically and emotionally exhausted. All she longed to do was fall into bed and bury her face in her pillow. But with all the excitement of the president's visit this week, and her own emotional turmoil, could she actually get to sleep?

Halfway to the staff quarters, a strange rustle in the bushes made Katelyn freeze. There were no animals on the island, save the cow and chickens. Maybe a large bird?

She jumped as a tall form stepped in front of her. "I must speak to you, Morning Dove. I've been a buffoon."

"Thomas? You nearly scared me to death!"

"I'm sorry." He took her hands and held them tight. His gentle voice beckoned her to listen. "Sara spoke with me. She told me how the conversation really went last night. I *have* misjudged you. Accused you wrongly. Please forgive this foolish, jealous man." Thomas tipped his head down and fell silent. As he did, a tear fell on Katelyn's hand.

Katelyn was so astonished at this abrupt change of heart that she didn't know how to respond. She had never seen a man cry before. Not her father. Not even her brothers. Her mind raced, and her heart melted.

"I do. I forgive you, Thomas."

When he looked up, his eyes glimmered with longing for her. She knew it. She feared it.

"This summer I've watched you struggle—but I've also watched you grow. I should have known better. I should have trusted you more." Thomas paused and sucked in a deep breath. "And I? I have my own weaknesses—jealousy, pride, and fits of anger. Faults that are worse than yours. I have no right to judge."

As he spoke, Thomas' cherry-colored lips and dimpled chin begged her fingers to touch them. Just once. She gazed into his dark eyes and wanted to assure him of all he had become to her, but she still stung under his accusations. She forgave him, but how could she forget the hurt?

"Thank you for saying that."

Thomas kissed her hand. "Can we start anew? Start fresh? Can you cast my misjudgments into the river and let them float to the sea? Will you, Morning Dove?" Thomas pleaded with his dark eyes. "I am reminded of what John Brooke said to Laurie, 'Over the mysteries of female life there is drawn a veil best left undisturbed.' I quite agree."

"You've read *Little Women*?"

"I've read a great many things in the frozen watches of the winter here, the Bible being the most treasured of all. I shan't be your judge, Katelyn, ever again. You have my word."

"Thank you, Thomas. I cannot truthfully say I wasn't wounded deeply, and I don't know if I can trust you not to hurt me again. But I will try."

"What more can I ask? I hope I can be the man you need me to be one day." Releasing her hands, Thomas planted a soft kiss on the top of her forehead. Somehow that simple gesture dispelled the hurt in one quick motion. His dark eyes stared deeply into hers until she had to look away. "Don't give up on me. Please."

Katelyn nodded. Thomas drew her close and held her as they both gazed into the darkening, velvet-blue sky, where a plethora of sparkling jewels danced around a golden ball.

"What a heavenly sight!" Thomas gave her a gentle squeeze before releasing her.

Katelyn looked up to see his tender eyes glistening in the moonlight. As he touched her forearm, as gently as a hummingbird's flutter, she melted. Before she could say a word, Thomas walked away in the direction of the boathouse. Katelyn didn't follow. Didn't question. She simply basked in the apology and act of forgiveness. It was healing enough.

CHAPTER 24

On Friday, Katelyn hopped out of bed even before the first rays of morning light, and the other girls soon followed. Sleep couldn't keep any of them from such an important day. The day they had all been waiting for, preparing for, worrying over. It had finally come.

President Ulysses S. Grant would arrive this very night!

The hard work the kitchen and dining room staff had already put in brought about a welcome surprise for Katelyn and Claudia. After breakfast, Mrs. Duncan sent them to assist the Crossmon and Angel teams in their final preparations for the Grand Affair.

Katelyn assessed the festive additions to Pullman Island as they stepped outside. A large platform with an awning covered much of the flat, grassy space, while a dozen or more men hauled tables and chairs up from the boat dock. Several large Pullman-car lamps and at least three hundred Chinese lanterns hung here and there, waiting to be lit. Water buckets sat under trees, near the tent, and around buildings, yet to be filled and at the ready in case any sparks or errant rockets landed on the island when the fireworks display commenced.

Claudia grabbed her arm. "Look at all this! So much has been completed just since breakfast with these strong men at work."

Katelyn nodded and squinted through the bright rays of sun. "Mr. Crossmon can't own all these furnishings. He must have borrowed buckets, tables, and chairs from every establishment within miles. And isn't that … Oh my!"

"Who? Who is here?"

Katelyn glanced at her before returning her focus to the man who'd caught her eye. "Mr. Stockton, the rogue reporter."

Claudia nearly jumped in front of her. "Where?"

Katelyn whispered. "There. In the blue shirt. Black hair and mustache. Oh …" At that moment, Richard Stockton looked at her and grinned that charming, exasperating grin.

"He's yummy." Claudia grabbed her arm and pulled her toward him. "So utterly handsome. No wonder you are taken with him. Introduce me. Please."

Katelyn dug in her heels. "Stop. It isn't proper. Besides, I don't care a whit for the man." She tried to disengage herself from Claudia, but the girl held her fast as, to her horror, Richard walked up to meet them.

"Well, hello there, Miss Katelyn. Who's your friend?"

"I'm Claudia Burton, the Pullman Island confectioner." Claudia batted her eyes and smiled demurely while drawing shockingly close to Richard.

"Are you now? And as sweet as the treats you create, I'm sure." He snickered.

Claudia giggled, and Katelyn rolled her eyes. "What are you doing here today, Mr. Stockton?" she asked.

"Crossmon's an old friend and needed extra help," Richard answered while eyeing Claudia from her curls to her toes and then back up again.

Katelyn shook her head at the two of them.

Richard turned to her. "Have you not received my letters? I've written a half-dozen or more and never got a response to one of them." He tilted his head and pouted like a forlorn puppy dog, making her feel like a scolded schoolgirl.

Claudia spoke before Katelyn could. She almost cooed. "She did, and I hear you're a wonderfully skilled and eloquent writer."

Katelyn shot her a horrified glance. "I … I've been busy. And we are busy still. I must go."

She turned in hopes of catching sight of Mr. Crossmon, but Richard grabbed her arm. "I hoped we could talk soon."

Claudia deftly looped her arm through his elbow, drawing him away from Katelyn. "I would love to hear all about the news business, Mr. Stockton."

"I must find Mr. Crossmon and attend to my duties." Katelyn shifted from foot to foot. "Where is he? Do you know?"

Stockton pointed with a raised chin. "Over yonder. By the bandstand."

Katelyn scooted away, leaving Richard and Claudia to get acquainted. She found Mr. Crossmon, paper in hand, pen at the ready. He spared a glance at her and frowned. "I thought there were to be two of you from the cottage?"

"Yes, well, she will be here presently." Katelyn's face flamed at having to cover for Claudia. As she awaited her orders, Mr. Crossmon spied the two and shouted. "Oh, Stockton, and you, miss, come and lend a hand, will you?"

Katelyn cringed as she, Claudia, and Stockton received the assignment to arrange tables and chairs. Together.

As they worked, Katelyn observed Richard. Dark hair and olive skin bespoke his Mediterranean descent, while double dimples and a quick-to-twitch muscle in his right cheek portrayed a sense of humor. His joviality disarmed Katelyn, even as his gregarious flirting with Claudia infuriated her. His eyes fairly twinkled with life and mystery, but his wide, white smile somehow failed to rise up to his dark eyes.

Richard talked just like he wrote. Charmingly. "I've come to fetch a story that will make the front pages of every paper in the nation, a real attention-grabber. I've been looking for *the* story since I took to the bloody battlefield of Gettysburg, but I always seem to be one step behind the others."

"I hope you find what you are looking for." Claudia's words were breathy, sensual.

Richard gazed at Claudia and then out to the water. "I'll continue to search for the story, but this river, the islands, the beauty of this place makes my heart yearn for a well-needed vacation, one where my mind can rest, and I can feel my heart beat a steady, slow beat of peace. I've not had such rest since before the war."

"Don't you enjoy the excitement of your work?" Claudia tilted her head and smiled. "This place bores me to death. I yearn for the thrill of the city."

Richard shook his head. "The world of the journalist is not for the faint of heart, whether on the battlefield or in politics. Both are a bloody mess of lies, intrigue, pain, and death. But it's true. The beat is exciting, enticing, and full of life. For me, I must write! I've been writing since the days at my mother's knee, reporting the birth of a new calf or a bullies' brawl or petty thievery. It doesn't matter as long as I report the news. It's in my blood."

Claudia tossed her curls. "Well, I hope you enjoy your rest, because I'm sure you're going to get more of it than lies and intrigue here on Pullman Island."

"Oh, I don't know about that," Katelyn blurted out. "I'm sure the lies and intrigues of the president's political scandals are tantalizing enough for you. Whether it's the Black Friday Gold Ring, the New York Custom House scandal, or the Star Route Postal scandal, there's plenty for you to write about, Mr. Stockton. I'm sure you didn't even have to come here to see our great president in person to help spread such stories about him."

Richard smirked, looking over her shoulder. Katelyn turned and saw Thomas standing behind her. Of course. He seemed to show up at her worst moments. His face was red as rhubarb, his fist clenched, his mouth tight. "Thomas, I …"

Thomas glared at all three of them, turned on his heel, and stomped across the pine platform to Mr. Crossmon. "May I please have another assignment? Those three have that duty well in hand." He tossed her an icy glare over his shoulder.

Katelyn started toward Thomas, hoping to explain that she'd intended her next words to Richard to warn him against circulating the type of rumors she'd spoken of, but Thomas put up his palm and shook his head. She stopped, sighed, and turned back to find Richard furiously writing in his pocket pad.

For the rest of the day, Katelyn only caught glimpses of Thomas. By twilight, the Pullmans, their guests, and most of the staff stood near the shore waiting for Mr. Pullman's steam yacht, the *Ida*, to convey their most honored guests to the Grand Affair: the president and first lady along with their son Fred, as well as General Philip Sheridan and Brigadier General Horace Porter. The thirty-mile journey downriver from Cape Vincent—following a long train ride from Washington, D.C.—meant that no one was sure exactly when they would arrive. Katelyn wondered if the important guests would even be interested in a party that night after such extensive travel.

Katelyn and Mrs. Duncan served drinks to the Pullmans, their extended family, and the other guests as they sat in the wicker chairs near the shore. In between, the staff stayed a good distance away and chatted about the days to come. Thomas seemed nowhere to be found.

The stars began to pop out of the velvet sky, and finally, around nine p.m., the moon peeked from behind a solitary cloud to ceremoniously reveal the steamer with its party chugging slowing toward the island. Even before the boat could dock and the guests set their feet on solid ground, canons pealed forth a welcome from Pullman and Nobby Islands as well as from Alexandria Bay. Soon fireworks illuminated the entire area, bursting forth in the sky among cheers of wonder and celebration.

"Beautiful!" Katelyn had never before seen fireworks, and her excitement nearly choked her. She turned to gauge Sara's reaction, but a voice on her left shouted in her ear.

"Isn't it wonderful?"

Twisting to see Richard, Katelyn scowled and took a step away from him. She scanned the crowd to see if Thomas happened to be nearby, and ignoring Richard, she turned to Sara. "Where's your brother?"

Sara didn't take her eyes from the fireworks. "Haven't seen him all day, but I think he's helping with this glorious display. Why?"

Katelyn shrugged her shoulders. "Just hope he doesn't miss the spectacle."

"I'm happy I can share it with you, Katie-girl." Richard was behind her again and placed his hand on her waist.

She slapped it away, her eyes darting to and fro to make sure no one saw. "Don't touch me!" Katelyn's heart beat wildly as she turned to walk away.

"There you are, Richard. I've been looking all over for you." Claudia sauntered up to him and slipped her hand in the crook of his arm. "Isn't this enchanting?"

Katelyn pursed her lips and painted on a fake smile, leaving Claudia to work her wiles. "I must get ready to attend to the president. Enjoy your time together."

Katelyn scurried to the safety of the dining room, thoughts bouncing between the bold Richard and angry Thomas. How could she manage such men? She didn't ask for Richard's attention, and she certainly didn't want his advances. On the other hand, she did want the attention of Thomas, if only to explain herself. After all, she loved her president and had intended to defend him against the rumor mill of the newspaper business.

After a long while of waiting, worrying, and wondering, Katelyn heard the party enter the cottage. McCarthy and Mrs. Duncan appeared, and she took her place beside them. Her heart pounded, her palms sweated, and excitement filled her. They waited in silence for what seemed like an eternity, but then heavy boots clomped on the wooden floor, metals clanged, and voices lilted in joyful chatter.

Katelyn shifted from one foot to the other, willing herself to face forward, though she'd much rather gawk at her president. Her president! Her president was here!

Mrs. Julia Grant entered first, her rounded figure resplendent in plum silk. She took the seat offered, and Mrs. Pullman sat next to her. The two women chatted as if they were old friends. The lilt of the first lady's gentle voice bid Katelyn to listen, although Julia Grant modulated her tone so well that Katelyn couldn't hear all of what she said. Her speech, posture, and proper mannerisms spoke of refinement, despite the distraction of one eye that drifted slightly.

When Mr. Pullman and the president rounded the corner, Katelyn sucked in a breath. Ulysses S. Grant was shorter than she expected. He sported wavy, reddish hair and beard, and his clear blue eyes surprised her, since she'd only ever seen black-and-white photos of the man. He walked with a slouch and held a cigar in his hand, puffing on it even before he sat down. Behind the president followed his son and the two generals, and they all took their seats at the same time, like a choreographed dance.

Katelyn released the breath she'd been holding, willing herself to act and move normally. As she helped serve a light supper, the dining room filled with chatter, laughter, and a blue haze of cigar smoke.

Katelyn had been assigned to retrieve the food from the kitchen. Several times, Claudia met her in the hallway with trays of tea as well as her hot yeast rolls and warm, spicy gingerbread. Next, she brought out fried fillets of haddock, two vegetable dishes, and a large bowl of stewed fruit—all of which the men heartily partook, while the women barely nibbled. Finally, Katelyn carried in a silver platter of fancy cakes, cookies, and other confectionary treats that nearly took her breath away as she handed the tray to McCarthy.

Between trips to the kitchen, Katelyn noticed that President Grant was quiet and soft-spoken, not like she thought a president or a general would present himself. He even seemed a bit shy. The president's fat cigar dangled from his lips, emitting a constant plume of smelly smoke.

"How did you hear about these islands, Pullman, old chap?" he asked his host.

Mr. Pullman swallowed and set his fork down. "My brother Royal found them in '64. When I visited him and saw this place, well, I had to buy Sweet Island and turn it into my own Pullman Island."

General Sheridan nodded. "And this cottage?"

"We call this 'Camp Charming,' for it is a charming little place, don't you think? I plan to build a magnificent, proper castle in a year or two."

"That will be splendid," Fred Grant said. "But what of the fireworks? How did you organize all this in such a remote spot of the world? The logistics make my head spin."

Mr. Pullman chuckled. "Our neighbors on Nobby Island, Henry Heath and his partner, C. S. Goodwin, spared neither pains nor expense for you. So did the little town of Alexandria Bay. Everyone wants to welcome you to these magnificent Thousand Islands!"

The president nodded and finished his cigar. But before long, he pulled out another, passing it under his nose, giving it a long whiff, and lighting it with more relish than he displayed for the gourmet dinner. As he puffed out more fumes, Katelyn tried not to choke.

"Pour the tea, Katelyn," Mrs. Duncan whispered to her.

Katelyn drew a steadying breath as she approached the president with the silver pot. So far, she had stayed a safe distance from him. But now, she could reach out and touch him if she dared. She bent to pour the tea into his cup just as he took a puff of his cigar and pulled his hand away, right into the path of her tea pouring. With a startled cry, Grant jerked back from the hot liquid, bumping Katelyn's arm and knocking the pot out of her hand, sending tea flying through the air and the silver pot crashing to the ground.

"Oh, sir. Sorry, sir. Pardon, sir." Katelyn whimpered in an attempt to restrain tears as she frantically began sopping up tea from the sleeve of the president's coat. When her head spun, Katelyn thought she might faint. But the president reached for her hand, stopping her.

"Please, miss. This accident was my doing entirely. No need to fret. I have seen much worse. Besides, after my journey, I'm in need of a good washing." Katelyn drowned in too much mortification to laugh at the joke. Grant must have seen the tears burn her eyes, for he patted her hand. "There. There. It is fine."

Katelyn croaked out a whispered "thank you," picked the pot off the floor, and stepped back in line with McCarthy and Mrs. Duncan. The guests chuckled and renewed their conversation as if nothing had happened. But Katelyn felt her face flame as she stared at the stained tablecloth, the puddle of tea seeping into the carpet, and the wetness of President Grant's coat sleeve.

The kindness of her president threatened to make her cry right there and then. His gentle touch. His humility. She would never forget this day, no matter how long she lived.

CHAPTER 25

Even at breakfast, Katelyn marveled that the swirl of fumes didn't choke President Grant as he continued his cigar smoking. After she poured his coffee—without incident—she responded to his wink with a relieved smile and stepped back in line.

Mr. Pullman took a generous slurp of coffee and set the cup down. "How did you fare the night, sir?"

The president stopped cutting his omelet and gazed wistfully out the window and then at Mr. Pullman. "My repose was most assuredly that of genuine enjoyment, a wonderful treat during this harried campaign. This blue bosom of the mighty St. Lawrence held me in its spell all the night long, enchanting me with a dream of a quiet piece of heaven and that of calmer affairs than I have had in a long while. Pullman, old chap, you respite on one of the myriads of gems you call an island. I call it a bit of paradise."

Mrs. Pullman sent a pleased glance toward her husband, who gave her a slight nod. "I am delighted you rested well, sir, and you are most welcome here anytime." She took one of the dainty muffins that Katelyn offered from a silver platter.

The first lady turned to Mrs. Pullman. "It is a delightful place. I should think every island here will be quickly scooped up by those who can afford such a summer's rest."

President Grant agreed and smiled so lovingly at his wife that Katelyn wondered if he would get up and kiss her at the breakfast table. "Did you know I spent four years stationed at the Madison Barracks in Sackets Harbor? It was beautiful, to be sure, but not like these islands." He went on to talk about the War of 1812 battlegrounds and the quaint little town on the shore of Lake

Ontario, not fifty miles from there. "It got mighty cold in the winter, and the snow? Never saw the like of it. One winter we had near ten feet of it, and a nasty blizzard nearly froze us all to death."

Mr. Pullman laughed. "Yes, that's why the Thousand Islands is only a summer spot."

General Sheridan cleared his throat. "Tell me more about this area. Perhaps I'll purchase a place for my retirement days."

Mr. Pullman sat up straight. "You'd be most welcome to, General. We determined that for a spot of land to be classified as an actual island, it must have at least one tree and stay above water year-round. The islands range from barely six feet in diameter to the size of a small city, and they number well over a thousand, perhaps closer to two thousand." Mr. Pullman paused for a sip of coffee and a nod of acknowledgment from Sheridan before continuing. "The farthest islands sit at the mouth of the mighty St. Lawrence, and they continue nearly fifty miles down the river. Some belong to Canada, but the United States—New York State, specifically—owns more than half of them. But when you're traversing the waterway, it's quite hard to know when you've entered the country of Canada."

"Such are the challenges of our international boundaries," President Grant said. "I haven't heard of any disputes about these waters, have you, Porter?"

The president's aide, Brigadier General Horace Porter, rubbed his ridiculously long—and Katelyn thought rather ugly—goatee and mustache with his hand. "No, the Canadians are right amiable neighbors and haven't brought a whit of consternation to your administration, sir."

President Grant gestured to General Porter. "This man is a walking encyclopedia and a mighty good chap. Do you know that he refused a $500,000 bribe during the Black Friday gold market scam and then alerted me to it? Couldn't have a more honest and brilliant aide, I tell you."

General Sheridan clapped his hands. "Bravo, General!"

Mr. Pullman snapped open his pocket watch to check the time before shoving it back into a tiny pocket in his vest. "We have a marvelous fishing expedition planned for this afternoon, for all who would like to partake. At noon, Mr. McCue, an expert fishing guide and excellent oarsman, will be here to escort us to the abundant fishing areas around these parts. Who would like to join us?"

The president, General Porter, and General Sheridan raised their hands like schoolchildren, and Katelyn grinned at the sight.

Grant tamped out his cigar and reached for a new one. "The press won't be joining us, will they? I dare say I'd be much obliged to have an afternoon away from their scrutiny."

Mr. Pullman shook his head. "No, there is just a handful on the island today. Several more will come for the evening entertainments, but my butler, McCarthy here, knows how to handle them."

By mid-afternoon, the men were off fishing, the women were resting, and everything in the cottage was put in order for the evening's events. Mrs. Duncan touched Katelyn's arm. "You can take two hours to rest. We will have a simple dinner for the president's party. Then Mr. Pullman's mother and brothers, as well as the Cornwalls, Waltons, Henry Heath, and Mr. Goodwin will join us for entertainments. I fear it will go on far into the night, so rest while you can."

"Yes, ma'am." Katelyn curtsied and left the cottage. A rest sounded wonderful. But on the way to her room, Richard popped out from behind the rose bushes.

Katelyn stopped in her tracks and clutched her chest. "You scared me, sir."

"It's Richard, if you don't mind. I've been waiting all afternoon to see you. Look what came this morning." He thrust a newspaper at her and beamed. "Let's sit a spell so you can read it."

Katelyn considered refusing him, but curiosity about both the article and the man got the best of her. The newspaper reporter's stray curls betrayed him, and she decided he could easily look like a ragamuffin if he didn't tame those locks with a generous application of hair tonic. He wore a pencil propped behind his ear, and a grin planted firmly on his face.

She pointed to the empty veranda. Once they settled into chairs, Katelyn surveyed the paper.

Richard reached over and tapped a lengthy column. "Right there. See my byline? On the front page of the *Watertown Daily Times!*"

His pride couldn't be denied, so she smiled weakly and turned to read it. The article's title read, "President's Scandals Widen." Katelyn glanced at the author.

"You're a good informant, Katie-dear." Richard's insincere smile grew altogether too wide.

Katelyn sucked in an angry breath and quickly read the piece. "I didn't say all that. I only …"

"Oh, but you gave me the inspiration for this topic, what with those beautiful eyes, angelic face, and the delicious suggestions of scandal that fell from your scrumptious mouth yesterday. All it took from me was a little research on the mainland. Perhaps you have more specifics to share today, Katie-dearest?" He reached over and touched her face, but she swiped his hand away and stood, stomping her foot in frustration.

"Don't touch me! I have nothing to share with you. I am not your source of anything. And it's Katelyn, if you don't mind!" She shoved his paper at him and scurried to the safety of the staff quarters before he could say another word.

Upon entering her room, she found Sara and Darcy fast asleep and Claudia primping in front of the tiny mirror on the bureau. Katelyn nodded a greeting and sat on her bed, hoping to be left alone. But Claudia turned and whispered, "You look upset."

"I'm just tired." She wasn't about to confide in her. Not about Richard.

"I'm going out to the veranda. It's too stuffy in here. Want to join me?"

Katelyn shook her head. "No, thank you. I'm going to rest."

"Suit yourself."

Claudia left the room, and Katelyn sighed in relief as she lay down to think. Yet after nearly an hour of restlessness, she got up. It was indeed stuffy, and her thoughts swirled around her head like a swarm of gnats. She redid her mussed hair and adjusted her uniform, careful not to wake Sara or Darcy. Hopeful to find Richard long gone, Katelyn decided to climb the turret.

But when she opened the door to the veranda, she found Richard and Claudia laughing and talking together. They turned to look at her, and Richard said, "Ah, there's the lovely Katelyn again. Come join us. We were just discussing what we liked and didn't like about our jobs. Tell me, what do you think about the newspaper business, Katie?"

She wanted to run, but she feared being rude, so she reluctantly joined them. "Though I do enjoy a grand adventure, the world of politics and intrigue does not sound like a tasty cup of tea to me."

Richard quirked his head and addressed her while glancing at Claudia. "And what do you think the president is doing right now?"

Katelyn noticed Claudia's pursed lips, sure sign of annoyance at Katelyn's arrival. But she had to give the newsman a safer topic to pursue. "Oh, Thomas told me all about it. Of the many traditions handed down by our St. Lawrence River fishermen, excursion parties are the most popular. He said that skiffs are attached to a small steamer launch, which takes the fishermen out to a favorite fishing shoal. Then the parties of two or three go fishing, while the steamer team sets up a buffet on a nearby island. When the fishermen return, they add their fresh-caught fish to the other delicacies, some of which you made, Claudia." Katelyn purposely paused and smiled at her. "And oh, they fly a white flag on the return voyage if they catch a muskellunge." Katelyn grinned.

Claudia wrinkled her nose. "Why?"

"They're the most popular sport fish. Literally hundreds of prize-winning muskellunge have been caught here on the river and mounted over the years. Mr. Pullman has one hanging in the dining room. I'd know because I have to dust it." Katelyn giggled.

"Please, can we be finished with such boring chatter?" Claudia's eyes darted from Richard to Katelyn, narrowing into angry slits when they landed on her.

"For certain. I'll leave you two to talk." With that, Katelyn scurried away before Richard could stop her. She strolled around the perimeter of the island, allowing the beauty around her to soothe worries about Richard's article from her mind.

"Oh magnificent Creator, how I love it here," she whispered as she walked. She could never imagine life on the mainland again. A life of cornfields and cows. Milking morning and night. Dreary, long winters with howling winds and ceaseless snow. And the spring mud. No, it had to be island life or at least one close to the shore. She would not, she could not, return to the farm! Ever.

But she did have to return to the cottage. Only she had forgotten her mobcap in her room.

When Katelyn approached the veranda, she could hear Claudia's sensuous, lilting laugh coming from the river's edge. There she saw Claudia wrapped in Richard's arms, while he sprinkled kisses in her hair and caressed her lower back.

Katelyn glowered, shook her head, and turned on her heel to retrieve her cap. *Foolish Claudia.*

After a dinner of fresh fish, angling tales, too much cigar smoke, and lots of laughter, the distinguished party retreated outdoors to a circle of chairs and small tables illuminated by Chinese lanterns and hurricane lamps. Katelyn stood at the ready to serve them while they enjoyed the cool evening breeze, the twinkling fireflies, and the sparkling wonder of a full moon.

A variety of entertainments ensued, including charades, music, and dancing. Katelyn—joined by Thomas in his dress uniform— was tasked with keeping the drinks flowing.

Fred Grant chuckled as he took a drink from Thomas' silver tray. "My, but you look different in that than you did as my fishing guide. Thanks for helping me bring in that muskellunge. That was an epic battle I'll n'er forget!"

Katelyn smiled, ready to congratulate Thomas as he nodded and stepped back, but his features grew somber when he saw her. "What's wrong, Thomas?" she whispered.

"Might'n you guess? I read the article in the *Times.*" He shook his head and walked away before she could respond.

~~~

Thomas knew he should be serving and smiling, but he stepped into the shadows to regroup. He watched as Katelyn floated around all the important people, performing her duties with grace—unlike him. She had become a true professional, and he couldn't help but be proud of her. Then he groaned and shook his head. Professional? Maybe not.

How could she break the confidence of her president and give that journalist the scandalous information for his article? Thomas had read every word of it after Richard Stockton thrust it at him. He had bragged about it all the way from the bay that morning when Thomas had picked the man up. Furthermore, Stockton had insinuated that because Katelyn was sweet on him, she would share more inside details of the president's visit as the week progressed.

He loved Katelyn. He knew it. But how could he reconcile the two sides of this exasperating woman?

~~~

Katelyn watched Thomas throughout the night, but the expression on his face failed to reveal his thoughts. How did he know about the article? What did he think she did?

Mrs. Walton tapped her arm, shaking her from her thoughts. "Say, miss, might you find me some headache powders? I seem to be afflicted with a migraine."

"I'm sorry you are unwell. I will get some for you right away." Katelyn laid her tray on a nearby table and hurried to the kitchen to retrieve the medicine. She found Sara near the cupboard.

"How is the party going, Katelyn?" Sara's eyes held eagerness mixed with a bit of sadness. Katelyn realized that her friend missed most of the excitement while working in the kitchen. Excitement that *she* got to enjoy.

"It's a lovely evening, my friend. But your brother is out of sorts again, and Mrs. Walton has a headache."

Sara patted her arm and retrieved the medicine. Then she poured the powders into a glass of water, stirring until they dissolved. "Here you go. Enjoy the party for me."

Seeing the wistfulness in her grey eyes, Katelyn hugged her friend. "It's not a party for me. It's work."

Before Katelyn could return to the Crossmon drink station, Thomas hurried up to her with a scowl on his face. "Where have you been? There are a lot of thirsty guests here. Mrs. Pullman wanted to know where you were, and I had no answer."

"I was getting headache powders for Mrs. Walton."

"Oh." He cleared his throat. "You should've told someone. The missus is vexed." Thomas swallowed hard, softened his tone, and touched her shoulder. "Sorry. A simple mistake. Go and give the woman her medicine."

When Katelyn handed Mrs. Walton the glass of headache powders, she drank them down in one long swallow, then paused for a deep sigh. "Thank you, dear."

Mrs. Pullman joined them. "So that's where you were."

"I have a headache and asked for the powders," Mrs. Walton explained.

Mrs. Pullman nodded and smiled at Katelyn, who curtsied and scurried off to the serving table. Picking up a silver tray of drinks, Katelyn swept around the party guests. President Grant reached for a glass with one hand while puffing on his cigar with the other. He looked into her eyes for several seconds and nodded a thank you.

Serving the likes of these fine folks is an honor. Maybe Sara does have a right to be a wee bit jealous.

CHAPTER 26

Early the next morning on her way to the cottage, Katelyn stopped to survey the beautiful pine platform and elegant lectern where the preacher would share his Sunday sermon that afternoon. She smiled at the clever use of several flags that formed the canopy above the makeshift pulpit. Though no roof would cover the worshippers, wide, spreading tree branches would protect them from the hot summer sun. Beyond the preacher's pulpit, the surrounding rocks and rising knolls created a picture-perfect place for a divine camp meeting to take place.

Peeping patches of blue sky caused Katelyn to blink as she pondered the historic day ahead. In just a few hours, dignitaries and ordinary people alike would descend on their island to enjoy the service and meet their president. Best of all, President Grant would give a short speech. She could almost hear his deep, crisp, and clear voice delivering the masterful lecture. What an honor to hear from him, not just hear about him! After all, she now knew her president personally.

This Sunday was bound to be a day like no other.

When Katelyn entered the dining room, McCarthy's sharp tone stopped her short. "Katelyn. We'd like a word. Now." He glanced at a scowling Mrs. Duncan, her arms crossed over her chest. McCarthy's eyes blazed, and his creased brow meant only one thing. Trouble.

Mrs. Duncan fairly shoved the newspaper in Katelyn's face. Then she wiped her hands on her apron as if to rid herself from some vile germs. "Heed what the Good Book says, Katelyn. 'He that is void of wisdom despiseth his neighbor: but a man of understanding holdeth his peace.' You, my dear, seem to have forgotten such wisdom, even though time and time again we have warned you and given you much grace in your errant ways. The time for grace has passed."

As Katelyn's heart thundered, McCarthy's face filled with anguish, and it appeared that he might cry. "How could you? Spreading such scandal with the likes of a journalist, and while in Mr. Pullman's employ? Yes, we know you are the guilty party. Claudia heard you with her own ears. Were it not for you, this article would not have been written, and it incriminates the president, the very guest under our roof. We cannot have such prattling staff. We cannot! You have put us all in a difficult place and endangered President Grant's re-election. Can you not see this?"

"But—"

"No excuses! Stop!" McCarthy swept his hand in a wide arc in front of her. Katelyn took a tiny step back, appalled at the accusation. "I have heard enough." He turned his back to her, attending to the items on the buffet.

Mrs. Duncan stepped up to her, very close, dipping her head as an angry blush rose from her neck to her forehead. "We cannot have you here this morning. When the Pullmans read this. When the president sees this." She shook her head violently and whooshed out an exasperated sigh. "You will go to your room and stay there. Do not show your face until the two p.m. church service, and then stay far in the back, far from the Pullmans and their honored guests."

"I—"

Mrs. Duncan shook her finger in her face. "I don't want another word, Katelyn. Not a word. Go!" She pointed to the door with an outstretched arm.

Katelyn curtsied and scurried out of the room. She hurried through the kitchen to the door, her head down, her tears dripping on the floor. The blinding sunlight slapped her in the face as she picked up her skirt and ran for her room.

Safe inside the isolation of her stuffy quarters, Katelyn sat. Wordless. Hopeless. Hurt. Yes, she had gossiped and prattled and spread rumors before this. But now? That article wasn't her doing! She was innocent. But now, she could lose her job, her reputation, perhaps even her future because of it. What could she do?

Katelyn fretted and prayed until it was time for the service. She listened to the hubbub of activity outside and steeled herself to join the gathering, hoping beyond hope to avoid any more accusations, scoldings, or worse. She chose a large oak tree at the very back of the crowded audience to place herself behind. She scanned the crowd. Only one person concerned her.

At the very front, President and Mrs. Grant sat facing the audience, and next to them, the Pullmans. From where Katelyn stood, she could see her president's head bowed in reverence and peace. He held no pretense of superiority. Indeed, this man who governed forty million people and who ran their great nation appeared as meek and lowly as the poorest of his fellow men. Katelyn's eyes filled with tears at the thought that he might believe she actually spread words to hurt him. She sucked in a whimpering breath and swallowed it so no one would hear her anguish. What if he judged her the villain? Oh how she prayed it would not be so!

The reverend began the service, and everyone stood to sing "Amazing Grace." Katelyn mouthed the words, but the boulder in her throat stopped her voice from making a sound. She swiped away tears as she thought about the words, "A wretch like me." As she sang, she prayed for grace, for God to be her shield from the accusations, for safety from the lies.

Reverend Street used John 13:7 to speak of the wisdom of believers fully trusting in God, even when they could not see what He was doing. The reverend said that God always did things for their best and that when they didn't understand why, they still must trust Him.

Katelyn couldn't conceive of a reason for her current predicament, but she imagined herself giving her difficulties and problems to God. No one could have noticed, but she actually raised open palms a fraction of an inch toward the heavens and whispered, "It's all yours, God. Do what is best."

The reverend concluded his sermon, and the pianist took up a rousing rendition of "Onward, Christian Soldiers" to close the meeting. Once the service ended, the president gave an eloquent and inspiring speech.

As each member of the audience paid their respects to the first family before each of them left the island, Katelyn continued to hide behind the tree, wondering if she should find Mrs. Duncan or stay in her room. Thankfully, McCarthy found her first. "Katelyn, I think you'd better stay near the staff quarters. Nothing transpired during breakfast, but Mrs. Duncan is still quite vexed."

"Yes, sir." Katelyn hung her head, trying to think of how to correct the mistake, but before she found the courage to speak, McCarthy hurried away.

The afternoon plodded on at a snail's pace as Katelyn wished she was working like everyone else. She felt isolated, ostracized, and judged, but she guessed that no one even noticed her absence. Even when she had seen Sara and Thomas for a brief moment after the service, neither had questioned her about anything. Moreover, both Claudia and Stockton had been prominently absent.

Katelyn would like to have walked off her angst, but McCarthy had told her to stay at the staff quarters. So she sat in the shade of a large oak at the corner of the veranda, wondering what would happen to her.

She must have fallen asleep, for when she awoke, the wind stirred the whitecaps and the treetops, warning of a sudden storm. Thunder danced a mighty war dance between the clouds and the churning river. A gust of wind tossed her skirts about her legs and pulled her bonnet from the pins that attached it to her hair. She chased it, forgetting the dangers.

A sudden thunderclap immediately followed by a bolt of lightning felt as if it struck the island. Katelyn fell to the ground and covered her head with her arms, frightened but also worried about losing part of her uniform. She looked up to see her cap carried onto the water by the raging wind. As if in slow motion, she watched it sink beneath the waves.

Katelyn got up and ran to her room to watch the storm from the safety of her window. A quick, torrential shower followed. It only lasted a quarter of an hour and left as quickly as it had come. Before long, the sun burst through the dissolving clouds, so she took her place again on the cool, breezy veranda.

Katelyn watched as fish broke the water, seeming to play tag in a joyful game. It reminded her of her childhood, of her friends. If she were a fish, she would surely be a wide-mouth bass, ugly and always fighting the desire to jabber, never able to keep her prattling mouth closed. She wished she were a rainbow trout, beautiful and desirable. But no, she was a bass, ever fighting and flapping her jaws.

The steady beat of the waves along the shore assured her that a divine heartbeat pulsed through this beautiful world that she was a part of. She had the power to choose. Right or wrong, she had to choose. It was terrifying to think of such power on the tip of her tongue. She could choose to speak life. She could choose to spread gossip and birth a deadly virus that could bring pain and hurt to many. She had the freedom to love others enough to hold her tongue or the freedom to hate and bring death. She even had the power to stay silent when faced with unfair accusations, as Jesus had done. Her choices might be terrible right now, but they were hers alone.

A wave of guilt threatened to engulf her. "Help me, Lord. I've been drowning in a sea of words I can't take back, in prattle that has poisoned, in gossip full of guile. And now, in false accusations because of my errant ways. Change me, Creator! Make me a new creation lest I die in the weeds of my own making. Take my tongue, my words, my thoughts, and my deeds, and make them Yours. Please."

Tears stung her eyes, and she allowed the dam to burst. Alone on the veranda. Alone with God. With only the river as her witness, Katelyn wept as she'd never wept before. For the loss of her mother. For the abuse of her brothers and her father. But most of all for her wretched tongue. The tongue that hurt others. That abused others with gossip, tales, and prattle that were untrue, half-true, or outright lies. Oh how she wished she could take them all back, rewind time, and make it all right.

"Forgive me, dear Lord!"

Just then, a gentle breeze swept over her, cocooning her in a blanket of divine love and forgiveness, in a moment of serenity she would never forget. A pure white seagull alighted on a nearby branch and looked down at her. It seemed to wait for her to respond to its presence, its gaze. Katelyn dried her eyes and stared at the creature. She glanced to her right and to her left, making sure no one was around.

~~~

Thomas had heard a forlorn sound come from the far end of the veranda. Weeping? Katelyn?

He watched from afar, keeping his distance, wanting to help but knowing he shouldn't. Somehow he knew that whatever she was dealing with, it was hers alone to bear. He hid behind a nearby rock outcropping, praying.

~~~

Secure in her solitude, Katelyn went down to the water's edge and scooped up a handful of water, pouring it over her head as a sign of both contrition and submission. Peace washed over her like a cleansing flood. From the tip of her wet head to the tips of her now-wet shoes, Katelyn knew. She knew she was a new creation, just like the Bible had promised.

Then she felt a burning on her tongue as if a hot pepper had burst in her mouth. She scooped up some river water and took a drink, hoping to calm the searing pain, but it didn't help. As she wondered about it, she remembered the sermon Pastor Olsen had preached just before she came to the island. It was from Isaiah 6 about when the angel touched Isaiah's lips with a burning coal and took away his iniquity. She had scoffed at the words that day. Not today. She fell to her knees, right there in the mucky water's edge, and bowed her head, silent under the weight of God's convicting yet healing presence.

She waited. She submitted.

She was clean.

When she opened her eyes, the coolness of the river water sent a chill through her. Yet she felt light as a bird.

Free.

Before she stood to leave the shore, a large flock of seagulls flew past her, swooping and diving in a beautiful dance. Katelyn smiled and whispered, "Thank you."

With the sound of crunching rocks, Thomas knelt down beside her, silent, but with a look of peace and contentment that she had never before seen on his face.

~~~

Thomas took Katelyn's hands in his, stroking the back with his thumbs. He questioned her with a raised brow. "You made your peace with God, didn't you?"

As she raised her chin and nodded, he noticed the glint of peace in her eyes. Her quivering lips told of pain. Her ragged sigh spoke of her newfound resolve. Then came fresh tears, begging for him to understand the war within her and her repentance.

There was no turning back. She had to be his.

~~~

As the sun began to set over the veranda, Katelyn marveled at the colors of orange, yellow, pink, and purple dancing gracefully on the magnificent river. The stormy day was giving way to a starlit night, and Katelyn felt hope sneak into her inner being with every breath she took. She sucked in the fresh river air, gulping, grabbing every molecule of life and hope.

She turned to admire the delicate pink roses, the deep purple hydrangea blossoms, the bluebeard, and the azaleas. They created a scented concoction that no New York perfumer could match.

Katelyn closed her eyes and breathed deep. When she opened them, she imagined the blossoms to be the colorful decorations for her own spiritual party sent by heaven above.

"Katelyn, might I have a word?" Mrs. Duncan stood beside her. Her gentle eyes and a slight up-curve of her lips told Katelyn she had news. Good news.

Katelyn nodded and waited for her to speak.

"I have misjudged you. We have learned that you were not the originator of Mr. Stockton's revelations. Furthermore, Claudia had misinformed us to purposefully discredit you. Forgive us."

Katelyn bit her bottom lip. "Please, Mrs. Duncan. My wayward words gave you every reason to assume the worst. Yet God has dealt with me this day, and I can say with assurance, I am a new woman. I, too, ask your forgiveness for all I have wrongly spoken these many months."

Mrs. Duncan took her hands and gave them a gentle squeeze. "Shall we both cast our errant words, thoughts, and deeds into the river and let them be swept away forever?"

Katelyn let out a nervous laugh. "Yes! Let's."

Mrs. Duncan took their joined hands and cast them toward the river, discarding their invisible, emotional baggage. "There. Let's start again." She laughed and turned Katelyn toward the cottage with an arm about her waist. "Now, we have much to do before the party returns from their moonlight tour. Can you imagine how beautiful the Thousand Islands are with the magic of twinkling lights along the mainland shore and dotting the islands? I hope to see such a sight one day." She turned to glance at Katelyn's face and grinned. "But this is a sight I don't want to see! Why don't you stop by the pump and wash away those tears? We want to see a pretty, happy face serving our president, don't we?"

CHAPTER 27

As President Grant's public reception got underway the next afternoon, Katelyn peeked up at the tree branches, grateful they would shade much of the island from the midday sun. Her heart beat faster as boats of all sizes and shapes came toward Pullman Island. Some anchored offshore, while others dropped people off, their passengers invited this fine Monday to shake the hand of the president and visiting dignitaries.

The crowd grew. So did the summer heat.

Relieved that the Pullmans had hired an Alex Bay laundry service for the busy week, Katelyn straightened the already-damp bodice of her best serving uniform and observed the modern dress of the many wealthy guests with awe. What if Thomas were one of them? She imagined him in a silk top hat like those adorning most of the men's heads. The gentlemen wore jackets styled a bit differently than years before—closer fit with narrower sleeves and lapels. Their shirts were a variety of colors and designs instead of the traditional white. Wide neckties, tied in a loose knot low on the throat, had squared, overlapping ends, and Katelyn thought them quite fancy. Thomas would make a mighty fine gentleman, of that she was sure.

Blushing at her vain imaginings, Katelyn glanced at Thomas as he stood next to her, also waiting to serve the crowd that quickly formed on the island. "I've never seen so many marvelously attired, important people!"

Her handsomely uniformed Thomas nodded and smiled. "Neither the whole town of Alexandria Bay, or even the entire population of Jefferson County, possesses a population so large. We are experiencing an historic moment, Morning Dove."

Katelyn's heart warmed at the term of endearment. "And just look at our regal president, Mrs. Grant, the Pullmans, and both generals, all waiting to receive them. How elegant they are!" She paused, deep in thought. "But how can this small island properly host such a mob?"

"I believe they'll come and go in the next few hours." Thomas had barely finished his sentence when McCarthy motioned for them to begin serving the guests.

Katelyn picked up a silver tray of exquisite crystal glasses filled with champagne and walked among the stylish people who mingled and chatted in small groups after shaking the president's hand. They laughed and bantered and took the glasses without acknowledging her, which was just fine with her. Once the tray was empty, she returned to take up another.

Thomas slid an empty tray onto the serving table at the same time. "Why don't you take the lighter tray of hors d'oeuvres, and I'll serve the glasses?"

Katelyn nodded and wiped her brow with her shirtsleeve. "Thank you. The glasses are rather heavy."

He winked, took up the tray, and disappeared into the crowd.

McCarthy smiled as he handed her the hors d'oeuvres tray, tilting his head after Thomas. "He's a fine young man, Katelyn. Couldn't do better."

Lowering her lashes, Katelyn felt her face grow warm. How odd. Was McCarthy encouraging her and Thomas? Granted, there were only a few weeks before they'd close up the cottage and her job would be done, so fraternizing would no longer be an issue. Katelyn shook her head and blew out a deep breath. She'd have to ponder that later.

As she wove in and out among the small groups of guests, Katelyn drank in the opulence. A well-bred lady sipped sparkling champagne. A cigar-smoking gentleman tipped his hat as he entered a group to talk. A frail, elderly man took a dainty teacake and popped it into his mouth, nearly swallowing it whole. The bustle of the group around her resounded with the laughter of many important people.

Suddenly a gentleman bumped Katelyn's arm, and the tray teetered, causing two tiny cookies to fall to the ground before she could set it right.

"Be careful, miss, or Cook will have your neck on that platter," Thomas teased as he passed her.

The guests sauntered across the green grass on their way to the tents. A few visitors strolled along the sloped lawn and among the wooded section of the island. Others meandered along the shoreline. But most stayed close to the main attraction—their president.

Then she saw him. Richard Stockton. Her heart skipped a beat as he stared at her, a grin on his lips and a gleam in his eye. Katelyn turned away from him to serve those in the opposite direction. *Such a bold man. How dare he!*

She focused her attention on the beautiful women she served. *What might it be like to wear such finery?* Many of the ladies sported dangling earrings and either black velvet ribbons secured at the back of the neck in a bow, often with a brooch or charm in the front, or a neck scarf tied in the front of the collar. Others displayed lockets or cameos on gold chains or long strands of beads atop their elegant jackets. Lace gloves encased their dainty hands, while frilly collars and cuffs drew one's gaze to their faces. Large bustles hid under the layers of wide overskirts, flounced underskirts, and full petticoats.

Katelyn shook her head, pondering how hot, heavy, and uncomfortable those elaborate dresses must be. No, a maid's uniform was much more practical, but even her clothes felt hot on this warm summer's day.

"You're as pretty as they are, Katie-dear." Richard had snuck up from behind, his lips nearly touching her ear as he spoke into it.

She stepped back, nearly bumping into a rotund gentleman. Katelyn curtsied to him. "Sorry, sir." He glanced at her, paying her no mind, as she gave Richard a scolding glare and scurried to the service table.

"Is that scoundrel bothering you, Katelyn? I will have none of it." McCarthy's narrowed eyes gave her pause and comfort at the same time.

"Thank you. No." Katelyn picked up another full tray and veered away from where Stockton stood. Thomas swept up next to her.

"What's Stockton up to? He'd better steer clear of you, or else." Thomas displayed McCarthy's same narrow-eyed threat.

"Thank you, Thomas. I'm all right. Really." Katelyn feigned a smile as she felt tears form in her eyes. He touched her arm before heading in the opposite direction. She watched him serve the guests with a dignified air. She'd never felt so protected and cared for in all her life.

"Miss Katelyn!" Florence and Little Hattie, accompanied by Bridget, surprised her as they tugged on her skirt. "We've been staying at Grandmother's cottage but are back for the party today and the masked ball tomorrow. We won't get to go to the mask, but we get to watch the people arrive in their ball costumes." The little girl glanced up to the second story of the cottage. "From the nursery window. How exciting!" Florence took a deep breath and sighed dreamily.

Katelyn nodded and patted their heads. "You little ladies look so beautiful!" The girls wore frilly dresses, one as yellow as a daffodil, the other as pink as a peony. Long pearls looped several times around their necks, causing Katelyn to worry that one or the other might catch such long strands on something and choke.

She addressed their nanny. "Hello, Bridget. I heard you were away. Have you met the president?"

"We did," Little Hattie said, "and he gave us a sweetie." She held out her chubby little hand and showed Katelyn a peppermint stick. "He's nice."

Bridget laughed. "Yes. He made quite an impression on these two, so much so that everyone seemed to think these wee ones—and not the president and his party—were the guests of honor."

Florence giggled, holding her hand over her mouth, but her eyes twinkled with pride. Hattie mimicked her sister. Katelyn smiled at them. "After the party is over, I hope to get a nice visit with you three, but for now, I must attend to my work."

Both girls hugged Katelyn's legs, causing onlookers to turn and stare. Katelyn's face grew hot with embarrassment, so she quickly said her goodbyes and went on her way.

"Be about your work, miss, and don't let those rascals distract you." The elder Mrs. Pullman smiled broadly as she took a small cookie, nibbling it with a wink before she walked away to join a group of chatting women. Katelyn smiled, knowing the girls' grandmother was well aware of their magic on her.

Sometime later, Katelyn froze as she passed a group of men and heard Richard's voice. "The beauty of these islands is matchless," he declared. She dared not turn and confirm it was he. She knew. "I've been the length of this east coast and seen none so lovely. The woods. The hills. The crags. The thickets and miniature forests. God surely smiled when He made this bit of the world. I promise you this, after I report on such a paradise, floods of folks will swarm like bees to fragrant flowers and suck out the nectar from even the tiniest island."

Katelyn's heart skipped a beat when she sensed he was glancing her way. She couldn't resist; she turned her head to find him smirking at her. The five other men stared and smirked too. She sucked in a breath and hurried off to the safety of McCarthy's table. "May I please visit the privy, sir?"

McCarthy smiled. "Of course, and then stop by the icehouse for another bucket. The ice keeps on melting in this hot weather."

"I will. Thank you." Katelyn ventured to the old privy and then to the icehouse, pleased to have a few minutes away from the crowd. She had to chip away at some of the ice, but most of it had already been chopped into smaller pieces. When her bucket was full, she turned and opened the door, but someone shoved her back inside and closed it behind him. As the darkness blinded her and she smelled a man's musky cologne, she cried out.

Katelyn tried to keep her voice from quavering. "Excuse me, sir. I must be about my work."

"Alone at last."

Stockton! What was he doing? As Katelyn's eyes adjusted, she could see his strong, whiskered chin and dark, lively eyes dancing a naughty dance. Something colored his casual demeanor. Something hid behind his haughty smirk.

Richard reached around her, and his fingers clamped onto her waist. Katelyn dropped the ice bucket and squirmed, trying to disengage from the man. His nails dug into her palms as he shook his head and narrowed his eyes in stormy displeasure. "Uh-uh-uh. You've been playing with me long enough. Now I claim you. Come away with me. Today."

Katelyn's heart raced as she realized she was in danger. Sheer danger.

"I am not for the claiming, sir. Let me go!" Katelyn ducked to the side as Richard lowered his head. Then, with a prayer on her lips and all the power in her, she stomped on his foot as hard as she could with the heel of her boot. With a yelp, Stockton released her, and she jerked open the door and bolted toward the safe haven of the crowd.

Tears welled up in Katelyn's eyes as she realized she had forgotten the bucket of ice. What would she tell McCarthy? She couldn't go back there, not while he was there. As she made her way up the hill to the reception, Thomas stopped her, his eyes ablaze with concern. "Are you all right?"

"The icehouse. McCarthy needs ice." She lowered her eyes. "I left the bucket."

On Thomas' face, confusion and compassion hardened into determination. "I'll fetch it. Here, take the tray."

Thomas thrust it into her hands and hurried down the hill toward the icehouse. Katelyn held her breath. He knew something had happened. At the open icehouse door, he placed his hands on his hips as he addressed the person inside. She couldn't hear what he was saying, but then he reached in, and Richard fairly flew out, hitting the ground several feet away.

"Be careful, Thomas! You'll lose your job," Katelyn whispered. "Oh God! Please help him. Help me."

"May we have a drink, miss?" Mr. Pullman's brother Royal called to Katelyn.

Steadying the trembling tray in her hands, Katelyn hurried to attend him, his other brother, and a group of couples who took all the glasses. She glanced over her shoulder but could no longer see Thomas. Biting her lip, she returned to the service table.

McCarthy stared at her as she stacked her empty tray. "Where's the ice, Katelyn?"

"I … I left it."

Coming up behind Katelyn, Thomas answered McCarthy. "Here's the bucket. I thought it was a bit heavy for her." Face flushed, he stole a glance at her.

"All right. The presidential party has been standing in the receiving line a long time since they were served. Please take them another round of refreshments."

Katelyn took the hors d'oeuvres tray and Thomas the glasses McCarthy indicated, and together they wove their way around the crowd to the receiving line. "Are you all right?" she whispered.

"I'm fine, but did he hurt you?" Thomas didn't look at her, but his tone indicated that he wanted an answer. Now.

"No. But he might have. I was so scared, Thomas." Katelyn's voice quivered, yet she knew she had to control her emotions. "Let's talk about this later. Please."

"I swear, he'll live to regret that he ever stepped foot on this island." His voice held an angry threat she had never heard before, but he nodded toward the president and his party. "You go first."

Katelyn squared her shoulders and stepped up to the president. "Care for some refreshments, sir?"

Cigar billowing smelly smoke, President Grant waved her to serve his wife first, then he took two hors d'oeuvres from the tray with his free hand. Neither Grant nor the generals said a word, but when she served the Pullmans, the missus declared, "Of all the people here today, my girls had to tell me they saw *you*. Whatever do you do to make them like you so much, miss?"

Katelyn pursed her lips and raised her eyebrows. How was she to answer that? "I don't know. I just love them, ma'am."

Mrs. Pullman gently placed her hand on Katelyn's forearm. "They know."

Mr. Pullman quirked an eyebrow and gave a harrumph. He helped himself to another teacake, popped it in his mouth, and mumbled, "Very good. Thank you." He gave her a slight, almost imperceptible wink.

When her tray was empty, Katelyn returned to the serving station. Thomas caught up to her, his tray empty too. "Well, well. I've never gotten a thank you from Mr. Pullman. How about that?"

Katelyn smiled a sigh of relief. "How about that!"

"We're not through with the Stockton discussion. Just so you know. He's a dead man, in my book." Thomas gave her a warning glare. "No one will treat you indecently. Ever!"

~~~

Thomas cleared the boulder that threatened to choke him from his throat. Never had he felt such rage, such hate, as he did when he saw Stockton in the icehouse. The very place his Morning Dove had just fled—upset and afraid! What had the blackguard done to her? Did he ... touch her? Hurt her? Worse? If so, his life was in danger!

He had to protect *his* Katelyn. He *would* protect her. Soon she would be safe ... in his arms, in his life. Forever.

~~~

Finally, the last of the boats returned the guests to the mainland or their islands. After cleaning up, Katelyn was sent to the dining room to prepare for dinner. Mrs. Duncan was already there, table set, poring over some papers.

Katelyn cleared her throat. "How can I help, ma'am?"

Mrs. Duncan looked up. "Ah, I'm just planning the after-dinner entertainment, cards and charades and such. The president and the generals are out fishing while the women rest, so please be as quiet as you can, but do tell me about the reception."

"McCarthy estimated that we entertained more than two thousand guests. Can you believe it?" Katelyn went on to describe the elegant fashions, the important people present, and of course, seeing the girls. She left out the icehouse incident.

"Well, this entire week is going just splendidly. We've barely had a hiccup, and I'm pleased as punch. Let's keep it going, shall we?"

Katelyn nodded, shaking off thoughts of Stockton and smiling as she drew strength from her superior's positive mood. She owed it to her president. To herself.

CHAPTER 28

A promising morning sun rose over the river where Katelyn found Thomas fishing on the dock, just as she had hoped. She had to speak to him before the busy day got underway. All night long, Katelyn's thoughts had been churning over what she would tell him. She didn't care one whit about that Stockton scoundrel, nor was she concerned about herself. But the anger she had seen in Thomas' eyes when he mentioned the incident scared her.

Although he acknowledged her with a nod, neither said a word. She stood so close to him she could hear him breathe and imagined feeling his heartbeat with her hand. Instead, she dared to tip her head toward his strong bicep and lay it there. He dropped a quick kiss on top of her mobcap, as natural as could be.

How wonderful to enjoy an unguarded moment with him!

Thomas cleared his throat. "Cook wants fish to add to the luncheon since the men are such hearty eaters." He grinned, and Katelyn returned a smile, but then he grew serious. "About Stockton. What did he do? Exactly."

Katelyn gathered her courage and answered. "He … he grabbed my waist and said that he claimed me. He wouldn't let me go. I told him I wasn't for the claiming, and when he tried to kiss me, I stomped on his foot. Hard."

Thomas stared at her for several moments before he threw back his head and laughed. "So that's why he limped as he slunk away to the boat dock yesterday. I thought I had done the damage, but my little Morning Dove put him in his place. Well done!"

Katelyn sighed in relief when she saw Sara hurry their way. Sara acknowledged them both and gave her brother a hug. "What a topsy-turvy week! Cook sent me to tell you not to bother with the fish. Apparently, the president made plans to go next door to Nobby Island for the day. Seems Mr. Heath is an old war friend."

Thomas put down his fishing pole and saluted her. "Flexibility is my middle name, and that's fine with me. I'll likely be taking the party over to Nobby since Shamus is under the weather again."

Sara's brow furrowed. "Is he unwell?"

"Poor Shamus is like a sailboat without the wind. He's so tired and weak. Can't get his strength back."

Katelyn shook her head. "But just last week he seemed to be on the mend."

"It appears that this busy week has tuckered him out. Seems he's set on retiring and moving to Buffalo to be with his sister once we close up the cottage."

Katelyn placed a gentle hand on his forearm. "I'm so sorry. I know how you love him."

Sara nodded in agreement with her friend and gave Thomas a kiss on the cheek.

Thomas stared at his feet and shoved his hands in his pockets. He cleared his throat, but his voice still sounded gravelly. "I do, and I will miss him terribly."

Katelyn surveyed the island she had come to love. "But who will stay on and be caretaker?"

"I've been asked to take his position." Thomas glanced at Katelyn and then at his sister. The two women looked at each other, eyes wide with surprise.

Sara turned to her brother. "Will you?"

"Maybe. Probably. We'll see." Thomas' gaze veered toward Katelyn again.

Katelyn wondered what such a job change might mean for Thomas, but she needed to focus on her own work today. She turned toward the cottage. "We'd better get to work. Tonight is the grand finale. The masked ball!"

~~~

Thomas shivered and blew out an unsteady breath. Would Katelyn be willing to join him on the island in the dead of winter? Would she forsake civilization for months at a time with nothing but him as her company? Could she?

After several sleepless nights and several conversations with Shamus, he had decided that he could no longer stand by and watch Katelyn be treated poorly by any man. Even her father. Or her brothers. And especially not Stockton. *No!* This would stop and stop with him. As soon as possible, if he could help it.

The sight of her teary, fearful eyes yesterday marked the point of no return. He had to speak with her. Soon.

~~~

With the guests gone to Nobby Island for the day, Katelyn worked on a variety of projects that Mrs. Duncan itched to mark off her list. As she bounced from task to task, she wondered if Thomas really would take Shamus' position and stay on the island all winter. She wondered if she could ever be so isolated during the cold, snowy months without much contact with others. And she cringed as she wondered if Stockton would appear later that day.

As the sun sunk to a fiery demise and tiny stars popped out on a blanket of blue, Katelyn changed, tucked a stray hair up under her cap, and smoothed her freshly pressed uniform, ready to serve the honored guests of the Presidential Masked Ball. The dancing on the lawn, illuminated by Chinese and brass lanterns, should ensure a glorious conclusion to the president's visit to the Thousand Islands.

Shooing gnats away from the crystal flutes that would soon hold fine champagne, Katelyn turned to McCarthy. "Doesn't the island seem magical with its twinkling lights, flags, and banners, and the fine guests now arriving by the dozens?"

"Indeed it does." McCarthy even seemed to twinkle as, having adjusted his bowtie, he clasped his hands behind his back like he so often did. Katelyn had become accustomed to his ways and now saw him as a friend. "It's been quite a week. I'm relieved that Thomas came to your rescue yesterday."

Katelyn didn't know how to respond, so she croaked out a simple "yes" and turned to survey the growing crowd. As darkness descended and a warm breeze arose, couples sauntered along the path in a steady stream. Cottagers from all the islands for miles up and down the St. Lawrence as well as many others from the mainland paraded arm in arm, their colorful finery reminding Katelyn of a lovely summer garden.

Thomas slipped up beside her and handed her a tray of elegant hors d'oeuvres. "You look fetching tonight. Let's serve the receiving line, shall we?" He held his tray of champagne flutes high overhead as if it were nothing.

"It's a good thing those huge Pullman car lamps light the waiting line so well. I fear it'll be awhile before all those people work their way through to meet the president. Just like yesterday."

Thomas stepped aside and waved for her to go first. "I doubt any of them will regret the wait. He's quite a man."

When the two arrived at the front of the cottage, Katelyn offered the Grants hors d'oeuvres. "Care for a refreshment?" When both declined, she noticed that President and Mrs. Grant appeared rather tired. She wondered if the week's fanfare had been too much for them.

A woman shaking the president's hand seemed to have lost her tongue. Her face grew red, and she stared at him as if frozen. Mrs. Grant grinned and took her hand, ready to chase away the woman's nerves. Katelyn supposed that many a guest might be intimidated into silence by such a man.

But then an elderly gent stepped up and shook the president's hand vigorously. "I do hope, sir, you will be re-elected. I shall pray the Lord allows it, for I favor the work you are doing for our country. And you mustn't worry about all the scandals them there journalists write about. The man on the street don't believe nary a tale."

President Grant quirked a brow. "Thank you."

Katelyn served General Sheridan, who chose a pastry as he laughed with a man and woman who held a small child. "This is a fine gathering, and on such a perfect evening. Your babe won't remember this night, but I surely will."

The mother nodded, smiled, and then thrust the baby into the general's face for him to kiss. The general complied and said, "I've kissed the baby, now how about a kiss from the mother?"

Everyone around them laughed, including Katelyn, and with much drama, the general proceeded to press a kiss on the woman's cheek, while General Porter guffawed loudly.

Katelyn caught Thomas' eye as he joined in the gaiety of the scene, and with a wink and a tilt of his head, he bid her to follow him to get new trays of refreshments. They walked toward McCarthy's table, but near a small stand of trees, Thomas pulled her aside. "Someday, I would like the honor of kissing *you*, Morning Dove."

"And I would be honored, sir." But such a thing should never occur without an engagement! Overwhelmed at the thought, Katelyn turned toward the front of the house, her face flaming. "Look, the receiving line is finished, and I'm glad. The president and the first lady seem rather tired, don't you think?"

Thomas touched her forearm. "They do. It's been a busy week for all of us."

Katelyn nodded as President Grant retired to the veranda facing the river, where the woman who had been tongue-tied stood alone in a far corner. When President Grant saw her, he went over to her. Katelyn glanced at Thomas and pointed. "That's so kind of him! That poor woman was too afraid to speak to him earlier."

"As tired as he must be, I applaud his concern for her." Thomas and Katelyn watched until Fred Grant joined the president and his shy admirer. Thomas nudged her arm. "You and I had best be serving the guests, my sweet."

With that, Katelyn and Thomas gathered fresh trays and proceeded to weave among the crowd. It was such a beautiful spectacle that she thanked God she wasn't stuck in the kitchen but got to be here, observing this magical night.

Before long, the musical ensemble tuned their instruments, struck the first chords, and played softly but gaily. It was time for the mask. Katelyn had only ever heard of such a special party, and what a sight it was!

All the guests wore or held masks up to their faces. Lace, feathers, and other embellishments covered the ladies' half-masks. Dance cards hung from delicate strings around their lacy-gloved wrists, just waiting to be filled. Intricate fans swung from the same wrists, and Katelyn smiled, wondering how the women managed all the paraphernalia.

Katelyn stood there mesmerized as fireflies joined in their own dance around her. A magical night to be sure.

Thomas cupped her elbow, shaking her from her reverie. "It is a wonderful sight, but come. We have work to do."

Katelyn went through the motions of serving the guests while beautiful music hung in the air, the notes creating a dance of their own, twirling around her, captivating her, enfolding her. She found it difficult to give the extra attention required to edging around the small clusters of attendees in the shadows of the evening. Though she knew a grand promenade would be forsaken due to the small dance floor, waltzes and reels filled the night air. Each time the band struck the first notes of a waltz, ladies batted their lashes and smiled, eager to dazzle onlookers with their skills.

And dazzle they did. The ladies reminded Katelyn of a flower garden filled with beautiful blue, green, pink, lavender, and yellow flowers twirling to the music. The silvery moonshine shimmered on the water, on the tree leaves, even on the elegant gowns, making the evening all the more magical as the wooden floor filled with couples swirling around one another.

"You're daydreaming again." Thomas grinned at her as he tapped her shoulder playfully, crooking his finger to bid her to follow.

Katelyn shook herself. "Sorry. It's so beautiful; I keep getting distracted."

Thomas chuckled. "I understand."

Working didn't prevent her from admiring the beautiful dresses. Mrs. Grant sported a pale yellow silk gown complemented by yellow roses and cream ribbons. Katelyn's favorite ensemble, she soon decided, was Mrs. Pullman's flowing gown of embroidered rose silk. The elaborate jewels around her neck twinkled in the moonlight, casting an air of royalty as she and her husband gracefully moved around the crowd, greeting each guest.

The women's hairstyles amazed Katelyn as well. Some wore their hair close to the sides of the head and high on top. Others sported a few careless locks and soft tendrils that fell around the face while ringlets hung behind a large, loose topknot held in place with elaborate combs. Some of the older ladies covered their center parts with small, frilly evening caps.

As if reading her mind, Thomas bent close to her ear. "You are even prettier; just you mind that."

Katelyn relished the flattery and returned some in kind. "And you'd make a mighty fine gentleman, Thomas." Her eyes darted from Thomas to the men she surveyed in the crowd. They wore plain black silk masks, white vests and neckties, and black suits that highlighted the ladies as they huddled in small groups holding their drinks and talking of the former Civil War, the present state of affairs, and the future of politics.

Clearly pleased, Thomas filled his chest with air. "Thank you."

Katelyn followed his lead to serve a group of guests on the other side of the dance floor. But he stopped to gaze at the moon shining brightly and the stars twinkling gaily on the navy waters of the great St. Lawrence. The wind danced through the trees, and fireflies swooped and soared all around, magically lighting their tiny beacons.

"Tonight, all of nature seems determined to add its own grand ambiance to the party, don't you think?" Katelyn giggled, as now Thomas seemed to be the mesmerized one. "Pullman Island is always beautiful, but tonight I think it's absolutely spectacular. And now that the breeze has stilled, it's one of those calm nights when the moon shines down on the quiet waters of the St. Lawrence like on a mirror."

Katelyn agreed. "And look, the other islands have light displays too!"

Thomas chuckled. "They've been lit all along. You've been too busy gawking at the beautiful women. And the handsome men."

Katelyn batted her lashes and quirked her chin. "You've nothing to be jealous of."

Thomas shrugged his shoulders, seeming to dismiss the comment. "I wonder why President and Mrs. Grant aren't dancing. But look at General Sheridan and General Porter's daughter. They've been dancing together much of the time."

When Katelyn and Thomas returned to gather new trays, the table was empty, so they waited for McCarthy to return.

"Thomas, go and check the water buckets," the butler directed. "The fireworks display will happen soon, and I want to be sure we are ready to drench any embers that might descend upon the island."

"Yes, sir." Thomas nodded to McCarthy before departing for the duty.

"Are you enjoying this event, Katelyn? I'm glad you're not holed up in the kitchen. It's sweltering in there." McCarthy blew out a breath and wiped his brow.

Katelyn smiled. "It's magical! Truly." She lifted a tray to go about the crowd, but McCarthy stopped her.

"Stay here until Thomas returns. I just saw that journalist skulking around the bushes." He pointed nearby and gave her a knowing gaze. "The crowd has had enough refreshment for now."

Katelyn gulped in a breath and craned her neck, peering into the darkness. She saw no Stockton. Still, she stepped a bit closer to McCarthy. She observed the party until the fireworks display began, lighting the sky with bursts of beauty. Katelyn jumped at the startling noise.

Then, as Thomas returned, she saw the culprit in the shadows. "Richard."

"Where is he?" Thomas demanded.

"Stay here. Please," Katelyn begged as she darted a glance in the direction of the bushes.

McCarthy agreed. "Yes, Thomas, stay. And both of you keep watch for stray embers."

Katelyn and Thomas nodded and scanned the perimeter of the island for embers and for Stockton, but the dance of colors shooting across the dark night pulled her thoughts to happier places. Worry of journalists and embers faded away as guests *oohed* and *aahed* over the ripples of light that exploded in the velvet sky and then gracefully sprinkled into the river.

When it ended, she turned to see Thomas dutifully scanning the earth below, brows furrowed, eyes darting to and fro, lips pursed. Always protecting, caring, concerned.

"Was it not heavenly?"

Thomas blinked. "What?"

"The fireworks."

"Oh. Yes. Of course." He never looked at her, but continued his watch, long after the ember-danger had passed. Stockton-danger was evidently on his mind.

The crowd began to disperse, and before long, the island fell quiet again. They gathered champagne flutes, and McCarthy sent Katelyn to help wash dishes.

"Where's Claudia?" Katelyn asked Sara as she entered the kitchen, wondering if the pastry chef's absence was the reason Katelyn had been called for.

Sara shrugged. "She's been gone for some time. I've been so busy I hadn't noticed."

Overhearing their conversation, Cook stopped scraping a dish. "I hadn't noticed either. Katelyn, go and see if she's sick in her bed, although she should have cleared any absence with me first."

Katelyn curtsied and hurried to their room. Lanterns had been extinguished, and she shivered at the thought that maybe, just maybe, Stockton hid in the shadows. She ran to the room and found it empty. Lighting a candle, she discovered a sheet of paper folded in half, lying on Claudia's pillow. Grabbing it, she gasped, covering her mouth with her hand. "No! She didn't."

CHAPTER 29

"I cannot believe Claudia ran off with that Stockton fellow. And in the middle of the President's Ball!" A clump of oatmeal fell from Sara's spoon, accenting her statement as she stared down the length of the staff table.

Darcy harrumphed. "It's shameful. I've never seen Cook so angry."

"I feel sorry for her," Katelyn added. "I fear she's making a terrible mistake." She scooped her last bite of oatmeal and licked the spoon clean. "I'd better hurry. It's time to say farewell to our president." She took her bowl to the sink, washed and dried it, and headed to her duties.

Mrs. Duncan greeted Katelyn as she entered the dining room. "Good morning. I can't believe this epic week is coming to an end."

Katelyn nodded, fluffed a napkin, and straightened a knife that was a tiny bit crooked. "I'll never forget it. Ever! So what needs to be done this fine morning?"

"Gather the juice, fruit, and muffins. If our guests are to be on the steamer by seven, I believe that everyone will be down soon."

Katelyn frowned, knowing that President and Mrs. Grant would soon be gone, bound for Ogdensburg, while the generals and the others would depart for the mainland and then on to parts unknown. *How quiet the cottage will be, and how uneventful life will seem from now on!*

As she carried in the tray of muffins, Katelyn heard the banter of the men as they descended the staircase. She hurried to set the tray down and take her place next to Mrs. Duncan.

Once everyone was seated, Katelyn served juices while McCarthy poured the coffee. The president clinked his spoon on the crystal juice glass. "Ahem. On behalf of all of us, I want to thank the Pullmans and their staff ..." He turned and gazed at each of them—at one point tweaking a grin at Katelyn. After that, she didn't hear anything else he said. She was dumbfounded that her president would bother to thank her, a servant, a nobody. The idea swept her away with its wonder.

Mrs. Duncan whispered a gentle scolding, shaking her from her thoughts. "Attend the ladies, Katelyn."

Katelyn hurried to pour the tea for Mrs. Pullman and Mrs. Grant.

"Thank you, dear." Mrs. Grant nodded and smiled at Katelyn, but she refused to think more about it. Instead, she curtsied and backed into her place.

Soon the dining party moved to the porch to say their goodbyes. Katelyn watched them from the window, and tears stung her eyes. "Epic. Mrs. Duncan is right. Epic."

Mrs. Pullman took Mrs. Grant's arm. "We will escort you to the steamer and then accompany you as far as the mainland. We have appointments in the bay today."

Once the entire group departed, the Crossmon staff appeared to tear down the party platform and the decorations and gather their serving equipment. The island staff put everything aright, and by mid-afternoon, barely a trace remained of the historic event that had transpired on their island.

McCarthy surveyed the surroundings and rubbed his hands together. "The Pullmans will be gone until late this evening, so I think the lot of you deserve the rest of the day off. I for one intend to take a long, long nap."

Mrs. Duncan laughed. "And I intend to put my feet up with a good book."

Cook scowled and shook her finger. "You young people had better keep down the noise. Us old folks need some rest." But at the end of her strict-sounding admonition, her lips turned up, almost resembling a smile.

With a glance at her elders, Katelyn grabbed Sara's hand. "We will. Promise. Come, Sara, Darcy, let's be gone."

Darcy nodded and followed, but said as they reached the veranda, "I'm just exhausted. If you'll excuse me, I'm going to take a nap too."

Katelyn and Sara bid her farewell as Thomas came up the pathway, hands in his pockets. "Well, hello, ladies! Will you join me at the water's edge? It's a lovely afternoon to dip our feet in the cool river. How about it?"

"Oh, let's, Katelyn. In celebration of the president's visit."

Without protest, Katelyn agreed, and they headed to the tiny beach below the veranda. Katelyn laughed as she and Sara plopped down on a grassy knoll. "Truly. It's been an incredible week, and I'll carry so many memories in my heart and mind for all my life." She covered her heart with her hands.

Sara frowned. "I'll take pleasure in the fact that I fed him and washed his dishes."

Katelyn patted her hand. "Sorry, I didn't mean to throw your kitchen confinement in your face."

"You didn't. It's fine. I would have fainted dead away if I had to serve the likes of such fine folks."

Thomas shook his head. "Sweet sister, you doubt yourself too much. You've grown so this summer. You have. You were like a skittish little fawn, but you're quickly turning into an elegant doe. Like your friend here. I think you could've served the presidential party just fine." He snatched a quick gaze at Katelyn and winked.

Sara smiled. "Perhaps. I hope so. But for now, let's enjoy the water a bit, shall we?"

They removed their socks and boots and waded into the cool St. Lawrence. Katelyn could feel her toes tingle, so she sunk them into the silty bottom. She held up her skirts and wiggled her toes until her feet were immersed up to her ankles. Sara and Thomas followed her lead, laughing and chatting about passing boats and billowy clouds flying overhead. Gulls glided on the breeze, squawking and chasing one another.

A gentle wind blew Katelyn's hair and pulled at the skirts in her hand as she tried to keep her uniform dry. As boats passed, waves splashed them, dampening her hem, but she didn't care. The warm summer sun, the beauty of the day, and the company made everything seem perfect.

Sara played with the surface of the water, swishing it around her. "Have you decided to stay on the island for another winter, Thomas?"

As her brother's eyes darted to Katelyn, uncertainty shone in them. "I think so, but I can't imagine being here alone … without Shamus."

Katelyn nodded. "We will all miss his funny Irish ways." A piece of her skirt slipped out of her hand and dipped into the water. "Oooh."

Sara waved a hand. "Don't worry. You'll dry. I shall miss you, brother, but personally, I'll be glad to return to the mainland. I don't think I'm an island girl after all, and I'm not sure I'm a kitchen maid either." She turned to Katelyn. "What about you?"

Katelyn's eyes danced from Sara to Thomas, to the island and the river beyond. "I've come to love it here, and my duties have been a joy. I simply cannot imagine going back to my father's farm." Sadness welled up inside her, threatening to overflow through her eyes. "I wish this summer would never end."

Katelyn expected Thomas to agree, but instead, he grinned mischievously and stabbed a finger toward the water near her. "Holy mackerel, girls! Don't let that huge fish bite your toes."

Sara and Katelyn squealed and pulled their feet from the murky water, looking for the mackerel Thomas seemed to be pointing at. They splashed themselves and each other as they fought to stay upright and avoid the sharp rocks on the river bottom. Sara lost her balance and fell face first into the water, but she jumped up, laughing cheerfully.

"Just kidding," Thomas confessed as he scooped his sister into a wet hug.

"You troublemaker!" Sara pushed Thomas away and splashed him in happy banter.

Katelyn joined in the fun, but before she was completely drenched, she scurried to shallower waters, beckoning the two to join her.

Sara slogged onto dry land and tried to squeeze out her skirt, but it was no use. "Look at me; I'm soaked. I'm going to change, but I'll be right back. You two behave yourselves." She wiggled her finger and giggled her way up the hill. Then she stopped and turned around. "No tomfoolery, Thomas."

Katelyn waved from the ankle-deep water she still stood in and looked down at her disheveled appearance. She was wet from her thighs down, and spots of mud speckled her uniform. Her hair hung half out of her proper chignon. She sighed and wiped drips of water from her face with the back of her hand. Then she hugged herself and headed to shore, watching the river bottom so she wouldn't trip in the muddy, rocky water.

When she got to the grass, Thomas took her hand and helped her sit in the sun on a grassy knoll. Katelyn sucked in a deep, satisfying breath. How she loved it here! The trickling water from a tiny stream nearby sounded loud in the silence of the moment. Thomas bent down, touched her cheek, and kissed her forehead so lightly that it was barely a brush. She tipped her head up and gazed into his dark, smiling eyes. Eyes that hinted that he knew something she didn't.

In a mere butterfly's breath, she realized that her heart belonged to him. He was more than her best friend's brother. She hoped the future would hold the promise of more. Much more.

He took off his outer work shirt and wrapped it around her shoulders. Then he sat beside her.

"I must be a sight," Katelyn said in barely a whisper.

Thomas wrapped his arm around her. "So beautiful! How I love you, Morning Dove!"

Katelyn snapped her head his way. "What did you say?"

He blinked and shrugged his shoulders. "I have four loves really—God, you, this river, and this island."

~ ~ ~

Thomas couldn't imagine living anywhere else. The beauty, the quiet, the solitude of the island breathed life into every pore of his being. He hoped to always be a part of it. With her.

He rose, but with a palm extended, motioned for Katelyn to stay seated. Thomas returned with a rose from a nearby bush. "For you, Morning Dove."

Katelyn's giggle rippled like the river's waves. Brilliant shafts of sunshine washed them in heavenly light and made the golden flecks in her gaze sparkle like jewels as she spoke. "I've come to love this island. This river." Suddenly, her eyes filled with tears, and she sucked in a deep breath. "I fear I will never be happy back on the farm. Without Mama."

He sensed her fear, her vulnerability, her pain, and his heart beat faster. No! She would not go back to the farm with the likes of her father and brothers. He would protect her, keep her safe, hold her close. Very close. Forever.

"I talked to your father, Katelyn. Last week when I was in the bay."

"You did? Is he unwell? Are my brothers?" Her eyes held a different fear, one of concern rather than sadness.

"All is well. I talked to him … about us."

"Us?"

"Your hand, precisely."

Katelyn blinked, her eyes filling with disbelief. Or was it fear? He wasn't sure.

He knelt in front of her, mere inches from her, invading her space and breathing in her breath. Slowly, he took her hand in his and kissed it, captured by her silent and wide-eyed gaze. Then he reached up to touch her cheek. He had memorized every fleck in her eyes, the tinkle of her laugh, and the nervous energy when she was worried. He loved them all.

"Will you? Will you be my wife? We can enjoy this wonderful island world together if you say yes. Please say yes."

Her eyes seemed to beckon him, so he bent closer and placed a gentle, tender kiss on her lips, guiding her with no demands. He felt her ease into him, returning the kiss with such abandon he feared he would burst with joy.

The sweat on his neck tickled, and his stomach tightened. Thomas felt his heart pump harder, nervous energy filling his veins and cutting off the oxygen to his brain. He watched as her eyes danced over his shoulders to the river and back to the island until they finally landed on his. Her tongue wet her lips as if tasting his kiss again, and she took in a deep breath just as a beam of setting sunlight burst through the tree branches and set her face aglow with warm and inviting reds and oranges.

Katelyn sucked in a full-lunged breath and held it. Lightning bolted from Katelyn's eyes as she nodded, releasing her breath. Thunder crashed in his heart. Another kiss, a deeper one, sealed the promise.

She finally spoke as her eyes asked the question. "But do you really want a woman with such an errant tongue? I am far from perfect, Thomas, though I feel the Lord is helping me change."

"None of us is perfect, love. I am far too critical and judgmental, and too easily angered. I shall love you as you are if you can love me as I am. I can't offer you a castle or even an island, but if you marry me, Morning Dove, I will love you forever."

"We don't need a shining castle or an island all our own. Life with you, wherever it is, will be a dream come true for me, and being your wife will seem like heaven on earth!"

~~~

Katelyn's heart filled with joy as she relaxed in Thomas' arms, taking in the awe-inspiring sunset. She drank in the wonder of the moment like a dying man would drink at a desert oasis. Soon she would be his wife.

Remembering all the errant words she had spoken, her heart had so recently been heavy, like an anchor. But now she felt feather-light and free. He would take her as she was, with all her faults and foibles. Katelyn looked at this man to whom she had pledged her love. She would no longer battle life alone but have a knight to walk with her.

As they sat together silently, cocooned in love, she watched the big, orange ball slip below the water's horizon, and bid it farewell.

She knew the struggles and temptations of her flesh would taunt and try her, but with God's help and Thomas' love, she would continue to gain mastery. Grateful tears slid down her cheeks, and she scooped one up with her tongue, tasting the salty goodness of it.

One last glimmer of sun burst through the cloudbank, splashing over her, warming her like a kiss from heaven. Leaves from the giant oak rustled in the breeze at the water's edge, and birds twittering overhead seemed to sing a love song just for them. Butterflies flitted on the rose-scented air, and Katelyn smiled to see fireflies awakening, twinkling their applause as they danced over the river.

"I think heaven is smiling down at us. I know your mama is." Thomas smiled gently.

Katelyn scooted closer until her nose nearly touched his neck. Eternity stopped as he turned her way. Breathless, she lowered her lashes and smiled. "I love you, Thomas."

"What's going on here?" Sara's voice held a tease as well as a question.

Thomas turned to her with a grin. "Sara, meet your sister-in-law to be!"

Katelyn smiled, feeling a blush rise on her face.

But Sara stomped over to them. She snapped her hands to her hips, quirked her head, and frowned as if in displeasure. "Really? Could you not have waited for her to change and fix her hair and feel like the beautiful woman that she is? I've taught you better than that, brother." She playfully pursed her lips together and stared at Thomas from under her lowered brows.

Katelyn looked down at her damp dress and then at Thomas, and both burst into laughter. "Sara, I've never felt more beautiful in all my life!" Thomas helped her get up and give Sara a careful hug, trying not to get her wet again. But Sara grabbed her and hugged her so tight that Katelyn thought she might break.

"Welcome to our family, sister!"

EPILOGUE

August 8, 1873
One year later

Katelyn enjoyed every moment with Florence and Little Hattie. She wasn't fond of not working, but at least she got to stay on the island with Thomas during his employment. Filling in for Nanny was one of her favorite treats.

As she and the girls sat on the dock, dipping their feet in the water, Hattie turned and gently patted Katelyn's swollen tummy. "When's the baby coming?"

"At Christmastime." Katelyn smiled and touched the wee one's cheek.

"That's Baby Jesus' birthday," Florence said.

"You're right, and it's also my first wedding anniversary with Thomas."

Florence pursed her lips and shrugged her shoulders. "I'm happy you married him. He had to wait too long for me."

Katelyn chuckled as Thomas steered the boat up to the dock. "Feet up, my lovely ladies!"

They all stood, and Florence proceeded to make footprints on the dock with her wet feet. Hattie stomped along behind her sister, mimicking her as she so often did.

Thomas tied up the boat and joined them. "I thought there were only three here, but look at all these footprints. Is there a tribe of elves around?" Thomas pretended to look for the creatures. The girls grinned at him as he scooped up Hattie and gave her a hug.

Florence raised her arms. "Me too!"

Thomas picked her up and galloped with both girls to a grassy spot before setting them down. Katelyn joined her husband, and they all plopped in the soft grass. "So, what have you girls been doing today?"

Florence hopped up. "We talked about babies and Christmas and your anniversary. What was your wedding like? I wish I had been there."

Thomas took her hand. "You could have been our flower girl. You too, Hattie. It was a lovely Christmas Eve service with snow falling gently and my bride as beautiful as any woman could be."

Katelyn swept a stray hair away from her face. "I'm happy it was a small and simple affair, and I loved having your family present, Thomas." She smiled at him and then looked to the blue sky, remembering how intoxicated and obnoxious her father and brothers had been. Thankfully, Ann, acting not only as caterer but as Katelyn's substitute mama, had skillfully sent them on their way home.

Katelyn shook herself from the memory and turned to Florence and Hattie, drawing Hattie onto her rapidly disappearing lap. "Oh, I would have relished you being there. I do so love being with you, and I'm sorry to see you return to the mainland so soon. By next summer, I expect you two will be so big, like little ladies."

"I could stay here with you," Florence suggested.

"Me too," Hattie added.

Thomas stole a quick glance at his wife before answering the girls. "Well now, that would be a treat, but Katelyn and I will be staying the winter on the mainland."

Katelyn sucked in a breath. "What?"

"I ran into Jude Keeler this morning. Do you know him?"

Katelyn nodded and then giggled as she recalled a long-ago memory. "I met him once when I was a little girl. I asked Mama what the name 'Jude' meant since I had never heard it before. When we got home, Mama took out the big family Bible and read me the book of Jude. Ever since, I think of him when I read it, especially when I hear the preacher read Jude's doxology."

Florence's brow furrowed, and she tilted her head. "The Bible is a book. How can a book be in a book?"

Thomas patted her head. "Good question. You're a clever one. There are actually sixty-six books in the Bible, so it never gets old. When you learn to read, you can read all the books."

"I know my ABCs and can write my name." Florence sat up straight and proud. "Maybe I can read it next year."

Katelyn winked at Florence as Hattie got up and whispered in her sister's ear. Katelyn turned back to Thomas. "So you met Mr. Keeler and …?"

Thomas grinned. "Sorry. These two can distract me faster than a fish can jump. He's been a widower for several years, and he used to be a teacher. Moreover, he's writing the history of Alexandria Bay, so he had offered to swap with us for the winter so he won't be disturbed while he writes."

Katelyn watched the girls play tag just feet from them. "I don't understand. Swap?"

Thomas scooted closer and kissed her on the cheek. "He'll take my place on the island and be caretaker for the winter so he can finish his work. He has even offered to let us stay in his house while he is here. It's just a block from the doctor and close to the river. I'm sure the Pullmans will be agreeable. This way you can have the baby in town and settle into motherhood before the spring comes. What do you think?"

Katelyn's heart raced with excitement—and a bit of relief. "I think it's a perfect plan, but can you stand to be away from the island without missing it too much?"

Thomas nodded. "We really should be on the mainland for the winter, especially with the birth of a new baby. Last winter the blizzards and ten feet of snow were a bit much. And with a newborn? I think it's best."

Hattie left the game of tag, ran up to Katelyn, and tugged on her shirtwaist. "Can I? I'll be bigger next year. Florence says I'm still a baby, but I'll be five."

"Can you what, wee one?" Katelyn asked.

Hattie stomped her foot and folded her arms over her chest. "I'm not a wee one, Miss Katelyn. I'm big. I want to hold your baby next year. Can I please?"

Both Thomas and Katelyn laughed at her request. Thomas grabbed her around the waist to pull her into a tickle hug. "Of course you can hold the baby next summer when you return to the island. You'll certainly be a big girl by then." Florence joined them, giggling and squealing until their nanny came to fetch them. Florence and Hattie gave Thomas and Katelyn goodbye hugs.

Hattie grinned. "I hope it's a girl. I like girls."

Florence glanced at Thomas. "I hope it's a boy and is just like Mr. Thomas."

Thomas waved the compliment away and motioned for them to return to Nanny. "See you later, girls."

Katelyn waved as they ran up the hill. "Thanks for the delightful company."

Once they were gone, Thomas handed her an envelope. "From Claudia." A shadow passed over his handsome face. Katelyn took it, carefully opened it, and read it in silence.

"Well?"

Katelyn blew out a breath. "She's a mother! Has a baby boy named Robert. She says she is well. They live near the newspaper office, and Mr. Stockton works for the *Evening Courier*." She looked at the letter and frowned. "But somehow I think she sounds lonely. It's not what she says, but what she doesn't say." Katelyn gazed at her husband. "Why would she write to me after all this time?"

Shrugging his shoulders, Thomas shook his head. Then he smiled, and his eyes twinkled. "I don't know. Perhaps to make amends or to justify why she left? Maybe because you brighten the world of everyone you meet or because you are the most wonderful woman in the world?"

"Shall I write her back?"

Thomas grinned. "With that heart of compassion beating inside of you, I know you will." He leaned in to kiss her deeply. "I love you, Katelyn. For all you have become. For all you are. For all you will be." He gently touched her belly.

"Thank you." Katelyn snuggled into his strong arms as the letter fell to the ground. "I love you, too, husband. Always."

Author's Note:
The Real Pullman Island

I fell in love with the Thousand Islands as a young girl, but it wasn't until the summer of 2016 that I felt inspired to write The Thousand Islands Gilded Age series. By then I had completed my debut novel, *The Fabric of Hope: An Irish Family Legacy,* a story set partially on the largest island, Wolfe Island, Canada.

That summer, my husband and I visited Wolfe Island, Pullman Island, and Singer Castle on Dark Island. We met some wonderful people who kept the intriguing Thousand Island history deep in their hearts, and I gleaned all kinds of valuable information and made special friends in the process.

Though Katelyn, Thomas, and other characters are fictional, I purposely included some fascinating historical information in *Katelyn's Choice*. Yes, the Pullmans were one of the first families to summer on the islands; they did invite President Grant and others to their island; and they did host a reception for the journalists' convention. Indeed, the events of the summer of 1872 successfully sparked the buying and building frenzy of the Thousand Islands Gilded Age.

In 1888, the Pullmans built "Castle Rest," a six-story, fifty-eight room stone castle rising a hundred and twenty-seven feet above the St. Lawrence River! Of the fifty-eight rooms, at least thirty of them were bedrooms.

In addition to the castle were several stone outbuildings, one being a powerhouse that held a coal-fired, steam-powered electric generator. This made Pullman Island the first island home that was fully electric—generating electricity for over five hundred electric lights, as well as for a pump, which delivered water to a supply tank high in the tower—a marvel for its time.

Castle Rest became a popular landmark in the Thousand Islands. The architecture and innovations were unique for the time. The wooden shingles, rough masonry, and careful integration of the structure into the natural landscape became a characteristic architecture style for the area, including building a tower on many of the islands.

In his will, George Pullman stated that the island could not be sold outside of the family and it had to be open at least six weeks out of the year. The castle cost more than one hundred dollars a day to maintain and operate, so during World War II it was used less and less. Then in 1958 the tax burden became too difficult to maintain, so the heirs razed the castle! In 1971, they had the will's restrictions altered, and the island was sold to a family outside of the Pullman clan.

The new owners have worked hard to restore much of the property that was left, and we enjoyed touring the island. The former servants' quarters, where Katelyn and the others stayed, has become the new owner's summer home. The family also uses the top level of the boathouse as guest rooms, and the original powerhouse equipment still remains on the island.

All summer long, tourists enjoy cruising around the Thousand Islands, passing by Pullman Island, and hearing the stories of yesteryear. As a historic landmark, Pullman Island is invaluable, and so are the stories that go with it. I hope you've enjoyed hearing one of them and learning about the "real" Pullman Island.

Made in the USA
Middletown, DE
13 February 2019